Graham John is 83 years old and has had several occupations including five years in the Royal Air Force as an engine mechanic (turbine). All other occupations have been as an engineer in one form or in another. He has written many poems and short stories, some of which are published. Graham is married with two daughters, three grandchildren and two great-grandchildren.

The Kindling Chronicle is the first of a series of five books already completed. He is currently writing a follow-up story, taking place some years after the initial series of books.

Graham John

THE KINDLING CHRONICLE

AUSTIN MACAULEY PUBLISHERS™

LONDON • CAMBRIDGE • NEW YORK • SHARJAH

A CIP catalogue record for this title is available from the British Library.

ISBN 9781398422940 (Paperback)
ISBN 9781398423671 (ePub e-book)

www.austinmacauley.com

First Published 2023
Austin Macauley Publishers Ltd®
1 Canada Square
Canary Wharf
London
E14 5AA

I would like to thank my wife, Barbara, who has proofread and supported me throughout.

Prologue

From 'The Apocrypha' 11 Esdras, Chapter 16, Verses 12 to 32:

The Earth quaketh; and the foundations thereof; the sea ariseth up with the waves from the deed, and the waves of it are troubled and the fishes thereof also, before the Lord, and before the glory of His power.

For strong is His right hand that bendeth the bow. His arrows that he shooteth are sharp. And shall not miss when they begin to be shot into the ends of the world.

Behold the plagues are sent and shall not return again, until they come upon the Earth.

The fire is kindled and shall not be put out until it consumes the foundations of the Earth.

Like as an arrow which is shot by a mighty archer returning not backwards: even so the plagues that shall be set upon the Earth shall not return again.

Woe is me! Woe! Who will deliver me in these days?

The beginning of sorrows and great mournings; the beginning of famine and great dearth, the beginning of wars, and the powers shall stand in fear; the beginning of evils! What shall I do when these evils come?

Behold, famine and plague, tribulation and anguish are sent as scourges for amendment.

But for all these things, they shall not turn from their wickedness, nor be mindful of the scourges.

Behold, victuals shall be so good cheap upon the Earth, that they shall think themselves to be in good case, and even then, shall evils grow upon the Earth, sword, famine, and great confusion.

For many of them that dwell upon the Earth shall perish of famine; and the other, that escape the hunger, shall the sword destroy.

And the dead shall be cast out as dung, and there shall be no man to comfort them: for the Earth shall be wasted, and the cities shall be cast down.

There shall be no man left to till the earth and sow it.

The trees shall give fruit, and who shall gather them?

The grapes shall ripen, and who shall tread them? For all places shall be desolate of men.

So that one man shall desire to see another and to hear his voice.

For of a city, there shall be ten left. And two of the field, which shall hide themselves in the thick groves, and in the clefts of the rocks.

As in an orchard of olives, on every tree are left three or four olives.

Or as when a vineyard is gathered, there are left clusters of them that diligently seek through the vineyard.

Even so in those days, there shall be three or four left by them that search their houses with the sword.

And the Earth shall be laid waste, and the fields thereof shall wax old, and her ways and all her paths shall grow full of thorns because no man shall travel there through.

Day One

There are some days when everything goes smoothly with no crises at all. It would be fair to say that this was not one of those days for the lorry driver travelling along the road between Corby and Market Harborough at the end of a long and frustrating workday. He reached the sharp dip, which is a feature of this road, and the engine cut out.

In a vain attempt to restart the lorry, the driver coasted down the hill, letting the clutch out from time to time to bump-start the engine. There was no success and the lorry came to rest at the bottom of the dip.

The driver sat in the cab for a few minutes, trying to restart the engine before he came to the conclusion that if he was going to get home on time, he would have to find the cause of the failure and repair it. The vehicle was one of those with a lift-up cab for easy access to the engine, so he set about undoing the securing bolts. He was partially underneath when everything around him was brilliantly lit up. He blinked hard to regain his vision and stepped back in an instinctive reaction.

From his new position, he could see that his lorry was badly scorched and on fire. The next instant, the vehicle was hit by a massive blast of wind which tipped it over and extinguished the fire. The driver was, for the most part, protected by the bulk of his vehicle, even so, his overalls were torn and he was rendered unconscious for an unknown period.

When he came to, he sat for a while in a dazed stupor. Smoke and flames were all around him, and the sky was dark except for the remains of a huge fireball on top of an ominous pillar of smoke. In front of him was his lorry on its side and with badly scorched and blistered paintwork on its uppermost surface.

As his senses cleared, he thought that he had initially survived a supposed nuclear explosion, thanks mainly to the protection offered by the broken-down vehicle. His first priority was to find shelter quickly if he was to have any chance of further survival. He started walking unsteadily away, fearing that he might already be too late to avoid fallout.

You can understand that the driver was still suffering from shock and not thinking coherently. He had gone a few yards when he realised that a few tools would be useful, so he returned to the lorry and collected a selection of tools from the toolbox he had opened and now spilled in the grass. He also collected his heavy jacket which he retrieved through the broken windscreen aperture.

Before walking away, he thought about the direction to take, and he headed towards the remains of a house which had been partially protected by the same dip in which his vehicle lay. All the other houses he could see were completely demolished, and there was no sign of life anywhere. The ruins of most houses were still burning fiercely, and his choice was limited to one.

This was an older property built of stone and was still largely intact, although some of the roof was missing. Its unique position had protected it from the heat flash, and the only damage the driver could see was caused by blast. The fire flash had passed over the top, as it could only travel in a straight line. This then was the haven to which the driver directed his shaky steps.

The devastation the driver could see around him filled him with utter despair. His vehicle was not the only one in his range of vision which had been affected by the massive blast. The larger ones had been merely overturned as his had been. The drivers of those he could see had been incinerated in their seats.

The smaller vehicles had just been picked up by the wind and smashed into tangles of twisted metal with no prospect of the occupier's survival. The tar of the road was smoking as was the remains of most of the vegetation that had not been torn from the ground by the blast. There were, however, some pockets of green showing through in the most sheltered places.

The driver realised that there was now a complete breakdown in civilisation as he had known it. Also, he suspected that most, if not all of the major centres of population would have been destroyed in the same manner as those in his immediate surroundings. The devastation must have included the city where he lived with his family, and tears were streaming down his face when he reached the house to which he was heading.

Most of the windows had been blown out, giving the driver easy access to the house. He climbed in through a ground-floor window and shouted to announce his presence.

Hearing no response to his calls, the driver ventured further into the house and began his exploration of his refuge. He discovered that the house was old and was provided with a cellar which contained most of the usual objects th these places are used for. He also found that the family who lived there had been keen on camping, and that, amongst other items, was a small picnic stove with spare canisters of gas available.

His next action was to check the rest of the house for things that would help him to survive the next few days and to move them down into the cellar. The kitchen was well stocked with food, but he realised that there was no gas, electricity or running water. There was still water in the hot water system. The lack of power meant that the freezer would no longer work, so the driver would have to use such food that the freezer contained first while it was still safe to eat.

He busied himself with items that would give him comfort he could expect under the circumstances. The items included a single bed and bedding, an easy chair and a small table, things like candles, matches and a torch. He searched the other rooms and found a number of books, amongst which was a small bible.

He included this without realising, and really in these conditions, he was able to make himself quite comfortable, at least physically. His mental comfort was a different matter.

Luckily for the driver, in the cellar was a quantity of wines he would be able to use in lieu of drinking water.

This was a luxury he did not expect, and it meant that he did not have to rely on the limited supply of water available to him.

The evening was well advanced before he finally settled himself into the cellar, and he was now able to take the time to prepare himself a substantial meal from the contents of the freezer. He ate a couple of good-sized pork chops supplemented with frozen vegetables and some potatoes he had found. He finished his meal with ice cream. This was a luxury, and he knew that he would not be able to keep up this standard for long.

It was just that he had an abundance of perishable goods which he had to use up quickly. He was able to drink wine, and of course, it was a candlelit dinner. His biggest regret was that he had no one to share it with.

He cleaned his utensils to the best of his limited ability. He had to be sparing with water, so he used kitchen paper as much as possible. Then he settled down to spend the night. While he had been busy with his initial tasks, he had not found time to grieve much. The desperation of his situation hit him very hard at this time, and he was filled with grief and depression, as he realised that he was probably the only living person for miles.

Despite the fact that he was a man and not supposed to show emotion, he couldn't help himself and was sobbing well into the night. He had great difficulty getting to sleep despite being desperately tired. He suffered badly from the effects of a long hard day during which his life, and that of any other survivors, had changed dramatically and permanently.

During the small hours and in complete darkness, the driver was troubled by the strange feeling that he was not alone. He rose and took the torch he had left by the bed to search the house but found no one—not even any animals. He went back to bed, but was still uneasy.

The strange feeling persisted and he felt that he had missed something vital. His inability to sleep continued as did the impression that he was not alone, and he began to get really worried. In the end, he shouted, "Oh God! What can I do?"

Then he realised that he had not prayed as was his custom. He was a firm believer and prayed often when he was depressed and worried. On this occasion, the work he had carried out and the effects of shock and grief had caused him to forget.

He rectified his omission immediately, first asking God to forgive him for his negligence and then asking God to accept the souls of all those who had died into His eternal kingdom. He finished by asking God to enlighten him and help him with his future actions. He was rewarded by a feeling of peace which allowed him to sleep for the rest of the night, and indeed, well into the next morning.

Day Two

The driver gradually became aware that light was filtering under the door and after a moment or two, during which he remembered where he was and what had happened to him, he prayed, "Dear God, thank you for letting me see another day. Please help me to face the future and help me to know what you want me to do. I only want to do your will."

He sat in the chair, trying to work out his next action. He decided to spend the next few hours after breakfast, taking in inventory of the contents of the house. He had already established that the waste from the toilet was working. Perhaps this was connected to a cess tank.

Anyway, the cistern had flushed once and drained away as normal. There was no freshwater to refill it, so he knew that this was going to be a great problem during the next few days. Some of the precious water from the central heating system would have to be used for this purpose.

Water must be preserved for the purposes of sanitation and personal hygiene only. All cooking must be done with the wine where appropriate and, of course, this was his sole source of liquid to drink apart from a few cans of lager and some bottles of soft drinks. When he worked out the food supplies, he found that, with care, he had enough to last him for three or four weeks. There was also a bottle of whiskey which he put aside, thinking that this might come in handy to help with fire lighting.

As the house was built of stone, the driver considered that he would probably be safe if he remained in the cellar apart from brief excursions to other parts of the building.

Up to that time, he had given no thought to the outside world, and he forced himself to look out of the upstairs windows. Nothing had changed from the day before. As far as he could see, the same depressing view was presented.

In reality, he could only see any distance on one direction only. This was because the house was situated on the side of a hill. Even this view was limited, as there were still large quantities of smoke rising from demolished buildings and from the countryside.

Before he started his exploration, he had prepared himself a reasonable breakfast. This was possible because he was forced to use those frozen and fresh food first before they deteriorated. He was fortunate that he had discovered the small picnic stove and spare gas cylinders. At least, he was able to cook the food he found.

Even so, the limitations of the stove gave him restrictions on the method of cooking. He could only fry or boil and decided that he would prepare some of the frozen meat to eat cold later. At least, by this method he could prolong the life of some of it for a couple of days, and then he would have to rely on tinned foods.

He had noticed earlier that there was a full range of camping equipment in the house, including a small two-man tent and typical utensils, together with a rucksack. One of the most important finds was a .22 air rifle in a case, together with some ammunition. The driver thought that this would be invaluable if he had to resort to hunting for his food.

He had already realised that he would not be able to rely on manmade foods for ever. His examination of the house had already told him that.

Another important find was one of the electronic gas lighters, the kind that worked without batteries, but induced a spark when a trigger was pressed in much the same way that a car ignition coil works. This simple and fairly small object enabled him to save his precious matches which were needed to light candles which he decided to use only for cooking and eating. This time he also used for reading in order to conserve the candles.

He spent the rest of the day in the very dim light of the cellar, the only light being that which penetrated through the open door. Because of this fact, he was unable to do any reading and could only spend the time reflecting on the position in which he found himself, and to try and determine what his future course of action was likely to be.

He began by thinking deeply about the events of the previous day, first the breakdown which had caused his vehicle to stop at the bottom of the dip in the road. The position of the final breakdown was such that it afforded him the best possible protection due to the contours of the ground. Secondly, he had been outside the vehicle and thus protected from the full force of the blast which had actually overturned the lorry. If he had still been seated in the cab, then he would certainly have been badly burnt and possibly seriously injured when the vehicle blew over.

The third stroke of coincidence was that the house in which he now found shelter was within easy walking distance. Another benefit was that the house provided him with all the necessary food for initial survival and for him to lead some sort of life in the future. All these things caused him to think about the nature of convenience.

He was forced to the conclusion that he was being protected. Why was he a survivor amongst so much death and destruction? If this was the case, then there was some purpose to his survival. It was, therefore, up to the driver to discover the reason why he had been protected.

He decided that this was all due to the will of God. Because of this, he spent much of his enforced idleness in prayer, seeking an answer.

After some hours of reflection, punctuated by periods of utter despair, he came to the conclusion that he was to stay where he was until the food ran out, and then he would have to leave and go where God directed him. What he was to do at that time was not revealed to him at this stage.

Day Three

The next day was spent in a similar way to the first, with meals cooked and eaten by candlelight, with some reading while the light was available. There was no change in the sky, still dark and with poor visibility, and in consequence, the cellar was almost dark when the candle was extinguished. The driver's main worry was the shortage of water for washing and sanitation. There were still great difficulties with the cleaning of his cooking utensils.

When night came, he lay on the bed thinking and praying; obviously, any future life was going to be vastly different to his previous reasonably comfortable existence. In fact, he had already started his new life, although he had no idea what would happen to him. If he was to survive at all, he realised that he would be unable to manage without help.

Where was he to get help? At the present moment, he had no one to turn to except God. Now, as never before, he must put his trust in Him. His trust must be absolute. He decided that if he had been saved up to that point in time, there must be a reason. The thought suddenly came to him that perhaps, he was destined to help others.

Anyone left would be likely to be in a similar position and struggling for survival in a devastated world. There was likely to be fighting for food and shelter. Life in this new world was not going to be pleasant. If any lasting survival was to be possible, the only way ahead was to be by mutual co-operation.

Such co-operation with mutual pooling of available resources would need some sort of co-ordinator. The driver's Christian background seemed to him to give the best chance of implementing such a policy. Not control!

There had been too much control of people's lives by powerful church men in past history, a gentle guidance seemed to be more appropriate. It seemed to the driver that someone should try, by mild persuasion, to bring people to believe and trust in the Lord.

The thought came to the driver that there would be few Christian believers left in the world, judging by the general decline in attendance at Church services that he had noticed, the driver thought that now, there would be even less who would be willing to accept God's protective umbrella.

He became more and more convinced that the task of bringing people together had fallen on his shoulders. This was likely to be a daunting task, but since he had already started a completely new life whereby everything had changed, he thought that nothing of his previous life had any relevance except for his belief in God.

Even his former name now had no significance. There was likely to be no one left who knew who he was. Further, if he was destined to spread the word of God's love to those who were left, then he, as a layman, would have to find something to make people interested in him to start with.

It was at this point that he decided to change his name and take one that might well inspire conversation. How this decision came to him, he never knew. It seemed that it was a logical solution that he would have to take in order to arouse interest.

He was by nature a shy and reserved man who did not force his opinions on anyone, so if he was to spread the word of God's love, then he would need a trigger to start a conversation. After much consideration, he decided that he would be known as Believer because that's what he was, a believer.

When he had reached this conclusion, he prayed to ask God to guide his footsteps in the future and to help him find the words he would need to persuade people, that the ways of peace and love were the only ways for mankind to continue. He also prayed that God would give him the health and means to carry out the task he was now sure God had preserved him for.

Day Four

With the next dawn, Believer awoke and after thanking God for another day, he carried out his ablutions and preparations for breakfast in the manner he had established the day before. After which he spent the rest of his waking hours thinking a great deal about the practical side of his future life.

The major problems soon became apparent. One, of catching his food, the other of lighting fires to cook his meals. The air rifle he found during his first full day would help with providing food, but he only had a limited supply of ammunition.

It was obvious that one of his most important tasks was to devise a way of replenishing this. He could think of no immediate solution to this.

As to the food itself, he reasoned that if God had a mission for him, then surely, He would provide him with enough food to enable him to fulfil it. The same would apply to the ammunition for the air rifle, he would be given solutions to both problems.

Lighting a fire would require some careful thought on his part, but there was liable to be a good quantity of wood torn from buildings and from damaged trees. Believer thought that it should be possible to start a fire with the aid of the gas lighter he had found if he used this in conjunction with the spirit, and used tinder or paper carefully dried out from the day before.

He was still very concerned by the lack of water for the next few days, and he prayed that the weather would change soon from the dull and overcast skies still heavily affected with smoke and ashes. In short, he prayed for rain. He suspected that even rainwater would not be safe to use for the first few days and that he would have to delay its use.

Days Five, Six and Seven

The next three days passed in a similar way, by the end of which, Believer's precious water supply was nearly exhausted. At this time, he felt dirty and unkempt. He had been unable to shave as the only razor available to him was an electric one, which was of course, no use to him at all.

He had now used as much of the frozen food he had found in the freezer as he dared. The rest he considered to be unsafe as there had been no means of keeping it fresh once it had thawed out.

Towards the end of the seventh day, Believer became aware of a gradual change in the sky. This darkened even more and a damp mist appeared. This turned to drizzle which during the night, slowly turned into a torrential downpour.

Day Eight

After a whole night and day of heavy rain, Believer felt that the fresh rainwater might be safe to use for washing, so he set to work catching as much as he could of the water pouring through the damaged roof. He filled the bath and any other receptacle he could spare.

The water fell in such volumes that within a short time, it reached the cellar where Believer had spent his first few days. Although there was a small drain in the floor, he thought that this would soon prove to be insufficient to keep his refuge dry, so he decided to move upstairs to the one bedroom unaffected by the flooding water.

He, therefore, spent some time in moving his precious belongings to this room, and was rewarded by his efforts in having more available light. Even so, to enable him to read, he had to sit with his back to the glassless window. He was fortunate that this window was facing away from the wind, and rainwater did not pour in as it did elsewhere in the house.

He now had an abundance of water but he decided to use it only for washing and cleaning. He still had wine and other bottled drinks for his internal consumption. He did not forget to thank God for his improving fortunes.

Day Nine

Throughout Believer's ninth day, the rain continued to fall at the same rate, but he was able to take advantage of the abundance of water that he was now blessed with to take a bath. The bath, of course, was cold but nonetheless invigorating, and Believer felt much better for it.

After attending to his personal needs, Believer set about washing some of the clothes he had been wearing. He was fortunate that the man of the house was of a comparable size, and Believer had been able to change his clothes when necessary. Under the terrible circumstances he had found himself in, he considered himself lucky to have found this particular house in which to spend the first few days of this new life.

Days Ten to Twenty

The heavy rain continued with no sign of abatement day after day. As Believer had surmised, the cellar had flooded, so he was glad that he had decided to move to the upstairs room. However, it became more obvious that each move he made was dictated by events beyond his control, and bearing in mind that he believed that God had a purpose for him, it was apparent that he was being guided to make moves in accordance with God's will.

With the increase of light available to him, Believer carried on making his plans for his eventual move away from the house and with the aid of a road map, he started to plot his future route.

What direction should he make for? He realised that he should avoid any towns and cities as these were most likely to be contaminated. Also, there would be less chance of finding survivors in the more densely populated areas. These were likely to have been the centre of the attacks, particularly as he suspected that even the smaller towns had been devastated.

If anything lived in the larger cities at all, these were most likely to be rats from the sewers carrying their own source of infection. Any human survivors would probably be dying from diseases like cholera and typhoid and infection from burns. Many, probably all, would be seriously affected with radiation sickness for which Believer could do nothing.

Believer spent a great deal of time in prayer and in studying the atlas, and found that he was able to plot a route which avoided the centres of population and only connected country districts and smaller villages.

His route would be mainly north and later north west, eventually heading towards the Peak District which Believer considered to be the most likely area in which to find small pockets of survivors.

He also realised that even though he was still in the summer season, he would have to restrict his walking hours to about five hours a day as he would have to spend some time hunting for food, cooking and finding shelter. He did not know the state of the roads but suspected that there would be difficulty with floods and damaged bridges, which would all add time to the journey.

Day Twenty-One

The available food had almost run out. There was only a tin of corned beef and another of mixed vegetables which, with care, might last Believer a couple of days. From now on, it was a case of hunt or starve.

Believer counted his blessings and was thankful for the possession of the air rifle and its ammunition. There would be no chance of practice with the rifle as the quantity of ammunition was limited. As with everything else that was consumable, there must be no wastage.

Believer carefully packed the rucksack he had found with all the spare clothing he could carry, cooking utensils and some sharp knives, some soap and including some detergent powder for washing clothes. By the time he had finished, the rucksack was getting very full and he tied the small tent and a sleeping bag wrapped in a plastic tablecloth to the top. He tied some cooking pans to the side and tucked a hammer into one of the side pockets. The air rifle he decided to carry separately.

When he had completed his preparations, he made a last meal from the remains of tins he had opened the day before. Then he spent some time in prayer before finally leaving his refuge for the past three weeks. As a last act, he buried all the potato peelings in the highest part of the now sodden garden, knowing that they might well grow and provide food for someone next year, even if the quality of the crop would be poor.

There was nothing left for him to do now, so he set off into the rain which had now abated somewhat. He had most of the day before him and decided that he should keep walking for as long as possible.

He walked on through the blackened countryside, finding as he walked that he grew more uncomfortable with the rain penetrating the clothes he was wearing. Because of the inclement weather and the necessity of having to wear a waterproof jacket, even his shirt was damp with perspiration. Discomfort was something he could do nothing about and by this time, it was obvious that he would have to find adequate shelter for the nights, if only to attempt to dry out some of his clothing.

Although Believer kept to the roadway as much as possible, progress was slower that he intended as he had to make several detours to avoid floods and other obstructions; like half-burnt and felled trees and also vehicles which had been affected by the intense fires or massive winds. The presence of these obstructions rendered travel by wheeled vehicles on the roads impossible, and Believer was glad that he had discounted the prospect of trying to find a vehicle to travel in. He would not have got very far at all.

The effort of walking with the heavy rucksack took its toll on Believer's energy resources as he was not used to this kind of exercise. Further, he had spent the last three weeks in relative inactivity, and he was forced to rest frequently, further delaying him.

During one of his enforced rests, he was sitting down in the lee of a partially demolished building, feeling thoroughly miserable and now soaked through, when he saw something which raised his spirits considerably. There was a gradual lightening of the sky and suddenly, the sun broke through and, in the direction, he was travelling, he saw a brilliant rainbow which only lasted a few seconds.

As the sun was again obscured behind the clouds, Believer was reminded of the rainbow that Noah had seen after his ordeal in the floods as told in the Bible. Noah was given hope by his rainbow and so was Believer, who knew that the sight of a rainbow usually meant a change in the weather. He was heartened by this thought as it meant that his clothing might get a chance to dry later.

He lifted the heavy rucksack onto his aching shoulders and continued on his way with a prayer of thanksgiving on his mind, and he experienced a period of inner peace that made his discomfort and tiredness seem more bearable.

He walked for the five-hour period he had allotted himself and came upon a small village which seemed to have suffered less damage that some of the buildings he had seen. Among the buildings was the village church, which was stoutly built and largely intact. Shouted as he walked through the village in order to attract the attentions of any survivors who might be there, but was met with the usual chilling silence.

Believer entered the church and looked around. Since this building was the most intact, he decided to spend the night in God's house. He had given up so much up to now and God had arranged for the church to provide shelter for the night.

Tomorrow he would check out the village thoroughly to see if there were any other survivors, but now he would take advantage of the shelter provided. Besides, he was very tired and wet.

He changed out of the wet clothes and arranged them in the church building to dry out as much as possible. He sat in one of the pews to reflect again on his future.

As he sat quietly in the church, the thought occurred to him that if he was going to be some sort of missionary, it would be likely that he might be called on to conduct services. As he was only a lay person, he was rather concerned whether he would be doing the right thing or would he be committing some offence against God and the church.

This took some considerable thought and prayer during which he reasoned that Christ's Apostles had been ordinary people prior to that memorable night when the Holy Spirit came upon them. Judging by the numbers of fatalities he had so far seen; ordained priests were likely to be few and far between.

In these circumstances, he felt that God would forgive him for his presumptuousness, and provided that he worked in the service of the Lord, then he must take the place of a priest in places where there were none available.

Having come to this conclusion, he felt as if a great weight had been lifted from him, and after a final prayer he settled down to a deep and exhausted sleep.

Day Twenty-Two

Believer's search of the village proved to be as futile as he had expected. He breakfasted on the second portion of the food he had brought with him and left the church in which he had spent the night. There was no one left alive as he already suspected, as there had been an overwhelming smell of death and decay.

This same smell had been present near every centre of habitation he passed and even, on occasion, in the open countryside. Nevertheless, he carried out the search diligently but with forlorn hope.

He was fortunate to find some tinned food, enough to last him for a further day or two. He was unable to carry more as he wanted to reserve some space in his rucksack for the books, he was likely to need in his mission. The books he chose were a prayer book, a copy of *The Alternative Service* book and a small selection of hymn books.

When he had risen that morning, he put on his damp clothes, reasoning that he should keep as many dry clothes as possible. Now he returned to the church and repacked the rucksack, ready to leave again.

If there was anyone to watch him, they would have thought that his next action was a very curious one. He searched for a piece of paper on which he wrote: *Believe in the Lord Jesus Christ. Only through him is the way to salvation and hope.*

He then pinned this in a prominent position on the church noticeboard and added the date.

He was now ready to leave and started to walk away, but at a slower pace than the day before. This was because his muscles had stiffened up and it was some time before they relaxed again.

He moved away from the village and stopped for his first rest of the day in the shelter of an old barn after washing in water from a flooded field. Then he took time to refill his water bottle with water he boiled using the last of the gas for the picnic stove which he now discarded.

The wash refreshed him somewhat and he continued his trek into the unknown, wishing he could have a hot bath. He realised that although he had not been wealthy before, his previous existence was luxury, compared with the life he was now to live, and he wished that he had not been forced to leave the house in which he had stayed for three weeks.

Then he reasoned that he could serve no useful purpose by remaining in one place. In the first instance, his food supply would run out, and secondly, if he remained in one place, he would meet no one, and would then be unable to carry out the task which he believed God had set him. He had to travel in order to perform his task.

Day Twenty-Three

On Believer's second walking day, progress was slower with more frequent stops to rest, due to the effect of his arduous walk the day before. Because of the time he had spent looking for survivors, he curtailed his walking time for the day to only four hours. It was late afternoon when he decided to stop for the night. This time, there was no solid shelter within sight, so he pitched his small tent in the driest place he could find.

Instead of using his precious store of tinned food, Believer decided that it was time that he tried out his hunting skills. There were a few crows around feeding on carcasses of sheep in the fields, so he loaded his air rifle and set off carefully in their direction.

When he decided he was close enough, he tried his first shot and missed. The birds were startled and Believer had to wait a while for them to settle again before he fired again. He missed for another three attempts, but the fifth was more profitable and he managed to bring down one crow which he was able to kill before it escaped.

Next came the task of making and lighting the fire in order that he could cook his kill. This proved more difficult than he had imagined since all the wood he could find was damp, but he managed to find a sufficient quantity. It actually took an hour to get a good fire going, using the gas lighter, spirit and some old newspaper he had brought with him.

He prepared the crow by putting it in the fire to burn off all the feathers, then he cut off the head and feet and opened up the bird. He cut out all the parts he didn't consider to be edible.

He roasted the crow over the fire, using a sharpened stick and made sure it was well cooked. He was pleased with the results even though he found the taste unusual. At least, he had proved to himself that survival was possible in this manner. Even so, he had found the work of preparing the bird to be distasteful, as he had previously only lived on food already partially prepared.

Gone now were the refinements of civilisation where anyone could go to a shop and buy a pre-frozen chicken or any other meat. From now on, any meat would have to be caught and killed. He had never done anything like this in his previous life, nor given it any thought.

Believer was very hungry when he finally got round to eating the bird and he ate every part of it which he considered edible. After cleaning his utensils and boiling up some water to replenish his water bottle, he crawled exhausted into his tent to spend the night in an eerie silence. He did not forget to extinguish the fire, and save some of the half-burnt sticks which he cooled and wrapped in polythene he had brought for the purpose.

The shooting of the crow had proved expensive in terms of time and ammunition and he prayed that he would prove to be a better shot as time went on. Also, he prayed that he would find the means to make more pellets.

Day Twenty-Four

A subdued dawn chorus woke Believer. Subdued because the number of birds had been greatly reduced since the massive fires and explosions which had caused so much devastation. Even so, Believer was pleased to hear any birds at all. This meant that more of the wild creatures had survived than he thought possible.

The weather remained damp and drizzling, and Believer made a small breakfast on some of the tinned food before breaking camp and continuing on his way, still stiff but slightly less so than on the previous day as his body was beginning to get used to the unaccustomed exercise. This day, he found that he was able to walk for longer periods before resting and so made better progress.

Towards the end of the day, he came across the ruins of a building which he found had been a workshop belonging to a firm of agricultural engineers. The workshop had been well equipped with tools and machinery together with various materials.

God had helped him again as here was the means of making a mould to form pellets for his air rifle. He achieved this by bolting two pieces of strip metal together and drilling holes along the seam with a drill bit that exactly fitted the bore of the barrel.

Of course, with no electricity, he had to turn the drill bit with the aid of a hand drill and this took time, but he did achieve his object. To make pellets, all he had to do was to hammer lead into the holes he had made and undo the bolt that held the strips together to remove the pellets thus formed.

The acquisition of lead from which to make ammunition should not be a great problem. Lead was available in considerable quantities as every house used some in the roof flashings and Believer had already seen houses with pools of lead among the rubble. The lead was now solidified, of course, but being a soft metal, it could easily be worked with the minimum of tools.

He was fortunate in finding the workshop which was still sufficiently intact to provide him with some shelter out of the rain, even if this was only one corner of the building. In addition, there was a propane gas bottle and a blow torch, so he was able to cook a meal from his precious store of food without having to light a fire. The bottle and burner were too heavy for him to take with him but at least, he could use them during the period of his short stay in the workshop.

Day Twenty-Five

The drizzle had eased. Believer was able to start the next day's journey without the discomfort which had been his only companion since he had first ventured out on his solitary walk. The wet clothing, he had been constantly wearing caused sore patches, particularly on his shoulders and legs, where he had been subjected to constant chafing to skin softened by the dampness.

For the second time, he had meagre breakfast before he started out. His time in the house had taught him how much food he needed to sustain him. He learnt rapidly after the first few days when the frozen food had run out and he had been forced to ration out the remainder, and although he did not realise this at the time, this had been a useful lesson to him.

He had even lost some weight, and to be truthful, he was fitter than he had been for a long time. If the soreness and chafing were to be ignored. What he was concerned about was that he now sported a growing beard and as he had always been clean shaven before, he felt dirty and unkempt. This was one reason why he tried to wash thoroughly each day and endured the cold water.

It is very difficult to suddenly adjust from a lifetime of reasonable comfort with unlimited supplies of hot water and soap, and of course, a good variety of food. All he had of these luxuries was soap and that was limited to an amount that he could carry.

Days Twenty-Six and Twenty-Seven

Two days later, still heading North and diverting to search for survivors at any likely place he came across, he found no one. He was feeling more comfortable and much of the soreness had eased. In different circumstances, Believer would have enjoyed the adventure.

He faced the evidence of death and destruction all around him and had had no company at all for the best part of four weeks now. These were not conditions to make for a happy walking tour, and despite his belief in God and the trust he now placed in Him, he could not help feeling despondent for most of the time.

He viewed every building he saw with hope that he might find someone alive, but the hope was dashed when he took time to examine the site. The most depressing fact was that each investigation revealed more dead bodies for which, as one man on his own, he could do nothing, not even attempt to make an effort to bury anyone.

Towards the end of the second day, he came upon a cottage in a little valley that was in far better condition than any he had seen so far. There was a brook running alongside the garden with the water almost up to the top of the bank, and there was evidence that the water level had been even higher.

Believer thought that even if there was no one in this place, at least he would have shelter for the night. He headed towards the building and noticed as he passed through the garden that there was evidence that someone had attempted to dig for potatoes and this gave him hope that he might actually find someone here. All the windows were intact except for one which was boarded over.

When he came up to the cottage, he found both back and front doors were locked, and although he knocked loudly, he heard no sound so he moved round to the boarded-up window. He pulled hard on the board and it gave a little with a creaking noise. More pulling and the board moved again. Believer paused because he thought he had heard a sound which he had not made.

He shouted and the faint noise was repeated. This seemed to be a faint knocking, and Believer pulled harder until the board came away with a final groan.

He looked through the window opening and at first could see nothing. As his eyes got used to the dimmer light within the room, he could see the back of an arm chair, and now he saw that there was a small skinny arm dangling over the side of it.

He completed his entry and went straight to the chair. In the chair, he found a small girl staring at him with frightened eyes. It was obvious that the child was very weak and thin from lack of food, and that hunger and lack of strength prevented the girl from making any positive movement. He said to her, "Don't be afraid, I have come to help you if I can. Is there anyone else here?"

The child answered in a very weak voice. "Mummy. Upstairs."

Believer said. "I'll be back." Then he went to search the rest of the cottage and found another small child in one room and two women lying in a double bed in another room.

Both these women were in a worse state than either of the small girls and Believer thought that they might have stinted themselves in order to feed the children whose condition was only marginally better. Believer started to pray for guidance. He was no doctor but thought that all the people he had found were mostly hungry and that food would help them most. He went downstairs to see what he could find.

There was no food at all in the cottage and Believer looked at his own meagre supplies. He had a little corned beef and a tin of stewed steak plus further tin of mixed vegetables, enough to make some sort of stew, but how to cook it? This was unlikely to be a quick job and he hoped that he would be in time. The kitchen was equipped with an old kitchen range and Believer went into a furore of activity.

He went outside and picked up as many pieces of scrap wood that he could find. Then he took a pan and drew water from the brook. He lit the fire in the old range, breathing a sigh of relief when he found that the chimney was clear. He emptied all the food available into another pan which he added water from his bottle which, luckily, he had pre-boiled.

It took some time to heat his weird concoction, but while it was cooking an appetising aroma filled the kitchen. When it was cooked, he divided into portions and started to feed his new charges. He gave slightly larger portions to the two small girls but had to spoon feed all the survivors.

It may seem a strange thing to feed the smallest the most, but Believer reasoned that these two were fitter than the two adults and more likely to get to their feet sooner. Besides, too much food, too soon, was likely to make the recipients sick and that would do no good at all.

He had already made sure that everyone had a sip or two of his boiled water, and spoke to the little girl he had first found the whole time he was preparing the food. He reassured her that everyone in the house would get better, and the frightened look she had when he first saw her gradually left her as she could see that Believer was trying to help.

Believer had taken time whilst he had been preparing the meal to wash the faces of the two older people and after he had fed them, he settled them all down to sleep. He hoped that he had done enough to start them on their way to recovery.

As for himself, he had eaten that day while he had been travelling, and decided that next day he would have to go out and find some food, sufficient for five people. Then, because he now had greater cause than before, he spent some time praying earnestly, not for himself this time but for the family who was in sore need of his prayers and assistance.

Before he went to sleep himself, he took the necessary step of checking the cottage to see what it contained to help him. The cottage had a bathroom that had been added to modernise the building. As in the house in which he had first stayed, the water drainage system was working. Believer considered that as they were underground, they had withstood the devastation to which most buildings he had seen had suffered.

The lounge was fitted with a solid fuel burner and Believer found some coke for this in an outhouse. This would keep the kitchen range in operation for a while, and he banked the range up in order to keep it going for the night.

In the bathroom, to his great joy, a packet of throw away razors and he was able to have a shave at last and now he had use of the kitchen range, he was able to boil enough water for him to have a hot bath.

The lounge contained a three-piece suite with a settee large enough for him to stretch out on, so he was assured of a soft bed for the night. There was also now-defunct television and video recorder, but more important to Believer's eye was an antique spinning wheel, and Believer could foresee the time when this would be pressed into service again.

It was obvious that such items would be needed, at least for a time, since anything that worked by gas or electricity would be useless for some considerable time in the future.

By the time he had searched the house, the water for his bath was ready and afterwards, with a change of clothing, he felt much refreshed.

He went upstairs to check on his fellow survivors and made sure that they were as comfortable as possible. All were now sleeping peacefully and on the same floor. He had moved the small girl he had first found up to the second bed to join the other young one and now, as the light failed, he went to sleep on the settee downstairs. As he drifted off to sleep, he gave thought to the dreadful responsibilities he was now facing.

Day Twenty-Eight

When Believer awoke, he wondered where he was, then, remembering, he built up the fire in the kitchen range and started to heat up the remains of the stew he had made the night before. While this was happening, he went to check on the four people he had found in the cottage when he had arrived.

He found both the younger girls still asleep. The other two were awake, but only slightly better than when he had first seen them. Neither was capable of much movement, so Believer started to attend to their immediate needs.

"My name is Believer," he said. "I am the only person here able to help you at all, so I shall have to do all sorts of personal things, no matter how embarrassing it will be to both me and you. The two little girls are alright, they are only sleeping. Now, do you need to pass water or anything? I will have to help you do that for a start."

Both women nodded and Believer said, "In that case, I shall have to help you use the pot." He had found an old Victorian chamber pot in the room and helped the older woman first. "Easy now, I know that you are very weak. I bet you never thought that you would have to use this in earnest." After the woman had used the pot, he went downstairs to empty it and repeated the process with the other woman.

"I imagine you feel better now. There is some food coming along in a minute, but first I must attend to the little ones. I shall carry them downstairs and they can sit on the toilet."

He found them both awake and gave them the assistance they required before he fed them all. There was no food left for himself. "I will have to go out and find us all some food," he told his charges. "I will be gone some time, but is there something like a village shop anywhere near here?" This, he asked of the two younger girls who had recovered enough to speak.

"There was a shop down the road." The girl he had first seen told him. "But Daddy used to take us all out in the car and we went to a big shop. Will Daddy come home?"

This was one question Believer had dreaded. "What's your name?" he asked.

"Sharon, this is Judy, my friend. Mummy and my sister, Joanne, are upstairs."

"Well, Sharon, you must be very brave, but I just don't know whether your Daddy will come home or not. He might not be able to. He may have gone to Jesus. You must ask your Mummy about it when she is better.

"Where is this little shop you were talking about? Just tell me where to go and I'll see what I can find."

The girl pointed in the general direction and Believer took his leave of the family. He walked about three miles when he came upon a small builder's yard and once again, he was given cause to thank God as he found, behind a wrecked shed, a small builders dumper truck, and in the wreckage of the shed he found a 45 gallon barrel of diesel fuel about two thirds full. Here was a means of transport he could use, as it was an offroad vehicle which could be started by hand.

He checked the machine for fuel and oil, and loaded the barrel into the skip of the machine by rolling it up two short planks which he also loaded. He also found a disc cutter machine with some fuel still in it. He loaded this as well.

Believer had taken the disc cutter as an idea was forming in his mind that he would have to make something like a cross bow for hunting, and he considered that the machine would be useful when he came to make the weapon.

He now had a vehicle of sorts and he drove along the road for a further two miles. As he had already found, the road was blocked in several places and there were times when he had to travel on the verge or even in fields to avoid a blockage. The ground off the road was still very wet and Believer just would not have been able to use an ordinary vehicle. Even then he had to travel in reverse because he found that the traction with the front wheel drive machine was better in reverse over very muddy ground.

He finally came upon the village shop that Sharon had told him about. As usual, he found no one alive and the shop was difficult to see at first among the other ruined buildings. The shop was partially demolished, but there was a store room at the back which contained a variety of food in tins. Some of the tins had their labels missing and Believer had to guess what they contained. He filled the rest of the space with as many likely looking tins as he could find, enough to last the family for several days. He also took some soap, detergent and as an afterthought, he added some packets of sanitary towels. Then he started back to the cottage.

He let himself into the cottage and checked on its occupants before he unloaded the dumper. He found the two younger ones slightly livelier, but both the older people were still unable to get up unaided. He cooked another stew for them all and this time included himself among the recipients.

When he had finished all his chores, he was very tired. He had to carry out all the work in the house, including fetching water and attending to the various needs of his charges in addition to his trip to find food. He found out for the first time how difficult it is to care for really sick people. He spent his usual time in prayer before he fell into an exhausted sleep.

Day Twenty-Nine

The sounds of movement slowly penetrated through to his sub-consciousness and Believer awoke feeling very drowsy. Then he realised that the bathroom was occupied, also that it was morning. He reasoned that the person he could hear must be one of the smaller girls. She must have risen and struggled down the stairs. Believer got up and stoked the fire in the range, then he put on some water to boil.

The little girl came out of the bathroom and Believer said. "Good morning, Sharon, how are you this morning? It's good to see you on your feet."

"Hello," she answered.

"Come into the kitchen and sit down. You can tell me about the rest of the household. How old are you?"

"I'm seven and so is Judy. She's my friend. She came to tea. We were going to Brownies together. That's why she came over to our house. There was a big noise and lots of things caught fire. Mummy started crying and wouldn't let Judy go home afterwards. My sister is 15. I don't know how old Mummy is. She's very ill, isn't she? And Joanne. Will they get better?"

"Yes, they will get well, you can help when you're stronger, but I shall have to do all the work until then. I brought some food in for us all yesterday. What about Judy, can she move about like you yet?"

"I think so, she has been very upset and crying a lot. She wants her Mummy and Daddy, but they didn't come, and my Daddy hasn't come home either. Do you think he will? He won't, will he?"

"Sharon, lots of people will never come home again. They've all gone to Jesus. We must be very brave and remember how good they have been to us. We must pray to Jesus and ask Him to look after them all."

Sharon started to cry then and Believer felt in much the same state. He was saved by the kettle which started to boil. "Can you tell me where I can find a teapot? I brought some tea back yesterday with some tinned milk. I haven't had a cup of tea for weeks. I think that a cup of tea will do us all good."

Believer made the tea and went upstairs to fetch Judy down. She was a little weaker than Sharon, but just able to get to her feet. He helped her downstairs and poured out the tea. The girls liked sweet tea, and Believer was lucky enough to find a small amount of sugar for them.

Sharon had helped her friend to the bathroom, and Believer was glad to see that she was trying to hold back her own tears while she helped her sad little friend. He thought that he would keep them busy helping out in the house. It would take their minds off the situation. When they had both used the toilet, Believer showed them how to flush it by using a bucket which he had filled for the purpose.

He busied himself with preparing a breakfast for them all and put out three equal portions for himself and the two small girls and slightly less for the other two. Sharon noticed this and said, "Mr Believer, why have you put out more for us than you have for Mummy and Joanne."

"Your Mummy and Joanne are still very ill and if I give them too much, they might be sick and that wouldn't do them any good, would it? You two can move about and you will be able to help me sooner."

Believer took the food upstairs and found the two older people slightly better and able to talk. He attended to their toilet needs as before, then he fed them. Afterwards, he said to the older woman, "I know this is Joanne, but Sharon has only referred to you as Mummy, what is your name? I am Believer."

"My name is Allyson, thank you for helping us. That is an odd name you call yourself. Can you tell me why?"

"I will explain later, when you are better. What I want to know just now is where I can find some more fuel for the kitchen range. Do you know if there is a foundry or brick works anywhere near here? Then I can go and get some today."

Allyson told him where she thought he might find what he was looking for and Believer said, "I've got to go out again today, you will have to ask Sharon and Judy to help if you need it. They are on their feet just but might be able to help a little. They mustn't do too much though, and I took them downstairs so that they won't have to come up and down the stairs, but if you really need them they will come. You two should sleep as much as possible and I shall tell the girls that they should do the same."

Believer went down stairs and told the two young girls what he had told Allyson. "Sharon, you're in charge. Your Mummy and Joanne are still very sick so you two must look after them if they need anything. There is some cold food there so you could eat some about midday and try to give the others some as well. Try to go to sleep when you feel tired, and don't go and bother your Mummy except to feed her or if she needs you."

He went out and checked the dumper for fuel, putting some in a gallon can he had found as an emergency supply. Then he started his arduous journey to the location Allyson had given him. The journey took him nearer to a large town and as he had suspected, the devastation increased as he drew nearer. He now knew that he was justified in not trying to return home, but the knowledge gave him no consolation for the loss of his family and all he had known.

He arrived at his destination and found that all the buildings had been demolished. This had been a foundry and these places used a great deal of coke. The coke store was among the wreckage and its contents were scattered over the site. In consequence, it took him some time to gather enough to fill his machine, and he was feeling the effects of his labours.

He diverted by the shop he had visited the day before and collected some more food which he put in a dustbin and tied on to the dumper. It was towards the end of the day when he arrived back at the cottage. He was cheered by the enthusiastic welcome the two small girls gave him.

They were much improved and had managed to keep the kitchen range burning. They had even managed to put some water on to boil.

"Hello, you two. How are you and how did you manage to keep the fire going?"

"We asked Mummy and she told us how. She told us to boil water to drink, so we've kept it hot all day, but Judy burnt her hand."

"Let me see that, young lady." Believer took Judy's hand and saw that there was a large blister on the back. "What have you done about it?"

Judy said, "I put my hand in cold water when I did it. We learnt that in the Brownies."

"Good for you. You must keep it clean now. I expect that it will be sore for a while, but it will get better in a few days. You will have to be very careful and not do it again." Believer went upstairs to see Allyson and Joanne.

"I'm back as you can see, are you feeling better at all? Can you sit up if I help?"

"We are a little better and thank you," Allyson told him. "Tell me; don't you feel embarrassed having to help us with everything, even with the pot?"

"Yes, perhaps a little, but since there is nobody else, it doesn't make any difference whether you or I am embarrassed, does it? The job has got to be done. Listen, God has directed my feet to this place as indeed. He has taken hold of my whole life from the minute the bombs went off and obviously for some time before. I didn't know that. But now I realise that if I was not doing the job that I was, then I wouldn't be here now.

"He has helped me every step of the way and provided me with all my needs and now He has sent me here to help you. Since He has sent me, then I must do His will. If that means helping you with your toilet needs, then so be it."

"Now I know why you call yourself 'Believer', but have you no other name?"

"I did have, but I use the name 'Believer' because my previous life has ended and now a new life has started. I must go where God sends me and carry His word wherever I go. There must be very many people of those that are left who have lost their faith or possibly never had it in the first place, so you see that if I use the name 'Believer' people will be as curious as you are.

"You have already asked why and others will do the same. Of course, I shall have to tell them.

"You are the first and perhaps because you have met me and seen that I have put my trust in God, then you might be able to see things as I do, you may even tell others what absolute trust means. Enough for now, I must go and get us all some more food. Then I shall get the little ones into a bath and have one myself.

"Tomorrow I shall stay here and try to do to some washing. If you two feel up to it, tomorrow, it will be your turn to have a bath. You'll feel a lot better for it."

He went to prepare a meal and found that the two girls were sorting out all the tins into similar types of food. Believer himself selected two large tins of pilchards and a tin of spaghetti which he emptied into a pan and heated all of this together. He dished it up into five portions and went upstairs with three of them, leaving Sharon and Judy to eat theirs in the kitchen.

He fed both his patients and alternated this with his own meal. While this rather odd meal was being consumed, Allyson said, "What sort of future do you see for us? Can we survive at all?"

Believer replied, "It seems that we are going to continue with our conversation. I don't want you to think that I am giving you a sermon particularly as you two are a captive audience. I can't make any explanation brief, but the way I see it is that hope is the greatest thing we have left.

"Without hope, there is no point in continuing. Where is that hope to come from? If we believe that God is still looking after us, then we can hope that there is still a chance for us.

"In the past, we have come to rely on material things and manmade products. We forgot that God made it all possible. We put trust in the hands of politicians and believed that they were going to do the best for us. It didn't work, did it?

"If we had all believed in God and obeyed his laws, all the wars could not have happened and we would not be in the position we are now. It will take many years for us to reach the living standards we used to enjoy, if ever.

"The supplies of tinned food will not last for long and we will all be forced to hunt for food for a while like our ancestors used to. I will stay until you have learnt to be independent of tinned foods and I shall teach you how to hunt. When you can do that, then I must go and find other survivors and take to them the hope that I have brought you. I am telling you now so that when the time comes, you will be prepared for me to leave.

"As a family man, I would dearly love to stay and set up home with a family somewhere. But I know that there will be many who will think that God has forsaken them. I hope to convince those that I meet that this is not so. If people don't believe, then there is no hope left.

"I believe that this is mankind's last chance to bury all our prejudices, and we must take it or fail God completely."

"How long can you stay?" Allyson asked.

"Until such time that I can see that you can look after yourselves and not depend on tinned food. I can see eventually a system of barter. Those who have crops will have to exchange any surplus for other goods or services someone else can supply, so when you are better, we can sort out what you have in terms of what you can grow and what you can do to help others.

"I see that you have a spinning wheel. Do you know how to use it? You may find that it will make a vital contribution to your own well-being and the well-being of others.

"Some time in the future, everyone will need new clothes. Everyone must learn skills new to them, but the old skills that have been lost will also have to be revived. Everyone will have to contribute, even the elderly, if there are any left, will have to teach the young. We must not lose the education that most adults have or there will be no progress."

The door opened just then and Sharon came in with some bowls of rice pudding which she had heated on Believer's instructions.

"Hello, young lady, do you think that you can feed your Mummy? Perhaps Judy can come up as well and feed Joanne, I have to go down and get a bath ready for you two."

Sharon shouted down to Judy and asked her to come upstairs and when she did, Believer went down and fetched sufficient water which he put on the hob to heat in some large pans. Then he checked in Sharon's room to find some clean night clothes for the children.

When the girls came down, Believer set them to do the washing up while he carried on with the preparations for the bath. By the time the washing up was finished, Believer had managed to get a shallow bath for them.

"Come on, you two, off to the bathroom with you. There are some towels in there. If you can get into the bath together, you can help each other. When you've finished and got yourselves covered up again, I will come in and wash your hair."

The two girls went into the bathroom, and Believer was pleased to hear a few giggles as they tried to wash themselves. He sat down at the kitchen table to think and pray, but fell asleep after a few minutes with his head on the table.

"Mr Believer. Wake up. Are you alright, Mr Believer?" He became aware that someone was shaking him and trying to rouse him. He shook his head and looked up, then he saw that Sharon was looking very worried and almost crying.

"It's alright, Sharon. I'm just tired, that's all. I've had a busy day." He struggled to awareness and went with the girl to wash her and her friend's hair then he took them upstairs and put them to bed. He looked in on Allyson and Joanne before he attended to the chores that were required for the end of the day and the last thing he knew was stretching out on the settee.

Day Thirty

Once again, the sound of movement brought Believer to wakefulness. He found that the time was about mid-morning. Sharon and Judy were looking at tins trying to decide what to have for breakfast.

"Good morning, girls," Believer greeted them. "How are you today? How are the other two?"

"We're alright, Judy's hand is still sore. Mummy and Joanne are sitting up, but I don't think they're very strong yet."

"Why didn't you wake me up earlier?"

"We thought that you must be very tired, 'cos you fell asleep while we were having our baths."

"That's right, I was very tired last night, but I'm not going out today. Instead, I'm going to try to do some washing. All our clothes are dirty, so are all the sheets and towels. There is a lot to do, but I don't know how good it'll be, I've got to do it all by hand."

"Mummy used to use the washing machine," Sharon said.

"I wish I could, but there's no electricity, is there?"

"I didn't think of that, aren't I silly?"

"No, you're not silly, you just forgot. We don't have any electricity, gas or running water, There's no radio or television. If we didn't have the kitchen range, we would be in real trouble, wouldn't we? Is the range still alight?"

It was, but only just and Believer had to coax it back into life before he could cook anything. While the range was heating up, he went to attend to the other two survivors.

Allyson and Joanne had struggled to sit up and were waiting for him. They had been discussing what he had told them the night before.

"Good morning. I'm sorry I didn't come up before. The girls didn't wake me and I slept in. I've got some water on and the girls are trying to choose something to eat.

"It's difficult, we only have tins to choose from. There's no bread or cereals, no flour either. We do have spaghetti and some other pasta products, so we will have to eat something like that. I will go and see to it when I've attended to you two."

"What did you mean when you said that we would have to learn to hunt for food to survive? What sort of things are we going to have to eat?"

"As you've realised, there are only limited supplies of tins and some of those are cat and dog foods. I doubt whether they will hurt us, but they might be difficult to face. The manufacturers used to say they wouldn't hurt us, they are merely prepared to a different recipe. There isn't much choice except to hunt. I killed and ate a crow on the way here and it didn't do me any harm.

"Any large bird will suffice, pigeons, ducks, pheasants, even peacocks or swans. Also, things like rabbits, squirrels, hedgehogs. We will have to use any vegetables we can find. Are there any in the garden? I haven't had time to look properly."

Allyson said, "There were a few potatoes, but we ate most of them. There are some carrots if they haven't rotted away. There was some spinach, but it all seems to have burnt away. There are two apple trees and some currant bushes, but all the fruit has gone from them, perhaps they'll come back next year."

"That's not very good, is it? We shall have to find some from somewhere else."

"You are painting a pretty grim picture. I don't know if we can do what you say, none of us have ever done anything like you are suggesting. I don't like the idea of having to kill things to eat, but I do see your point. If you hadn't come along when you did, we would probably all be dead. Thank you."

"You will have to do a lot of things you've never dreamt of doing before, some that would have horrified you before all this happened. Everything was done for you in shops and supermarkets. Now you will have to do it all for yourselves. Listen, I had never killed or prepared a bird to eat before I ate that crow.

"I decided that I had to learn to do it, so I did. I must admit that I felt very queasy when I was doing it, but I forced myself and I have suffered no after effects. I'm still here, so it didn't do me any harm."

"What about radiation?" Joanne chipped in for the first time.

"That's where trust in God comes in. I reasoned that if God has a purpose for me, then He wouldn't let me die or even become seriously ill. I prayed befor eating that bird as I pray for guidance in everything I do. I pray when I am walking or even driving that dumper. All the time when I am not actually concentrating on the job in hand, I am thinking of my immediate future problems and asking for guidance.

"So far, I have received that help according to my current needs. I found shelter from radiation and from the rain. I found appropriate clothing and food to enable me to survive. I have an air rifle and the means of making more ammunition.

"I have prayer books and hymn books, also a bible. I have all I(need to travel. I was directed here when you desperately needed help and since then, I have been provided with the means of fetching food and fuel. All these things I have received after prayer, so how can I not believe that God means me to travel and try to help anyone I find.

"You four are the first people have encountered in about 40 miles, and I came along in the nick of time. All through the will of God."

Believer left the two women thinking about all the things he had said and went back downstairs to find the girls struggling to open a tin. They were finding the task rather difficult. Sharon was trying to use the opener while Judy was holding the tin down. The seven-year-old didn't have enough strength to close the levers of the opener and turn the key at the same time, and Believer had to smile at their efforts.

"Give that to me, you'll have it all over the kitchen. Find me a pan and another tin, one won't be enough for all of us." Believer prepared the meal and once again he put some out for the girls to eat in the kitchen and carried three portions up so that he could join the others.

Allyson said, "I used to attend church before, but not as often as I should have done. I didn't think I have met such an ardent believer as you. Were you always like this?"

"No, I was a regular churchgoer, but because of the nature of my work, I was rather a lone wolf. I had a wife and family and we were all believers. I never had the courage or opportunity to talk as I do now.

"Since the bombs fell, I have spent a lot of time thinking and now I know that I was never alone. Indeed, the first night that I was alone, I felt God's presence and came to know how to recognise it. I couldn't sleep until I had prayed, and I came to realise that He has a purpose for me as he has for all of us that are left.

"He has a purpose for you as well, although I don't know what it is. It is for Him to tell you, so you must listen to Him. He will come to you when you least expect it and you will come to know what He wants you to do. Believe and trust in Him and you will know His purpose for you."

"Does that go for me as well?" said Joanne. She had not spoken much at all as she had left her mother to do all the talking.

Believer said, "Of course. Actually, I think that you will end up being the hunter and provider for this family. At least until Sharon and Judy are older, but by that time, I suspect that things will be less desperate than they are now. You seem to be the obvious person for that job as you are young and resilient.

"Obviously, the other two are too young and Allyson will have to look after the cottage and the girls. I know that you are a girl, but you will be a woman as soon as you take responsibility.

"I will take you out with me when you are better and we will see what we can do. You must remember that God provided for the needs of the tribes of Israel when they were wandering in the wilderness."

Joanne was very worried about the prospect of being the provider and said, "I just can't see me doing all the things you say. I'm not very brave and I don't like the thought of killing things for food."

"I'm afraid that it is going to be necessary, just to stay alive, particularly in the coming winter. There will not be enough vegetables for a while. You will have to try and grow some. You must keep some of every vegetable crop for seeding and replanting.

"Plant the best of the crop and eat the rest. Plant potato peelings as well. If they have eyes, then they will produce something the next year.

"You may find someone later who can produce cereal crops, but you will have to survive the winter first, and someone will have to do the hunting until then."

"You can't stop over the winter, then?" Allyson asked.

"Probably not. By the time I leave here, you will be able to survive by yourselves. I will see to that, but don't you understand? I will be needed by other people who might be less able to cope than yourselves. They will also need the help that I might be able to give them, with God's assistance and guidance. Would you deny others the chance you have now?

"You have a spinning wheel. If I find someone with sheep, you will be able to spin the wool for them. They might be able to do something for you in return.

50

perhaps let you have some of the wool for your own use. I must spread God's word, but at the same time, I can pass the word to different communities of useful talents or services for everyone's mutual benefit."

Allyson thought about what she had just heard, then she said, "I don't know how to use the wheel, but I will learn. I understand all the points you have made. I can see why you say that you will have to leave us. Also, I appreciate that we must all co-operate as never before. Can you teach me to pray and to turn to God as you do for everything we shall need?"

"I can't really teach you, that must come from within you. What I do is to think about a problem for a while, then I pray and the answer seems to come, or perhaps the problem seems to solve itself. There always seems to be a solution and God will provide it if you ask him. It may not always be the answer you expect, but there will be one."

"You seem so sure, you seem to speak with the conviction of knowledge, not just belief."

"True. Belief and knowledge go hand in hand. If you have knowledge, you can't help but believe. You can believe without knowing, but I have found that belief turns into knowledge, and that in turn, intensifies the belief. So, you see that one feeds the other.

"Oh dear! It does seem that I am giving you a sermon. That wasn't my intention. I was only trying to explain why I must believe and do what I have been saying, and why I must leave you when the time comes. Oh, how I would like to stay here with the pleasant company I have found you all to be.

"I know that I would be useful to you if I stayed, assuming that you would even want me to. I have a greater compulsion about which I have no choice."

"I understand. What can I do to help?"

"Nothing for now, just get better. If you can, teach the children to believe by your own actions and love of God. That reminds me, I must go and see what they are doing."

Believer collected the dishes and went downstairs. He was greeted by the younger girls, who asked him if he wanted them to do the washing up. "Yes please," he said.

"Sharon better do the washing while you dry, Judy, you've got to look after that hand of yours. I bet is still sore. It's a good job you put it straight into cold water. When you've done that, can you try and find all the dirty clothes. We're going to turn this place into a laundry."

51

He started the task of drawing water from the brook and put plenty on the hob. After which, he spent time rigging up clothes lines. For detergent, he had picked up some non-automatic washing powder as he reasoned that the supplies in the cottages were not appropriate to hand washing.

The washing took about four hours, and Believer's hands were sore and blistered by the time he had finished. He said to his young companions that he would never be any good in a Chinese laundry as he considered that the results were far from perfect. In spite of his doubts about the efficiency of his work, a lot had been done, and when the clothes dried, the family would have the benefit of having fresh clothes to wear and linen to sleep on.

"I don't suppose there is one of those old-fashioned irons around," Believer said to Sharon. "You know, one of those that don't work with electricity, like your great-grandmother used to use."

"I think there's one in the garage. Daddy used to prop the door open with it, but it's very rusty."

Rusty it was, and Believer put it by to clean for the next day's use. Then he started to prepare the main meal for the family. This was another stew followed by some tinned fruit.

After the meal had been eaten and the washing up completed, Believer spent the rest of the evening cleaning up the old iron with the aid of some soap filled scouring pads and some sandpaper he had discovered. He found that the iron was badly pitted and it took some hard rubbing to remove any rust which might affec the clothes when it was used. A long job which did nothing to help his sore hands

Day Thirty-One

"You seem to be a very capable person. You seem to think of everything and be able to turn your hand to anything, cooking, washing, hunting and searching for food," Allyson said when Believer took out the morning meal and attended to the needs of her and Joanne. "Is there anything you can't do?"

"With God's help, nothing is impossible. Without Him, I would be a very ineffective person. You haven't seen the results of my laundry efforts yet. You'll probably be horrified as I know I haven't made a good job of some things.

"As to coping, who else is there to get things done? No one else is fit enough. Only me, therefore I must just get on with things. I ask for strength and guidance and then I get on with the work. I do have some material help, though, Sharon and Judy are getting better day by day, and they do a lot of the easier things."

"How is the food holding out?"

"Enough for about two weeks at the present rate, but we will have to be independent of tinned food long before it runs out. We will have to go back to prehistoric methods of hunting and gathering, and it will probably be years before there is a return to any kind of civilisation.

"It will be disastrous if we ever go back to the situation we had before. The world will not stand another major war. The only real way forward from here is to follow the teaching of Jesus and to believe in Him. That is the way to salvation. I'm convinced that there is no other way."

Allyson said, "You're beginning to convince me, anyway."

"That goes for me as well," Joanne added. "What do we have to do to be as strong a believer as you are?"

"You must put your trust in God and Jesus completely. Pray and ask for guidance and you will receive it. Jesus said, 'Whatever you ask for in my name, you shall receive.' The only proviso is that you must believe that it will happen.

"I have talked enough for now. Rest now and later, I will get you downstairs and give you both a bath. You will feel much better afterwards."

"I shall be embarrassed," said Joanne, with a nervous squeak and a very red face.

"I shall be embarrassed as well," Believer answered. "But in view of the circumstances, I see no other course of action. Both of you need a bath. I don't know how long you've been lying there, but I'm afraid that it is rather noticeable.

"I've found some clean linen and will get the beds made up at the same time. Perhaps Sharon and Judy can do that. They can try anyway. Since there is only me strong enough to get you downstairs, I shall have to do it. At a time like this, I must simply regard it as another job to do and put any inhibitions I might have aside."

"I must admit some apprehension myself. But I do see the need, as you say, it must be rather obvious," Allyson said. "We've been in bed for some days now. We were giving most of the food to the children, hoping that someone would come and help us. I started to get dizzy first and then Joanne, from lack of food. Somehow, the children must have got us upstairs."

Joanne said. "I helped you up and got you into bed when you collapsed. I think that the effort drained me. I don't remember after that. Sharon and Judy were helping then everything went blank.

"I suppose that I must have passed out and the girls got me into bed. After that, I got weaker and couldn't get up. You were delirious, and I imagine that I went the same way."

"I can imagine how frightened the little girls must have been. When I arrived, you two were unconscious and so was Judy. She was in the other bedroom. Sharon was conscious, but only just. She knocked on the chair and attracted my attention, otherwise. I might not have stayed.

"Thank God you did," said Allyson.

"Exactly. Thank God. I'm glad He led me to your door in time. I also thank Him that I had some food with me and was able to give you all some fairly soon You've all gradually got better and the girls are quite mobile now, but they stil get tired.

"They have had a bath but they managed to wash each other. You two are weaker and I shall have to help you. Anyway, I shall come and get you later, res now, and don't worry. I shan't take advantage."

Believer collected the dirty dishes and carried them downstairs.

"You've been up there a long time. Are Mummy and Joanne getting better?

"Yes slowly, they are going to have a bath later. Do you think that you can make the beds when I am helping them."

'We can make the beds. Is there anything else we can do?" this was Judy. The poor child had not said much up to now. She was the most affected by the disaster as she had no close family left at all.

"Well, you can wash up the dishes while I make a start on the ironing."

Believer gathered the items that required ironing and made a start on the task. He had decided that, where possible, it would be better to try and live up the standards most folk were used to, even if there were no normal facilities to use. He saw no reason to not having clothes looking as good as possible and even during his walk to the cottage, he had attempted to wash his socks and underclothes in any water he found on the way.

He found the task of ironing very difficult with the old iron he had worked so hard the night before, as he had to stop at regular intervals to re-heat it. "Oh Grandmother, you must have had a very hard life," he said.

"Why did you say that," said Judy. "That's a funny thing to say."

"I was thinking of my grandmother. Do you know, she didn't have any of the modern things you were brought up with. In her early days, she used to have an iron like this and she would have had to use the kitchen range all the time like we have to now.

"She had no electricity or even wireless. She must have had a very hard life. We will have to live like that for a long time. Everything we had has gone and we have to start again."

"My Daddy took me to a place where people worked as they did in the old days. I think it was some sort of museum. I didn't think we would ever have to live like that."

Believer smiled at her and said, "Now you can see how difficult it was in those days. I bet you have learnt more of how they must have lived in the past few days than you did at that museum."

Before the ironing was finished and during one of his enforced pauses whilst the iron was heating up, Believer started to draw water from the stream and put it on the hob to heat for the baths he had promised Allyson and Joanne. When the ironing was finished and the bath prepared, he went to fetch Allyson.

He had some difficulty in negotiating the stairs with her and when he was halfway down, he realised that there was no chair in the bathroom so he shouted down to Sharon to put one in quickly. The girl rushed to do it, and Believer managed to get her mother into the bathroom. Fortunately, she was under weight and not too heavy. He undressed her and eased her into the bath, then he took his turn on the chair in order to get his breath back.

Allyson asked, "Are you sure that this isn't too much for you?"

"Even if it is, it's still necessary, so it must be done," he replied. "In your condition, you are not too heavy, it's just that I'm a middle-aged man and not as fit as I used to be even though I have lost a bit of weight myself and certainly done more exercise in the past few days than I used to."

He started to wash her, making a thorough job and including her hair.

"I haven't been pampered like this for a long time," said Allyson. "Doesn't it affect you, seeing me like this and washing me like you have?"

"Of course, it does. I'm just as human as anyone else. Being a believer doesn't alter my physical reactions. It's simply that I must regard this as a necessary job and I must control my emotions."

"Thank you for that, you are so kind and gentle. I wish I was strong enough not to put you to so much trouble."

"No trouble. It's a pleasure being in a position to help, also, although you don't know it, you have helped me enormously, simply by needing help. I had been alone for some weeks before I came here. Alone with no person but God to share my grief of which, like you, I have had plenty. Finding you has clarified the purpose for which God has for me, and shown me that I must help others as much as possible when I meet them.

"I am still convinced that I can't stay here for ever. There are other people I am to meet and bring God's word to. Much as I would like to stay, I must move on when He tells me to. That won't be until you become independent of me, so I can enjoy your company for a while longer."

"You said yesterday that you long to stay, but must go eventually. You also said that you couldn't be sure that we would want you. I'd like you to know that you are very welcome to stay for as long as you can and not just for the things you do for us. We, all of us, like you very much and shall be sorry to see you go."

"I shall be sorry to go, but when I do, I shall try to find someone I can send to you to help. I think you will need the presence of a man around you to help in case you get any undesirable people around. Four females on their own might be an easy target for some people.

"I keep praying that such persons will be enlightened before long, and that everyone who is left will see the need for total co-operation. Perhaps you would like to add your prayer to mine. If our belief is strong enough then it will come about."

Believer lifted her out of the bath and wrapped a towel round her. He carried her into the lounge and laid her on the settee before fetching Joanne, and giving her the same attention, he had given her mother. Joanne was silent throughout the bath and was obviously very embarrassed at the thought of being bathed by a man she had only known for a short time.

When Believer washed her hair, he said to her, "That wasn't so bad, was it? I bet you feel a lot better for the bath, don't you? Sharon and Judy have made the beds for you all with fresh linen and there are some clean clothes for you to wear.

"Tomorrow, I am going to bring you both downstairs. If you want to move about, you might be able to use a chair as a walking frame. That way, you might be able to use the toilet by yourselves. You should be able to manage that by then."

"Thank you," Joanne said. "You are right. It wasn't really so bad. I could see that you were just doing a job, but it was very embarrassing."

"And for me, if you only knew," he said with a smile. "I'm glad it's over too." He carried her into the lounge to join her mother and helped both of them to get dressed in clean night clothes. Then he carried them up to the bedroom in turn and let them rest before he disturbed them with a meal.

"Sleep now," he said. "I think that you have done enough for today. It's been a hard day for you, and I've just about talked your ears off. Goodnight,"

Downstairs, he found that Sharon and Judy had got themselves ready for bed and he went up with them to tuck them in before going down to sleep himself as the light was now fast fading.

"Dear God. Thank you for sending me here and for providing all the comforts we have here. Please send your healing spirit to help these four people and bring them to complete recovery. Particularly, help Allyson and Joanne so that they can, in turn, care for the little ones. I know that it is your will that I must leave here when it is time. Please send someone to guard them from all harm when I have left. In the name of Jesus Christ. Amen."

Believer had made his final prayer for the night and knowing that he was always answered in some form, he drifted off to a sleep which was troubled from time to time with the image of a man with a gun. The figure was shadowy and he couldn't make out a face. It was not clear whether the man was friendly or not, and Believer could not, at that time, make out the significance of his dream.

Day Thirty-Two

Believer was still troubled by his dream the next morning. He rose and washed, making do with a cold-water shave and carried on with the morning chores of raking out the ashes and stoking up the fire. He drew water from the stream as usual and put plenty on to boil.

He was taking the common sense precaution of boiling all water that was going to be used for drinking, and had impressed on Sharon and Judy the necessity of not drinking any water unless it had been boiled. Since his arrival, he had made sure that there were adequate supplies for the needs of all the occupants of the cottage during the days when he was out.

He was glad to see that they had followed his instructions and he found that there was always a pan of water on the hob. In fact, they had been doing just that when Judy had burnt her hand. That injury was getting better. The blister had receded and the skin was dry and showing signs of rapid improvement, although Judy told him that her hand was still sore.

He thought that the two little girls had coped with the situation remarkably well, although they were still prone to tears at odd times when they thought of all those they had lost. He suspected that Allyson and Joanne cried at times when no one was about, particularly since they had more time to think than anyone else.

The two small girls came down whilst Believer was preparing the breakfast, so he left them to carry on while he went upstairs to see Allyson and Joanne. He found them much improved and sitting up in bed waiting for him.

"Do you think that you're well enough to spend the day downstairs? It would be easier for all of us. It might be better if you changed beds with Sharon and Judy, rather than sharing this double one."

Allyson said, "I think that the answer to both suggestions is yes, but don't you think we ought to ask them first?"

"I'm sure they will agree. I suppose it is Sharon who will have to move out of her own bed. I assume that you, Joanne used to share the room with her and

59

as Judy was only visiting when the bombs fell, she has taken your bed. If they share the big bed, they can comfort each other.

"They have been very brave so far and seem to have a lot of sense for girls so young. Anyway, I must get you two downstairs now."

Believer carried them down and helped them to the toilet. He settled them in armchairs and gave them the breakfast the girls had finished preparing. He took the opportunity to eat with them while the girls ate in the kitchen.

With the conclusion of the meal, Believer told them all that he was going to the ruined shop again and this would be the last chance. Sharon and Judy took on the task of washing up, and Believer once again checked the dumper for fuel and left the family to their own devices.

While he was on his way, he remembered that he had seen something in the building site that looked very much like a generator. It, like the dumper, had been partly buried under rubble and at the time, he had been more concerned with retrieving the dumper and also with the prospect of finding food for the stricken family he had found. He had left the machine to investigate another time.

Today he had time, so he returned to the site and found that his surmise was correct. The machine was a generator and was powered with a small diesel engine. It took him the best part of an hour to move it, and in fact, would not have moved it at all without the help of the dumper which he used to pull the generator free from the rubble.

Another hour was used to find a starting handle which fitted. Fortunately, the machine started without a great deal of effort and he tested it with an electric drill he had found amongst the general wreckage.

It took him some considerable time to load the machine into the dumper as it was quite heavy and he was tired from moving a large quantity of rubble. Nevertheless, he felt that the machine would prove to be invaluable as long as the diesel fuel held out.

At the shop, Believer loaded the last of the available food which included bottles of various sauces. Items like soap and detergents, matches and as many candles as were not destroyed. Firelighters and a supply of medicines and wound dressings. Some bags of smokeless fuel. In fact, anything at all that he considered might be of use he loaded into the dumper.

When he finally filled the dumper to his satisfaction, he set off towards his temporary home, driving very carefully in order to avoid spillage on the way back,

On his arrival, he was greeted enthusiastically by Sharon and Judy and also by Allyson who had been worried by his long absence.

The two young girls had prepared the meal duly supervised by Allyson from the armchair in which she had spent the day, and Believer gratefully accepted the meal after having a wash to remove all the dust with which he was covered.

When the meal was over, he enlisted the help of the two girls in unloading the dumper. They started on the food and the smaller items as Believer moved the heavier pieces. The generator gave him as much trouble as it had when he loaded.

He overcame the problem by driving the machine to a low wall and tipping the skip onto it. He was then able to wheel the machine through the garden and into the garage where he also kept the dumper.

"Mister Believer," Sharon said. "Why have you brought tins of cat and dog food. We haven't got either?"

"I'm afraid that's for us if we get desperate. If it's good enough for cats and dogs, it will keep us alive and we can't be too careful what we eat from now on. We will have to trust the manufacturers and God. We are going to need all the food we can get and soon we will have to go into the countryside to hunt and catch wild animals to eat."

"Yeuk! I don't fancy that. Do you mean we will have to eat rabbits and things?"

"Oh yes, there's no doubt about that and we shall have to find out how to catch them. That will be Joanne's job when she's better. We will have to learn to grow all kinds of vegetables to help us eat properly.

"I passed a barley field while I was out and there's still a bit left in a corner. When it is ripe, we will have to harvest it and perhaps we will be able to make some kind of bread.

"I hope you've been behaving yourselves while I've been out. How have your Mummy and Joanne been?"

"They've been much better since they came downstairs. Mummy has been showing us how to knit. We undid an old sweater and started to make squares for a blanket."

"That's a wonderful idea. Blankets are going to be needed for sure. We shall have to look for old woollen clothes whenever we go out. I didn't think of it before, but there's some wool in that shop, I'll pick some up next time I go that way, then you girls can start making clothes and blankets for trade."

Believer went into the lounge and found that Allyson and Joanne were much improved, although they were not capable of maintain any sustained activity. In fact, Allyson was very tired after her efforts in trying to show Sharon and Judy how to knit.

"Hello, you two, Sharon told me about the blankets, that's a wonderful idea. I've had a bit of luck. I've brought back a diesel generator. It's old, but it works. I can connect it up to the electrics and we can use it to work the washing machine. We shall have to fill the hot water system by hand so that the machine can take in water.

"I shall rig up the generator in the garage as it makes a lot of noise and we don't want to attract the wrong sort of people. I'm afraid that human nature, being what it is, there are bound to some that will think of robbing for food and other possessions. We must pray hard that any we meet will be turned from ways of violence and come to understand that they must co-operate in order to survive."

"That thought has occurred to me as well," Allyson said. "What can we do to protect ourselves?"

"Not a lot at the moment. We have no weapons anyway. When we have started to hunt for food, we shall have to hide any tins that we have left so that there is no temptation for others."

Allyson said, "I thought I saw a gun in your belongings. Isn't that any good?"

"Not much, it's only an air rifle I have kept for hunting. In any case, I don't believe in killing people. Enough have died as you can understand. Killing is totally against my principles.

"I will have failed God if I have to resort to shooting at anyone. If we are to love everyone as Jesus taught us, how can we do this with a gun?

"I don't even like killing animals for food. But I'm afraid that will be necessary. Even before the disaster, I was totally against fishing and hunting for sport. But as we are carnivores, I can see the need to hunt for food only. Besides, I very much doubt if we could find enough vegetables to sustain us in our present circumstances.

"I used to hate seeing rows of anglers trying to catch fish which they would only throw back into the water after ripping out their mouths. Some sport! The fish can't even fight back."

"I never saw it that way before. In fact, my husband used to go fishing and his tackle is in a cupboard upstairs. Will it be any use to us?"

"Of course, provided that we only use it to catch food. It is possible that there will be plenty of fish in the rivers as there will be few anglers left. It will provide us with another source of food."

Allyson said, "You must be very tired. You've done everything for us. You've been working all day and evening too. That settee you're sleeping on can't be very comfortable either. I wish I could offer you a proper bed to sleep on."

"Don't worry. It's a luxury compared to some of the places I've slept in. I've slept in a church and a workshop and in a tent while I was on the way here. So, I'm living in luxury for a while. I am pleased to be in your company, and so pleased that God has given me the strength and courage to be able to help you all. Believe me, I am happy to be here for a while."

"You've lost everyone yourself. How do you cope with it?"

"With God's help, but of course I miss my family and friends and feel full of grief at times. It was very hard at first, particularly when I was alone. Meeting you has helped. Knowing that there is a task for me has given me purpose and that makes things easier."

Believer helped the two older people to their beds and settled the youngsters into the double bed as he had discussed with the family. He went to bed himself but was again troubled by the dream that had disturbed him the night before. This time, the man with the gun seemed to have a name, Eric. Believer remembered that he had prayed for someone to come and look after the household after he had left, and he concluded that the man, Eric, was to be that person. He slept better afterwards.

Day Thirty-Three

Believer woke to hear Judy calling for him. "Mister Believer. Can you come quick? Sharon needs your help."

He rushed upstairs and found that Sharon was trying to help her mother down the stairs but were both sitting halfway down. "Why didn't you call me sooner? You know that I would only be too glad to help."

Allyson said, "I suppose that this is my fault. I wanted to be a bit independent so that I could help you more. You've worked non-stop since you came, even doing the housework which I should be doing. I feel very guilty about not being able to do my share.

"I'm not as strong as I thought I was and had a dizzy spell. Joanne feels the same way. She was crying just now and said she wanted to help."

"Don't you worry about the work. Someone has to do it. Besides, I have Sharon and Judy to help and they have been tremendous, haven't you, Sharon?"

Sharon blushed and said, "I've only done a little bit."

"Your little bit has made it possible for me to do the rest. Otherwise, wouldn't have managed and you wouldn't have any clean clothes to put on. O you go and get dressed now, and I'll see if I can find something for you to do."

"What about Joanne and I?" Allyson asked.

"You are obviously too weak to do much, but you can supervise Sharon an Judy. I'm sure that if you tell them how to do things, you will find out just wha little treasures you really have. You know that they cooked all the food for us a yesterday and they have been boiling water for us to drink.

"They've done quite a bit of washing up. They tell me that they wer Brownies. They have earned a lot of Brownie points and will earn a lot mo yet."

"They've only been Brownies for a few months but they were both very kee Sharon joined first and Judy a few weeks later. Since they both becam Brownies, they have become inseparable.

"They do everything together. Judy came round here, the day the bombs fell and we tried do what we could till help came. Nobody came, except you."

"I'm afraid there aren't many people left at all, judging by my experience. I suspect that all the towns and cities have been devastated. All the villages are badly damaged and it is not a pretty sight out there.

"As you know, I went near Derby to collect that coke and it's just a big hole in the ground. That reminds me, I shall have to go and get some more to lay in a good store for the winter.

"I shall have to fill the dumper right up again. I shall take a broom with me next time as it's well scattered. If the girls were fitter, I would take them. I think they would be better employed here where they can take a rest whenever they feel like it."

"Can you help me down the stairs now, please? I will see that the girls will do what they can."

Believer helped her down and into the bathroom and after into the lounge. Then he went back up for Joanne, passing Sharon and Judy on the stairs.

"Good morning," he said to her. "Your mother says that you've been crying because you can't help more."

"Yes, I listened to you talking to Mum last night and I suddenly realised how much you were doing for us."

"Don't you realise that your time to help will come very quickly? As I see it, your job for the near future and for some time to come will be the most difficult and dangerous. You will have to go out most days for food and to gather anything edible, like blackberries.

"I am going to make you a crossbow and you will have to learn how to use it. That will take some time. An air rifle would be better, but we only have the one I brought with me, and as I said, I can't stay forever. God keeps telling me that there is work for me to do elsewhere and when you are able to carry on without me, I must leave."

Joanne said, "I know that you have said that before, but I never quite realised how difficult it was going to be. Can't we just go on finding tinned food like you have so far? No, I don't suppose we can. I see now that it won't last for ever, but what did you mean about being dangerous?"

"I'm very much afraid that people are not all kind and friendly. There are bound to be some that will want to rob and steal from those who have managed to survive and have food. Some will not be particular about how they go about it. You must be careful when you are out.

"Also, there will be animals that will be hungry, rats, dogs and even more worrying, what has happened to all the big cats that were kept in zoos? Some of them might have survived and may be loose.

"You will have to move carefully around the countryside as will any other survivors. I am very worried that the main hunting job will be left to you as your mother will have to look after the house and the little ones. You are the obvious choice for hunter as you are young enough to learn and to take up a completely new existence, but big enough to be able to do it. You will also have to teach the younger girls so that they will be able to help you later."

"You haven't made me feel much better, you know, telling me about all the dangers."

"I know that I have painted a pretty terrible picture of the future, but I don't see any viable alternative. I will send someone to help out as soon as I have found one, I can trust. In the meantime, I keep praying for a solution for all the problems."

"You've given me an awful lot to think about. I'm very frightened of the responsibility I'll have. It's alright for you. You believe that God will help you if you pray. I'm not so sure that I can do that," Joanne answered with some apprehension.

"Only believe in God and Jesus, and He will help. The proof is all that has happened to me since the bombs fell. I have felt that He has been with me often and all my prayers have been answered so far."

"Can you teach me how to pray?"

"Not too difficult. Just ask God to help in the name of Jesus. Look, I will say a prayer for you now.

"Dear Lord. Please help Joanne to face the difficulties she will meet in the near future. Give her courage and wisdom. Guide her in the way you wish her to travel. Help her to have the strength of mind and faith to trust in you. Let her know that you are near at all times and calm her fears. Help and protect her and all this household. In the name of Jesus Christ who died for us. Amen."

"Thank you, I feel better now."

"You see, it's working already. God is here and helping now. Just believe and trust in Him. Don't forget to thank Him for all that He does. On my first night, I felt so scared, lonely and worried that I didn't know what to do.

"I couldn't sleep and felt that I had not done all that I was supposed to do. It was some hours before I realised that I hadn't prayed and when I did, I was able to sleep peacefully for the rest of the night.

"After that, when I had to decide on something, I asked for help. Each time, I have been rewarded with an answer. I have felt his presence often since then. Because of all this, I can't help but believe. He has helped me in so many ways, so He will help you if only you ask."

Believer helped her down the stairs and found that after his long conversation, the two young girls had once again excelled themselves. Under Allyson's supervision, they had prepared breakfast.

Allyson said, "You've spent a long time with Joanne. Is she alright?"

"She's fine. I've been scaring her with tales of what to expect for the future. She will need a lot of help and support from you. I think that she has realised the extent of the task facing her. Her job will be the most difficult of all."

Joanne came out of the bathroom and Believer helped her to the table. After saying grace, they ate the meal that the two girls had finished preparing.

After the meal, Believer left the washing up to Sharon and Judy. He filled the dumper with fuel once again and set off for the foundry. On the way, he stopped at a wrecked garage to collect some oil for the engine.

He looked around the forecourt with interest. He prised open one of the plates covering the tank filling points and checked the dipstick. He was delighted to find that the tank was three parts full of diesel fuel. He had only to devise some method of extracting the fuel and Allyson would have a supply for some considerable time.

He carried on to the foundry and started sweeping up the scattered coke. Then he noticed that there was evidence that someone else had been collecting the fuel that was lying about. It was obvious that the person had come on foot as Believer found signs that a bucket had been filled.

If the person had come in a vehicle, then there would have been evidence of tyre tracks. A bucket was of convenient size to be carried easily on foot.

Believer wondered who had been collecting coke as he filled the dumper. He was undecided to know what to do about his discovery. Should he spend time to search? What direction to try?

Surely, if the other survivor had been near while he was working, that person would have heard the dumper. Would he make himself known or would he be frightened? After much thought, Believer decided to return to the cottage and hope that the other person would be able to find it and join them if he or she wished.

He resolved that if the person did not make an appearance before he left, then he would come in this direction and see if he could make contact. With the decision made, he started the return journey.

There was a meal waiting for him prepared by the two little girls under Allyson's supervision and he noticed that she was very tired. Joanne's condition had improved and she was looking a little better.

Believer said to Allyson. "What have you been doing? You know that you shouldn't do too much yet. I bet you've been doing some kind of work."

Allyson admitted it and said that she had been trying to clean the house.

"Tomorrow, don't do anything except eat. You've got to build up your strength. If you work too hard too soon, you will undo all the benefit of the food you have eaten. That won't help me much, will it?"

Allyson apologised and Believer said, "I'm sorry, I seemed to be telling you off like a schoolgirl. I am simply concerned about your welfare."

"No, you're quite right, I should have thought about that. I just felt so guilty about letting you do all the work."

"Why should you feel guilty? Surely, if you found me in the same condition, wouldn't you do everything you could to help? That's a silly question. I know that you would.

"If you are the sort of person to feel guilty about not being able to help, you would undoubtedly do everything you could if the positions were reversed. You would obviously feel the same way that I do. That is to do everything time and ability would enable you to do. Please take things very easy tomorrow and you too, Joanne."

Believer told them of his find at the foundry, saying that he thought the other survivor probably needed help if only Believer knew where to look. He said that he had decided to leave things as they were for the present. He thought that they were only a small group, and were probably living on tinned food in much the same way that he was feeding Allyson and the family.

In these conditions, a small group was liable to survive longer, and there was little point in trying to join forces at this stage. It was going to be hard enough to provide food for the family as it was.

When the meal was cleared away, Believer busied himself with the generator and wired the machine into the main power supply. Now, when the generator was run, all the power points would be operative, and therefore, all the appliances the cottage contained would work, with the exception of the television and radio.

It was possible to use a video machine in conjunction with the television, but of course, there was no broadcasting. In the same way, music could be obtained from the Hi-Fi set with tapes or compact discs, but again, only when the generator was running.

The next problem was to check the water system and see whether this could be adapted to admit water to the washing machine. The hot water tank was of the kind that contained a hot reservoir above a cold tank, and Believer found that the system could be used provided that the tank was filled by hand.

Believer was extremely pleased with the acquisition of the generator and this one item had cut the future work load considerably.

"Mr Believer," Sharon said excitedly, "Will the telly work?"

"The set will work, but I doubt whether anyone is broadcasting. We've tried the portable radio with the batteries we took out of the torch and we didn't get anything. Anyway, we will have to be careful of the fuel and we must only use the generator when we really need it.

"Also, it makes a lot of noise, so I shall have to muffle it a bit. We should only run it when the washing machine is working and then only because there are five of us and we make a lot of washing between us. I know where there is some more fuel, but I shall have to think of a way to get it out. That won't be so easy."

Allyson had been listening and said, "I thought you said that you wanted to meet people."

"I do, but as I told Joanne this morning, not everyone is reasonable and there will be some who will try to take what they want by force. I'm afraid that unless they can be persuaded otherwise, they will present a danger. Those who take without giving will destroy everything in the end. They've got to be shown better ways of survival.

"Allyson, do you know much about growing vegetables or what wild plants are edible. I do know that things like dandelions and nettles are edible, but I don't know how to prepare them. There must be many others, but knowing which is safe is a big problem."

"That's something that I never thought about. We do have some books on wild plants, they might tell us."

"We will have to make do with vegetables we know about until we can find out more."

"We tried to get what we could from the garden, but there wasn't much," said Allyson.

"I saw that you'd dug up some potatoes, but when I arrived, I saw that most of the garden had been underwater. I've seen the remainder of some current bushes and strawberry plants, but their season is over. There will be some blackberry and elder berries later but they will take some finding.

"Your apple trees have all been stripped by the blast. They might produce next year. That won't help us now. We might find some potatoes when the ground has dried out. By the way, what did you do with the potato peelings?"

"We threw them in the dustbin. Why did you ask?"

"I know from experience that if you plant the peelings, they will produce small potatoes next year, especially if they have eyes and you put them all together. I'll see if I can rescue them. How did you manage to cook them?"

"We used the range, but we had a bit of a job with it at first. The worst thing is that we were going to a supermarket the next day and we hardly had any food in the house. Of course, all the food that was left in the freezer was ruined after the first few days.

"We used to depend on that a lot and we didn't know how much until there was no electricity. We had to throw most of it away and the crows ate it."

"Perhaps you should have eaten the crows. They would have kept you alive Tomorrow, I am going to start making a crossbow for hunting. It will take a day or two, and of course, I shall have to make some bolts for it. There are some six inch-nails in the shed. They'll do for the bolts.

"There's a van on its side up the road and it's got leaf springs. I'll go an take them off and I can use them to make the cross bow. I should like to mak more than one, but it won't be easy."

"Is there no end to your talents. So far, you've done so many jobs, you seer to be able to do anything," Allyson asked with awe.

"I do have my limitations. I believe that we can do anything if only we kne how. We will all have to do things we have never done before and we hav already started. Sharon and Judy have used a kitchen range which I doubt the have done before.

"You would not have let them near it, they are so young. Joanne will have learn to hunt. You will have to learn to live in a house without electricity. You' already started that. That spinning wheel is another problem to overcome, and later you will need to learn how to grind grain for flour.

"I will have to learn how to make a crossbow. It will have to be accurate. I've got some ideas, but I've never tried to make one before. You can help by praying for me. I want to make some sort of windmill to work a car alternator.

"That's another thing I shall have to learn how to do. If I can do that, there are things like refrigerators in caravans that run on 12 volts. I shall have to find one of those. What I can't do is to make a television work with no broadcasting. You see, there are things I can't do."

"My husband worked in an office, but he did like to make things out of wood. He had several tools that you can use if you need."

"Thank you, I've seen them. Don't you think you should try to learn how to use them? There are quite a few repairs needed to the house and I won't be able to do them all. Also, you will have to learn how to look after the dumper and generator and how to start them."

"Won't you take the dumper with you when you leave? I should think that you could get a long way on it."

"No, it'll be more use to you here. Besides, if I travel with a vehicle, there will be some that will covet it, and I would be in more danger than if I was walking. You will probably need something to carry things to trade with later on, so I'll leave it here and go with only the things I came with."

"You should know that I keep wishing you could stay here and not have to leave here at all. I feel that if you could stay, our life would be quite comfortable, considering the circumstances. I do respect your need to travel as I know that you believe that God has a purpose for you. How long can you stay?"

"About two weeks after you are fit and well, but that will depend on how well Joanne makes out with the hunting. I want her to use the crossbow well and hit what she is aiming at. So, she will have to practice a lot first. Thank you for your compliment, I wish that I could stay, but that is not to be.

"I must carry out the mission God has given me. It seems like a daunting task, but I must try. I know that I will have God's help, so perhaps things will not be so hard."

Allyson said, "Do you realise that it's getting darker. I didn't realise that we had been talking for so long."

"It's the lack of sunshine that makes it get dark so soon. There hasn't been much sun since the beginning of July, before the rains started. I know that it hasn't rained much since I started walking. The torrential rain we had before that has been good for us as it has helped to clean up the ground.

"The water has washed a lot of the radiation away, but I don't think it will be safe for us to venture into the cities. Those of us that are left must stay in the countryside and make our living here. We shall have to learn to live off the land, and I suspect that the winter will be a bad one.

You should be alright here, provided you can find enough food to eat. Everyone will have the same problems, but if the winter is bad, there won't be much travelling until the spring and I think by that time, we shall all be desperately in need of green vegetables. That's why I mentioned the wild plants that are edible. They will be the first to grow and it'll be very important to know which are poisonous."

By this time, it was completely dark, so Believer lit a candle from a spill he ignited from the range. He banked up the range for the night. Then he helped Allyson and Joanne upstairs and got them ready for the night while Sharon and Judy got themselves to bed. As for Believer, he settled down to do some serious reading of his bible before he became too tired to concentrate and went to sleep himself.

Day Thirty-Four

Allyson was up first, waking Believer with her movements. He rose and found that Allyson was just going out to fetch water.

"Don't you think that I had better get the water in for breakfast?" he said. "You don't want to tire yourself at the beginning of the day."

Allyson came back and let Believer do the heavy work. Instead, she busied herself with the kitchen range, raking out the ashes and adding coke to the still glowing embers. When Believer returned with the water, she said, "I thought that it was time that I started pulling my weight in the house instead of having you do it all."

"I appreciate your efforts, but I don't expect you to leave me with nothing to do. Anyway, how are you feeling today? You are looking better."

"I get stronger every day, mostly thanks to your help, also the food you have supplied us with. I vaguely remember someone spoon feeding me with some sort of stew. That must have been when you first came here. I have just realised that you must have given us all the food you had with you on that day.

"Were you not out for most of the next day? I wasn't conscious for most of it. I remember being lifted and then silence until I heard some sort of machine. That must have been when you came back with the dumper, then after a while, you fed me again and from that time, I started to get better. You seemed to know exactly what to do and have played the part of doctor, nursemaid, cook, dishwasher and many others."

"As to doctor, I'm certainly not that. However, I asked for help as soon as I found you all. If I seemed to do the right things, it is only because God has guided me, as he has done for a long time. I didn't know I was being helped before I was suddenly left alone. There was no one to turn to for help and advice except God and Jesus who have guided me here in time.

"I am not the only person for whom God has a purpose. All of you are now involved. Perhaps you ought to start asking Him to guide you. I think that your job is to start producing food and other items to help other needy people.

Yesterday, I was given the idea that a market garden would be a good place to find. Judy said that she thought that there might be one somewhere around here and I think that if there is, it might be a good idea for you to take it over. There might even be some vegetables left in the ground to be harvested next year.

"There is a field with some barley left that is nearly ripe and we should be able to make some sort of bread. But you must save some of the grain for replanting. All this means that there is a great deal of work to do for the future.

"I don't see it as my task though. I have been given everything I need to travel, so it seems that that is what I must do. Only staying here and at other places to give a little help where I can and where it is most needed."

Allyson said, "You say only a little help, but I know that none of us would be here if you hadn't come. In the first place, you gave us the last of the food you had with you with complete unselfishness. Secondly, you nursed us back to the health we enjoy today, doing all manner of unpleasant tasks.

"You washed and bathed us and carried us up and down the stairs. You foraged for food and many other things that we needed all on your own with no thought of your own safety. All of this and you are no young athletic man either. Just how old are you?

"I know that you have said that you had grown up children. I am sure that there are many stronger men who wouldn't have bothered or cared enough to try. You not only tried, but you have succeeded so far."

"I'm 54, and as to the help I have given, it is only a little help which I could not have achieved but for the help that I have received. My strength of mind and purpose comes from the Lord. I pray to Him constantly, and it is He who drives me on. I attempt nothing new without first asking for help.

"My only regret is that I didn't realise how much He has helped me in the past. He not only helps me, but you as well. Someone must carry His message of peace and love to the people that are left and someone must start providing food for others. I think that is you and your family.

"I don't think that you can do that without His help or the help of others and I know that you will get that help since I have prayed hard for a solution. I have been rewarded with a dream of meeting a man after I have left here. This man will have strengths that I do not possess. You see, I have not the temperament to give you any physical protection for how can I preach peace and love and react violently if it should be needed.

"The man will come and will be able to meet violence with the correct action. I even know his name, although I have yet to meet him. He will be able to help you in the way of trade and agriculture, and will be able to fill any gap that I will leave."

Allyson sat quietly for a moment or two and then said, "You are so sure and you know that these long talks are getting through to me. I find that I am beginning to pray more often now. The main reason is that I know that you are completely sincere in what you say. All I can say for now is thank you for stopping here on your journey.

"The worst thing is that I am getting very fond of you. I say the worst thing because I know that there is no way in the immediate future for that fondness to grow and develop into love which I know will come because you will have to leave here sometime. What I do know is that when things are better and sane sort of order returns, I shall follow you and try to find you."

It was Believer's turn to be silent for he was very surprised at Allyson's words. "That was the last thing I expected you to say. Thank you very much for the compliment. I feel a strong attachment to you myself.

"It was the last thing that I wanted to happen because it would be completely unfair if I took advantage of you, knowing that I must leave in the future. I think that it would be wise to prevent our relationship from getting any closer while I am here.

"If you want to follow later I can't stop you and indeed would welcome it, but do wait until travel is easier and safer and also when the girls are older. You have a duty to them. I might be difficult to find, though, I will only be able to give you a rough idea of my long-term plans of direction and location.

"I think that it is likely that I shall wander through the old National parks as these areas are more desolate and are likely to have the most survivors that will need my help. I shall try the Peak District first, then the Pennines, Lake District and the Yorkshire Moors.

"You will have to look first in those areas, but I really don't know where I shall go. It depends on where I can do the best."

Allyson said, 'If your actions here are anything to go by, you will leave a trail of people who will remember you. None of us here will ever forget you. Breakfast is ready, will you call Sharon and Judy? I will go and get Joanne down."

Breakfast was another scratch meal from tins and afterwards, Believer checked the dumper and started it. This time, when he left, he took his air rifle with the intention of doing some hunting while he was out. His main purpose was to procure some batteries to go with the alternator he had acquired the previous day.

He set off, determined to explore the local roads and lanes to find out what was available near at hand. Previously, he had been too busy providing essentials to take back. Now, he was looking for items of less immediate necessity for future use.

His first find was a small transport yard with some lorries that had been parked at the disaster time. These had been blackened by the heat flash, but two had intact batteries which still had the remains of a charge in them. These he removed, feeling very pleased as they were both heavy duty.

He added an empty 25-litre oil drum and two others which he filled with diesel fuel he drained from the fuel tanks of the lorries. In the damaged workshop, he found some rolls of insulated wire used in vehicles and various nuts and bolts which he added to his acquisitions.

Then he turned his attention to the damaged houses nearby. In this instance, he was looking for an old type spin drier. He was disappointed in the first, but was luckier in the fourth.

A caravan dealer's premises provided him with the refrigerator he wanted but he had to take this out of a smashed caravan. Now, he had the materials he needed for providing battery power and means of preserving a small amount of food. The next task after he had made the crossbow would be to make a wind driven source of power to drive the alternator.

On his way back to the cottage, he stopped in open country where he had seen same crows feeding on something which had died in a field. The dead animal turned out to be a sheep, but this had been dead too long to be any use to him, so he took the air rifle and waited by an old tree for the crows to settle again after being disturbed by the arrival of the dumper. His patience was rewarded and he managed to shoot two of the scavenging birds.

Well satisfied with the results of his excursion, he started the dumper and returned to the cottage where he was greeted with a great deal of curiosity concerning the various contents of the machine.

"What on earth do you want that old spin drier for? We have no electricity" Joanne asked him as she was completely mystified to see it.

Believer laughed and said, "Not to use with electricity, but to help provide it. You see, I am going to dismantle it and use the drum on its bearings to turn the alternator. The drum will spin easily without the motor and if I fit vanes to it.

"I hope to make it turn the alternator to charge up these two batteries. That will work the fridge which is dual voltage and will run off 12 volts. I can also rig up some lighting with the wire I brought back."

"I should like to see that," said Joanne. "Do you really think that you can do it?"

"We shall have to see, won't we? But first, I will have to make the crossbow I promised and that will take a few days. Allyson, do you think you can do something with these crows? Perhaps a casserole.

"What I did with the one I ate on the way here was to put in the fire to burn all the feathers off, then I cut it open and threw away all the bits I didn't fancy, I roasted the rest over the fire. I was too lazy to try to pluck it first."

"I'll do my best, but I have never done anything like this before. I suppose that I had better get used to it."

"I'm afraid so, I know it won't be pleasant for you, but I must get on with making that crossbow. First though, I will start the generator up and you can use the washing machine after I have filled the water tank. While I am sorting that out, perhaps someone can gather up the dirty clothes to wash."

Believer started the difficult task of filling the tank with water from the stream. He found that lifting the heavy buckets up to the top of the tank a very taxing job as the tank was in a confined space, but he was successful in the end with the help of Joanne and the two young girls. Then he changed the hot and cold water connections to the machine. He blocked off the unused pipe so that any water taken in would not drain away through the redundant water pipes.

Joanne loaded the machine and Believer started the generator. He told Joanne how to check on the fuel in the generator and the water in the tank from time to time as he didn't know how long either would last.

He turned his attention to the task of making the crossbow. He used the disc cutter to dismantle both springs and carefully cut the main leaf of each down the centre line. He was then left with four powerful springs about a yard long and about one inch wide. He had considered that a spring of this size would not be too difficult for a fit person to bend.

By the time he had finished preparing the springs Allyson had cooked the meal and the family sat down to a crow casserole to which she had added some canned vegetables. She had used considerable ingenuity, and the meal looked and smelled most palatable.

The family seemed reluctant to start eating, so Believer said, "Thank you Lord for providing the food we eat." Then he added, "Since I brought the crows, then perhaps I should be the guinea pig." He started eating.

"You know, it's really quite good. You all will have to get used to this kind of meal, no matter how much you are worried about what it is. "Allyson, you really have made a good job of the cooking, It looks good as well. Won't you join me in sampling your cooking?"

"You provided it and I did the cooking. So yes, I will eat some. Come on you lot, have some faith in us," Allyson said, then she looked at Believer and added, "And in God our Father."

'Well said, but it is God and Jesus you should have faith in, rather that Allyson and I. Remember that God fed all those thousands of Israelites in the desert after Moses brought them out of Egypt. Remember also that on more than one occasion, Jesus fed a multitude with just a little food that seemed totally inadequate.

"God has looked after us so far, so do you think that He would let us be poisoned now. I can't believe that, can you?"

Allyson started eating, quickly followed by Joanne and the two girls rather diffidently. After they had all eaten, Believer said, "That wasn't so bad, was it?"

"Well, it was different," Joanne answered. "But it wasn't terrible like I thought it would be. I could get used to it quite easily."

"That's the spirit. You have a new life to lead that will be entirely different to whatever has gone before. The food you eat will be mostly what has been hunted and killed and whatever vegetables you can grow or find. Vegetables are another problem.

"We really must find out what we shall be able to plant and when to do so We should find that old market garden, and all go there and see what there is in the way of crops we can use now or save for replanting. Allyson, how is the washing doing? I want to turn the generator off soon."

"It's nearly done. I've managed three loads and the last one is on its final spin."

"Good, that generator can be heard for miles in the evening, or at any time suppose, now that there is no industry. The dumper makes a lot of noise as well Tomorrow, if you and Joanne feel up to it, we can have a driving lesson."

Allyson said, "I can drive, is that machine so difficult?"

"No, quite easy for you, except that it is rear wheel steering which can be a little tricky at first. Joanne will have to start from scratch though. You will both have to learn how to start it and also how to look after it."

"Are you going to make mechanics of us as well as all the rest you expect us to do?" This was Joanne.

"I am not going to make you into anything. I am merely telling you what you must do to survive. I will teach you as much as I can, then it will be up to you. You will learn some from me.

"Other things you will pick up as you go along, just like any other survivor. You must put your trust in God, pray to Him often and you will get answers to your problems. Remember that the answers you will get will not always be the ones you expect.

"Your first concern is your own survival, but at the same time, think and ask God how you can help others. Have you not already seen that you are being guided along that road. You have the spinning wheel. There is a market garden nearby and the stream is quite wide and deep. There should be fish in it.

"Perhaps Sharon and Judy could learn to fish. You have coke for the range and a dumper to collect more when you need it, and also to carry produce when you can grow it. I think that you will end up being gardeners and hunters, knitters and weavers. The four of you and any others that come along will be Jacks and Jills of all trades.

"I am sure that you will be producing vegetables and fruit to trade for wool and other necessities. Why don't you ask God for guidance tonight before you go to sleep?"

"Can you teach us to pray as you do?" Allyson asked.

"I am not so sure that I can, praying can be very personal and everyone is different and so will pray differently. I can't say that anyone actually taught me to pray. I just ask God for help and He hasn't failed me yet. All I can say is that you should be sincere and believe."

The washing machine finished its programme, and Allyson went to attend to it while Believer turned off the generator and the two girls did the washing up.

'Believer, what shall I do with all the rubbish from the birds, all the bits and pieces I cut out, before I cooked them?" Allyson asked.

"I suggest that you burn them in the range, otherwise you might attract predators that you don't want. Later perhaps, it might be beneficial to put rubbish in the field and see if it will attract crows to shoot. Talking of crows, you did a fantastic job with the two I brought back, particularly as it was the first time you had cooked them. I know that there will be lots of first times for all of us. I know that I have had a few up to now.

"I am very much afraid that we will all return to a primitive life and forget about all the luxuries that we used to have. There will come a time when we will forget what things like tea, coffee and cocoa taste like. There will be no more imported fruits and vegetables for a very long time.

"I sometimes wonder what has happened to the rest of the world. I imagine the war was global. If any nations have escaped, they will probably be in South America and Africa.

"The economy of these countries depended on others for their survival and no doubt will be struggling to sort themselves out. I suspect that other countries will have enough to do without bothering about anyone else. Poor old England can't expect any help from outside, so no foreign trade. Therefore, we will have to help ourselves."

Allyson thought for a while, then she said, "I hadn't considered that aspect of life before. We have been enjoying tea, ever since I can remember, even since you came. I never thought that we would actually run out. Of course, if there are no imports, we won't be able to get any more."

Believer could provide no answer to this, but as the evening was drawing to a close, he said a final prayer.

"Lord, help us to look forward to the future with new hope. Give us peace this night, and in the days to come, help us to start producing food for us and for others so that we can all continue to live in Your love and glory. Give us You're blessing in the name of Jesus your son. May you and the Holy Spirit be with all of us now and for ever. Amen."

After the prayer, Allyson and the girls went upstairs and Believer settled down as usual on the settee. He reflected that he had taken an important step towards a situation, whereby he might be called upon to conduct same kind of religious service with groups of survivors.

He had no ambition to displace any ordained priest, but he felt that God had chosen him to be some sort of travelling missionary, particularly to isolated communities and would therefore, have to conduct any kind of service requested of him.

He realised that same might regard him as some sort of charlatan, but he hoped that he might overcome this by working with any regular clergy he might came across. Where there was no priest available, he hoped that he would be accepted for what he was. Just a devoted Christian who wanted to carry out God's work to the best of his ability.

Day Thirty-Five

The morning was half finished by the time all the usual chores were completed. This included the normal scratch meal and attention to the kitchen range and fetching in the water. Believer considered that it was time to introduce Allyson and Joanne to the mechanics of the dumper.

As the machine was started by hand, he tried to show them how to turn the engine over. Sharon and Judy thought that Allyson's first few attempts were a huge joke, particularly as she failed to start the machine. Believer told her to rest for a while and let Joanne try.

Joanne's efforts were equally unsuccessful and Believer said, "The trouble is that you both are still a bit weak and it is quite a knack. You are just not turning it fast enough before you work the decompression lever. This time, you turn the engine, and I will work the lever." Joanne was successful at this attempt but was very breathless.

"That's better," Believer said. "You can try again when the engine has warmed up and you have got your breath back." He stopped the engine and helped Allyson in the same way and she was successful this time. When the engine was warm, both were able to start it unaided.

Allyson said, "I didn't think that it would be so difficult. I've seen you start it with precious little effort, you made it look easy."

"Perhaps that is because I've done it before. I am stronger anyway. I have not been ill and half-starved like you two. You will find it easier with practice and increasing strength. If it takes two of you to do it, don't worry."

"Allyson, would you climb on and have a go at driving it? It's got the same pedals as a normal car and the steering wheel works the same as a car, but the rear wheels turn instead of the front."

Allyson put the machine into gear and moved off a little erratically at first and causing a fresh round of giggles from Sharon and Judy. She soon began master it and after about ten minutes was managing to control the driving line quite well.

Joanne found the exercise much more difficult as she hadn't driven anything before. In fact, she stalled it a couple of times, but being young and resilient as well as determined, she was able to drive it tolerably well in low gear after a while.

Believer was well pleased at the progress that had been made. Then be turned his attention to the two young girls. "Now, it's your turn. I'm not going to get you to drive the dumper because you are too small to reach the pedals. As you have had such a good laugh, I am going to try and teach you some fishing. I have got some tackle in my kit, but didn't I see some in the house."

"Daddy used to go fishing, his rod is in the bedroom, shall I go and fetch it."

"That's a good idea, Sharon, off you go and be careful of the hook."

"Do you know? I used to get fed up when Jim used to spend a day fishing," Allyson said. "I never thought that fishing was of any use at all. I didn't imagine that we would ever have to fish for food. Now, I am glad that he had the tackle. What do you think the girls will catch?"

"I don't know but children often have a knack of catching fish when adults can't. I don't know why, but when I was a boy, I used to go fishing with just a bamboo pole for a rod and I often used to catch fish, but as I grew older, I caught less.

"I've seen many men fishing since, but never saw anyone catch one. Children do seem to be luckier. I hope that the girls will prove my case.

"By the way, I've changed my views about fishing since those early days. It must be cruel to catch fish, pull the hooks out of their mouths and then throw the fish back. Fishing for us is now a necessity and the girls will be fishing for food.

"In these circumstances, they will not be thrown back. Any caught will be eaten. I think that they will only manage coarse fish. I doubt whether they could manage trout even if there are any.

"They will have to catch a lot to make a meal, four or five for each person, but it will keep them occupied for a while and they will think that they are helping, which of course, they are. I shall have to go off with Joanne to hunt for the rest of us. Can you keep an eye on them while I am away?"

Sharon returned with her father's rods and Believer spent the next hour showing them how to bait the hooks, cast and watch the floats. During this time, Judy actually caught a roach, so Believer showed them how to kill it and remove the hook before he left them to their task.

83

"Do you know where there is a pond? There might be some ducks, around," he asked soon after he had left with Joanne.

Joanne did and directed him to a large pond she knew of. She had seen water fowl on it several times and thought that there was a good chance of finding them this time.

As they were walking, Believer noticed that she was crying, but trying to hide her feelings. "What's the matter? You can tell me."

Joanne replied, "Sharon and Judy told me that it was bad out here, but I never thought that it would be like this. I didn't let myself believe that there would be all this destruction around. I just was not prepared for it at all."

"I am very sorry that I had to bring you out here for you to be upset. That was not my intention, but it's not all bad, there is hope for us. Not everything has been destroyed. Some trees have survived and will bear leaves and flowers next year, possibly fruit as well.

"There is still some grass in sheltered spots, and look here, see this patch of burnt ground! Can you see the new shoots trying to come through? Next year, you won't know this place.

"God has already started to restore the vegetation. And who knows? Maybe the countryside will look even better than it used to. Particularly as man won't be doing much building in the future. No new houses or motorways all over the place.

"I should think that it will be a very long time before another new road is built. We have more than enough for the few of us that are left. Houses as well. Aren't those potatoes growing in the corner of that old wall over there? We will see if we can collect some on the way back. Is it far now?"

"We're nearly there, thank you. I'm sorry that I cried."

"Don't apologise. I've cried a lot since the bombs. It's a release of emotions God give us the means to cry, otherwise we would end up hardened and not have roam for love in our hearts. If there is to be any hope of salvation at all, it will be through love of each other, of all living things and above all, the love of Jesus."

Joanne thought for a while and then said, "You've given me a new insight. realise that you are right. Love is the answer. Do you know that Mum says that you are the sincerest person that she has ever met. That includes Dad.

"Do you think that there is any chance that he could have survived? I suppos that Leicester was pretty well devastated."

"From what I have seen, I wouldn't hold out much hope. As I have said before, a completely new life has started. I remember my family with love, but I have realised that I have to look to the living and I must carry on with the mission God has set me. As will you.

"At least you have your mum and Sharon, also Judy. She needs more help than any of us. But as I told your mum, you must look out for Sharon. She has been so busy looking after Judy, I don't think that she has found time to grieve for herself. She hasn't cried since I've been here and I am worried about her.

"I don't think that Judy would have recovered so quickly without Sharon's care. What about you? I don't think that I have seen you or your mum cry either until today."

'We've done our share of crying. A lot at first and later when we were getting better. We always gave more to the little ones than we had. We were hoping that someone would find us sooner.

"Nobody came, then Mum collapsed and I tried to get her into bed. That was too much for me and I passed out as well. By that time, there was no food left. We hadn't known how to go and find food. What should we have done?"

"I don't want you to think that I am reproaching you, but I think that you should have decided which of you was stronger and after it had rained for a few days, that person should have gone out to find food.

"Possibly, if any food was found the person who was out should have eaten something straightaway to keep her strength up. I did. I realised that I mustn't allow myself to get weak so that I couldn't return. That may sound selfish, but in reality, it was practical.

"For the same reason, I fed Sharon and Judy more than I gave you since they were marginally stronger. It made sense to get them mobile to take some of the load off me. Besides, you two would have only been sick if I gave you too much and that would have done no good at all.

"Is that the pond over there? When we get closer, we should stop talking and move very quietly. We don't want to frighten any ducks away. By the way, have you ever fired an air rifle?"

"Only at fair grounds and then I wasn't very good."

"Not many people are very good at fair grounds. My observation is that most people lean on the counter when they fire. I was taught to shoot when I was in the forces, and I found that if I applied what I had learnt, I was fairly accurate.

"As soon as the stall holder saw that I was holding the rifle properly, she tried to put me off. That was my last attempt at firing any sort of gun before now. I have been fairly lucky since.

"Shall we stop here for a while and I'll show you how to hold the gun? Then, if I manage to get a bird, perhaps you can have a go. There are a lot of us to feed and there is not too much meat on a duck, so two will be better.

"We only had those two crows yesterday, enough to keep us alive, but not to build up our strength. Are you right or left-handed?"

Joanne told him that she was right-handed, and Believer spent about ten minutes showing her how to hold the air rifle. "Remember to hold it tight into your shoulder with your left hand and squeeze the trigger, don't pull it. Are you holding it tight?" Believer took hold of the barrel and shook it.

"You will have to hold it tighter than that. I shouldn't be able to move it easily. Let's try again. This time, hold it so that it is nearly hurting you. That's better. I can't let you practice firing it, we mustn't waste ammunition. You can practice in earnest when we already have one duck."

They approached the pond and saw that there were some ducks on the far side, so they moved away from the shore and walked around at a distance before coming within range. Believer loaded the air rifle and the two of them crept as close as they dared, taking advantage of some bare tree trunks.

Believer then stripped down to his underpants before aiming at the nearest bird. He wounded it with his first shot, then passed the gun to Joanne so that he could enter the water and swim after the disabled duck. He retrieved it and killed it instantly.

The remaining ducks had flown off in a panic, so Believer dried himself off as best as he could. Then he said to Joanne, "Look, I've got to take these pants off. If you are embarrassed, look away." He quickly removed them and dried himself with his shirt before he dressed again.

Joanne had turned bright red and Believer said to her, "I'm sorry about that. I could hardly go home with them still wet. Besides. I don't think there is anything wrong with the human body. It is what God gave us and if it's good enough for Him, it's certainty good enough for me."

Then he continued, "It is only convention that causes embarrassment and convention seems rather silly in these circumstances. Besides, I washed you the other day, as a matter of necessity. We had better move away for a while and see if they came back. Then you can try to get another one."

"I'm sorry that I was so embarrassed. I hadn't thought how you were going to get the duck from the water. I suppose that you will do it again if we get another. I shall be expecting it next time and I will try not to be so surprised.

"It does seem rather silly to worry about you when you stripped me and washed me, and my Mum, of course. We couldn't stand at the time and we did feel much better afterwards."

"Of course, you did. If you feel comfortable, that is an aid to recovery. I might say, you did whiff a bit when I found you, but you were too ill for a day or two, and I daren't move you much at first, only help you with the pot. That must have embarrassed you then, but it had to be done, particularly after you had eaten and drunk a bit."

While they were talking, they had moved away from the pond and busied themselves with plucking the duck Believer had shot. They kept a watch on the pond from a distance, but had to wait about an hour before the ducks or perhaps some others came back. The hunters moved towards them as before, and Joanne asked if she should go into the water for any bird she happened to kill.

Believer said, "There is not much point in you risking a chill. Besides, you are not fully fit yet and I don't want to risk you getting into difficulties. That wouldn't do us much good, would it? We've got to get back yet."

Joanne took the rifle and Believer stripped off again and moved as close as he dared to the water but keeping himself covered with the clothes he had removed. The girl took aim at the nearest duck but missed. This time the birds did not fly away, but were made uneasy by the splash of the pellet in the water beyond them and actually moved closer to the bank.

Joanne quietly reloaded and her second shot was more successful. Believer was able to fetch the injured bird and kill it as he had before. He came back to the shore and dressed again.

"We should eat well today, but we should never be greedy and shoot more than we need. I'm sure that if we take too many, they will fly away and not return. We must vary the sort of animals and birds as much as possible.

"You did very well with your shooting, perhaps you might be able to get hold of an air rifle sometime in the future. In the meantime, the crossbows will have to serve. They will have more killing power, but will probably be less accurate. The main advantage is that the bolts I shall make will be re-usable.

"You will have to practice a bit before you go hunting. It won't be easy, but with prayer and effort on your part, you will do it, mainly because you will have to in order to survive and to keep the family fed."

Joanne replied, "I was terrified that I would frighten them away, but so pleased that I hit one. What do we do now?"

"1 think that we should head for home, don't you? The others will be wondering where we have got to. Besides, I have to do some more work on that first crossbow before it gets too dark. It's four o'clock already and you are looking very tired. We've some miles to go, and I think that it is starting to rain again."

The couple started on their homeward journey with the rain increasing as they walked. They stopped at the place where they had seen the potatoes and Believer used his hands to dig enough to provide two or three meals, filling all his and Joanne's pockets. By the time they returned, Joanne was feeling very tired and Believer had to support her for the last quarter of a mile.

Allyson insisted that they both change into dry clothes and while they were drying out, she started preparing the birds. Sharon appeared and seemed eager to speak and when Believer was dry and able to listen, she told him that she and Judy had managed to catch nine small fish during the day. Believer was pleased to hear this and said that he wished that they could have them on toast for breakfast, but as there was no bread, they would have to find some other way.

Joanne had dropped off to sleep on the settee and Allyson was rather concerned about her.

Believer said, "Don't worry, she will be alright. Perhaps today was a bit too much for her. She is still weak. After the meal, she will be much better. She must rest tomorrow and I shan't take her with me.

"She will make a good huntress. She shot one of those ducks and we found those potatoes. There are some left, but don't forget to save the peelings and bury them in the garden for next year."

He left her with the cooking and took himself off to the garage where he started working on the stock for the crossbow. He spent some hours completely absorbed in the work and was startled when Sharon came to tell him that dinner was ready. He found that Allyson had roasted the birds and had laid the table as if for a festive occasion. She had even found some wine and candles.

"How marvellous, a candle lit supper. I had forgotten what it was like to eat in style like this. What is the occasion? Is it someone's birthday?"

'Well, it's mine actually," Allyson said. "I thought that we would celebrate a little. I'm sorry that it is not better. I would dearly like to make a really good meal. I used to be quite a good cook and would like to show you what I can really do, but resources are rather limited. There are so many things that we haven't got."

"Considering the circumstances, I think that you have done very well. This is as good a banquet as we are likely to see for a long time. Many Happy Returns to you. Will you say Grace?"

Although the meal consisted of only one course. It was thoroughly enjoyed by all, and they sat and talked until it was completely dark, and Joanne was falling asleep again.

"It looks as though it's time for bed. Let's settle the girls, all three of them. Look, Sharon and Judy are not much better than Joanne, they are nearly asleep as well. We will do the washing up between us, then we can get to bed ourselves."

This they did and while they cleaned the dishes, Believer said, "That was really a lovely surprise tonight. I must say, it was the most pleasant time I have had since the bombs fell. I regret that I couldn't get you a gift or a card, but, in any case, I couldn't have done much about it since there are no shops.

"I think that things like presents will be very difficult to arrange. We are living at a time when everything we have is around us already. It wouldn't be the same to try and give gifts when we have seen all that there is.

"In the old days, we could go and buy something, even if it was only a box of chocolates, but now I think that the only gifts we can give are those that we have made ourselves. I didn't know that it was your birthday and I think that Joanne forgot as she didn't tell me. I don't know, even, if I could have found the time to make you anything. Nevertheless, I can only offer you my good wishes, but if there is anything that you would like me to try and make, then I will have a go."

"You needn't worry on that score., I know the situation only too well and I didn't expect anything. I just thought that we should just have a time when we could relax and talk for a change. We all seemed to be busy over the last few days, you in particular.

"I know that you and I have had a chat now and then, but you were always doing something while we talked. I wanted to get you to stop for a while. You know, I've seen you nearly ready to drop yourself. Now that we are all a bit fitter than when you first came, we can all help and ease your burdens.

"You won't be with us much longer, will you? Tonight, was the first time that I could show you what I could do with the food that you have provided and that I can make the best of things as well as you."

"I shall be here for some days yet, there is so much I want to do. I don't know yet how I shall manage, but with God's help, I will. Thank you for that meal. It was delicious. I thought that duck would be nice for a change.

"Do you know anything about chickens? There must be a few about. Some day you will have to try and catch some and a cockerel. Then you will get a supply of meat and eggs.

"Talking of eggs, ducks will be laying around next April or May. You will have to try and find their nests. They are funny birds, several will lay their eggs in the same nest and one bird will took after all the ducklings that hatch out. When you find a nest, there might be a dozen or more eggs in it.

"There will also be geese and swans during the winter months. I can't see that all the birds from the frozen North will have been destroyed and they will migrate South as usual. Just another source of food.

"Even so. the winter months will be the hardest, but by this time next year things should stabilise a little, and we should know what to expect and what we can store in readiness."

Both Believer and Allyson were beginning to fall asleep themselves so they retired to a better night's rest than they had had for a long time.

Day Thirty-Six

Breakfast next morning was a surprise. Believer had gone straight out to the garage after drawing the water and stoking up the kitchen range. He was working on the crossbow when he was told that the meal was ready. He discovered that Allyson had prepared the fish that the girls had caught the day before.

She had served them up with what looked very much like fried bread, but it was actually portions of sponge pudding that Allyson had found in a tin. Believer thought that this was a marvellous piece of ingenuity and he told Allyson so. She thanked him but seemed strangely silent during the meal, so while the girls were clearing away and washing up, he drew her aside and asked her what was bothering her.

She said, "I'm a little surprised at what you did while you were out with Joanne yesterday. She told me about your swim."

"I am sorry that you seem to doubt my intentions. I was in a bit of a quandary. How was I to retrieve a duck I had shot without swimming for it? I didn't want to get all my clothes wet and there is precious little undergrowth out there to strip discreetly.

"I would have, in preference, taken someone of the same sex. But since there was no alternative, I was left with Joanne.

"I think that if you ask Joanne to tell you a bit more, she will say that although I did strip in her presence, it was for one purpose only—to retrieve ducks that were only wounded. They had to be collected quickly or be lost. That was why I stripped before the ducks were shot, so that I could get into the water straightaway. I considered that it was a necessity and in those circumstances, embarrassment must be put aside."

"Would you do the same if it had been me or Sharon and Judy?"

"Yes. if the conditions were the same. Look, I have seen all of you naked. I've had to wash you and Joanne in the bath. Then, it was something that needed to be done.

"In the same way, I had to get the ducks and also keep my clothes dry. The fact that a girl of 15 saw me naked seemed to me to be of little importance against the possibility of losing a valuable source of food. I hope that you will forgive me for the occurrence, but I have to say that should the need arise, I will do it again. The only difference is that any companion would be expecting it."

"I see your point and I'm sorry that I raised the question. As you say, food is the most important thing at the moment. Can you forgive me for being worried about it?"

"There's nothing to forgive you for, is there? Your reaction was the natural one of any mother to protect her children from harm. I do assure you that I have no intention of causing anyone harm or distress. It was just a task that had to be done.

"I wish now that you had been there as I'm sure that you would have taken it in the right way. Hearing it second hand does not give full credit to my motives. I have done my best to be discreet here in the house as I am sure you will agree.

"Here, though, I have the advantage of separate rooms. Not out there in the field."

Allyson said, "Thank you, you've put my mind at rest. How is the crossbow coming along?"

"Another two hours should do it, but I've got to go out and get some more food. I hope that you won't mind if it's crow again. They are the most plentiful at the moment."

"I think we must be thankful for what we can get and be satisfied with whatever you bring back."

Believer said, "Perhaps you would like to come with me today. Joanne is probably too tired for another trip, but she should be able to look after the girls."

"I'd love to come if you will have me. I haven't been out since the bombs came. I suppose that we have been lucky as the cottage is in a sheltered spot and missed the worst of the blast. How bad is it out there?"

"Bad, almost complete destruction. Not only buildings, trees and bushes are gone. The leaves have gone off most of the surviving ones and most of the undergrowth is gone which is why I said that there is no cover out there.

"On the good side, there are pockets of old vegetation in sheltered spots and where the ground was laid bare, new growth is beginning. What is a little worrying is that small animals like squirrels have almost disappeared. There are some rabbits in odd places, but the best time to hunt them is at dawn or late evening. They are usually underground during the day to keep away from predators.

"I think that it will be unwise to take too many of one kind of animal as that might kill them all or drive them away. As for larger animals, those which survived will be scattered over the countryside as a lot of hedges and fences have gone. I suppose that there must be sheep, cattle and goats, likewise chickens.

"There are also predators, dogs, cats, foxes and possibly larger animals escaped from wild life parks. They will be a big worry when winter really bites.

"I should think that any of the bigger animals are feeding on escaped farm stock and carrion at the moment, so I don't anticipate much danger from that source yet. I seem to be painting a pretty bleak picture, don't I? It you get ready, you can see for yourself."

Allyson came back after a few minutes dressed in old jeans, an anorak and wellington boots and the pair set off. This time in the direction of the old market garden.

Although she had been warned, Allyson was appalled by the change in the landscape. So different to what she had known previously. All her nearest neighbour's homes destroyed, wrecked vehicles, some with the deceased occupants still visible.

In many places, the smell of decomposing bodies, both animal and human still detectable after over a month. Believer could see that she was getting more distressed as they walked. He did his best to comfort her, but at every turn, they came across fresh scenes of devastation.

"It's far worse than I ever imagined," she said with tears running down her cheeks. "How could you have stood the strain of coming out into this almost every day. After seeing this, I'm not sure I want to face the future. It will be years before things get bearable again.

"To think that you walked through all of this to reach us. I think that if the positions were reversed, I would just have given up. It seems so hopeless. Look round, there seems no sign of life and no prospects of any future."

Believer let her cry. Her sobbing lasted a good half hour, during which time he remained silent. He was unable to think of anything he could do to alleviate her sorrow.

"Listen to me," he said after Allyson had brought herself under control. "I cried like that at first even though convention said that men should control their emotions. I don't mind admitting the fact. First, I cried for my lost loved ones, then for myself.

"Finally, I cried for man's arrogance and stupidity that this should have been allowed to happen. Then I felt anger and thought that if I found any politicians, I would strangle them with my bare hands. After that God got through to me and made me realise that now when we are all in the same state, facing a desperate struggle for survival, it is up to each and every one of us to do our utmost to live at peace with each other.

"If we can do this then we can build a better world than mankind has seen for thousands of years. Now is our chance to put things right. Our last chance. If we make a mess of this, then there is no hope.

"God gives us hope and we must build on that with all the love that He gives us. If we do His bidding and refer constantly to Him, He will help us all."

"I feel a bit better now, shall we go on?"

"Yes, come on, I've got something to show you. Sharon and Judy told me about the place we are going to when we were all out together. The sight you will see will be daunting, but perhaps you will see the hope that I did."

They carried on walking, past the place where Believer had removed the road springs for the crossbows and towards the market garden Judy had told him about.

"Here we are, do you remember this place?"

"Yes, it used to be a thriving place. I think that they grew vegetables and sold them to wholesalers. Can we make it work again.?."

"Not just by yourselves, but with help, you might. When you feel completely fit, you will be able to make a start. If you can grow anything at all, it will help Other people will move into the area as larger groups split up to find food.

"I think that you will get your help that way. I'm sure that, in time, everyone will see the sense of working together to provide food. Who knows? You might even be able to produce a surplus and be able to trade.

"Everyone has skills of some kind or another and those who have the skill to produce food will trade for other different goods supplied by different talents.

"People will develop new skills to the advantage of all. In the field near the old van, the one I robbed, there is still some standing barley. It will be ripe soon and must be harvested.

"Some grain must be kept for re-sowing but you should be able to make some kind of bread from it if you can find a way of grinding it. I think that you will have to find a stone to make into a quern."

"What on Earth is a quern?" asked Allyson.

"I don't suppose that there are many around here now, but querns are used by primitive people where there are no mills. It is a hard flat stone that is used when mills are not available. Corn is placed on it and ground into flour with another stone. I believe that it's a slow process.

"The Egyptians used them and they didn't do so bad, did they? The point is, that like it or not, we are all primitive people now and must use primitive means to survive. We must use methods and processes that have not been used in this country for hundreds of years.

"Only a few have the necessary skills, most of those worked in working museums. There won't be many of those left. We have just got to re-learn those lost skills or die."

"You are a mine of information, aren't you? You seem to know something about most things."

"You've heard the old saying, 'Jack of all trades, master of none.' That's me. I used to be teased because I seemed to be good at general knowledge questions. I used to fill my head with useless information, snippets and facts that seemed to stick somehow.

"Now, perhaps, they are not so useless. Do you not see God's hand in all this. It seems that it was a talent which I didn't really know existed, and I am sure that God will help me to put it to good use."

They carried out a thorough investigation of the old market garden premises, crunching over the smashed glass from several greenhouses. In one place where some panes had survived, they actually found a tomato plant with some tomatoes nearly ripe. These they duly harvested.

'We must try to propagate some of the seeds from the fruit. It should be possible, if so, you can have some for next year. We've got to start somewhere, as with the potato peelings.

'Sort out the fruit, keep the best for re-planting and eat the rest. Are you ready to leave now or shall we look around the fields to see whether anything is still growing?"

"Let's look around some more, I want to make the most of my time," replied Allyson.

"That's the way, that's a lot better than your attitude a while ago. I thought that you would get some hope from this place. It obviously has possibilities and I can see the difference in you. Look, potatoes here and spinach.

"Not much, but spinach keeps on growing, so if we take as many leaves as we can carry, there will be more later. It will keep us in green vegetables for a while. The only trouble is that it cooks down a lot."

They picked about two pounds and were lucky enough to find some carrots and parsnips. They could not carry any more so they started homeward, diverting to inspect the barley field to see how much could be harvested later. Suddenly, a croaking noise was heard and Believer motioned to Allyson to keep silent while he set the vegetables on the ground.

He quietly loaded the air rifle. The noise occurred again and the remains of the standing corn rustled before a bedraggled cock pheasant stalked out. Believer took careful aim and was able to bring the bird down.

"Something else for us to carry," he said as he went to retrieve it. "Look at this, he was badly singed, I don't think that he could fly. He was probably on the wing when he was caught by the blast.

"Do you know, I have never eaten pheasant before. This is luxury indeed. We should eat well tonight. I'm sorry that we didn't get the crows I promised."

Allyson burst out laughing and gave Believer a whack across the shoulders. "Oh you, you're impossible. You shoot a pheasant and complain that you haven't got any crows. What you have done is to cheer me up no end. That's the first time I have laughed for over a month.

"From now on I am only going to look at the bright side of life, and I am going to try to see the funny side of things more often. I really do think that things will get better from now on."

They set off home in far better spirits than when they had left in the morning They arrived back about three o'clock, loaded down with the spoils of the day Like Joanne the day before, Allyson was very tired, so Joanne said that she would cook the dinner if her mother would tell her how.

The small girls said that they wanted to help, so Believer asked Allyson to show them how to use a potato peeler so they wouldn't waste too much. "W must make the best use of the food we have been given. From now on there mus be as little waste as possible," he said.

Believer then went to complete his work on the crossbow. This took all o his ingenuity, particularly in fixing the spring to the stock and designing a efficient trigger mechanism. When he had finished, he turned his attention to making the bolts.

For these, he used six-inch nails from which he removed the heads. He then split the blunt ends with a small hacksaw and added plastic flights which he cut from an old ice cream tub. Now, he had an acceptable looking weapon ready for its first trial.

He took an old plastic sack and stuffed it with earth to use for a target and went out to the nearby field to practice. He found that he was able to hit the sack from a distance of about 30 yards and was surprised by the accuracy. Most of his efforts landed in an area of about a square foot but some missed so he decided that he must show Joanne how to make more bolts. He became aware of a feeling of being watched and turned to find that Allyson had come to fetch him for dinner.

"Congratulations, that looks a pretty lethal weapon, what size animal can it kill?" she asked.

"You must have heard how dangerous they are. Given sufficient accuracy, I think that it is capable of killing something as big as a cow. It would take a lucky shot, but it is quite capable of killing a man. Pray to God that this will never be necessary, but never forget that it is a killer.

"They were used in the middle-ages but were not as effective as an English longbow which was quicker to fire, and could penetrate a suit of armour at a distance of about a hundred yards. The crossbow was more accurate though. More of my mine of useless information."

"Shall we go in now? Joanne can have a go at it tomorrow. I'm looking forward to that pheasant. We'll throw the remains into the field and see if it will fetch some crows around. If so, we won't have to go out hunting."

The meal was a success, made more so by the addition of spinach as a green vegetable, although, like all small children, Sharon and Judy were a little reluctant to try it. When Allyson explained that there was a shortage of vegetables at the time and that they should be grateful for any that came their way. They would be likely to be ill if they did not eat whatever they could find. The girls ate reluctantly and discovered that the taste wasn't so bad after all.

After the meal was cleared away, they all sat down to discuss their future plans, particularly how Allyson was going to deal with the market garden.

Believer said that the first thing to do was to try and salvage as much glass as possible. One day, they might be able to rebuild some of the greenhouses. If not, cloches could be made of some of the larger pieces. Once the glass was cleared away, then a start could be made to dig out and prepare the ground for the growing of much needed vegetables.

"It will be a daunting task," he told them. "Much of it will fall on your shoulders, Allyson. You are going to need a great deal of help, fairly soon. I don't know where that is going to come from, but I'm still convinced that I will be able to send someone soon after I leave here.

"One thing I am worried about is education for Sharon and Judy. Allyson, Joanne, you will have to try and set some time apart to teach them all that you know. Otherwise, in a few generations, education will disappear and mankind will degenerate into a primitive existence.

"We have nearly gone back to that state now, hunting for our food and gathering what we can in the way of vegetables. The young must be taught with any knowledge and skills that you have and that you gain in your new lives."

Allyson said, " I will do what I can in that respect. I suspect that there will be times during the winter months, if we can have some light for the longer evenings."

"That is my task for tomorrow. I am going to try and rig up a 12-volt system with the alternator and the batteries I brought back. If it works, the caravan fridge can be used and I will certainly be able to rig up some lighting.

"I shall have to go out and rob a few cars for some bulbs and bulb holders. I think that I can use the existing wiring, but the hardest thing is to make the alternator spin."

"Do you really think that you can do all that? What are you going to turn the alternator with? It won't go by itself."

"I've got ideas. It's just a matter of putting them into practice. I'll sleep on it tonight and say a few prayers, then I will know what to do. It's been a long day, shall we go to bed now? Sharon and Judy are nearly asleep."

Allyson said, "You're right, it has been a long day, and eventful. Today, though, I laughed for the first time. Your joke about the pheasant was a big boost after the depressing sights out there. Tell me, were you always making jokes before?"

"More than now, but I don't suppose that they were always appreciated. think I must try to get my sense of humour back. To tell the truth, there isn' much to laugh about, is there? I used to see the funny side of a lot of things, so suppose it will come back eventually."

Day Thirty-Seven

After breakfast, Believer showed Joanne how to load and fire the crossbow and she went off to practice with it, while Believer started work dismantling the old spin drier. He removed the outer casing and other parts until he was left with the drum which was still connected to the internal framework and spinning freely on its bearings. He greased the bearings with some Vaseline and then attached the drum, on its frame to a wooden structure to which he added the alternator with the aid of an adjustable bracket.

He was interrupted in his task by Joanne who came to tell him that there were some crows in the field where the remains of yesterday's pheasant had been thrown.

"Shall I try to get them with the crossbow? I don't really think I am good enough with it yet or are you going to use the air rifle?" she asked.

"Suppose that you use the rifle," he replied. "After all, you are going to be the hunter and as the birds have come to you, you might as well have a try on your own. You'll find the slugs in the left pocket of my anorak and you know where the gun is. Just remember how you shot the duck and put what I told you into practice."

Joanne went off to fetch the rifle. Believer told Allyson, Sharon and Judy to keep very quiet and to keep out of sight of the field whilst Joanne made her first attempt at hunting on her own. He then returned to his self-imposed task.

He carefully cut one of the rescued oil drums in half lengthways and fitted the two halves on either side of the spin drier drum so that they made two vanes to catch the wind.

He added a long drive belt he had removed from one of the lorries which he had already robbed. This was long enough to pass right around the spin drier drum as well as the alternator pulley. He now had a wind driven alternator and he was pleased to see that it worked quite well when he set it on top of the garage.

All he had to do now was to fix it securely, construct some form of cover for weather protection and to arrange the wiring. That was a task for the next day. Today was already half gone and he had plans for the rest of it.

Joanne returned from the field. She had been successful and had shot two crows and a magpie, but confessed that she had used several pellets. She was worried that Believer's supply was getting low.

He said, "Don't worry about it. Look at this tool I made. I can use it to make as many pellets as I like. The ones I make aren't quite as good as the originals, but they will serve me. They will have to. You have done very well, perhaps your mum will do as good a job at cooking them.

"She is pretty good at that. That little trick of putting out the scraps won't work too often as crows are very crafty and they will soon learn not to come around, so we mustn't drive them away altogether."

Believer called the others and suggested that it might be a good idea if they all went off to the wrecked nursery and made a start to clean the place up. Everyone was in agreement so they all put on old clothes, and took a broom and spade. The three younger people climbed into the skip of the dumper and Allyson sat on the wing. The journey to the market garden was uncomfortable, but they all regarded it as an adventure and the trip really lifted their spirits.

Allyson asked, "Why have we taken the dumper today when we walked here without much trouble yesterday?"

'We will need the machine for clearing up. That is one of the reasons it was built for, generally moving rubbish and other things about. I think that Joanne can drive it while we are there.

"You and I will do the heavy work and the girls can do anything that they can manage. I thought that the trip would get us all out together. Something different to just cooking and eating."

"It is a good idea, the girls are enjoying it already, but their clothes will be mess after this, can we get the washing machine going again tomorrow?"

"Yes. I'll see to that for you, also I think that we will all need baths again tonight, so that will have to be considered as well. I don't think that the generator should be used more than once a week as the fuel won't last for ever. We've only got about 30 gallons. The same thing applies to this dumper.

"From now on, we must never be wasteful. The tank on the dumper takes gallon and a half and the generator, three quarters, but they are pretty economical

I will try to get you some more before I leave. Anyway, we've arrived, where shall we start."

Allyson looked around and then said, "Don't you think that we should start with the largest pieces of glass and stack them up somewhere? Sharon and Judy can do some sweeping up for a while and if Joanne is going to drive. She will have to keep starting the machine because, as you said, we mustn't keep it running all the time."

"Good for you, Allyson, that shows that you are thinking, but I'll just show Joanne how to tip the load and give her a try at starting the engine. Then as you say we can start on the big pieces. Joanne can shovel the glass the girls have swept up for a while at least.

"One of us can take over when she gets tired. I think that we are all going to find muscles we don't know about yet, that is why I suggested a bath tonight."

They all worked hard for about three hours and made considerable progress. Believer, Allyson and Joanne took turns at filling the dumper while Sharon and Judy did a marvellous job with the sweeping. They took turns and really seemed to enjoy themselves, particularly as some of the glass broke into smaller pieces while they were sweeping and made a good deal of noise which added to the girl's fun.

Believer made sure that no one worked too hard for he said that there was plenty of time. Really, they had the autumn and winter before them to prepare for spring planting, weather permitting. It would take a full year before they discovered everything that was in the ground.

They did find that there were several root vegetables already starting to re-grow their foliage after the flash fire that had occurred. The hard-working group realised that these were going to be invaluable during the long winter to come.

Joanne became quite skilful in handling the dumper, and Believer and Allyson had made a good stack of re-useable pieces. At the end, everyone knew that they had done a good afternoon's work and returned home tired but contented at the progress they had made.

They even tried to sing some hymns on the way back. This was started by Believer and the others joined in. They all found that they couldn't remember all the words, but that only made the singing more fun.

Everyone felt that they had contributed to the work and thought that they had made a start to get life back to an easier state of living for the future. Really, this was the happiest time they had experienced since Believer had found them so weak and near to death.

When they returned, Allyson started to prepare the meal while Believer drew water from the stream. He filled the hot water system ready for the washing machine to be used next day, and carried on to fill as many pans as Allyson didn't need to prepare for the baths they were all looking forward to.

The evening was spent in a joyful mood and before they retired, Believer said a prayer thanking God for all the good things they had achieved that day. Particularly, he thanked God for the joy and happiness they had experienced, and the feeling that they had done something towards the future.

Day Thirty-Eight

Believer arose early, before first light. He awoke Joanne quietly, telling her to put on her hunting clothes as he thought that it would be good idea if the two of them tried to shoot some rabbits for the day's meal. They set off and headed for a sheltered valley Believer had seen earlier on his travels.

Believer was armed with his air rifle and Joanne with the crossbow, which she insisted on bringing. She said that since she had spent a lot of time practising the day before, she might as well try to use it in earnest.

Believer agreed but said, "I know that you practised hard and got quite accurate, but you made your fingers very sore, didn't you? Are they up to more strain now?"

The girl replied, "They are still a bit sore and the work yesterday didn't help much either, did it? If I am going to be the provider in the future, then I shall just have to put up with the inconvenience of sore fingers and stiff limbs. I expect that there will be days when I can't catch anything, particularly in the winter. What shall we do on those days?"

"I don't know, we've been very lucky so far. During the winter, your hunting days will be shorter. Also, the weather may keep you indoors at times. I think that you might have to consider making some snow shoes to get about with.

"You will have to be very careful to dress warmly and you will have to be careful of frozen lakes. They will be a hazard and you will have to be very careful that any ice you venture onto is thick enough to bear your weight.

"I would suggest that if you are after water fowl, you carry a coil of that strong nylon rope and tie it to something solid on the bank before you venture on to any ice. Also, lie down on the ice to spread your weight as much as possible. You will have to think about these things when the time comes, but now we only have the problem of never-ending sunless days with some rain thrown in.

"I did see the sun, once on my way here, also a rainbow. A sign of hope, don't you think, but it only lasted a second or two and we might not see it again until the frost comes. By then, the weather will be really cold. I shall have to get you some more coke before I leave, but you must also gather some wood to help out with the fuel."

"You keep saying that you must leave. I wish that you could stay and so do the others. I know that Mum will miss you terribly. She says that she is going to follow you. She misses Dad and cries for him.

"We all do, except Judy, she has her own grief. I think that Mum loves you as much as she did Dad, perhaps in a different way, but I am not so sure about that either. Can't you reconsider and change your plans?"

Believer was silent for a while. In fact, he was praying silently, when he had finished, he said, "I really wish that I could stay, but there is so much for me to do elsewhere. God keeps telling me that I am needed in other places. How can I do His work if I don't contact others?

"You all know that I believe wholeheartedly in Him, I have told you that He has kept me alive to fulfil a purpose. This I cannot do with just one small community. I must tell you that sometimes, I cry myself at the idea of having to leave such a lovely family and the comfort of living with you all.

"I include Judy in that, since circumstances have compelled her to join you and you have all taken her into your care. I am subject to emotions just like any other person. I am no superman, nor am I hard hearted. When you are able to cope by yourselves, then I must go, for there are others who need help.

"There are others who above all, need hope. The hope that only the love of Jesus and God can bring. I must tell them of this love so that they may grow in His knowledge and in turn spread the word to others so that all may share a new life of peace and love."

Joanne was a bit petulant at this and said, "You never seem to forget God, do you? How can you even think of leaving when we need you so much? I don't know how we shall cope without you. I'm not even sure that I want to go on with all this hunting, particularly now." Then she burst into tears.

Believer stopped walking and sat down on the remains of a stone wall. Joanne, when she saw that he had stopped, went a few yards further on and sat with her back to him, sobbing as though she would never stop. After ten minutes or so, Believer moved along and sat beside her. She didn't move away, but kept her back to him, still sobbing, though not so violently.

Believer remained silent, thinking that if he spoke, he would only provoke another outburst. Instead, he let the girl cry out her anger. When she finally stopped crying, she remained silent for a while, then she turned to Believer and buried her face in his shoulder.

He asked if she was finished and she said, "I'm sorry, I just don't know what came over me. I feel so ungrateful after all you have done. We have you to thank for our survival, how can you ever forgive me?"

"What is there to forgive? Yours was a natural reaction. You have just come face to face with the reality of the magnitude of the task in front of you. You've just realised that you must provide the food for four people at a time when it will be difficult to obtain, even vegetables.

"Then you realised that I really do have to leave. I tell you, that would be a daunting task for me, let alone a 15-year-old girl, who, two months previously was living in a situation where food was easily provided and with all home comforts. You were suddenly deprived of all these things.

"You must believe and trust in the Lord. That way you will have hope. Faith and Hope are two of Saint Paul's virtues. There are two others—love and charity. If you have faith and hope, you will be able to face the world ahead. If you have love for Jesus, God and your fellowmen and women, then your way will be much easier."

The girl replied, "How can you be so sure of what you must do? How do you pray? I know that you have said prayers with the family, but you pray often and silently. I want you to help me to pray and believe the way you do."

"It's not easy to explain, but in my case, I came to know God while I spent three weeks alone in a house. At least, I thought that I was alone, then came the feeling that someone else was there. That impression grew stronger until I realised that God was talking to me. Not with words, but in my mind.

"I started praying and found that all my questions were answered in one way or another. He even told me when to leave that place, simply by letting me come to the end of the available tinned food and the gas I was cooking with. I found that if I was to survive, I could not stay any longer.

"I packed what food was left and arrived here some days later. You know the rest. What about you? What were you thinking about when you were lying there so ill? I bet that you kept asking in your mind for someone to come and help you. Am I right?"

"How did you know that? I had just about given up all hope when I realised that someone was feeding me with some kind of stew. I didn't know or care who it was. All I knew was that someone had arrived and right from that moment, I felt at peace, knowing that I would survive."

"You had been praying unconsciously and God heard your desperate plea for help. He sent me in order to carry out His purpose for both of us. I know what He wants me to do. He will, no doubt, tell you and the family His purpose for you all.

"To find that purpose you will have to choose a quiet moment when you are free from distraction, then just ask Him to send the Holy Spirit to tell you what to do. Ask this in the name of Jesus and you will find that you know what to do and what to say, if necessary. Only believe and your answer will come. I will keep praying for you in any case."

"Thank you, I feel better now and I will try to do as you say. Shall we go on now?"

The pair continued to their destination, a grassy bank which had somehow escaped the ravages of the fire that had destroyed most of the surrounding countryside. Believer had seen the evidence of rabbits during an earlier visit. He had seen the burrows and fresh droppings so knew that some had survived.

He also knew that the coming winter would be extremely harsh, and that not many of the people and animals which had survived the holocaust would survive the cold. Food for vegetarian animals would be scarce because so much had been destroyed. Fewer animals like rabbits, meant less food for all carnivores including man.

He thought that Allyson and her family would have to depend on migrating wild fowl, and that is why he had told Joanne about snow shoes and the danger of thin ice. He hoped and prayed that she would take heed and prepare herself for the rigours to come, but all this would be beyond his control. As an ex-city dweller, he had done remarkably well so far, but as for teaching Joanne the art of hunting, it was a case of the blind leading the blind. Only his common sense and faith in God had enabled him to carry on.

Like all men and women, there were times when he felt that things and events were too much to cope with. He had felt like giving up many times. Indeed, he had felt utter despair when he realised that he would have to provide for the immediate needs of a family.

He had prayed and persevered in the end, proving himself successful in a way that would have been incomprehensible to him before that fatal July day.

his heart, he knew that success was due only to divine guidance he had received at crucial times. This had given him the encouragement to carry on.

Meanwhile, Joanne was thinking about the middle-aged man who had come into their lives at such a critical time. After her outburst, she had begun to realise just what and who was driving him to carry out the tasks he had done since she had first felt him supporting and feeding her. She suddenly thought that he had not only done it for her, but also for her mother and sister, also for Judy, the poor child who had been forced so abruptly into her family.

She thought hard about all she had seen him do. She also thought about the things she hadn't seen when he was out of her sight. She remembered that she had never seen him angry in the presence of the family.

Sometimes he had looked very sad, particularly at those times when anyone, herself included, had given him cause for anger. The last occasion being just half an hour previously.

It was a severe jolt to the girl's thinking process when she realised that Believer had suffered as much, if not more than any of them, except Judy. He too had lost all he had loved. All his ambitions and hopes had come to naught. She didn't even know his real name, for he had never revealed it.

All she knew about him was that he had lived in Coventry, and had been on his way home when his journey had come to a sudden end. The name he had chosen, she now thought, was indeed serving his purpose as she was forced to think about the implications.

What did this man believe? She knew because he had told her. She thought that as his whole life was governed by his beliefs, there must be a great deal of truth in them. If there was truth in someone else's belief, then it must follow that she believed as well.

Suddenly, Joanne found that she was praying herself for God's forgiveness for her own selfishness. This was followed by a feeling of peace and calm such as she had never felt before. She knew then, at that moment and without any shadow of doubt, that God did indeed exist.

She knew also that God was making her aware of Him. She now felt that she would be able to put her faith in God and Jesus just as Believer had done earlier and a great weight was lifted from her.

At this time, they were approaching the area where the rabbits lived. Bearing in mind that the dawn sky was lightening rapidly, Believer cautioned her to keep silent. They loaded their weapons and crept up to the top of the bank until they could see the grassy area where the rabbits had come to feed.

They could see several and Believer picked out one that seemed to be keeping watch as his target and Joanne chose another. They had prearranged that they should fire at the same time, and this Believer achieved by counting down with his finger on his left hand. Both shots were successful.

The one that Believer had chosen died instantly, but Joanne's was only wounded and was squealing in agony and distress. This upset Joanne, but Believer told her to go and kill it and put it out of its misery.

He said to her afterwards, "I'm sorry that I had to make you do that, but if you are hunting for food, then you must realise that you have to do the killing as well. Injured animals must not be allowed to suffer longer than necessary. Also, we must not be too greedy and kill more than we need from day to day.

"Since God has kept some alive for us to hunt, we must only take them out of necessity. Greed has been man's downfall in the past.

"Greed is the cause of most of man's iniquities, greed for riches, for land, but most of all, greed for power. Just think, if all the politicians on both sides of this last terrible war had not been so greedy for power, then none of this would have happened at all. Going back to the rabbits or anything else that we kill.

"We must retrieve them as soon as possible. There must be predators about that are just as hungry as we are and you will lose a kill if you are not quick enough.

"I don't think you saw it, but there was a fox around when we shot the rabbits. I saw it running away as we stood up. I think that a fox will be harder to kill than a rabbit, but don't discount the fact that they contain valuable protein if you get really desperate."

"Do you really mean that we will have to eat foxes? I don't think I could," Joanne had a horrified expression on her face.

"Possibly, also dogs, cats or even rats. Remember that the Pekinese dog was originally bred in China for food. Some primitive people eat grubs and caterpillars. In some parts of Africa, children used to catch mice and small birds

"These were a valuable source of extra protein and were actually a part of their survival pattern. The tribes actually thrived on such a diet. Think of this whatever has happened to the world, the primitive tribes in Africa, Asia, South America and the Arctic are far better off than we are now. They know how to survive in adverse conditions.

"We don't, and have to learn it all from scratch. Our only advantage is that we have had technology. We know things can be done. If they have been done once, they can be done again.

"It will take some years to recover, and the conditions will be almost as bad as any primitive tribe has to endure. For all I know, It may be to no avail as it is possible that we may all be sterile. Somehow, I don't think that that is the case.

"I am sure that God would not have preserved some of us if there was no one left who could reproduce. We must remember that God is on our side and will give his help when needed."

"Everything you say is true. I realise that now. We have had food every day since you came. At first, it was only tinned food, but then you started hunting for us and we have had fresh meat ever since. We have even had some vegetables.

"I am beginning to see that we have had just enough food to last us from day to day. This area seems to have just enough food to support the five of us, with no excess. I can also see that being greedy would not benefit us in the long run as there might not be enough left. Aren't you going to get that little fridge working? Won't that mean that we will be able to keep food a little longer?"

"Yes, but as you say, it is only a little fridge. It might be sufficient to let you hunt every other day, but it won't keep things for very long. It will just help a bit. Come on, we must go back as I have to finish that windmill off and install it.

"I've also got to rig up some 12-volt lighting, so I must take some bulb holders and bulbs from some wrecked vehicles on the way back. We won't be able to use anything until the batteries are fully charged. That will be tomorrow or the next day and that depends on whether the wind keeps up. It is only a breeze, but it has been steady for a few days."

The pair started on their homeward journey, stopping now and then for Believer to remove some of the items he needed from various vehicles on their way. When they returned, they found that all the family were up and the chores already started. Allyson had even managed to start the generator and had begun to wash the clothes that they had dirtied the day before.

"I wondered where you were," Allyson said. "But then, I remembered that you said you were going to try for rabbits today, I see that you have been lucky again."

"Not lucky, Mum," Joanne said. "I realised today that we had God's help. I have decided to trust Him as Believer does. I behaved very badly to him today and he had every right to be angry. Instead, he just looked sad, then he comforted me after I cried.

"Mum, he really does have to leave us soon. I know because the hope he has given me has made me see that he can't give it to just a few of us. There must be many other people who will benefit from meeting him, and we must not be selfish.

"I know that he doesn't want to go, but I can see that he is being driven on by love and hope. Love for the Lord and hope for mankind."

Believer stood beside her looking acutely embarrassed, but at the same time he was pleased that Joanne was beginning to see things the way he did. He left the room to wash in order to avoid the rest of the conversation.

Allyson was a bit surprised at Joanne's statement, then she said, "I know. I've known all the time that he would have to leave. He came to us when we desperately needed him. He made us love him just by being here and doing so much for us unasked and for no reward.

"I have seen him so tired, he could hardly stand up. Particularly at first, when he did everything for us. He has talked me into seeing things his way as well. I am still going to find him later as soon as you are capable of looking after the children.

"I want to help him if I can, but for now, I have made a breakfast from left over vegetables. We've had ours as we didn't know when you would be back, so come and eat it now, you must both be hungry."

Believer and Joanne ate a thoroughly appreciated meal, after which Joanne helped her mother while Believer finished the work on his windmill. When his makeshift machine was securely installed on the garage roof, he spent time converting the house lighting circuit to 12 volts. He used the existing wiring but connected the fuse-box to the two batteries wired in parallel.

He had already connected his windmill to the alternator but left the fridge and the lights switched off, in order to let the batteries charge before any load was imposed upon them.

Evening was on them, by the time he had finished and Allyson had prepared a very appetising rabbit stew. Joanne insisted on saying some prayers thanking God for their survival and for providing them with their daily food. She also thanked God for Believer's timely intervention.

This was part of a pattern that Believer had originated right from the time that anyone could sit at the table. It was the beginning of a tradition that th family were to continue for the rest of their lives, even after Believer left to search for other survivors.

After the meal, the household spent the rest of the daylight hours in discussion about God and Jesus. Sharon and Judy asked many questions which Allyson and Believer did their best to answer.

At the end, Believer said, "I don't know everything, no one does. What I know about religion is mostly what I have gleaned from reading the Bible I have with me. This is in addition to the knowledge I have gained from church attendances and what God tells me. When I speak on the subject, the words I use just seem to come without thinking. I am being guided even when I speak."

Allyson asked, 'Will you be able to hold some form of service before you have to leave us? I really miss the thought of not being able to visit a church if I should want to. I would like to feel that I had attended something of the sort again."

"I will give the matter some serious thought and prayer during the next day or two. I will start tonight. By the way, has anyone noticed how dark it is? I think we'd better go to bed before we can't find the way."

Day Thirty-Nine

The household arose in the usual haphazard manner, first one, then another. Believer and Joanne were the last to rise as their previous day had been longer than the others and they had, therefore slept longer. However, all were up and about within an hour of the dawn.

The day was dull yet again with some wind and rain. There was no sign of any break in the clouds, and the small group were resigned to another sunless day.

Joanne went off, armed with her crossbow and taking the two young girls with her. Believer started his working day by checking that his windmill was working and that the two batteries were accepting the charge provided by the alternator. He found that both of them were fairly well charged, and that he was able to connect the refrigerator and the makeshift lighting circuit he had rigged up.

Allyson busied herself cleaning around the house and Believer started work on the second crossbow. This task seemed easier as he had already completed one and the method was known. Even so, progress was only slightly better and he worked throughout the morning, completely absorbed in the task of shaping the wooden stock.

Gradually, he became aware that someone was watching him. He looked up to find that Allyson had come into the garage. She was standing quietly and was obvious that she had been thinking hard.

She tried to speak, but with some difficulty. Believer could see that she was struggling with her emotions, so he put down his tools and motioned to her to come into the house where they sat down.

"I can see that something is troubling you," he said. "Perhaps, we can talk about it and see if we can solve the problem."

Allyson gave a great sigh. "You're right as usual. It's just that watching you working has made me realise that your time here is almost finished. You ha provided us with adequate comfort, considering the circumstances. After the bombs fell, I never expected that we could have electricity so soon.

"We have light and the fridge is working. I've checked and ice is beginning to form on the icebox. We have nothing to put in it yet, that is up to Joanne. She has started to go out daily now, and today, the little ones have gone with her.

"With you working out there in the garage, I felt quite lonely so I came to find you. Then I saw that the second crossbow is well on the way. That made me think that there is not much more for you to do here, and I nearly started to cry. I can see that you will probably be gone in less than a week, and I don't think that the others have realised that fact yet.

"They all know that you will have to leave sometime, but I'm sure that they don't understand how soon it will be. For my part, I can hardly bear the thought that when you leave here, it will be the last I ever see of you. That is why I have said that I will follow you later, and I will find you no matter how long it takes."

"Thank you for all that you have said. I do appreciate your feelings for me. To my regret, I have also realised that I have nothing much left to do here. I saw it some days ago because I knew what progress we were all making.

"Joanne more than any of us. The girls are young and will have to make a life of their own.

"I doubt if they will forget me, but their memories will mellow in time. It will be more difficult for us older people. I am sure that we have both known and loved people with whom we have lost touch and never saw again. We have already experienced similar partings.

"I am talking about our previous lives, not this one. The circumstances are completely different now. Our losses are the result of war and mostly final, so I can understand your determination to follow me. I feel the same way about you. I suppose that we could call it mutual attraction.

"I would dearly love to stay here, but I must go, for God is calling me. I would be extremely happy if you could come with me, but that is impossible because there are the children to consider.

"I think that it has fallen on your shoulders to teach the younger ones about life and Jesus, and the love that God has for us all. Joanne knows. You can see it in her face and by the way she has changed since yesterday morning. Even so, she still needs her mother as an anchor and teacher.

"Your burden is as heavy as mine, perhaps more so as you will worry about their safety when they are out. That will happen quite often as Joanne will have to go out most days, probably with one of the girls. I think that it would be best if she took one with her every day.

"That way, they will both learn. One from you and one from Joanne because we must not forget their education.

"Because we now live in primitive conditions, it is vital that they learn as much as you can teach them, for they are the future. The more the youngsters can learn, the quicker we can overcome the tragedy that has befallen us."

"I had not thought things out quite like that. Nor had I considered that one day I would have to be a teacher and a market gardener as well. I have just remembered what you said about growing things for other people and us to eat.

"Do you really think that is what God wants of me? The task seems daunting. However will I manage it?"

"If you pray hard, you will have far better help than ever I could give you. Remember that, with God's help, nothing is impossible. Pray for His help in all things. In fact, put your trust in Him and His Son, and you will find that there is always an answer to your problems. Perhaps not quite the answer you expected, but an answer of some sort."

Allyson was quiet for a moment, then she said, "You really do know, don't you? I listen to you and I can tell that you speak with such positiveness that it is from knowledge, not speculation. You know that we will survive. Can you explain how the knowledge comes to you?"

"Explaining is difficult, but I suppose in the old days, it would have been regarded as clairvoyancy. That is not quite true. God lets me see a little of the future now and then. Possibly not the future so much as the results of certain actions.

"I know that if I obey God's will, then certain things will come about. I believe that I have already told you that you will get help of the human kind in addition to the help that God will give you. No, that's not correct. The help that God will give you will be in the form of practical assistance from some other person or persons.

"You and your family will provide help to others who will arrive here. To them, God has given help in the same way that their help to you is God given. This all sounds very complicated, but don't you see?

"When I arrived here, guided by God, then the help I gave you was God given. Similarly, you have helped me, since your house provided me with shelter

Your state of health gave me an immediate purpose. First to provide for you and then to communicate.

"This was tremendous help to me, as I had been alone before I came here. You must see that we have helped each other. Since I was guided here by God, then the mutual help each of us gave the other was God given."

Allyson opened her mouth to speak, but was stopped short by a joyful shout from Sharon. 'Mr Believer, Mummy, we're back. Come and see what Joanne has got for dinner."

Allyson and Believer went outside. Sharon and Judy were out of breath and very excited. Joanne was only just in sight, and it was obvious that the young girls had run on ahead despite having a bag of vegetables each. Joanne could be seen to be carrying something quite large and when she was close enough, the others could see that her load was a Canada goose.

"Praise the Lord," Believer said when he saw it. 'Were there any others around?"

"There was quite a flock of them," said Joanne. "I remembered what you said, yesterday about being greedy. Anyway, one was hard enough to kill. This one took three bolts to stop it. The first only stopped it flying and it started running away. Even the second didn't stop it, and it was only just in range when I fired the third. We picked up some vegetables on the way back, so we should eat well."

"Well done. It's a good job the fridge is working now. We can't eat it all in one day, and at least, you won't need to go out tomorrow to hunt. Not for food anyway."

Believer was pleased that the girl had done so well and he said to Allyson, "This is just what I was talking about. God gave me the skill to make a crossbow and Joanne the skill to use it. Just think, she shot three times at a moving target. She had to reload twice and that takes time. As for accuracy, that is tremendous. Both skills are God given."

"Co-operation," Allyson replied. "That's the answer. I didn't see it before, not in this light, anyway. Prior to this, we all survived by co-operation. Everyone has different talents and we lived by all of them.

"When we worked, we supplied our skills in return for money which we spent on items other people had provided with their own, but different skills. They had, in turn, worked for money. I never realised before, that everyone was selling their skills and time. It took a disaster to really bring it home to me.

"What we have been doing all the time, is co-operation. Now, it seems more personal than ever before."

"While you and Joanne have been out providing for us, I have used my skills at housekeeping to turn what food you have provided into palatable meals. Even the two little ones have done their share. We have all contributed to our survival. At least, since you, Believer, arrived and helped us back on our feet again. I think that now, I can see God's hand in it all.

"Before, when we were starving, I didn't realise that some wild animals and birds had survived or that we would be able to catch and eat them. I suppose that I thought they would be all radio-active. Believer, how do you know that they aren't?"

"I don't know, myself, I just put my trust in God. My reasoning is that if God provides us with food, then it won't harm us. So far, my trust has been justified and I have no doubt that it will continue to be so.

"The most important thing to remember is that God has a purpose for us all. If so, then He will provide us with the means to fulfil it. He won't kill us with poisoned food, will He?"

"You know he's right, don't you, Mum?" Joanne chipped in. "I suddenly understood it yesterday when I got angry with Believer. When he comforted me afterwards, I had such a feeling of peace. Then we found the rabbits.

"I realised that everything Believer had been saying made sense. Believer knew we would find rabbits and we got two of them. We haven't been hungry since he came to us and today, I brought that goose home. That is proof that I can do it on my own." She stopped talking as realisation of what she was saying and its implications came to her.

Allyson took up the conversation. "Yes, that's right, you can do it. I can cope as well. You've just thought it out, haven't you? I was watching him work just now and came to the same conclusion that you have.

"We will not need him here to help us much longer. His task here is nearly finished and you have just realised what that means. We are nearly independent or as Believer would say, we are only dependant on God now.

"We were dependant on God all the time really. That dependence meant that God sent Believer to us when we needed the most help and someone else will need him soon."

Joanne was crying now. Believer had quietly left and was working in the garage again to avoid the embarrassment and trauma she was going through. "How long, Mum?" Joanne said between her sobs. "How long?"

"Less than a week now," Allyson said. Tears were running down her cheeks now. "Come on, we must prepare this goose. The work will help us. The girls can help us with the vegetables later, but that bird will take a lot of cooking, about five hours, I should think. We should try to make this a very special meal tonight, don't you?"

"Oh, Mum! I know he can't stay, but I didn't think that it would be so soon. I found that I could go hunting and take responsibility for the girls. I felt that Believer had let me go to prove to me that I didn't need him with me. What I can do once, I can do again and again.

"I prayed that God would help and He did. I felt joy and elation. In fact, I was quite pleased with myself, but God brought me down with a bump, didn't He. He made me see that if I could do the hunting, then Believer needn't do it.

"If that is the case, then his time here is nearly finished. I suddenly thought, days, not weeks."

"I was the same. He has about half finished that second crossbow, but I really think that he is only doing it to keep himself occupied. Although we could probably do with a second weapon, we could probably make one for ourselves. We have a pattern, and Believer says that nothing is impossible with God's help.

"When he goes, we will be forced to turn to God whether we like it or not. There will be no other help for us for a while. Believer says that he will send someone else as soon as possible. He seems to know that someone is coming, and by what he says, that person will not be of the same character as Believer.

"Not mild and gentle as he is, but someone who will be able to defend us if we need it. Another thing that Believer says is that we will not always be isolated as we are now. There will be some who will want to impose their will on us. The man who is coming will protect us in a way that Believer, with his nature, can't."

"Does Believer really know that? How can he know? Unless God told him."

"Exactly. I'm sure that he prays far more often than we realise. He must, of course, have prayed for our welfare when he will not be with us. You know that he has always said that his prayers have been answered, although he can't always explain how the answer comes.

"You must have seen that he always seems to know what to do. He is never any doubt. He just does things with a surety that what he does is right. For

117

instance, take the hunting. Do you know that he had never killed and eaten any creature before he set out to look for other survivors? How is he when he is out?"

Joanne thought for a moment, then she said, "He's completely confident and seems to know just what to do and where to go. I have never seen him go wrong. If he has never done it before, he must be guided by some sort of inner sense, I see now that it must be God's guidance.

"What bothers me is whether we can get the same sort of help to give us the same confidence. Now I think of it, I prayed before I went out and look what I came back with. Not just the goose, but the knowledge that I can do the hunting. The proof is there in the oven."

"Believer says that my job is to be a teacher to you and the girls. He said that it would be best if the girls took turns to go out with you, so that I can teach the one who stays behind during the day. I will have to do that in between tending the market garden.

"We hope that that will prove to be another source of food for us and for others. We will be able to use any surplus for barter for anything we might need. Above all, I must teach them and you of the love of God and Jesus.

"You obviously know some of it, for you've felt it yourself, haven't you? We must work to find out more."

The conversation continued whilst the goose was roasting in the kitchen range. Allyson called the two young girls in and told them of Believer's impending departure as kindly as she could. Even so, both girls were deeply upset and cried for about an hour. They did not stop until Allyson and Joanne persuaded them to start preparing the vegetables they had brought back from their hunting trip.

The meal was served and Believer was called in from the garage. Allyson said the Grace. Sharon looked at Believer and immediately burst into tears. "Why must you go?" she said, half choking with her sobbing. "I thought that you would be here for ever."

Believer was saddened by her outburst, and for a moment was at a loss for words. Then he said, "You two little ones always do what grownups tell you, don't you? You think that we older ones know what to do all the time.

"Really, we don't, and sometimes we even do the wrong things. Every now and then, we have to do things we don't like. Sometimes, you are told to do things you don't like, but you do it anyway because a grownup has told you.

"That is what is happening to me now, only it's not a grown up telling me what to do. God is like a grown up to me, and to him, I am just like a little boy. He tells me what to do and I try to do it as well as I can.

"I didn't want to wake up from a bump on the head to find nobody else around. I wanted to stay there and cry, but God told me to get up and walk. He sent me to a house where there was shelter and food. When that was finished, I didn't want to leave.

"God told me to, so I did and He helped me all the way 'til I got here. I didn't know what to do to help you all, so He told me. Every day, He told me new things, and now He tells me that I must go in a few days.

"I don't want to go, but I must. He wants me to help other people and since He has helped me such a lot, then I must help Him now. I know He loves me as He has told me so. He loves you all just as much, so you must help him by letting me leave when He tells me to. Now dry your tears and eat up or that goose will be swimming away again."

They all ate the meal, but the conversation was rather weak. No one was eager to disturb the thoughts of anyone else with the result that the occasion was not as memorable as Allyson had planned. Really, it was quite a sad event and Believer said afterwards.

"Thank you, Allyson, that goose was really cooked magnificently. I have never actually eaten one before and didn't know that it would taste as good as that. Don't you think that it was nice, girls?"

Believer said to Sharon and Judy. "Let's show Allyson how much we liked the meal she made for us by washing up, and after that I will tell you two a little about Jesus."

When the washing up had been done, they all sat down in the lounge and Believer opened up his precious Bible. He read to them some of the stories of the miracles that Jesus had performed.

Then he asked, "Do you think that Jesus went around just performing miracles? I bet that you wish you could do things like that. Do you know that Jesus never did anything without first asking God, His Father in Heaven for help? Don't you think that sometimes God asked him to do things He didn't like?"

Believer then told the story of Passiontide leading up to Easter. "You see, there were lots of times when Jesus didn't like what he was told to do. More than we can ever imagine. Think of the sorrow and pain Jesus suffered. This was all for us.

"Do you know that Jesus wasn't the only man to perform miracles. Moses did it and Saint Peter and the other disciples performed them as well. They could do this only after praying to God and with His help.

"If you really believe then you might be able to perform miracles, but only with God's help. If you ask for God's help in the name of Jesus, then anything can happen. Miracles, little ones, happen all the time. Ask Allyson about babies.

"I'm sure that she will tell you that every birth is a little miracle. Ask Joanne how she managed to catch a goose for us to eat today. She prayed to God and we were able to eat well today.

"If God is so good to us, don't you think that we should do what He tells us to do? Jesus did, and although He died on the cross, He did it for us and lives now with his Father in Heaven. Should we do less than Jesus? No, we must obey God and He will look after us. He will help us to perform little miracles as well. Let us say a little prayer now.

"Father God, please keep telling us what to do and help us to obey you. Help us to see that what you tell us to do is for our own benefit and help us to carry out those tasks you set us which we do not like. Grant us the patience and fortitude to take all the knocks and sorrows we encounter. Come into our hearts that we may know you better.

"Grant us also the knowledge, wisdom and energy to help anyone who needs assistance and comfort. Give us the words to use to bring others to know and trust you. Receive our prayers in the knowledge and love of your Son, Jesus Christ who gave the ultimate sacrifice for our sakes. Amen."

This prayer was the last significant piece of conversation that night as the light was fading fast. Everyone went to bed, thinking about the events of the day from their own viewpoint. They had all been both elated and sorrowful at different times and really, nobody slept well.

Believer, in particular, was deeply concerned with the sorrow he had caused. He knew this would happen again when the time for him to leave actually arrived. Both he and the family had known that departure would eventually take place.

He regretted the mutual attachment between himself and the loving family he had been living with and wished that there was some way he could remain. There was no solution to this problem at all.

He had much to think about prior to his leaving. What would he need to provide for the family? There was still a good quantity of coke for the kitchen

120

range, but Believer felt that the coming winter was liable to be severe, and he resolved to make another trip to the foundry to collect more fuel for the dumper and generator was another problem.

He thought that there were possibly several sources of fuel. He knew of a wrecked filling station with a good supply. This was stored in an underground tank and obviously there were no pumps to bring it up. This was the problem which kept him awake for some time.

Day Forty

Believer was first up and after tending the fire and fetching the water, he sat down in the quiet of the morning before anyone else joined him. He spent the time thinking and praying about the problem of the diesel fuel. After a while, he rose and looked at the small refrigerator.

This was working well and the uneaten portion of Joanne's goose was as cool as he hoped. Then he went to look at his wind driven alternator. The rotor he had made from the old spin drier was spinning freely in the breeze that was blowing across the valley in which the cottage was situated.

He thanked God for the inspiration of using the spin drier without its motor, then he realised that the drier had been fitted with a motor and a pump which would take a small-bore hose.

There was a garden hose hanging on the wall of the garage, and Believer wondered whether the pump would be capable of lifting the fuel from the wrecked filling station. He decided to experiment. He spent a while studying the motor and the pump, working out how to fix them so that the belt would be tight enough to drive the pump. Then he started to make a frame to hold both the units.

Allyson was disturbed by the noise of work so early and came to find out what Believer was doing.

"You're working early today, what's all this for? Is there no stopping you? Isn't that the motor from the spin drier?"

"Yes," said Believer, "and the pump. I am going to try to get some more diesel fuel today and some more coke."

Believer thought for a moment. "I think that it might be a good idea if you came with me today. The girls won't have to go hunting as there is enough o that goose in the fridge to feed us all day. If this idea works, we will take th generator and go, and fill a couple of barrels when we have found them.

"Can you rustle up a little breakfast? I think that there are left over vegetable from last night. You do wonders with all the cooking you do in these primitiv conditions."

Allyson realised that Believer was concentrating hard on the task in hand even though he had spoken to her. He had carried on working throughout the brief conversation and she quietly left to start the breakfast.

In the meantime, Believer had finished the crudely made frame-work and was working on the wiring for the motor. He paused only to eat the meal that Allyson had provided, then went straight back to his work. He moved the generator near to the stream and connected it to the electric motor.

Then he fitted the garden hose to the pump and dropped the end into the water. He started the generator and watched his contraption hopefully. Although the pump turned, nothing happened. He thought that the pump might need priming so he poured some water into the outlet hose.

He was rewarded by a jet of water which soaked him, much to the amusement of Allyson and the girls who had come to watch this new wonder of ingenuity. Believer laughed with them, despite getting wet. Really, he was pleased at having solved another problem.

He was satisfied that his idea worked and he carefully drained all the water from the pump and set the pump and the generator aside. Then he and Allyson set off on the dumper after checking it for fuel and oil. The pair made better progress to the wrecked foundry which had, on two previous occasions, provided the household with coke for the kitchen range.

Although there was plenty at the house, Believer was thinking of the coming winter and he was trying to ensure that Allyson and her family would be provided with sufficient to last.

When they arrived at the site, Believer found further evidence that someone else was using the supply of coke and he pointed this out to Allyson. "Whoever it is, they are only taking small quantities at a time and carrying it in a bucket. I would think that there is only one person involved. When we have filled the dumper, we will sweep a pile ready for him. He must have been finding things very difficult with it scattered all over the site."

Allyson looked at him and said, "You never cease to amaze me with the things you do. You always seem to put others before yourself. At least you have since I have known you. You have come out here purely for the benefit of myself and the girls as you know that you are leaving soon. Even now you are trying to help someone you haven't even met."

"It's not a big thing that I am doing. since we are equipped for dealing with scattered coke, it seems reasonable that we should help another survivor by piling some up for him or her. I think that I shall leave a message for him when we've finished. Something to show that we are friendly."

The work of filling the dumper was completed much faster with the two of them working, one sweeping and the other shovelling. It was a simple matter, afterwards, to heap another pile ready for the unknown survivor to collect. Having done this, Believer carefully swept a patch clean in front of the pile he had made. Then, using a piece of coke, he wrote in large letters, the words:

Jesus lives. Believe and trust in him and all things are possible.

Allyson said, "I wondered what you are going to write, why those words?"

"As I said, piling the coke up for him was only a small thing. If he sees the words and as a result, begins to believe, then that beginning is the best gift anyone can give to another other than the gift Jesus gave, Himself. Besides, I have a feeling about this person.

"I think that this man is your future help. He has already proved that he is resourceful. I think that he comes some way to collect his coke and on foot as he only takes it away in a bucket.

"I think, also that he is frightened of people as he must know that we've been here, but he doesn't seem to have made any effort to contact us. Mind you, haven't been any better myself. I haven't made any serious effort to find him either.

"I suppose that I could use the excuse that I have been trying to provide for five people and I have been constantly busy. God and Jesus teach us that w should make time for all people. I do feel a little guilty though, hence th message. There are really two messages there. The first is obvious, the secon lies hidden in the words.

"Consider, if you had suffered a bad experience with other survivors an were living alone in chosen seclusion as a result. Then you found that someor else was using coke from a place you had found. What's more, the other persc was collecting the coke in a vehicle which you might have seen or heard.

"You might not be very keen on meeting them. What if you found a messa; written by a Christian which my message so obviously is. Also, if the pers who left the message bad piled some coke up to make it easier for you to colle then the message is a first contact without obligation by either party.

"If our friend wishes, he can come and look for us and I will try to find him when I leave. I do believe that I shall find him, and that he is the person who will come to help you in the future. I think we had better leave now, in case he is watching and feeling a little nervous."

They started their machine and set off back to the cottage, stopping only at a derelict farm to collect some empty 40-gallon barrels which they balanced precariously on top of the coke. Allyson shared the driving and they arrived sometime in the middle of the afternoon. Believer unloaded the dumper and reloaded it with the two barrels, generator and the pump he had made.

Believer added a selection of tools to the other items which he thought would help him to undo the tank covers in the ground and they went back to the old filling station. Believer found that although some tanks still contained petrol, one held diesel. His first task was to fill both the barrels with the ramshackle pump which he had primed with some loose diesel. He also took the time to fill a small can with petrol which he thought might be useful later.

After the barrels were filled and the covers replaced, Believer and Allyson were sitting resting before their journey home. Allyson started crying, then she hugged Believer tightly, kissing him fervently. Believer started to respond, but after a moment, when both stopped to catch their breath. Allyson noted that tears were running down his cheeks.

"You are too," she said. "I was crying because you will be leaving us soon. Is your reason for crying the same?"

"I don't know," he replied. "I'm afraid that I was crying for purely selfish reasons because I have to leave. I want to be able to stay in the comfort we have all been used to for a while. No, that's not all really. I am crying because I have come to love you as I think that you love me.

"I know that I cannot let our love develop into a natural fulfilment since I have to go. I must not permit any further sexual attachment now. I think that you will have an exceedingly hard life ahead of you when I leave, and I can't afford the risk of getting you pregnant. Besides which, I am old fashioned enough to believe in love and marriage.

"At least, in our present situation, a permanent relationship since we have no priest to perform a ceremony. I will not permit us to indulge in any sexual intercourse which I know would have been very easy for both of us. I know that we both wanted it very badly. That is why I am crying."

"I'm sorry," said Allyson, crying again. "I knew in my heart that you would say no, but I want you so badly. Many men would have taken advantage and I did want it to happen, nor did I care about the consequences. You are stronger willed than I am, and now that you have explained your principles. I won't let the situation happen again.

"As to getting pregnant, do you really think that it will be possible after all the radiation? I always believed that radiation made everybody sterile, so perhaps I wouldn't have conceived anyway."

"I don't know, I'm not a doctor, even if I was, testing for fertility requires specialised equipment. There isn't any of that around. Think of this. We five survivors are of both sexes, there are doubtless others, both male and female. I think that possibly the older ones among us, you and me, those that have already reached full puberty before the catastrophe may well be sterile.

"God, in His wisdom, has left both male and female of all ages. Some of us will certainly be fertile, if not now, then later when the younger ones are older. If God had meant the human race to become extinct, then there would have been no survivors. Those that are left will surely be able to breed.

"Possibly not until some sort of civilisation has formed again. That is why I believe that only the young ones will be able to conceive.

"Even though I think that, I don't dare to take any risks with you in case we are both fertile. You will need all your strength during the coming winter. This is likely to be hard as there is only just enough food for us now.

"Even if we have enough now, there will be less available in the winter. There always was, and now, it will be worse. Any one pregnant through the winter is either unlikely to survive or at the very least, run the risk of a miscarriage and other complications. These will need medical facilities which will not be available, so it is better not to take the risk."

"You said you were crying for selfish reasons. I can see that really you are the most unselfish person I have ever met. When you stopped us just now, it was to save me from future difficulties.

"I really understand now how hard it was for you, since I feel the same. It is very difficult to say no, but as you say, we must."

"Thank you for understanding, but you know, the odd thing is that if we had met in previous times, I doubt whether we would have given each other thought. I am a scruffy lorry driver and you are a very attractive person who obviously had enough money that you didn't have to work."

Allyson thought for a moment, then said. "I suppose you're right, but what a rry driver you are. It just goes to show that you can't judge people by)pearances, can you?"

"I'm afraid that lots of people were judged that way. People with the oddest •oks have turned out to be really kind hearted. Unfortunately, the reverse)plies. Some who looked really nice and well-dressed turned out to be vicious 1d mean.

"I have always tried not to judge people until I got to know them, but I must)nfess that I failed several times in my life. I have made mistakes as to a 2rson's character. Look, we have stopped for long enough. I think we should 1rry on with the work.

"I intended to take this fuel to the market garden and hide it. It will be needed 1ere in the spring for the dumper. There is enough of the diesel at the cottage 1d on the way back, I want to collect some of the barley we saw. I want to <periment with it and try to grind some into flour. We will have to do it by hand, 1t we might be able to get enough to make some kind of biscuits."

They took the diesel fuel they had collected to the old market garden and iried the two barrels under piles of rubble in two different places.

"I know that what we have done seems like looting and hoarding, but if you ant to make that garden productive and feed yourself and others, you must have 1uipment. Drastic action must be done to achieve this. You will have to be)aring in the use of the generator and this dumper. Fortunately, neither machine ies much fuel and you should be able to keep going for quite a while."

On the way back to the cottage, they gathered about two armfuls each of the pening barley. This task made their hands very sore as they had to gather it by and. The leaves of the barley seemed to have an excess of sharp edges so eliever said that they had to be very careful to wash thoroughly when they turned.

Due to the absence of proper medical care, cleanliness would be the best)rm of preventive medicine available. Believer had so far been careful to be as ean as possible after the disaster as he realised that there would be no help vailable should he become infected in any way.

The only risks he had taken had been with food. He had no way of knowing hether any fresh food he and the family had eaten was contaminated. He had ut his trust in God's hands and so far had been proved right. All along, he had :lt that he had been kept alive for a purpose.

If so, then God would provide him with sufficient wholesome food. If he ha
been kept alive for a purpose, then so had Allyson and her small family and t
same rules applied. In actual fact, only his faith in God had prevented him fro
giving up.

He hoped that Allyson would come to share the same faith. He knew th
Joanne did, but he felt that, so far, Allyson had shown more faith in his ow
ability and not God's. He knew that her love for her children would drive her c
as she had already proved this by starving herself so that the girls could have t
greatest share of food.

This had proven to be a near fatal mistake. With this in mind, he stopped t
dumper some way from the cottage.

"Allyson, will you promise rue that you will never again starve yourself
feed the girls?"

"That is a very strong promise to have to make, and it was a bit sudden
you to ask it, and why now?"

"It's simply that I know how much you love them and that you will c
anything for them. You've already proved that, haven't you? I know that t
coming winter will be hard and I won't be here. If you are all short of food, yc
must work together to provide it.

"If one gets too weak, then all will suffer. That is why you must all sha
what food you have to keep up the strength and morale of you all. When t
winter hits hard, you will all have to go out hunting for food, or fishing. Whatev
is necessary for you to survive, you must do it.

"Don't forget that any animal will provide valuable protein. This applies
predators as well as rabbits and wild fowl. If you see a fox when times are har
shoot and eat it, it might keep you all alive.

"Don't forget that if one of you falls ill, all will be affected because t
remainder will be worried and so perform their tasks less well. Suppose th
Joanne was worried because someone was ill. She might well miss a shot wi
her crossbow.

"That might mean a day without food and that would do no one any goo
will it? Don't forget that God and Jesus will help, and that has already bee
proved."

"I see the sense in what you say and I will make that promise to you becau
I know that you love us all. I know that when you leave here you will rememb

us, and you will leave with a lighter heart because of the promise I have just made. Will you promise me that you will look after yourself.

"I know that you have proved to be pretty capable, but you have had us worried a little because I've seen you get overtired several times, particularly when we were so ill.

"The same thing that you have made me promise applies to you in a different way. You have worked yourself almost to a standstill just to look after us. You were never likely to starve, just collapse from exhaustion and that is just as bad. How can you help others as I know you will if you are too tired?"

"I promise. It makes a change for me to listen. I seem to have been doing most of the talking since I've been here and now you are giving me back something in kind. Thank you for reminding me of my responsibilities. You are so right. I have been very tired at times.

"I thought that you were too ill to notice. Obviously, I was wrong. Shall we go on? I think we have got some cold goose to eat and we've had a very long day. We've also got a lot think about."

Believer started the dumper and the pair finished the journey to the cottage to find that Joanne and the girls had prepared a meal of cold meat and vegetables.

During and after the meal, Allyson told the girls of some of the conversation she had had with Believer, particularly the portion about all sharing the work load and the food so that everyone received sufficient. She told them about the coke and how Believer had piled some up to help the other unknown person who was also using the valuable material.

When she finished, she looked around and saw that the three girls had tidied the house. She made sure of thanking them for their efforts.

They all carried on talking over the events of the day until darkness and tiredness combined to send them all to bed.

Day Forty-One

Joanne was first to rise and left at first light in order to try to hunt for rabbits. The two young girls and Allyson were trying to work out how to set a trap for pigeons they had seen flying around. They eventually came up with the idea of setting a bucket on a stick to which a cord was attached. The simple trap was baited with a little of the grain Believer and Allyson had brought back the day before.

Believer spent some time finishing off the second crossbow. Then he searched around the locality until he found a large flat stone and a smaller round one. He experimented with the wheat he and Allyson had collected.

He was trying to find the best method of producing flour. After a long period he managed to obtain about a pound of rather gritty flour which he gave to Allyson.

"See if you can make some sort of biscuits with this. I know that it may be a bit gritty and tasteless, but perhaps you can use some of the dripping we got from the goose. There is no other cooking fat.

"If you succeed, can you save some for tomorrow? Can you look out some sherry or other kind of wine? I know there is some.

Allyson agreed, then said, "You are going to hold a communion service tomorrow, aren't you? Are you allowed to do that? I thought that only ordained priests were permitted to give the sacraments."

"In normal circumstances, I'm sure you're right, however, ordained priests are few and far between. Since vicar and priests are normally ordained by bishop who are even scarcer, I'm sure that God won't mind if I try to carry on with the traditions that Jesus started at the Last Supper.

"Besides, if I am to be some sort of missionary which seems to be the way in which I am being directed, then I will have to hold services. I want to make plain that I would no way wish to work against any ordained priest I might find. Rather, I want to reach people who do not have the privilege of a parish still existence.

"I understand that if a man and a woman are completely isolated from any priest and no chance of any to marry them, then they would be considered married in the eyes of God. Such marriage would naturally be ratified by any priest who came along afterwards. Would not the same thing apply to me? Surely, it is better for someone to take the part of a priest where there are none available than to forget completely all that Jesus did for us so long ago."

"I agree with what you say, but following your train of thought, would not God consider us married in our present circumstances?"

"Undoubtedly yes, had we made love and consummated the relationship. We both realised that it would be unwise to allow ourselves to behave as man and wife because I have to leave soon, and there can be no lasting relationship at the present time. That particular situation does not exist with us. There is no marriage agreement between us.

"I wish there could be. Maybe later, if we ever meet again. In that case, I would welcome it."

The conversation was interrupted by a shout from Sharon. Mummy, Mummy, we've caught one, what shall we do?"

"It would seem that your idea with the bucket has been successful," Believer said as they went outside to join the excited girls.

Sharon and Judy had indeed caught a pigeon under the bucket, and Believer removed it at the expense of a few pecks from the frightened bird.

"Listen, girls, you do understand that you have caught this pigeon for food and that we will have to kill it. One small pigeon will not really feed us all, so you must be very patient and try to catch some more. Was that the only one around?"

"No, there were some more. A lot came down to feed on the corn we put down, but that was the only one that came near the bucket."

"Try again, but put the bucket somewhere else and make sure that the string around the stick is fairly tight so that it only takes a little pull to drop the bucket. It's a good job the birds are hungry. they might come round again. Still, we only want pigeons or birds of a similar size, try not to catch sparrows or starlings, they would only be a small mouthful.

"Perhaps, when winter comes, you may have to eat the smaller birds, but not now. By the way, Allyson do you know how to dress and cook pigeons?"

"I never have, but I've got a good cook book which tells how to cook lots of things. I'm sure I can find out how."

Believer resumed his work with the wheat grinding and produced a similar quantity which Allyson said would make some sort of dumplings. Joanne returned with a rabbit she had shot with the crossbow, saying she was sorry that she had only managed to get one. This wasn't enough to feed the whole household. She was relieved to find out about the pigeon which Allyson was now preparing. This was supplemented by another one, some vegetables and the dumplings Allyson made with the wheat Believer had ground.

Believer said afterwards, "As soon as it is possible to feed animals and birds with crops you grow, you should consider plans for domesticating such creatures you find. You will have to build rabbit hutches, chicken runs and a dove cote. It will be necessary to catch cattle, sheep, male and female of each species to start breeding.

"I doubt that they have all been made sterile. You will know in the springtime, if you start seeing baby rabbits. Don't forget that cattle and sheep were still breeding after Chernobyl in North Wales and Cumbria, even though the government banned the use of these animals. At that time, we had alternatives. Now we don't."

"You mean that we will have to start farming again, right from scratch," Allyson said. "I don't know much about it. I suppose we will have to catch sheep and cattle, and we will have to learn to look after them, and also learn how to milk cows and goats."

"Sheep as well. They give milk in the right circumstances. It might not be as bad as you might think. I suspect that most of the survivors will be country folk, there should be some people amongst them who will be able to pass on their knowledge.

"The fact that you and I are here is proof of that. We were all in the country when it happened. We know that there is someone else near here and there are doubtless others.

"All these people will begin moving about and a lot of skills will be passed on. Farming will start again. It will have to. You have started already. I bet you never thought that you would have to use that old kitchen range again to do all the cooking. For my part, I have hunted, made weapons and done a few things never thought I would do.

"Look at Joanne, or should I call her Diana, the Huntress. It will be thanks to her not inconsiderable skills that you will have enough to eat. She has a natural talent for hunting. Sharon and Judy have proved that they are resourceful.

"They have done their bit and that is quite a lot when you think about their ages. Their contribution is as important as anyone's. They have provided meals on at least two occasions, and what about the work they have done around the house? Particularly when you and Joanne were under the weather.

"This family is living proof that cooperation works and you are an example to all and with God's help, I will be able to spread the idea of self-help and co-operation to some of the others that I meet."

"In that case, the sooner it all happens, the better for everyone and the quicker we will be able to contact you when things settle down. We shall be very sorry to see you go, in fact, I don't know how we shall bear it, but we must."

"Don't forget to ask for God's help whenever you need it. He will help as you already know, but look, it's time for bed now, doesn't time fly."

He turned to Joanne and said to her, 'Don't go out early tomorrow, there is something we must do."

With the rest of the household upstairs in their respective rooms, Believer prepared the settee for his own rest. Before retiring, he sat for a long time in the darkness, thinking and praying. In actual fact, he was feeling very depressed because he realised that the next day would be his last full one under that roof.

He had come to love the family, including Judy who was not related to the others at all, and they had all come to mean so much to him. He knew that he had gained the affection of them all, and that fact made his imminent departure the more difficult to come to terms with. Just how does a person walk out of the lives of people who love him and who are loved greatly in return.

In the middle of these bouts of depression, he seemed to see a play back in his mind of all that he had done since he had arrived at the little cottage. It had been protected from destruction in its own little valley and provided a shelter for its occupants and later for himself. He remembered how he had found them and nursed them back to health by providing food for them, first with tinned food and later with fresh food he had hunted. He thought of the crossbows he had made and how proficient Joanne had become at using them.

He thought, now that there was little left of a practical nature he could help them with. It was obvious that his presence was not needed any more. He knew that he had to move on and was being told to go despite any sorrow he might feel. He prayed earnestly that after he left, the family would have the benefit of God's help, and then he drifted off to sleep and to dream.

Day Forty-Two

Believer awoke with a start and then realised that he had been dreaming of church bells. Thinking back to the events of the last few days, he could not relate the dream to anything he had said or heard except, perhaps, his conversation with Allyson the night before. He took his dream to mean that he was required to hold some sort of service.

When he had slept in the partially ruined church on his way to the cottage, he had collected some useful books that he thought he might need sometime. Even at that time he had thought that he was being prepared for life as some form of missionary. He had included, amongst his finds a copy of the Alternative Service Book along with a standard prayer book and a couple of different hymn books.

In the time before the family had woken up and joined him, he spent time working out how to use the books to best advantage and which parts of the service were applicable to the particular circumstances in which he found himself.

Allyson joined him and as she was aware of Believer's intentions, added her contributions to his arrangements and helped him to choose the hymns they were to try to sing. Believer laughed a little at this and said to Allyson, "I know my voice isn't the best, but it is the best male voice available, so I suppose that we must try to make the most of it."

Allyson said, "I know that you are going to hold a communion service, but who is going to receive the sacraments. You and I, but Joanne has never been confirmed and Sharon and Judy are too young to understand what's going on."

"Joanne believes, therefore I am sure that God will accept her, but I will say a prayer especially for her before we start. I agree with you about the others, but they will be included in the service and I will ask for a blessing for them. I have always believed that children should be included in all services so that they get to know what goes on, and they are ready to take a further step in their religious education when they are old enough."

When all the household had come downstairs, Believer explained to them what was going to happen. Allyson fetched the biscuits she had made and a bottle of sherry. Believer put one of the biscuits on a plate and poured a minimal quantity of the wine into a large goblet.

Allyson was curious why only such a small quantity if wine was to be used and Believer explained, "Once God has been asked to bless the wine and the bread, in this case, the biscuit which is the nearest we have, all of it must be consumed. The blessing that God gives is very powerful and if it gets into the wrong hands, it can be used for evil purposes. Like God, Satan is always around and looking for opportunities to turn God's good works to his evil purposes.

"Unused bread and wine, once blessed would be a prized acquisition for his minions to acquire. That is why, at a communion service, you will always see the priest consuming all the bread and wine that has been blessed."

"I always wondered about that, no one ever explained that to me. I hadn't really thought that if you believe in God, you must believe in the Devil as well. But what about the small amounts that are used for people to take communion at home."

"That is the only exception. Even that small quantity must be consumed by the participants and this has always been **so.**"

Everyone in the house had a feeling that somehow, this day was to be different to all the others. Even the two seven-year-olds could sense the change in the atmosphere.

Believer gathered them all together and started by saying, "This is a very special day. Today, I am going to try to hold a service which will alter the course of my life. Also, Joanne will have a new beginning and Allyson will be affected as well.

"You little ones should watch what goes on and try to learn what it all means. You are too young to take the step that Joanne will make, but I hope that your turn will come when you are older. I wish to set a precedent which I hope that Allyson will follow on Sundays in the future.

"I would like you all to set aside some time for God once a week when you will all be together and pray together. That doesn't exclude you from praying at any other time, but just make a special time at least once a week. That means that you, Allyson, as the senior person here will have to take over when I have left, and try to keep a sense of religion within your community."

"I hadn't thought of that," Allyson said. 'Will I be able to? Won't I be offending church laws or something? I just haven't considered what was going to happen when you left, at least, not in the matter of religion."

"The same applies to you as it does to me. I am only an ordinary person. I am taking the role of a priest because there is no one else available. Surely, as the most senior person after me, you will be teaching the younger ones from your own experience and education.

"Won't you be able to extend your teaching to include religion. Surely, that will only be a short step for you, after all you believe. You know that much of what I have said is true. You have experienced that truth.

"As to you being a woman, what difference does that make? It was a woman who first carried the news of our Lord's resurrection to the disciples and in any case, who is it who does the teaching during the first years of a child's life? From whom does a child learn about life right up to their teenage years?

"Their mother or mother-figure in their lives. It will be up to you to continue to ensure that faith is kept up by whoever is most able. Since we are all here and ready, we might as well start straight away."

The family agreed and Believer started by saying, "Lord, we are gathered here in this house to hold communion with you and Our Lord Jesus, your Son. We know this is not a church and that you will not mind, considering the circumstances. We thank you for our survival with all our hearts.

"You have guided us and nurtured us and we pray that you will extend your valuable assistance to all who are in need of it. We pray that you will cast your blessings on this house in order that we may regard it as a holy place during the period of this and other services to be held later."

After this initial prayer, the group sang the hymn: *'Just as I am without one plea.'* Believer had chosen this because he felt that the words were appropriate to their present situation. They were just ordinary people trying to carry on with the tradition of their former religious experiences.

When the hymn was over, he asked Joanne to kneel before him. "Joanne, do you accept the knowledge and guidance of Jesus?"

"Yes, I do."

"Will you continue to worship God the Father, God the Son and God the Holy Spirit and do your utmost to spread the Gospel with whoever you can?"

"I will."

Believer placed his hands on her head and continued. "Father Almighty. You have heard this young person confess her faith in You and Your Son, Jesus. We ask that You accept her fully into your church. Guide her in the ways of love and gentleness.

"Protect and help her at all times, especially when she is hunting for the family. Joanne, you can stand up now. I think that we should all hold hands. Father, we in this house, three adults and two young children affirm that we will try to spread the knowledge of you and your love for us.

"We will try to love others and show mercy to any we meet, whatever the circumstances. In this task, we will ever be in need of your guidance. We know that sometimes, it will be difficult to be always tolerant. We ask that you will always remind us when we feel intolerance to try to see another point of view. We ask this in the name of Your Son Jesus. Amen.

"Joanne, I have asked God to accept you into His Church. As I trust in Him, I know that He will. You have confirmed your trust in Him. As far as I am concerned, you should regard yourself as a full member of His church and as such, you should feel free to take the sacrament of the Holy Eucharist whenever it is offered. Now we shall continue with that service."

Believer followed the sequence of the service in the Alternative Service Book. Each of the three adults read a lesson and Believer decided not to give a sermon on any particular text. Instead, he just spoke about his feelings on religion generally.

He made the point that each of them had been guided and had experienced God's touch in some way or another. He said that they should continue with their faith and that they would receive His help if only they would put their trust in Him.

The intercessions were also slightly different from the printed version in that Believer felt that certain specific prayers no longer applied. For instance, he felt that to pray for the Royal Family and the Government was no longer relevant. Instead, he prayed for unity and love between all survivors wherever they could be found.

That such love would result in everlasting peace, between small communities and between larger international groups. He prayed that mankind had at last learnt the lesson of the futility of war. Then he prayed for all survivors who were sick or injured, that they would recover as God willed. The remainder of the prayers were as printed and the rest of the service followed the regular form.

During their breakfast, which they had mutually decided would take place after the service, Believer asked Allyson, "Do you think that you could carry out such a service on a regular basis?"

She seemed a bit doubtful and said, "You made it seem so easy, the way you spoke, I felt that you had been doing it all your life. As for your sermon or talk, it seemed inspired." She then realised what she was saying and thought for a moment before continuing.

"I suppose it's obvious really, knowing you and how you think. You must have prayed for help beforehand and it is evident that you received it. The funny thing is that I felt compelled to listen to every word. What is more, the words seemed to make more sense than ever before."

"And me," Joanne joined in. "When you put your hands on my head, I felt elated and strange at the same time. Also, my scalp was tingling."

"Anyone else feel the tingling?" Believer asked.

"Yes." This was Allyson. "I felt it two or three times during the service."

"My head felt funny," piped in Judy.

"And me," from Sharon.

"I'm glad you all experienced that, I am no exception. I've felt this before, sometimes before the disaster. Then I didn't know what it was. Now what I think it is that the Holy Spirit is making His presence felt. Although He is with us always, there are times when He makes us aware.

"I find this a great comfort. What I am not sure of is, whether at those times, I am meant to do something special. This morning, I felt the tingle at the same time as Joanne and I think that, in this instance, the Spirit visited me and passed on to Joanne directly and then to the rest of you. We may have all been affected at the same time.

"The point is that it happened and there is no reason to question the fact. We should all recognise it in the future and we should draw comfort from the fact that He is with us."

When the meal was finished, Believer said that he would spend the rest of the morning hunting with Joanne. If they managed to catch anything in good time, then they should all go again to the ruined market garden and see what was growing. Perhaps they could prepare some soil for planting. At least they could do some planning for the following year.

All were all in agreement, so he and Joanne set of on their hunt. Believer was carrying the newly finished crossbow in addition to the air rifle he had always used because he wanted to try it out under field conditions. Joanne was, of course, armed with the original weapon which she had used to good effect.

As they walked, the two hunters talked about how they felt about the future. Joanne was very apprehensive, but rather than try to console her, Believer said, "You do realise that things are going to be very difficult for you in particular? First, because you are a young and very attractive girl. So far, we have not actually met any other survivors. Others may not be of my temperament or faith.

"This means that you may be called upon to defend yourself and the family. I hope that, if that happens, you will ask for God's guidance and that you will not try to hurt or kill anyone.

"Above all, try not to let anger or revenge cloud your judgement. Remember that the crossbow you are carrying is a lethal weapon and is really far more dangerous than my air rifle. There is no animal that could not be killed by the crossbow if the bolt hits the right spot.

"It should even be possible to kill an elephant with it, although not easy. At the right distance, one of those bolts could go right through a man. If you should be in danger, try to remember that, please."

"What about self-defence?" asked the girl. "I might have to act very quickly and might not have time to aim properly. What should I do then?"

"Pray first. 'God help me' is sufficient in time of danger. He will guide your next action. Never forget that revenge and greed has got us into this mess that we are in now. Also, anyone who has survived has done so only by God's will, therefore that person has a purpose to fulfil which probably only God will know.

"Anyone who is killed from now on will be a loss to the rest of us. That person will have some skills to contribute. If not a skill, a talent which can be used to help others."

"I see what you're getting at, but what about children like Sharon and Judy? I know that they help Mum around the house. I suppose that their skills haven't developed yet."

"Don't forget that, young as they are, they have also contributed to the food we have eaten. They have caught some fish and a pigeon or two, all the less for you and I to provide. Now that you are adult in every way apart from age, they provide a comfort to your mother. They give your mother purpose to carry on.

"A mother's purpose in life is to bear children and provide for them. Before you say that that is a sexist thing to say, I did say a mother's purpose, not a woman's. It's sexist only in that it is impossible for a man to bear children. As

139

soon as woman becomes pregnant, she becomes a different person with responsibilities.

"There is no escaping the fact that children learn first from their mother. Poor old dad never got a real look in when it came to teaching the children. In a man's world, he was always the one going out to hunt and to provide what food he could for his family.

"This applies to modern man since for the most part, that a man has been the main provider and has had to work for a living. It's the same thing really, using his skills to earn money to buy things. You see, man and woman are equal until she falls pregnant. From that time on, no man could be a woman's equal.

"A mother is many things, cook, nursemaid, manager, financial wizard, laundress, you name it, a mother is all of these things and if a man could do them all then he would become a superman.

"There is an old saying that says that women's work is never done. That is not quite true, for a woman alone without children could usually manage to finish her housework and be able to spend a good deal of her time on her own activities. Not so a mother. Her work continues for years.

"With regard to Sharon and Judy, they will learn both your skills and your mother's. They will end up being more capable that either of you, especially if you take them out hunting. I advise that you take them out in turn. They will learn your skills and add their own in time.

"Both are very bright in their own way. When they are your age and you are eight years older, you won't be able to match them because, when I have gone, you will only have your mother to learn from. They will have both of you as well as each other. Be pleased for them when that happens, for they will need more and more skills to cope with life when civilisation starts to return.

"They will learn skills that you cannot imagine at the moment. At best, I have only improvised, using what is available. Your future lies in your ability to adapt to both the old and the new. Sharon and Judy will surpass you as you have already surpassed your mother and possibly me.

"I am only a bodger, a man with a modicum of skill to put what little knowledge I have into practice. Look at us. You have great skill with the crossbow. It was made by a man who is a complete amateur and in primitive workshop conditions.

"I am fairly skilled in the use of this air rifle, but it was made with the finest of engineering skills and accurate tools. That is why I say that you have already bettered me in some respects. I doubt that I could use that crossbow as well as you. I know that you have hit moving targets. I have to wait until they are stationary."

Joanne said, "Surely that is because the crossbow has more killing power. You've said yourself, how lethal it is. The bolts do far more damage than the pellets you fire so therefore you have to hit the right spot. I have only to bring the target down.

"I've seen you, don't forget, one shot is enough for you. You kill things with the first shot, I don't always."

'You've missed the point, I think. The rifle is a precision instrument and you could use it as well as me. You have done. Your weapon is certainly not precision built but you have a natural feel for it and can fire it at a moving target.

"You seem to know where the target is going and where that rather inaccurate crossbow will fire. It would take me a long time to use it as well as you do, if ever. Don't forget that you have used the rifle and hit something. I used to miss at first so I am no better than you. I've just had more practice."

"But I couldn't have made the crossbow in the first place, so what would I have done without it?"

"If the possibility of hunting had occurred to you, I suspect that you would have thought about bows and arrows. I believe that you could have made something like that and learnt to use it well. By the way, you now have two crossbows. Teach your mother to use one as quickly as possible.

"It would be better if there was more than one person who could use one. The girls are not strong enough yet. You should always leave one behind unless you are all out together. You've seen me make the bolts. Do you think that you could make some?

"You should have a few in reserve. You are bound to lose some."

The pair walked on in silence as they both had much to think about. Joanne was thinking about the implications of the conversation they had just finished. Believer was thinking about his impending departure and worrying in his mind about what was to become of the small family after he left.

He was concerned about whether there was anything else he should have done for them. He decided that while there were many tasks he could have done, nothing was left unfinished.

He prayed silently that God would spread His mantle of protection over them and send someone soon to help them and look after their interests. At this time, the image of the man with the gun came back to him and he realised that there was no menace in the apparition. He had a strong feeling that the man with the gun and the person who had also used the coke at the foundry were one and the same person.

He decided that he would head in that direction in the hope that he would make contact with him. He was sure that this man was the one destined to replace him as protector of the family he had come to love.

Believer's reverie was interrupted by Joanne who touched his arm and pointed. Her attention had been caught by some crows that were feeding in a field. By means of signals, they worked out which birds to aim for.

Believer shot at the crow he had selected, and noted that Joanne had delayed her shot by a fraction of a second. She still brought down a bird and they went across to pick up their kill.

They were surprised to find that the crows had been feeding on the remains of a chicken.

Believer said, "Chickens. Listen, where there is one there are probably more. When we get back, we must try to build a pen for them, then as soon as you can, you must try to catch some alive, also a cockerel. If you can them you just might be able to get some fresh eggs, provided of course, that the birds are fertile.

"Sharon and Judy should be able to help. Their pigeon trap might work on a bigger scale You've got to try before predators get them. If you can breed chickens, you will have a valuable food supply for yourselves and for trade. Let's hurry back now and tell the others of the news."

They went back and while Allyson started preparing the crows, Believer and the others worked feverishly to gather materials to make a chicken run. They had to use the dumper and visit the builder's yard and were able to obtain timber and wire netting from there.

The wire netting was somewhat tangled and took some unravelling, but there was sufficient for Believer's purpose, and he started to build the chicken coop immediately on his return, ably assisted by Joanne and the two young girls. The work carried on until the evening was nearly finished with only a short break for the evening meal which Allyson had prepared.

When the work was finished and Sharon and Judy had been settled into bed Joanne said to Believer, "Why have we worked so hard to finish this today. Couldn't we have waited until tomorrow?"

Believer said in reply, "Tomorrow is another day and I have a feeling that something important will happen. I thought that it would be best if we could finish as much as possible. It will serve its purpose at the moment and you can improve on it later."

Believer realised that he was getting some sort of message, a premonition of the nature of his dreams about the man with the gun who had come into his mind on several occasions in the recent past. Premonitions like this were to govern many of his future actions, although he did not fully understand the implications at that time. All he knew was that his life would take another turn the next day.

Day Forty-Three

Believer was, as usual, the first to awake and could not escape the feeling that the day would be special. He carried out the usual chores, raking out the kitchen range and opening the vents so that the fire would draw, fetching the water for the toilet cistern and the cooking. While he was working, the rest of the household joined him one by one.

Allyson prepared a light breakfast from the leftovers from the day before. The atmosphere during the meal seemed to one of apprehension.

It was Sharon who noticed that the light was gradually becoming brighter. The sky was lightening and was now lighter than it had been from the time of the holocaust. The survivors had experienced nothing but gloomy skies interspersed with rain since that time.

The brightness increased until, eventually, the sun broke through. The wind was blowing from the South East, and the little group could see the patch of sunlight gradually spreading along the road which ran in a North Westerly direction.

Believer said to Allyson, "Can you please come into the lounge? I have something I have to say to you first. It will be very difficult and I shall need your help later."

Allyson followed him into the lounge and they closed the door behind them.

"I think you know what I am going to say," Believer said. Allyson was fighting to control her tears and could only nod.

"That first sight of sunlight is a sign and it has shown me that it is time to go. Not only that, also the direction I must take. Now I must pack my things. Will you help please?"

Allyson regained control and busied herself with collecting some of the items Believer would need in his travels. Believer had stored most of them in a box with a lid which had served as an extra seat at times when the house had been full.

When his rucksack was packed, he turned to Allyson and said, "I've come to love you and your family as much as I had loved my previous family, and I feel exactly the same as I know you do at having to leave. Most of my feelings are urging me to stay. God is telling me now that I must leave, that I am needed elsewhere.

"I must obey. Please help me when I tell the others. I'm sure that they suspect what is happening and they will need your strength to help them face the inevitable."

Allyson said, with a tremor in her voice, "I meant what I said earlier, I love you and I will follow you when the children are older. Perhaps, things will be better then. When I catch up with you then we will be together for the rest of our lives. Until then, I shall think constantly of you and I shall pray for you."

"Do that please, and I shall pray for you. I won't forget you and your family either. We should go and face the others now. I think that you know that this is the most difficult thing I have ever done," Believer replied. Then they kissed with a long and breath-taking embrace.

The two saddened and subdued people went into the kitchen to find the others waiting in anticipation.

Joanne said, "You're leaving now, aren't you? I thought that when the sun shone, that it was pointing the way to go. I told Sharon and Judy that I thought God was calling you and that you must go. I could see that you have been busy finishing things off here during the last few days.

"I knew that your leaving would be very soon and when you worked so hard on that chicken coop. I thought that you only had the one day left. We are all upset that you are going, but you've said all the time that God was guiding you, and when the sun came out and shone along the road, it seemed proof of all that you have been saying."

"Now you know, as well as me, the difference between knowing and believing. You know that God is there. No. Not there. Here. I am relieved that you know why I must go and that I would stay if I could."

Allyson had been busy while this conversation had been going on and Believer found that she had packed a few vegetables in an old paper bag.

"I can't take these, you will be short for the family."

"Don't worry about that, we will get some more. Please take them, otherwise you will leave with just what you came with. You have given us so much. You have worked day in, day out for our comfort and survival. You have given us life

145

and hope. We haven't much to give, but a little food will help and it is all we can spare."

"The widow's mite," Believer said. "In that case, I accept and thank you. Now I must go."

He took the hands of each in turn, saying, "The peace of Christ be with you now and forever." He kissed them all and hoisted the rucksack on to his shoulder to start the next stage of his journey. He knew that he had left behind four people with tears in their eyes.

He was no different. When he was almost out of sight of the little cottage, he turned, waved once and continued.

He walked on with a heavy heart for about five miles then he stopped and prayed hard for guidance and strength of will to carry on the task that God had set him. Also, he prayed that God would protect and help the family he had just left. Then he carried on feeling only slightly easier in his mind.

He walked steadily throughout the day, stopping only to shoot a pigeon for his evening meal. He cooked this on an open fire and pitched his tent just as night was falling. Then he slept away his exhaustion after the long walk.

Day Forty-Four

Believer's first thought on waking was how much he wanted to turn back and retrace his steps. Then he felt that someone was telling him to go on because he was needed elsewhere. He prayed again for strength of mind to enable him to continue.

The weather had reverted to the overcast sky that he had been used to over the past few weeks. Also, rain was falling in a light drizzle which added to his discomfort and longing to return.

He sat up in the tent and thought of all he had done since he had first woken up beside his overturned lorry. He remembered how he had been helped every step of the way since then. He had been guided to shelter in the first house and had found all the equipment to keep him alive. Later, he had spent time with a family he had come to love, and saved their lives by arriving at an opportune time.

He reflected on the tasks he had done while he had stayed with Allyson. He realised that although he had been completely ignorant of many skills, he had achieved everything he set out to do. The most important being the training of a 5-year-old girl in hunting skills with which he had no previous experience himself.

He had done this after nursing them all back to health after near starvation. Under normal circumstances, all of this would have been regarded as the work of a near superman, which he certainly was not.

He reflected that a middle-aged man, as he was, could not have performed all the tasks without inner strength and forbearance. He had not been particularly fit at the time of the disastrous war, but the work he had undertaken and the necessary rationing of available food bad made him fitter and stronger than he had been for years.

When he considered all these things and that he had God's help to perform them all, he felt that he was now prepared to continue his journey to search for more survivors. He prayed that he would be able to bring them God's word of peace and hope.

He packed up the tent and rucksack and continued on his way, now feeling that he was not alone. Despite the rain, be was now able to face the future with much more confidence.

After he had walked for several hours, he found that he was nearing the foundry where he had collected coke for the people he had just left. It was in the foundry that he had seen evidence of at least one other survivor, and he had directed his footsteps in this direction in order to make contact. The time was now about four o'clock and Believer had not eaten that day, so he pitched his tent in a corner of a field where he had seen the evidence of rabbits.

He had not seen any sign of any other person and was sitting at the entrance of the tent when he was startled to hear a voice say. "Keep very still." He looked up and saw a young man about 20 years old, standing by the tent and pointing a shotgun at him.

The young man said, "I'm hungry and I want some food. What have you got to eat?"

"Not much yet. Would your name be Eric, by any chance?"

The young man was taken aback by this and said, "How did you know that" Who are you anyway?"

"The first question is difficult to answer quickly, so I'll answer the second first. My name is Believer. That is the only name I shall ever answer to. I ha another name once, but decided that when my life changed so abruptly, then would change my name as well.

"I will explain why, later, if there is any later for me. I don't wish you an harm and in fact I came this way hoping to meet you, so I would rather prefe that you point that gun somewhere else."

"Why should I?" Eric said. "I'm not afraid to use it, I have done it before an I want some better answers than you have given me so far. Also, I want son food."

"All I have are a few vegetables, only about two day's supply. No tins at a If you will be patient for an hour or two, we might be able to get a couple rabbits."

"But they will be contaminated and so are the vegetables, we'll get ill."

"I'm still alive and have been living on natural foods for some time now with no ill effects, so if you will be patient, I will be pleased to share a meal with you. Please turn that gun aside now."

Eric rested the gun butt on the floor, but was still very watchful. "I suppose if you can eat food like that, then so can I. Tins won't last for ever and I didn't know what I would do if I couldn't find any more. How are you going to catch rabbits? I haven't seen any around. How do you know they are here?"

"Again, second question first, you're not very observant, are you? Look at the ground. Their droppings are everywhere. As to catching them, I shall shoot them."

"You mean that you have a gun. How do I know that you won't use it on me?"

"If you look just inside the tent, you will see a gun case. I would like you to take the weapon out and examine it."

Eric did this, but still watched Believer closely. Believer remained seated. When he had seen that Eric had examined the weapon in question, he said, "You will have seen that it is an air rifle. With that, it is very difficult for anyone to inflict a serious incapacitating injury on anything as large as a man. It would require a very good or very lucky shot.

"While you have that shotgun, it would be a foolish risk on my part to try anything, wouldn't it? If I were to shoot you with that, it would be extremely doubtful whether I could injure you enough to stop you shooting me afterwards. If you want to share a meal with me, you will have to trust me. After all, you have a shotgun and can afford to take the risk."

"Why don't I shoot the rabbits?"

"Several reasons. I intend to get two rabbits. If you use that shotgun, you might get one. In that case, it would be full of lead pellets. Secondly, if you missed, there would be no rabbits because your gun will make a lot of noise. Thirdly, if you used the air rifle, can you guarantee to hit anything?

"Also, what would you do with the shotgun? I might try to take it off you. It seems logical on all counts that I use the air rifle while you watch me. Are we agreed?"

"Yes, I see your point. How long will it take? I can't see any rabbits yet."

"They will come out at dusk so we will have to cook them in the dark, makes life interesting, doesn't it?"

Eric considered for a moment while still watching Believer, then he said, "A thought has just occurred to me. You have said that it would take a good or lucky shot to stop a man with that air rifle. Then you asked me if I could guarantee to hit anything with it. You went on to say that you intend to shoot two rabbits.

"That implies that you are a very good shot, possibly good enough to kill a man. How do I know that you still won't turn the gun on me?"

"Good you're thinking, but in answer to your question, what did I say my name was?"

"Believer," was Eric's reply.

"Exactly, that is my name because I am just that. I believe in God the Father, God the Son and God the Holy Ghost. I believe wholeheartedly and I know that even before the bombs fell, God was looking after me and pushing me along his way. The teachings of Jesus tell us that we must love our fellowmen and women.

"We should help each other as much as we can. How would it serve His purpose if I tried to shoot you? Even if it could loosely be described as self-defence.

"Anyway, you haven't posed any real threat to me, have you? You spoke to me first when you could have shot me without warning. I sensed that you didn't want to do that. In any case, as I believe, then my life is in God's hands, not yours.

"If it is His purpose that you shoot me then you would still be affected by our meeting because you will have found in my possession, some religious books and by them God's purpose would have been fulfilled.

"He has other uses for us both. My purpose is to travel and contact as many people as possible. To spread His word and bring His love to all. You are the fifth person I have met so far, and I believe that it is your mission to join up with the other four to help and protect them."

"After that, what can I do but trust you. Now what can I do to help you, start the fire or something. Where and when will I meet the others?"

"All in good time. Before that I have much to tell you and I'm afraid that it will sound like a sermon because I sense that you are a little sceptical of my beliefs. I must tell you that God has sent me dreams or visions of you. In those dreams I learnt your name.

"That is how I knew that it was Eric and also that you wouldn't harm me. Now we must gather some wood for the fire and I suspect that some of it may well be damp, so we shall have some fun getting a fire going."

The two men set about gathering the driest wood they could find. A difficult job in the circumstances. By the time they had finished, it was almost dusk and Believer asked Eric to be very quiet as it was nearly time for the rabbits to come out of their burrows.

First one, then gradually more. As Believer promised, he was able to shoot two with the air rifle. Then he started the fire with some dry tinder he had saved from his previous efforts. A small quantity of the whisky and the gas lighter he had kept from his first refuge started the flame and after careful coaxing and much smoke, he finally got a good fire going.

It was completely dark by the time he had prepared a stew with the vegetables and rabbits. The two of them settled down to talk with only the firelight to provide any illumination.

"Was that you driving some sort of vehicle in the old foundry?" asked Eric. "I heard it two or three times but could never get close enough to stop anyone. I did shout last time, but the driver didn't seem to hear."

"Yes, that was me. I got hold of a builder's dumper. I never heard anyone shout, the machine is very noisy and I was practically sat on top of the engine. I take it that you were the man with the bucket."

"I was, and I read your message. I thought that it was left there by some crank. I'm not so sure now that I have met you. You really do believe all that stuff, don't you?"

"I admit that I can't take it all in just yet. I am not sure that any God would let all this happen. All those people dead and the injured as well."

"You've posed a difficult question and it is not easy to answer. God has told us time and time again to love each other. He gave us free choice to follow and trust Him. Each time man has rejected him.

"Several times, God has given us the chance to make a fresh start. Each time Man's greed and animosity has brought him to terrible consequences. None more so than this last one. Man went to war, not God.

"If you were in God's place, what would your reactions be if a race you created insisted on trying to destroy everyone with a different creed or colour? How many times would you forgive before you said enough? If they want to destroy themselves, so be it.

"Perhaps God has said just that, but then He is ever forgiving and has left a few of us to start again. Perhaps for the very last time. We must make a go of it,

151

this time because we can't be sure that there will ever be another. I believe that the small number of survivors are the chosen ones.

"We have got to learn to live and work together. Of course, we are a mixed bag of abilities and temperaments. If we don't work together, we simply won't survive.

"If we go about with guns for the purpose of killing our fellowmen, what hope is there? On the other hand, if we follow Jesus, we will not want to kill anyone. We will try to help each other instead. Even then, it will be very difficult.

"You and I have made a start. You didn't kill me and I have no desire to kill you."

"Are you saying that I should get rid of this gun and go about unarmed? I only have it because I was with a group who were all armed. They found another group and a battle started. I didn't like the idea and said so.

"Their reaction was, that if I was not with them, I was against them and they turned on me. I fired on them and ran away. I think I hit someone, but I'm not sure if I did any harm. Anyway, I hid for a couple of days and then made my way over here."

"I didn't say that you shouldn't carry a gun, only that you should not have any intent to kill anyone. It may well be that such a weapon is necessary as there may be large predatory animals escaped from zoos. Perhaps, later, packs of dogs, so keep that gun if you wish.

"Only if you try to kill anyone with it, then all I have said has been wasted on you. I don't think that is God's purpose for you, do you?

"God has directed our paths so they cross. That being the case, both our lives will be affected to a greater or lesser degree. There is no going back to the situation that was in force before our meeting. You will remember what I have said and I must try to find the people who were fighting and stop them, or at least try."

Eric was alarmed by this and said, "But they will shoot on sight. They said that there was only enough food for their group and they would shoot anyone else they saw.

"Greed again, what were they living on? Tins, I suppose. I agree that there are not enough tins to last any group indefinitely. What do they think they will live on when all the tins are gone? They must be short sighted idiots.

"You and I and the other group have proved that we can live without tins. When you meet them, you will find that one is a very accomplished hunter another is a genius with a cooking pot. I wonder what your talents are. God will find them and put them to good use. The people I have left will tell you of my talents, poor as they are."

The two fell silent whilst they ate their rabbit stew, leaving enough in the pot for a meagre breakfast. When they had cleaned their utensils by washing them in a small brook, Believer put the fire out. He showed Eric how to keep some dried-out sticks and half-burnt wood to start the next day's fire.

"These Believer carefully wrapped in plastic when they were completely cold. Then they settled down for the night, sharing the tent and Believer's sleeping bag as best they could.

Eric said, "You really do believe in God, don't you? I have never met anyone who was so convincing. You don't seem to be any sort of special person at first sight, but when you start talking, I can tell that you are completely serious.

"I never went to church much except as a child, but if I had met anyone like you, a sincere believer, I think I might well have been persuaded."

"People like me were there. Every church I have ever been in has its ardent believers. I fear that perhaps, they didn't use their talents as they should have done. I am no exception to that. I am very far from perfect, like everyone else.

"You see, the world was full of people like me and you. In my case, I believed but didn't know how to ask for guidance. You had been told many stories about Christianity, but never really tried to find out more, did you?"

"You're so right. Can you teach me?"

"I will have to say no to that as time is too short. Besides which, I don't know everything myself. I can only tell you about my beliefs. Only God can teach you. Everything from now on will be a lesson directly from Him.

"If you think that I am telling you now, you are mistaken, for I am a very shy and reticent person. Where do you think that all this confidence comes from? I tell you, I could not have spoken in this manner in my former way of life.

"I have to say to you that God has made our paths cross. God directs each of my footsteps. The difference in me now is that I know He is directing me. Before I only stumbled along.

"Now I talk about Him with ease. I don't think of the words I use, they just come. Once I start, it is very difficult for me to stop. I chose the name Believer because it opens up a path for conversation.

"Look, when we met, I told you that my name was Believer. Straight away, that needs explanation. Either I would have to explain it or you would have asked me anyway. The end result is the same.

"I start talking and whoever you are or whatever your beliefs, you have heard me. There is no way you will forget everything for ever. Someday, something I have said will come back to you. God will make you understand what He is saying through me.

"I suggest that you read any religious books that you can. Perhaps, then you will have a new understanding. I shall do the same and I shall learn as well. It's getting very late now so try to sleep. You might well understand more in the morning and I, for one, am very tired. Goodnight."

They drifted off to sleep but Believer received a premonition that Joanne was going to face some terrible danger. So strong was the feeling that he resolved to send Eric to assist her as soon as possible in the morning.

Day Forty-Five
(Believer and Eric)

The pair awoke and breakfasted on the remains of the rabbit stew. Believer remembered his premonition about Joanna and said to Eric, "You know what I told you that I dreamt about you before I came here. I had a similar dream last night. I must act on it as I believe that it is a message. I didn't tell you about the people I have just left.

"They are a family of four, a mother, Allyson; her two daughters, Joanne and Sharon and another small child by the name of Judy. Joanne is the one who is doing the hunting. She is 15 and the other two girls are only seven. I dreamt last night that Joanne is going to be in some terrible danger and needs your help. Will you give it?"

"What sort of danger? Do you know that? I will be glad to help if I can, but you will have to tell me how to find them."

"I don't know what form the danger will take, only if you do as I tell you, you will be in time. You have the best part of two days journey and I shall have to get you something to eat on the way as you haven't the means of lighting a fire. I will have to cook whatever I can catch for you to take with you.

"It looks like crow, I'm afraid, but they are not too bad. You see where I threw the remains of the rabbits, some crows have come down and you will have to take one with you cooked and cold."

Eric pulled a face at this idea and was still not happy about even when Believer had brought one down and was cooking it on a stick.

"Do you really expect me to eat that?" he said. "I don't think I can."

"Listen to me now. I have eaten crow. I've had to in order to stay alive. So have the people you are going to next. It is imperative that you keep fit and strong for your journey. You must go as soon as the crow is cooked or you will be too late."

"Why don't you go back yourself and take me with you? Surely, it would be better if there were two people to deal with the danger you say is coming."

"I would like to do that very much. You don't know how much I have prayed to have been able to stay there or how much I would like to go back. I get the answer every time that I must go on and meet other people.

"You are, in a way, the answer to a lot of my prayers. You are the person to take my place in that household. You will be able to help them in ways that I cannot.

"I would have liked you to stay with me for a couple of days so that I could have explained more about how I feel and how I am motivated. I know that your presence is needed there and to my great sorrow, I am needed in other places,"

Eric was still feeling a little dubious, but he gathered his meagre belongings and prepared himself for the journey ahead. He was partially convinced, but was surprised by the suddenness of it all. He sensed that Believer was sincere in his belief that this unknown girl was going to be in danger.

He suddenly understood that Believer trusted in God absolutely and took no action without first praying. Therefore, if Believer really thought that he, Eric, was desperately needed, then he was in no position to refuse the request.

When his preparations were complete and he had studied the directions Believer had given him, he was ready to make a massive change in his life.

Believer clasped him firmly with both hands and said, "Go in the peace of Christ. May He guide and protect you in all you do and give you wisdom to make loving and compassionate decisions. Eric, if you are ever undecided, don't be frightened to ask God for His help through the love of Jesus."

Eric thanked him and told him to look after himself, and set off to retrace Believer's footsteps. He looked back and was surprised to see that Believer was on his knees in an attitude of prayer. This was a sight that he was to remember for the rest of his life.

Eric's first day was uneventful except that he wasn't sure how to regulate his pace. He understood that his mission was urgent and felt that he should run. He recalled that Believer had told him that there was a journey of nearly two day This meant a long trek, so running wouldn't do any good.

He decided to walk at a steady pace which he was able to keep up all day and until well into the evening where he found shelter in a partially demolished building. He ate the cooked crow that Believer had given him which he washed down with water.

He settled down to sleep and to ponder over the events of the previous two days. Must of his thoughts centred on the middle-aged man he had left that morning. Never had he met such a man as this. A man who had so convincingly told him about God.

Believer had seemed, at first glance, just ordinary. Eric realised that he must be a very capable survivor. He sensed that when he met the people he had been sent to find, he would hear some very interesting tales. He wondered whether they had been influenced as much as he had been.

He resolved that night to try and find out as much as he could about the religion that Believer embraced and to try prayer as a solution to his own problems. He had two major things to occupy his thoughts. One was of his future survival.

The other was the danger to the teenaged girl that Believer had warned him about. He worried whether he would be able to cope with the emergency when he came across it and what form it would take. He made a big decision then, perhaps the most important in his life. He decided to pray for God's guidance and fell asleep with a sense of calm that he had not experienced for a long time.

Day Forty-Six
(Eric)

Eric woke feeling hungry but now had no food left. He washed himself in a small stream and continued on his way with a feeling that he was no longer in control of his own destiny. In fact, he realised that he had not been for some time. Ever since the bombs had landed with such total devastation, his life had been controlled by events.

First, his disagreement with the group he been with. Then his battle for survival on his own, followed by the most unusual meeting with Believer, more than a day ago. Now, he was walking towards some unknown danger, the like of which he could not imagine.

He had much to think about and had been walking for all the morning, steadily feeling hungrier and wondering where his next meal was coming from. He heard a sound which jolted him into immediate awareness. The sound he heard was a scream produced only by a feminine voice. Remembering Believer's words, he said, "God help me," and headed in the direction of the sounds of distress.

When he got within sight of the originator of the sounds, he saw that a girl, aged about 15 was struggling with two youths, both a little older than she was. As she was weaker than the other two, she was losing the fight. Eric came closer, the youths pulled her to the ground and began forcibly removing her clothes.

The attention of the attackers was centred entirely on the girl, thus enabling Eric to approach. He was about ten yards away before he was seen. Eric realised that he should get even closer because he didn't dare to use his gun for fear of hitting the girl.

He shouted, "Save some for me when you've finished."

The girl heard this and her struggles increased, causing the youths to concentrate more on her. This enabled Eric to close the gap sufficiently to be able to hit one of the eager youths with the butt of his gun. This one was disable completely and Eric placed the barrel of the shotgun against the ear of the other. The would-be rapist was terrified into immobility but was still lying on top of the girl who was now partially undressed.

"Get up slowly," Eric said and when the youth complied, continued, "Go and look after your mate."

He watched him carefully while he said to the girl, "I think you better get dressed."

The girl was naturally in tears but she did as he suggested. Eric could not help noticing that she was quite a beauty, also that some of her clothes were badly torn. He turned to the youth he had threatened with the gun and told him to remove his jacket and give it to the girl to put on.

The girl said, 'Watch them, they both have guns."

Eric saw that nearby were two packs and two rifles lying near the place where the fight had taken place. Slightly further away was a dead goose and a crossbow.

"Is that yours? Are you Joanne? Believer sent me. He told me that you would be in danger and was so right. Now, have you any cord or rope? Yes, there is a coil there. Is that yours as well?"

"Yes, I'm Joanne. Thank God that you met Believer. Now what do we do?"

"First, we must unload their weapons, then we must tie them up so they can't threaten us. Is that crossbow lethal? Yes, I can see it is, you shot that goose didn't you. Load it and keep those two covered while I sort out their rifles."

Eric did this, then he took the rope and the rifles and tied the two youths in such a way that their arms were behind their backs and the rifles tied between arms and bodies. By this time, the one he had hit had recovered consciousness. Eric's method of tying deprived the youths of the use of their arms and rifles at the same time.

He said to Joanne, "You'd better show us the way to your home. Is it far?"

"About two miles and thank you again for your timely arrival. We may get help soon. When I was attacked, Judy ran off; so Mum will come with the other crossbow. We'd better start now. I'm not really hurt, just a few bruises, so I'll be OK. Thank you again."

Eric said, "Believer told me about you, but only that you were here and would be in trouble. I expect there are some stories to tell about him. I never met anyone like him before. I am surprised that he would leave four females without protection."

This conversation was taking place as the procession made its way towards the cottage where the family had endured so much hardship before Believer arrived.

Joanne answered Eric's previous statement by saying, "But he didn't leave us without protection, did he? We were left in God's hands, and as you see, we were protected, you came along."

Meanwhile, Allyson, alerted by Judy, had picked up the second crossbow. She set off to try and rescue her daughter, guided by Judy and accompanied by Sharon. About a mile from the cottage, she heard voices, so she motioned to her two young charges to hide while she herself stepped behind a ruined building to wait.

She saw a small group of people coming slowly along the road. The two in front were tied up with rifles behind their backs to prevent their arms being used.

The third person she saw was Joanne wearing a strange combat jacket over jeans that were obviously torn. They were accompanied by a young man who was carrying a shotgun and covering the two bound young men. These two were not walking as well as they might since they could not use their arms for balance.

Also, the packs they had been carrying had simply been hung around their neck in any way that Eric had managed to place them. Understandably, he had not been particular as to the youths' comfort.

"It's alright, Mum. You can come out," Joanne called. "This is Eric. Believer sent him to us."

"What happened? Judy came running back and said that some nasty men had grabbed you, so I came out to help if I could."

She turned her attention to Eric, "It seems that you, Eric, have saved my daughter from a lot of harm."

"Mum, they tried to rape me, then Eric came along. He asked them to save some for him and then the next minute, he was in control and I got dressed. I've not asked him about that yet, but he has been very courteous to me since."

Eric said to Joanne, "I'm sorry about that. It was only so that I could get close enough to take action. It worked because you struggled harder and took the attention enough for me to get near enough to do something."

"Thank you, Eric," said Allyson. "Now, what do we do about these two? Personally, I feel very angry and I wouldn't blame Joanne if she felt the same. I'm tempted to shoot them now, but I keep thinking of Believer and wondering what he would say. You've met him, what do you think he would do, Eric?"

"Well, I don't think he would shoot them, but how can we trust them?"

"Mum, we will have to send them away, I don't feel like trusting them either. How do we know they won't come back? If they stay, I don't know whether I can catch enough food for them as well as us. We have a big problem."

Allyson turned to the two youths who were showing sign of severe discomfort. "Your names, please? What do you think we should do with you? You tried to rape an innocent girl, and would have succeeded but for Eric's timely arrival."

"I'm John, this is Dave and I think he's got a headache. He was hit pretty hard. I suppose we have given you cause to be angry. I'm only surprised that we are both still alive. In other circumstances, we would be dead.

"Who is this Believer you talk about? He seems to be some sort of religious crank. Why don't you kill us anyway? We've got no food and there are not very many people left, so I don't see how we can all survive. We only attacked the girl because we thought we wouldn't live long anyway." He was hysterical when he said this.

"Believer is the most wonderful person I have ever met," Allyson replied. "He believes wholeheartedly in Jesus Christ and God, but he is very far from being a crank. He is practical and a very hard worker. He saved all of our lives and taught us how to live in these circumstances.

"He has saved your lives as well. If Eric had not met him before he came here, I suspect that you would both be dead now. Eric looks the sort of person who would shoot if he felt it necessary. Is that so, Eric?"

"Yes, before I met Believer, I might well have killed them both. He influenced me before I even met him. He piled some coke up for me and left a message."

"So that was you with the bucket. I was with him that day. His actions don't surprise me. He only does what he believes in."

"What about us?" John whined. "My shoulders are aching and Dave's just been sick."

This was true. In fact, he looked very ill. "I think he has concussion," Allyson said after looking at him. "I can only pray that he gets better. There are some aspirins in the house, we will go there now. John, I think we will leave you tied up for now, until you get there. We'd better help Dave as he is so ill.

"Joanne and I had better go on ahead because I've got to prepare Joanne's nose and she wants some more clothes on, no thanks to you. There should be

161

enough for us all to eat. Come on, Jo, we will think what we are to do on the way back." She and Joanne departed, leaving Judy and Sharon to guide the rest of the party.

Progress was slow for the rest of the way back. The last mile was covered with some difficulty, due mainly to the fact that Dave was getting weaker as they moved. Eric had been forced to untie him and let him stumble along as well as he could.

Eric, himself, was now encumbered with Dave's pack and rifle as well as his own equipment. He partially solved this by asking the two girls to carry the extra rifle in turns.

"Can I carry it first?" said Judy. "I went to fetch Sharon's mummy."

Eric gave it to her first and was then able to help Dave along, despite the extra load. This helped progress a little, but it still took best part of an hour to get there.

Allyson was waiting when they arrived. Joanne had washed and changed, and was finishing off plucking the goose she had shot.

"Joanne and I have been talking about what we should do with these two," indicating John and Dave. "We've had an idea, but don't know whether it's practical. John, Dave, we are living in a time of great hardship. Food is difficult to come by as you doubtless know.

"Since Believer came into our lives, we have lived in fair comfort. There is not room enough for us all here. Jo and I are prepared to forgive you for what you tried to do to her. We won't forget it, though. Who could?

"We are prepared to share our lives with you as much as we dare. It won't be easy and you would have to earn our trust from now on. We all have to work hard for our survival, so if you are prepared to help us and work hard, then we can feed you as much as we can. Please bear in mind that everyone who is left must work hard to survive.

"What I propose is this. There is a market garden near here that was completely devastated. We have started clearing it as we shall need the food we can grow there. Now, if we helped you to build a shelter, would you be prepared to help look after it and guard it if necessary.

"There are, of course, no wages, What use is money, anyway? All we can offer is a share in our food and whatever else we have. If you agree to this, I will untie you. Other than that, you will be taken far away tomorrow and left to fend for yourselves. In either case, you will not have your guns. Which is it to be?"

John considered this and turned to Dave, who was, by this time, deathly pale and asked him what he thought of Allyson's proposition.

Dave said, "What else can we do? We've nowhere else to go. We can't go back and I thought that we would be killed for what we did."

John said, "I don't understand why you should let us go. Where we have come from, we would have been shot instantly. We will agree to what you say. We would like to share a bit of company. We've been wandering about for some time, and now I've seen what type of people you are, I think I would like to stay."

"You can thank a man called Believer, although you may never meet him. He told us to love our fellowmen, whatever they did. Sometimes, like now, it is difficult, but it is possible," Allyson said as she untied him.

"Now I am busy with the cooking. Will you look after your friend here. I have a few aspirin but if he still feels sick, perhaps he had better not have them yet. You must keep him awake for a few hours, and perhaps we can make some sort of broth for him to eat later."

She turned to Eric and said to him, "Thank you again. I'm sorry that I seemed to ignore you, but I had to resolve the problem of John and Dave. I haven't asked you what you want to do or whether you agree with what Jo and I have decided. You are very welcome to stay here with us. We need a few men here, but before you decide, take the little ones and have a good look around."

"I will, thanks," replied Eric. "Come on, you two, show me what there is here."

Judy and Sharon went with him and showed him over the cottage and garden. Eric was intrigued by the odd-looking wiring system and was pleasantly surprised to find the generator and also the alternator which was still turning and providing 12-volt lighting and power for the small refrigerator. Then he returned to the kitchen.

"I'm amazed, how did you do all this?"

"Believer did it all before he left. He left us as comfortable as he could. I said that he is a very capable man. He also taught Joanne to hunt and the girls to fish. He gave me hope and I love him. Now do you want to stay with us?"

"Please," said Eric. "Believer influenced me as well. I only knew him for one night. Actually, I threatened him with the gun when I first met him because I was hungry. I had been living on tins and run out, so I was going to rob him.

"He just sat there and asked me if my name was Eric. I was so surprised. Then he persuaded me to let him shoot some rabbits for food. While we were eating, and afterwards, he told me of God and how he had been helped all the way.

"I didn't know whether to believe him, but next day, he told me that Joanne needed me. I thought that if he knew my name, then he might just be right about other things. I left to come here and the last thing I saw of him was that he was on his knees, praying. I found Joanne in trouble and now I believe him. I've got to learn about God, though."

"Haven't we all?" Allyson said. "What a joy it is to have met a man like that. I've boiled some water. If you men would like a bath, Jo will show you what to do. You will have to share the bath water as it takes time to boil enough.

"There is cold water in the tap marked hot as we have filled the hot water tank. The drain and toilet cistern work but we have to fill the tank between flushes. We fetch water from the brook outside and that is our first task each and every day.

"We use the generator when we want to wash clothes and I will do some for you all tomorrow. Do have a bath if you want to."

Both Eric and John complied. Dave was too sick at that time. They put on their cleanest clothes ready for the meal which was nearly ready. During the meal and afterwards, they all told of their adventures since the bombs fell and surprisingly found it easy to tell of their rather unsavoury lives up to the events of that day.

John and Dave had behaved like bandits taking what they wanted at gun point and their tale was quite horrific at times, but they all felt that it was desirable under the circumstances to tell all as John and Dave thought that they had been given a chance to start a new life. This was despite the attempted rape of Joanne who remained quiet throughout most of the conversation.

Dave recovered slowly through the evening and by the time they all retired, he had retained his colour. He was put to bed on the settee, but because of the shortage of beds, John and Eric had to sleep on the floor. As a precaution which proved unnecessary, all three guns and both crossbows were taken into Allyson's room. John and Dave realised that they had, as Allyson had told them, to earn the others trust and so caused no trouble.

The next day, Allyson took the men out to the market garden where John and Dave had agreed to stay and work was started to build a hut for them to sleep in It wasn't completed the first day and they returned to the cottage to spend the second night.

Day Forty-Seven
(Believer)

As Eric walked away in the direction from which Believer had come, Believer sank to his knees and prayed for the safety of Joanne, about whom he had his premonition of danger. He prayed earnestly that Eric would be in time after his long journey. The worst thing was that he did not know the kind of danger she would be in and neither would he know whether Eric would be successful in averting it. However, after praying for a while, he felt a sensation of relief and he knew that his prayer had been answered.

He felt comforted and began to pack his things before he continued on his way in a north westerly direction. He passed a few devastated villages in which he found no sign of life, but towards the end of the day, he began to feel hungry. He shot another crow, this time for himself. He cooked it in the open and ate it before he made his way towards the tower of a church he could see in the distance. He thought that if the tower was still standing, then he would have shelter for the night.

When he arrived at the church, he found that it was mostly demolished, but the tower was still there as this is normally the most robust part of a church. There was still some roof left over the nave and sanctuary and some of the choir stalls remained. Believer felt the need to sit and reflect on aspects of his life and future in what remained of God's house.

He brushed dust from a seat and sat down. He remained there for a while in private meditation and gradually became aware that he was being watched. He looked around, but saw nothing. He carried on with his thoughts until he caught sight of a movement at the corner of his eye.

He looked around again and saw a door partially open leading to what he surmised was a vestry in the base of the tower. He knew, then that the door concealed someone who seemed reluctant to reveal his or her presence.

Believer returned to his thoughts but kept half an eye on the doorway. His vigilance was rewarded when he saw the door move slightly. He called out. "You can come out, now. I won't hurt you. Come and join me."

The door opened slowly to reveal a small boy Believer judged to be about 14 years old. He was dirty and wearing ragged clothes.

"You look as if you could do with a good square meal and a change of clothes to me. Come and sit by me. You've got a story to tell, I'm sure."

The boy made his way along the aisle, avoiding rubble that was strewn there. He still looked nervous and sat down at the opposite end of the choir stall from Believer who watched him with interest.

Believer said, "The peace of the Lord be upon you now and for ever." The boy relaxed at this, so Believer continued, "Now that we've met, who are you?"

"Please mister, I'm Jimmy Ellis. I've been living in the tower. No one ever comes here because there's not much left in the village, no food, nothing. I have to go out and steal what I can get and sometimes it's only scraps. No one knows that I live here, they would kill me if they knew."

"My name is Believer and I won't kill you. Tell me, why do you feel safe here?"

"I used to come here a lot, not in church. My Dad used to beat me. He used to get drunk and hit me and my Mum. He used to say that he had no time for religion and busy-body vicars. I used to run away and listen to the singing, just from outside.

"When the people started to come out, I would go away. I knew that my Dad would get angry if he caught me. I never dared to go inside. I wanted to, the singing was so good. Now, there's no one to stop me is there?"

"That is a very sad story. If only you had come in. I'm sure that someone would have welcomed you. I would have done and do now. I am a missionary of sorts. You know what that is, don't you?

"I am going to go around and tell people about God. I came here today to pray and think because this is God's house—what's left of it. I have nowhere to sleep tonight, would you mind if I stayed here with you. Come on, show me where you sleep."

"I was asleep when you came in," said Jimmy. "That's why I was in the room. I would have hidden if I had seen you coming, like I do when anyone else comes, but nobody does much. There were some men who took away some cups and things, but that was some time ago."

"Aren't some people fools? I suppose that the chalices were silver. What a waste of time and effort. I suppose they thought that they were valuable. They were once, not now, like money. What use is it? You can't eat it.

"It won't buy anything now. There are no shops. It's a bit of a joke, really. If someone gave us a lot of gold and silver, what would we do with it. We could sell it for money, but what would we do with the money?"

Both Jimmy and Believer were laughing as they picked their way back to the vestry. "Do you know, I could have had as much as I wanted. I've seen enough money and valuables to have made me very rich in the old days. I took only things of real value, clothes, this air rifle, pots and pans, cutlery.

"This air rifle is worth more to me than all the gold in the world. A tin of corned beef is worth more than a ton of gold, so what's the point of being rich. I tell you that I am richer than most. I have God."

When Believer saw the vestry, he was a little sad to see its condition. It was very untidy, so he set about putting things in order so that the two of them would have some room to sleep.

"Do you like living here on your own, young Jimmy? Do you want to go on stealing your food? You are scared of everyone, even me. How would you like to be a missionary's assistant? It won't be easy, there will be a lot of walking, but you will get food regularly and some more clothes, yours are pretty tatty."

"I think I'm comfortable here, thank you," Jimmy answered. Believer sensed that this was nervousness. If Jimmy were to join him. It would mean a further upheaval for him. The lad had settled here in the church which had been a place of refuge to him.

He had even come here to escape from his drunken and violent father. Just standing in the churchyard listening to the music and not daring to go inside. He had been far away when the bombs fell and like Believer had found temporary shelter. He had gradually made his way back to the one place where he had been happy, even if only while he could listen to the music.

He had stolen what food he needed and had been nearly caught several times. He had even been fired at. Only his small size and agility had saved him. Here he felt safe and reluctant to move on.

"Don't you think that someone will find you here someday? How long do you expect to hide out? It can't be forever, can it? Also, your food supply will dwindle. It's nearly all gone now and you've got to go out and steal some more, risking your life again."

Jimmy thought about this for a while, then he said, "What's the point of going away? There aren't many people left out there. Those I have seen don't want to see me or help me. Nobody has helped me for a long time. Why should I help you anyway? I've only just met you."

"What makes you think that nobody has helped you? Someone has been helping you all the time and you are in His house now. He has seen your need and sent me to help you now if you will let me. I must tell you that God's way is not easy.

"You may have to do things that will cause your personal suffering. I know that only too well. If you give yourself to God then you will have more help than you thought possible. Look at me, I was just a lorry driver doing my job when my world was suddenly taken away.

"I was shown the way to shelter, given food and clothing and the means of my continued survival. I turned to God then, and I must go out and help people to know that God's love will help them as I have been helped. I won't be able to reach everybody, therefore, I must have help.

"Someone to work with me for a while and then go out to other places where I can't get to on my own. You are very young yet, but by the time you are 18, you will probably be able to cope on your own if you believe as well as I do.

"The task will be dangerous at times because there are all sorts in the world. Some will not listen at first. Our job is to convince them. Does the adventure appeal to you? You've already proved to be resourceful. Anyway, sleep on it and tell me in the morning."

Day Forty-Eight

Next day, Believer kitted Jimmy out with some of the clothes he had found and washed the previous day. Enough had dried for him to wear. The clothes the boy had been wearing, together with some of Believer's, were washed in an old bucket in the same way. Believer and Jimmy went hunting and caught a rabbit for their meal.

At the end of the day, both rucksacks were packed for the next day's journey. Believer made sure that he included a number of service booklets to take with them, together with the last of Jimmy's tinned food.

Day Forty-Nine
Part One

For the first time for over six weeks, Believer had someone to keep him company on his travels between groups of survivors. He regarded Jimmy as a permanent assistant who would learn God's way, and eventually, when he was older would go his own separate way and reach people that Believer would never be able to reach on his own.

Believer started out towards the place Jimmy had been shot at, the last time he had tried to steal food. They walked for much of the morning and afternoon, only stopping to eat and rest when they needed.

It was late afternoon when they first saw any sign of population. This was when Jimmy saw someone running away along the road, obviously to warn others of their approach. Believer had made sure that his air rifle was secure in its case, and he and his companion walked down the middle of the road to try and give the impression that they meant no harm to anyone.

A while after they had seen the first person, they found that their way was blocked by two armed men. Believer and Jimmy sensed that others had stepped into the road behind them.

"This seems to be very like an ambush," Believer said to the men in front of him. "Peace of the Lord be upon you. I suppose the people behind us are armed as well. It is very sad that you find it necessary to behave like this to two strangers."

The man who seemed to be the leader said, "You are a stranger, but the boy isn't. He has been stealing food from us and I think we ought to shoot the pair of you now."

"Before you do that," Believer replied. "Just think how you acquired the food you say he stole. I should imagine that you didn't ask anyone for it, yourself. Isn't it a case of 'He who is without sin casting the first stone'?

"Don't you think that there has been enough killing without adding to the death toll. We haven't come to steal your food. You are obviously part of a community, and therefore, you will need all the food you can find. No, we want nothing from you, we are self-sufficient as you must try to be if you want to survive."

"If you don't want food, what have you come here for. We have nothing to spare. There isn't much of anything left at all."

"You could say, I suppose, that I have come for your souls. That isn't really true. I have come to see if I can help you in any way or perhaps give you some advice on how to survive. How are you going to manage when all your tins are gone?

"You can't have much left, can you? I saw that there is no food left in any of the villages we passed. Incidentally, the village that Jimmy here was living in was completely cleaned out."

Believer mentioned the name of the village and was told that the man's party had raided that village for food. "Jimmy was living in that village when you went there. You didn't bother to ask his permission before you took everything away, did you? So who stole from who?"

"You have a point, I suppose," The man grudgingly replied. "How can you help us? Have you got any food?"

"At the moment, no. I would like to meet all of you. I don't wish anyone any harm, but in order to help, I have to talk to you and I would much prefer to speak to you all at once. This would save me repeating myself. Can that be arranged?"

"It might take some time. I want to tell you who I am and what I believe in. Then I will see if I can help you with some advice."

A woman's voice behind him said, "I think we should give him a chance. He doesn't look as if he's starving and he says that he doesn't want anything from us. Anyway, I am interested in what he has to say to us. We could all meet in the old barn. It will hold us all."

Believer turned round for the first time and noted that the two behind him were a man about 30 and a woman about the same age. Both were holding rifles.

"Thank you, young lady, could you perhaps direct me to this old barn you spoke of. I'm surprised that it is still standing, but there are always a few buildings partially habitable, aren't there?"

The small party walked into the remains of the village and to the far side where there was a Dutch barn with most of its roof still intact. The rest of the people, alerted by a shout from the man who had first spoken, drifted in by ones and twos until there were nine people in the barn, plus Believer and Jimmy. Believer asked whether this was the whole community and was told that there was a teenaged boy and girl on watch. Believer said that he would see them later.

He found an old bench and stood on it. "The Lord be with you," he said, and was pleased to receive an answering response from one of the women. He continued, "My name is Believer. You will never know me by any other name and I shall only be here a few days.

"I will not ask for any food from you, instead, I shall try to provide some. Jimmy here and I will be away some of the time, I would ask for shelter at nights though. We do have a tent but we would rather spend our nights in your company. Now, can I know who you are?"

The man who had stopped him on the road said. "I am Nick, the other men are Peter and Tony. The ladies are Christine, who you have already met, Shirley, Tammy, Emma, Eileen and Paula. The missing two are another Emma and Jason. Our ages range from 14 to 62. What about you?"

"I've told you my name. I suppose that I would call myself a missionary since that has been my task for the last six weeks. I am no theologian and have much to learn myself. I can tell what I know about God and Jesus.

"Some of you might think that I am some sort of crank, so I will try to tell you what has made me what I am now. Before, I was just a lorry driver doing my job. The vehicle I was driving developed an engine fault in just about the worst place possible, or so I thought when it broke down.

"I was right at the bottom of a sharp dip in the road. I was outside the vehicle trying to find out what had gone wrong when the whole sky lit up and the lorry caught fire. I was actually shielded by the flash and heat by the vehicle, but was unconscious for a while.

"When I recovered, I made my way to a house that was still almost intact. There I found enough food to keep me for a while, clothing and camping gear stayed there until after the heavy rains had stopped. I thought that I was alone but gradually became aware that God was with me.

"It was in that house that I came to know God as I had never done before was filled with the knowledge that if I turned to Him and trusted Him, then would be guided and shown what to do. I came to realise that if only I follow Him then my purpose in life would be revealed.

"He told me when to leave that house. I took some food, the last I had and set off looking for other survivors. I saw no one for a few days, but one day, I shot and ate a crow." This produced some gasps of horror from some of the women, and Nick asked whether Believer had been worried about radiation.

"I'm still here, aren't I? I have not suffered any after effects. If God wants me to spread word of His love, then I have to trust Him to provide me with food. Anyway, that crow helped me to keep the little food I had left for someone else who, when I found them, were in desperate need.

"The people were starving and the little bit of food I had gave them their first meal for days. For a while, I foraged for food for them. Later, we were eating natural foods, rabbits and birds, even some fish which were caught by two seven-year-old girls. When I left them, the hunting was being done by a 15-year-old and all were healthy. So you see, it is possible to live without tinned food."

"How will that help us? None of us knows how to hunt. What about vegetables? We need them as well," Nick asked.

"Excuse me for a moment." Believer walked out of the barn and picked some wild barley he had seen on his way in. He returned and held it up. "You see this. Before there was any cultivation, grasses like this were the only source of cereals.

"All your wheats, oats, barley and rice are cereal crops and are grasses. I am not a botanist, but it must be possible to grow cereals such as this from scratch. The cave men did. You have the advantage, you know it can be done. Between you and the rest of the survivors, there are many different skills. Even the most unlikely can help in some way."

He rubbed the grass between his hands and the wild barley, being almost ripe, separated, leaving the grain in his hands. "This is wild barley. You've all seen it. When I was a boy, I used to pick the ears and stick them up my sleeve. The ears would crawl up my arm. The whiskers on it vibrate with movement, causing the ear to move. That's how it propagates itself.

"The ears move along the ground with any slight vibration. Also, the ears catch on animals and drop down later. The point is that it grows anywhere. The grain I have here is edible and it is just one source of food which God provides.

"In lots of places, there are still root vegetables. These must be cultivated, eat some. Choose the worst to eat and plant the best. If you find potatoes, plant the peelings. If they have eyes, there will be a crop next year, even if it is poor quality. It is still food.

"There are sheep and cattle running wild, so animal husbandry is possible. Where I helped the other people, I found evidence of chickens. There are ducks, geese, pheasants and pigeons. Not so many as there used to be, I admit.

"They are there if you look for them. Crows are quite common as there is a lot of carrion for them to eat. What I suggest to you is that you find ways to hunt these valuable sources of food.

"You are a small community of mixed sexes. If you split yourselves up and hunt in different directions, you should be able to find enough food to eat. I strongly recommend that you try to make quiet weapons to hunt with, otherwise you will scare off game and your hunting will be more difficult.

"I use an air rifle and have made a tool for making pellets. Bows and arrows can be quite easily made. I made two crossbows for the last group I was with and the 15-year-old is using hers with very good effect.

"It can be done, but you won't do it by staying in one place and trying to exist on tinned food. You all know that you can't live much longer on that supply alone. Now, what sort of occupations did you have before the bombs?"

Nick said, "I was a bricklayer, Peter was a miner and Tony here is an engineer. Paula was a nurse, Eileen a housewife, Christine a telephonist. Emma and Shirley were office workers, and Tammy was a shop assistant here in the village. The young ones have no trade, of course."

"That's a fair mixture. You have someone who can build, an engineer who can make things, one who understands stresses and props, a doctor and someone who can cook."

"Who is the doctor?" Paula asked. "I was only a student nurse in my third year."

"You are the doctor, Paula, of all the people here, you are the one with the most medical skills and in the absence of anyone more skilled, that makes you the king pin. As for the two who are office workers, perhaps you can learn to be the hunters or farmers. That's not so daft as it sounds as you are both young and fit.

"I didn't tell you before, but the hunter in the other group is named Joanne so there is no reason why you can't do what she does, she is only 15. You have only to say to yourselves 'I can do it' and you will manage.

"Eileen, housewife and mother no doubt. You are older, perhaps you can be the teacher if there are any children later, Tony could help you there. As an engineer, he should know things like physics and maths.

"Perhaps, though, God has a different purpose for you now. I noticed that you responded when I said, 'The Lord be with you.' You used to attend church regularly, didn't you? What do you believe in now?"

Eileen thought for a minute, then she said, "I had serious doubts after this calamity. I thought that no caring God would allow this to happen. All the suffering and now the starvation which might still come.

"I had begun to think that there was no God, but you came along. You obviously believe because you call yourself Believer. Do you really think that God is helping you?"

"I know He is. I believe because I know. There is a difference between knowing and believing. You can believe without knowing, but it is impossible to know and not to believe. So, as I said, I know, and if you start to believe again, you will find that you know too.

"While I am here, I will hold a Service of Thanksgiving for any of you who would like to come. Eileen, when I leave here, perhaps you would like to carry on with the religious aspect."

"I don't know about that. I am a Roman Catholic and it seems that you are asking me to be some sort of priest. I don't think that my religion would allow that."

Believer said, "You were a Roman Catholic. I was Anglican. Can we not now be just Christians? It seems to me that now is the ideal opportunity to do away with different sects.

"Don't you think that there was something wrong before when each different sect believed that their religion was the only right one? All were partially right and all were partially wrong. I was brought up in the Anglican faith and the form of worship suited me.

"What about all the atrocities committed by all sects in the name of religion? I regret to say that many sins have been committed by all sects in the past. Jesus said, 'Love thy neighbour,' and we didn't, did we? As to being some sort of priest, don't let being a woman put you off.

"My feeling is that if God decides that you are a fit person to spread his word, who has the right to say otherwise? If God gives you the talent to make others listen, take it."

Nick spoke up then, "It's all right for you and Eileen. You are both religious. What about the rest of us? I don't believe in God, particularly now. It doesn't seem relevant."

Believer said, "I can't make you believe anything, but you have seen me and heard me. I have spoken for some time and have much more to say. Think about this. You seem to be the leader here. You are a bricklayer.

"Tony is an engineer. I should imagine that he is more highly educated than you. Why are you the leader and not him, or Eileen for that matter, she is older? No, I am not stirring things up for this community, but I say this, despite your feeling of disbelief, you have a talent for leadership which Tony doesn't have.

"That talent is God given. All of you have different talents which must now be used for the benefit of all. If you, Nick, are the leader here, then by all means use your talents. You will be better at it if you believe and trust in God."

Nick said, "It seems that you are leading us now. Why should we listen to you? I feel as if you have taken over and you've only been around for a couple of hours. You are telling us what to do. How is it that you seem to know best. You said that you were a lorry driver, how does that make you better than me?"

"I am not better than you or Tony or Paula, or Eileen or anyone else for that matter. I'm sorry that you think I am taking over, but I did say that I was only staying for a few days. I want to help you if I can. Perhaps give you some ideas.

"Most important, I know that God has helped me. I want Him to help you as well. He will, if you let Him and ask for His help. Tell me, Nick, have you ever asked God for His help? I didn't much, before the bombs fell, but when I was in that house, it seemed that someone was trying to contact me.

"I couldn't believe it at first, then I stopped to listen. To be precise, I started praying and answers seemed to come to me. I still pray and the answers I receive I try to pass on to anyone I meet.

"You said that I was only a lorry driver, very true. Why do you think that I was only a lorry driver and not the owner of the lorry? It is because I was not a leader. Now, how do you think I can talk to you all like this? You seem to think that I am now a leader.

"What, then has changed me, a mere lorry driver, into someone who can talk to nine perfect strangers and keep their interest for a couple of hours? You lot haven't interrupted me much or shouted me down, have you? It is because I am being helped right now by the greatest leader of all. Every word I say is direct inspiration. God has made me talk and you to listen.

"I will be here for only a while as there are others I must visit. When I leave here, you will still be leader here. I hope that you will listen to others as they will contribute to the survival of you all."

176

Tony spoke up then. "Nick, he's right you know. You are leader here because no one else has taken the crown. We don't want to either. We are quite happy that there is a strong person to lead. I don't want that responsibility.

"Believer, here, is something different. Can't you see that he is talking with utter conviction. I, for one, don't want to miss such an opportunity as this to see what we can do for ourselves. You also know that we have only three day's food left and then what are we to do. Go and raid someone else?

"That would start a war all over again. A war with some other survivors who are in the same position as ourselves. We can only delay the inevitable that way. Believer says that it is not inevitable and we can survive.

"Let us listen and do as he says, at least for a while. You know, I didn't believe either, but then I never met anyone like Believer before and doubt if I ever shall again. If anyone can convince me, he can. He walked right up the middle of the road with complete confidence.

"Poor Jimmy was scared stiff., I could see that. We could have shot them both at any time. It was as if he knew we wouldn't shoot. I would have been as scared as Jimmy was.

"It is that, above all, that has convinced me that he has got something to say, and even you have listened. Frankly, he has talked a lot of sense. We must find an alternative source of food very quickly or we shall be reduced to cannibalism until there is only one left. I don't want that. Let us listen to him and try to grow as a community."

"That's some speech for you, Tony," replied Nick. "I admit though, that I couldn't help listening to him myself. I do know about the food. That is why I tried to stop Believer joining us. If he can help, he can stay. I was a bit worried at losing the leadership to a stranger, but I think that I would have stepped down after all that talk."

To Believer he said, "You are welcome, perhaps you can show us how to hunt and anything else you can think of. I'm still not sure of God. Perhaps you can help us there as well."

Believer said, "Thank you, but I can only tell you about me. Eileen can tell you about God. She has been taught it all her life and is more qualified in that respect."

To the oldest member of the group. "Eileen, you have heard Nick ask for spiritual help. As the most able, are you prepared to help him when I leave, and the rest too? I don't necessarily mean that you should teach Roman Catholicism. There may be some things the priests taught you that don't seem to fit now.

"Just teach Christianity. It is time for the world to go back to the first principles of the teaching of Christ. After all, there were at least two Christian religions before the Romans. The original church founded by Peter and the Apostles in Israel.

"Also Saint Columbo was active in Scotland before Constantine permitted Christianity in Byzantium. Ask God what to do, He will tell you."

Eileen was a little shaken by the turn of events, then she said, "You are asking a lot of me. It will be very difficult, particularly as my religion does not believe in women priests. Also, priests are celibate and must not marry. I have been married."

Believer said, "I said before, If God gives you the talent, has any man the right to take it away. With regard to celibacy, as an Anglican, I cannot see why a priest who is not allowed to marry is expected to give advice on family matters. Surely the best qualification for that job would be as a member of a happy family group.

"You were a housewife and a mother. Who better to look after the spiritual needs of this larger family. You know a lot about the Bible and also how to look after a family and this one needs your help. Nick has already asked and I think Tony will listen to you. He sounds interested.

"If you think you have a hard task, think of Paula. She has just found out that she is the nearest thing to a doctor for miles. She will need your prayers more than anyone. As 'doctor', she may have to travel to other communities to help them.

"What I am trying to do is to help groups of people look after themselves. any of you has any skills that can help others, then I will pass on the information. For instance, if medical skills are needed, then either Paula could travel to other groups or they would come here.

"The point I am trying to make is that everyone has something to offer and all survivors can be helped. If groups can help each other, all the better. It is only by co-operation that civilisation can ever hope to grow again. Now, I think that I have talked enough. Tony, will you show me around the village, and perhaps we can come up with some ideas for your future comfort.

"Jimmy, see if you can talk to the two young ones outside. They are your age. Tell them what we have been doing and what you are going to do in the future."

Day Forty-Nine
Part Two

The small group broke up and Believer went with Tony to see the village. The two men discussed how the group was divided. It turned out that they were living in various cellars and ruined buildings that still had some roofing, mainly in four smaller groups.

Eileen, Shirley and the two teenagers in one place, Paula, Emma and Tammy shared a cellar. Pete and Tony occupied a ruined cottage while Nick and Christine had taken another similar shelter. It appeared that they all shared meal times together with the exception of the teenagers who spent most of the time on watch, eating later when they had been relieved by those who had already eaten.

Believer asked about sanitation and water supply. He was told that the water came from a stream flowing through the village. All drinking water was boiled before drinking at Paula's insistence, but sanitation was fairly poor and consisted of a latrine pit dug some distance away so that the stream was not polluted.

Few improvements had been made. Since the main consideration was for food and the necessity of keeping watch for unwelcome visitors. There had been one attempted raid, but that had been beaten off with no further problems.

Tony told Believer that Jimmy had been chased off a couple of times. Nick had fired at him really to scare rather than kill him for which Believer was glad.

The group had come together within days of the war and had, up to now, survived on what tinned food they had been able to find. They were down to only three day's supply, so now they were getting desperate.

Believer told Tony that apart from the food, the group had two major problems, adequate shelter and clothing for the coming winter. He said that these two problems should be regarded as priority. He suggested that Nick, Tony and Pete should consider building a communal shelter for them all to use during the winter.

One building would be easier to heat and in extreme cold, the whole group could huddle together. He also said that it might be possible to provide piped water to the building when it was completed. There were plenty of second hand materials for building. Clothing was another matter. Believer suggested that old blankets could be made into suitable winter clothing.

He told Tony how to make crossbows for hunting and bolts for ammunition. He told him of his achievements at Allyson's cottage. At the end of his tour Tony had received quite a few ideas and said that he would discuss them with Nick in the morning. The two men returned to the centre of the occupied area.

Believer then contacted Emma and Shirley, and asked them if they would join him the next day to go out and hunt for food for the community. Both girls were worried at the prospect and Shirley voiced their feelings with a great deal of apprehension.

"You mean that we have to go out and actually kill things to eat? Why us?"

Believer said, "I've chosen you two because you both have office skills, you must admit that they are not all that much use at the moment. The men have to start building in preparation for the winter. Jimmy will be with us. Paula might be needed at any moment and as we worked out, Eileen has a great deal to think about and is too old.

"Christine seems to have attached herself to Nick and if he is leader here, he needs all the help and support anyone can give him. Christine can supply a great deal, and perhaps, she has her own problems. It must be very difficult to provide support when Nick is so obviously worried. It is not the easiest thing to do.

"Young Emma and Jason are doing an excellent job with their watchkeeping, although I think that Jason should be more careful. I saw him running to warn somebody when I came today. A raiding party might have stopped him before he got back.

"That seems to leave you two and possibly Tammy. Don't worry. If a girl of 15 can do it, so can you, you look pretty fit to me. Someone has to do the providing, so why not start tomorrow?"

The girls agreed. Then Believer asked them about the general relationships within the group.

Emma said that when Christine joined up with Nick, she and Shirley thought she was trying to advance herself as much as possible and were not too happy about it. As to other relationships, there were none at the moment. They had all been too busy surviving.

181

Now Believer had pointed out Nick did need support, so perhaps Christine was not just on the make and the two of them had been over jealous. Christine's attachment to Nick might not be all roses after all. If she could support him and comfort him, then perhaps she was doing a useful job. Emma finished by asking whether there would be any babies.

Believer said, "Only God can answer that one and He will do that in his own good time. Surely, if some survivors are left, it is inconceivable that there will be no more births. Hope in that respect will rest with the younger survivors who have not reached puberty.

"It is the young ones who are the future and if I am right, this will give communities the chance to settle down before any great numbers are born. I imagine that a pregnancy now would be unlikely to succeed. The present restrictions of diet will cause problems. There will be a strong chance of miscarriage or a still birth. A baby born now, even if it survived the birth will be very difficult to rear and the winter is liable to be bleak."

Emma, who was the more extrovert of the two girls, asked Believer about his previous existence and Believer said that he had been a family man before, but felt that there was no hope of any survivors in the cities. What he had seen of the towns bore out his suspicions.

He had thought initially of trying to return to the city where he had lived, but reasoned that if the smaller towns like Market Harborough had been destroyed, then there was no hope at all for the cities. Although, he grieved for the loss of his family and friends, there was no logical reason to return. Anyway, all those left were in the same boat. All had lost most of the people they loved, and Allyson had been extremely fortunate to have two daughters still surviving.

Emma said, "What about Jimmy?"

"Jimmy hasn't had much of a family life. When I found him in the church where he was living, he was very scared. It took some persuasion to encourage him to leave his shelter and come with me.

"He has joined me in my mission. There is no relationship other than friendship and compassion between us. Why did you ask, Emma?"

Emma was very embarrassed. "There is a shortage of men in the community. I have always liked men's company. I was fishing a little. I hoped to meet a man I could take up with. I'm sorry if you think I am too forward."

"Thank you for the compliment. I have told you a little about Allyson and her daughters. I found them starving and helped them to survive. If I could sta anywhere, that is where I would make my home. God has need of me elsewhere, so I had to leave.

"As I told them and as I have told you, I cannot stay in one place long, all the family and myself were in tears when I left. In fact, Allyson vowed that she would set out to find me when the children are older and things settle down. I very much regret having had to leave.

"I know that Allyson had come to love me. She told me so. I wanted to return her love and I miss her very much. It was not to be. God called me and I had to leave.

"So you see, I will not form any lasting attachment to any other woman and if I could retrace my steps, I would return to her now. Please don't be offended if I seem to reject you, let us just be friends."

"Thank you for explaining things to me," the girl replied. "I can understand what you say and now that you have explained your situation, I won't be so impertinent again. I am also sorry for thinking that, perhaps, you and Jimmy had some sort of relationship. I think that the society we have lost caused everyone to think the worst of people."

Believer said, "Perhaps, now is the time to change all that. People's relationships should be a matter between the people concerned and no one else. In the past, the media thrived on gossip and were always trying to make stories out of next to nothing.

"I wonder just how many marriages were broken up by irresponsible reporting. If anyone in the public eye was seen with someone they were not married to, some newspaper would be sure to create any sort of illicit romance. This must have started many suspicions in families. Suspicion feeds on gossip and people are very quick to believe that there is no smoke without fire.

"One case in my own life, which I won't relate, opened my eyes to malicious gossip. It made me realise that people will make rash statements that are not based on actual knowledge. I prefer to take people as I find them and not believe anything that is said of them without proof to me.

"Now we have no media to fan the flames, let's just get on with surviving. I guess what I am saying bears out what you said about Christine. Let's look at her life now. Like all of us, she has lost everything. If she feels that she can get some solace from Nick, then good for her.

"We all deserve as much happiness as we can get. There is precious little hope for that, with the worry about providing food. As to Nick, don't ever think that being a leader is easy. Some who take that road are just bullies. They are not leaders, they are pushers. A true leader is one, who by his actions, does the best he can for his followers.

"By what I have seen, Nick is one of that kind of person. He has succeeded so far. He is, I know, extremely worried about the food situation and that is why I am trying to help with advice for a few days before I move on. If I can set you all on the right lines for survival, then you will all have ideas which can only improve your conditions. In the next few weeks, things will get better.

"In the meantime, you two will learn to hunt. Tony is going to make you some weapons. He, Nick and Pete are thinking of building and making this a permanent base. When you are proficient hunters, you can teach Jason and the other Emma. Paula will want to pass on her medical skills. I don't know yet what Tammy can do, have you any ideas?"

Shirley spoke up for the first time. "Tammy has taken charge of what food we managed to find. She rations it out and makes sure that everyone gets something. She has helped Eileen to try and keep our clothes clean and dry. In fact, she helps out wherever she can. In a way, she has made us two feel ashamed as we don't seem to contribute much."

"Another talent comes to light," Believer said. "Tammy is obviously good at being a storekeeper, but then, she did work in a shop. What she is doing is a vitally important as anything else. Since you two feel that you haven't done much yet, now is the time to find your talents as hunters.

"I will be teaching Jimmy at the same time so I can't promise much first time out. We must also look for vegetables so will you try to find some sort of bag. hope that we will be able to fill it with something. Now I think that we should try to get a good night's sleep. If you see Jimmy around, tell him that we are going out tomorrow."

Emma and Shirley left him and he sat for a while to ponder about the developments of the day. He thought that he saw Emma heading in the direction of Nick and Christine's shelter to which place he headed himself some ten minutes later.

When he arrived, he told Nick what his plans were for the following day and that he would be leaving at first light with the girls and Jimmy.

Nick asked, "What weapons are you taking?"

"Only my air rifle and God's protection."

"Don't you want one of the bigger guns to take. We have several and some ammunition."

"No, they only make a lot of noise and will frighten any game away. Besides, the ammunition you have is in the same category as the food. It will run out sometime and you won't be able to replace it indefinitely, whereas, I can make more pellets for my air rifle for a long time to come."

"We have an old air rifle which hasn't got any ammunition, I'll fetch it for you." Nick did this and Believer was pleased to see that it was the same bore as the weapon he had been using. All it needed was a good clean which Believer did straight away.

"Thank you," he said. "I'll teach the two girls how to use it and that will set them up for the future. I will have to show Tony how to fabricate a tool to make pellets for it. He should manage that all right."

Nick invited Believer and Jimmy to spend the night with him and Christine, and Believer was glad to accept the offered accommodation. There was a separate room for him and Jimmy to use, but before they all retired, he spent some time talking with the leader and his companion. He told them about his conversations with Tony, Emma and Shirley.

"What did you say to Emma and Shirley?" Christine said. "I had a pleasant surprise just now. Emma came to me and apologised for her behaviour. They have been unpleasant to me ever since I took up with Nick here. It was so bad at times that I thought of leaving."

"I pointed out to them that Nick, having taken on the burden of leadership, had accepted the hardest job of all and he needed all the help he could get. Also, he needs time away from all his worries when he can relax. You provide him with help and comfort he needs to carry on.

"You may not realise how much you have helped him, whatever your relationship with him, you have helped him to prepare for each new day and I wonder if he could have done so well without your help."

Nick spoke up, "Thank you. It seems that you have made things easier for us already. I'm a little surprised that you, a strong believer that you obviously are, should not question our relationship. It must be obvious that we have a sexual agreement.

"That is probably the main reason behind the unpleasantness shown to Chris. I would have thought that you would condemn such a relationship since we are not married."

"Who am I to condemn anyone?" Believer answered. "I'm no better than anyone else. Besides, if you wanted to get married, who would perform the ceremony? There are no registry offices or active churches in the area as far as I know. You two have decided on forming a relationship and if you have any thoughts of making it a permanent agreement under these difficult circumstances, why not?

"In a situation like this, where a couple set up home together with no possibility of a marriage service taking place and there are no other reasons why a marriage should be forbidden, then in the eyes of God, you are already married. If you are not closely related, which I understand, you are not, and neither of you has a living spouse, which is difficult to prove or disprove, then I am sure that God will bless your union.

"If not with children, then, perhaps, with happy companionship and mutual comfort. Of course, should a living spouse be found, then the previous marriage would take preference. How you feel about each other is your own affair and a matter of concern to no other person than God, so be happy together."

"Thank you, you've made us feel so much better, We have both felt the jealousy and Christine has suffered a great deal from it ever since she moved in with me. We hadn't really thought of a marriage or a permanent relationship. We've been together for about four weeks and I would be happy if the situation carried on for a long time. How about it, Chris?"

Christine said, "I would like it, I think. Up to now, I hadn't considered that it is already like a marriage. I don't know whether my husband is alive, but he was working in Sheffield, so I suppose he's dead. You know that your wife is gone, you buried her yourself.

"Believer, you said that you would hold a thanksgiving service before you left, would you conduct any service? What about a marriage service?"

"I'd be glad to, but I hope you realise that such a service would not be recognised by an ordained minister. I would even sign some sort of certificate for you, and I would hope that should some properly ordained clergy come along then perhaps he or she could repeat the service. That way the marriage would be recognised by other church people.

"Aren't you rushing things a bit, though, we've only just been talking about possibilities. I suggest that you discuss things together and if you still feel the same way, come to me before I leave and I will see what I can do for you. Now I have a long day tomorrow so I think I will get my head down.

Jimmy is already asleep. The day has been a bit much for him. For me, goodnight and have a good think about our conversation."

Day Fifty

Believer arose at first light, shook Jimmy awake and prepared for the hunting trip he had arranged. He had to find the two girls who were living in separate ruins before he could set out with a rather sleepy trio. Jimmy carried the second air rifle while they left the village.

Later, before they had gone very far, Believer asked the girls if they had ever fired a rifle of any kind. Emma said that she had tried at a fairground stall but hadn't achieved very much.

"How did you hold the rifle? Did you lean on the counter like most people? Let me give you a few pointers. First, are you left or right-handed?"

Emma said, "Right-handed."

Believer said, "Contrary to general belief, if you are right-handed, when you use a rifle, it is the left hand which does all the work. The right one just works the trigger. Take the rifle and let me see you hold it. Now, with your left hand, pull it hard into your right shoulder.

"An air rifle doesn't kick much, so it won't hurt. Now for your feet, put one slightly in front of the other and slightly apart. That gives you stability in two directions.

"Now choose a target and bring the sights in line with it, hold it steady with the left hand. Bring your right hand up and place your finger around the trigger When the sights are lined up, squeeze the trigger, don't pull it."

Emma did all this with the unloaded weapon and Believer said, "Do you see what I meant about the left hand? Now you have a go, Shirley."

Shirley did this and was surprised at the result. She said that it seemed quit easy to aim like that. Believer agreed and showed them how to fire in the sitting kneeling and prone positions, but as he wanted to preserve his supply of pellet: he said that they should only be used on real targets.

"That rifle is yours. Nick gave it to me yesterday. Here are some pellets. Yo must keep it clean. At the moment, it is the best means of providing food fc everyone.

"It is relatively silent and if you miss, it won't scare other animals, so you might get a second shot. When Tony has made the tool for forming new pellets, get some practice in. For today, I want you both to try to hit something when we find it.

"I shall try as well so we will have two chances. Tony will be making some crossbows. They are less accurate, but have greater stopping power, so you will be able to hunt better. Long bows are easy to make and if you practice a lot, you will be proficient in all the weapons."

The small party moved on, checking gardens and farms as they went for any vegetables that had survived. Diligent checking yielded quite a good supply, but Believer told them that some must be replanted to provide food for the future. He said that when they returned, the group would have to start cultivating a patch. Everyone should be involved.

"There are 11 of you, so you should be able to do it. Make a party of it, a day out, sing a few songs, tell a few jokes. The country people used to do it in the old days for harvest and haymaking. Why not revive a few old and pleasant customs.

"Everyone needs as much happiness as they can get. Particularly as we all grieve for someone dear to us."

The hunting expedition took them to a small lake where some ducks were swimming. Believer told the party to wait in hiding for the birds to come to the shore. They did eventually come to the side, but some distance away from the hunters.

Believer told Shirley and Jimmy to stay still while he and Emma crept around the lake towards their quarry. When they were close enough to fire at the birds they had each selected, they both tried to shoot a duck. Believer hit one, but the one that Emma had aimed for showed no signs that it had been hit.

All the remaining birds panicked and headed for the water, taking off as soon as they could. Believer swiftly reloaded and tried again but missed the rapidly moving birds. He retrieved the downed bird and killed it, after which he and Emma re-joined the others with their prize.

Emma was in tears and said that it was all her fault they had only got one duck.

Believer said, "Don't worry. There is no blame. Even two ducks would not enough to feed all the group and we would have to go on anyway. You would've been extremely lucky to have managed to be successful on your first attempt in earnest.

"Besides, I don't really know how accurate that rifle is, I haven't used it myself. The ducks ran and flew away when one was shot, not because you missed. You may have hit it anyway, but not in a vital place. My second shot was taken in haste so I didn't do much better, did I?

"Let's look at the bright side. At least you aimed and fired. Last week, you wouldn't even have thought about it, would you? Success only comes to those who try and you have both been pushed into the action, haven't you?

"You two girls should take turns to fire, you've got to practice. It's the only way. What we are really after is something like a goose or a turkey. There must be some around, all running wild. There will also be pigs, cattle and sheep. These must be captured alive, if possible, for future breeding."

The hunt continued. Shirley took the next shot at a crow and was more successful than her friend. Believer had let her try first, but was ready in case she missed. The others, of course, all flew away, leaving the injured one behind. Believer sent Shirley after it. She was reluctant at first but Believer was insistent as he had been with Joanne earlier.

He said, "The purpose of hunting is to provide food for 13 people. This lifestyle is going to be the norm for the immediate future. The unpleasant task of killing small creatures is necessary. You have to put aside all your squeamishness and the sooner the better.

"How do you think that you are going to manage when I am not here? Besides, it is cruel to shoot animals and birds and leave them injured, nor will such actions fulfil any useful purpose. You have to kill the creatures that you injure, so you must start with this one."

Emma had more success with her second attempt and managed to hit squirrel. Later the group managed to get a couple of rabbits, Jimmy adding his contribution to their efforts. After a long and tiring trip, the party returned to the village and gave their spoils to Eileen and Tammy to prepare.

While the meal was being prepared, Believer busied himself with making more ammunition for the air rifles. He set some aside for target practice and encouraged the two girls and Jimmy to try while they were waiting for the meal. Tony was very interested to see how the tool was made and used. He set himself the task of making one as soon as possible.

Lead for the pellets was readily available as most of the ruined houses had lead flashing on the roof. Also, there was a builder's yard nearby which had a roll of lead sheeting partially melted by heat which could be readily worked

Believer made enough for the next day's hunt, and Tony resolved to make a good stock for Shirley and Emma to use in the future.

Whilst the four hunters had been away, Nick, Tony and Pete had been working hard. Tony had been looking around with a different point of view to see what mechanical devices could be made to improve the community's comfort. Nick and Pete had started to prepare a building for renovation so that it could be used for communal living.

It had to have enough rooms to ensure privacy for all the lesser groups. This was, of course, a long-term project but Nick had drawn up plans which be showed to Believer.

"Congratulations," Believer said, when he saw them. "This is a good first effort. I can't comment on the viability of the plans since I am not a builder so the matter is in your hands. The concept is very good and it will give the whole community the incentive to better their existence.

"You have taken my advice to consider the problems that you have. Shelter, which you are now dealing with. Food, hunting is only a short-term solution, so you must consider cultivation and farming generally.

"Clothing is another problem. Someone here should try to find out how to cure animal skins. To start with, there are two rabbit skins and a squirrel. Their skins will help to provide warm clothing, perhaps Tammy can gather together all the clothes in the village and see just what resources there are. You have already done this with the canned food, so the same principle must apply to everything you need."

Pete said, "I will work on that aspect as Nick is concerned with the building and Tony is working on mechanical improvements."

Both Nick and Pete said that they would enlist the help of any of the others when they were doing nothing else and all of the community said that they would help where and when they were needed. The conversation ended when Eileen and Tammy told them that the meal was ready and the whole group, including Believer and Jimmy, gathered in the old barn to have a communal meal which they all enjoyed.

None of them, except Believer and Jimmy, had enjoyed this kind of meal before since they had all existed on canned food after the catastrophe. Even though Eileen had been somewhat limited, she had made a large casserole type meal with the vegetables and small creatures the hunters had brought back.

Despite the different griefs of everyone present, a new feeling of hope and comradeship developed throughout the course of the meal, and when it was finished, Nick stood up and said, "Yesterday, we were all very worried and concerned about our chances of survival. Most of us thought that our chances were pretty slim. We were faced with the prospect of foraging further and further afield for food supplies. Then a man and a boy walked into our lives with a different message.

"Believer came and told us that there was a way, a better way than ours. I, for one, was sceptical, but Believer went out with Shirley and big Emma. They came back with food for us all. When he came, he said that he only wanted shelter from us, not food.

"Not only has he not taken any food from us, he has provided us with the first meal which has not come out of a can. I am very grateful. Not only that, he has made us see that we all have uses in this new world of ours. He has shown us that if we all work together, then we can hope for a better life.

"He says that God is guiding him. Again, I was sceptical, but his attitude is completely unselfish. He said that he had come to help us and by God he has."

Believer stood up, saying, "Thank you, Nick. Do you realise what your last words were? You said, 'By God, he has.' That may not mean much to you, but to me, that phrase which you used as an expletive means everything to me.

"Without God's help, I am just an unemployed lorry driver. You have thanked me for providing you all with food. Don't thank me, thank God for making it possible. I do, regularly. Today was easy, but there will be times when small animals will be difficult to find.

"Although it is only September now, winter may come before you realise it. Things will be very different then. We have already had a long period of rain and cloudy skies lasting well over a month. I have seen the sun briefly on only two occasions.

"One of these produced a rainbow which made me think of the one that Noah saw. That one brought him hope that the world would not be totally flooded again. The other occasion showed me that it was time to leave a refuge where I had been as happy as I could be.

"I was told to leave and shown the way to travel. Apart from those two brief bursts of sunshine, the sky has been completely overcast with rain in various degrees. The rain is God's way of cleaning the land to make it fit to live in again.

"I think that most cities and towns are completely uninhabitable and will be for years. It is only in the country areas like this where there is any chance of survival at all. It will be very hard, but God can make it easier for you if you ask him in prayer.

"Tomorrow, I propose to hold a service of thanksgiving here in the barn before I go out hunting with Shirley again. I would like you all to come, whatever you feel about religion. I want you to feel the presence of the Holy Spirit as I often do.

"Some of you may not feel it, but if we are all together, then I am sure that some of you will have an experience which will surprise you. I know that the other small group I was with became aware of His presence and will continue to pray even though I have left.

"I know that the Spirit is with me frequently when I pray and I am carried along by that knowledge.

"What I pray for most is that everyone who is left will learn to live in harmony as never before. It is the last chance for the human race. We must live together or not at all. Thank you for listening to me.

"Let us now try to do something to cheer us all up. I think we should end this evening of hope with some sort of party. Anyone know any jokes or poems, perhaps a song or two?"

Jokes proved to be rather scarce but Tony produced a harmonica and the group tried to sing some well-known songs, after which they retired to their various shelters with a great deal of hope.

Believer and Jimmy again spent the night in Nick and Christine's ruined house, and the four of them sat up talking before the darkness forced them to retire.

During their late-night talk, Nick apologised to Believer for using God's name in the way that he had earlier. Believer said, "Don't worry. It gave me the chance to explain what the words really meant. That way I was able to further God's purpose. I am sure that you will think about the words you use in future.

"When you say things like 'Thank God', you are really uttering a prayer, even when you don't realise that you are doing so. Perhaps, if you think what you are saying, then the prayers may become conscious ones. You will be surprised at the results."

"Every time you speak, you seem to put a different thought into my head. I'm beginning to understand you, I think. I do believe that when you talk about religion, you mean everything you say.

"I am still not sure how it will work for me. I haven't really believed for some time and when the bombs fell, I thought that they had put an end to religion for all time. You seem so sincere that I am beginning to change my mind.

"What's all this about feeling the presence of The Holy Spirit. It is all nonsense, isn't it?"

"Come along tomorrow and see. Since you are perhaps losing your scepticism, you may well be one of those who will feel the Spirit come to you. Here is a thought for you to go to bed with. You are asking me questions, Why?

"If you don't believe, you are showing considerable interest. Perhaps you a getting a little push, otherwise, why are you asking so much. Good night to you both."

Day Fifty-One

To Believer's surprise and pleasure, the whole community was present in the barn soon after first light. He had seen them entering in ones and twos while he washed at the stream and when he joined them, they all seemed to be waiting eagerly to hear what he had to say.

He began by saying, "The Lord be with you." He received the response, mostly from Eileen but one or two of the others tried to join in.

Then he said, "Thank you, Lord, for enabling us to meet together in this place. Thank you for our survival and for the food you have provided. Grant that we may be able to find sufficient for our needs in the future.

"Grant us the wisdom to take only that which we need and not to be greedy for more. Grant us also, to show compassion to our fellowmen and women and to help all who are in need no matter who they are and what they believe."

Then he went on, "Today, I am hoping that the Spirit will come to more than one of us here in this barn which God has left for us to use as a meeting place. Now, while I am talking, some of you may feel something. I don't know what the effect will be on each of you since we are all different.

"I shan't tell you what the effect on me is, as I don't want to influence you by suggestion. If any of you feel any odd effect, anything that you didn't feel when you came in, please raise your hand. Say nothing. Don't think that you have to raise your hand because someone else does. There is no shame if the Spirit doesn't touch you on this occasion. He might; anyway but you may not recognise it as such.

"For a start, try asking God to help you with your talents so that you put them good use to help the community you are in and any others that need your help. Do this silently and in your own way for a couple of minutes. Then we shall say the Lord's Prayer' together, and afterwards we will try to sing a hymn or two."

The whole community was silent during those two minutes. One hand was raised, that of Eileen. Believer had expected this in a way, for she had been religious all her life and he felt that she would be the most likely person to recognise the presence.

Believer moved over to her and led her to the front of the group. Then both knelt on the floor to continue their private prayers.

During the period of the Lord's Prayer and the hymns, two more hands were raised in addition to Believer who now felt the familiar tingle in his scalp. Jimmy was one and Paula the other. Believer led them both out to the front to join Eileen. Then he asked them to describe what they had felt.

Eileen said that she had felt a deep peace which had moved her to tears. Jimmy told them that he had heard music as if from a cathedral even though there were only a few people present. Paula's experience was that she felt that she was going on a journey, but she didn't know where. Believer told them about the tingle he always felt on occasions like this and whenever he was talking and thinking about God.

"There are four of us who have experienced something at this time. I know when the Spirit is with me, it is usually when I am singing or talking about God In truth, I felt it as soon as I started speaking at this small service. I didn't raise my hand then as I wanted any of you who felt something to acknowledge i spontaneously.

"I only put my hand up when some of you had responded. You see, we ar all different and God will choose His own way to make himself known to you. will tell you now that God has called you many times in the past, but you hav not listened because you did not know how to.

"Now the next step is to ask Him to tell you how and when to listen. I thin you will all experience His presence sometime in the future. Ask Him now help you recognise him when He calls.

"When I have left here and at any odd time, you will suddenly feel a ne sensation and you will think, 'Ah! that's what Believer was talking about.' Thre of you have already felt that call. Perhaps the three who will need him most a soonest.

"Eileen, because she will be your teacher. Paula, your journey has alrea begun. I know that the time will come when you will be greatly need elsewhere, and I feel not too far in the future. As for Jimmy here, this is not t first time he has been called and he knows it.

"He knows when and how often. Perhaps he will tell you what he used to do and why I found him where I did. Jimmy is also starting on a journey. In fact, he started several years ago but didn't know it. Jimmy, tell them about it now."

"I don't like to," Jimmy replied, rather timorously.

"Ask God first," was Believer's prompt reply.

Jimmy was silent for a while, then he suddenly found the confidence and told his sad story.

When the lad had finished, Believer said, "Do you not see? God was calling Jimmy even then. The one place he felt safe was outside that church listening to the music. He was too scared of his father and also of the people in the church to do anything about it.

"He knows now that he would have been welcomed in the church. The people would have accepted him in time. The point I am making is that when God calls, act upon it. It will change your life in ways that you cannot imagine."

The service continued with more hymns and the Blessing in which Believer used the word 'us' instead of 'you' as in the service books. After he had finished, he called to Eileen and said, "You know what your task in life is now. As I said before, you will be the teacher. Have you any books to help?"

"I do have a Bible, but not much else."

Believer said, "There are quite a few books in the church where Jimmy was living. I'm sure that God won't mind if you borrow some to keep His church intact."

"Do you mean that we should go there to worship? It's a long way."

"Not at all. As I told Jimmy, the church is not the building. It is the people who believe in Jesus who make the church. This barn is the church in this village. Why? All the people have gathered here to thank Him for survival.

"Some who believe and some who don't. Also, some who don't know what to believe, perhaps, God has gathered us all here and I know that The Holy Spirit touched at least four of us today. He was with me all the time I was speaking and also, now.

"I feel that we should sing one more hymn before we split up. You will find the words in the Mission Praise books I brought with me. The hymn I wish us to sing is 'Bind Us Together' and as we sing, we should all hold hands."

The small group did this and Believer noted that everyone seemed to be smiling and happy when they were leaving the barn to go about their tasks for the day.

197

Believer gathered Emma, Shirley and Jimmy together and organised some target practice for the air rifles, using some of the ammunition he had made the night before. After the practice, the small group set off on their daily hunt. This time, they split up into pairs. Jimmy went with Emma in one direction. Believer and Shirley took another course, each pair taking an air rifle.

Shirley asked Believer what sort of animal they were looking for. Believer said, "Any animal or bird small enough to knock down with an air rifle. I doubt whether we could kill a sheep. Anyway, sheep must be caught and reared if possible. The same would apply to cattle, deer and llamas, if they could find some escaped from a zoo."

Shirley was a little alarmed at this. "You said things like llamas could have escaped from a zoo. That means that there might be other animals out there, lions and tigers perhaps."

"Possibly," said Believer. "What about all the safari parks. The fences will have been damaged. Places like Longleat which I know is a long way away. There, lions roamed free in parts of the estate, so they could well have strayed. Not as far as this, I doubt, but there were other places."

"What if we meet one? You're teasing me. I don't like that idea at all. We've only got an air rifle and you've already said that it won't kill anything big. What will we do if we find one?"

"We will just have to trust in God, won't we? I do, and so must you. When Tony has made some crossbows, they will be better for killing larger animals but they will need a lot of practice before they are used. As to the air rifle not killing anything big. That's not strictly true.

"A very good or lucky shot could be lethal but very unlikely. It might be better to shout at it. In your case, scream directly at it. Did you know that no man, however loud he shouts, can produce more decibels than a woman's deliberate scream. I saw it proved once on television.

"The presenter got an army sergeant major to compete against two young girls using a decibel meter. He didn't stand a chance. The girls, particularly the youngest, practically bent the needle on the meter. They sent the instrument off the scale while the sergeant major only managed about 80 decibels.

"If ever you get in that position, you may find that a scream is your best defence. You do know that it is possible to shatter glass with the sound of a voice. Think what a deliberate high-pitched scream would do to an animal's ears.

"I didn't realise it before, but telling you made me understand that a woman has been given a high-pitched voice as a defence. Still, the fact remains that we have to trust God for food and protection."

The pair continued their hunt and found a few crows, one of which was shot by Shirley and another, later, by Believer. They collected a few vegetables and returned, hoping that Jimmy and Emma had fared better.

They had nearly returned when they saw the other two on their way back with some rabbits. The biggest surprise was that Jimmy was struggling with a sheep he had on the end of a rope.

The girl and the young boy had found the animal tangled up with some barbed wire. They had chased a dog away and rescued the sheep. The animal had several superficial cuts but was still able to walk.

Believer was astounded and remembered that he had been talking about sheep to Shirley. Once again, he had received some sort of premonition about future events.

"Thank the Lord," Believer said. "It's a ewe, isn't it? Now, Emma, Shirley, you must look for a ram when you are out. If you find one, you will have food and clothing for the future. It must be kept alive. Paula will have to clean the wounds up. It looks like she will have to be a vet as well a doctor."

The party were now joined by the rest of the community who had been warned by Jason that the hunting party had come back with a sheep.

Nick said to Believer, "Are you some sort of miracle worker? You have provided us with food for yesterday and today, and now you have come back with a sheep. We haven't anywhere to keep it yet. There is some limited grazing, though. What are we going to do with it?"

"Only God works miracles," Believer said. "Thank Him first, then thank Jimmy and Emma, they found it. Shirley and I only managed some crows and vegetables. What you must do now is to organise some fencing around the field here.

"Until you've done that, you will have to keep it tethered. It will have to be guarded day and night. Nick, can you organise that? I would suggest that you watch over it in pairs, one being a responsible person with a weapon. There will be both human and animal predators to look out for.

"Jimmy said that he chased a dog away. What I am really worried about is packs of dogs, but if you can catch a single dog, you will have some help with the watch keeping. You will have to consider the extra problem of food for the animal.

"If you could find more sheep, particularly a ram, you might be able to build up a flock which will provide food and clothing for the future. Allyson, who I stayed with before, has a spinning wheel. Before I leave here, I will tell you where to find her. That way, you two groups will be able to help each other.

"If you can produce the wool, Allyson can spin it into yarn. You could then share the yarn between you and help each other that way. It must be possible to get some sort of barter system going between groups. Each group will have to be self-sufficient for food, but you should be able to trade for other things."

While this conversation was taking place, Paula was doing her best with the sheep's wounds, and Eileen had taken charge of the food the hunters had brought back.

Believer told Nick, "You will have to think about storing winter fodder for the sheep and some sort of shelter for it if the weather should turn really harsh. You should also try to find pigs and cattle. If you can, then you will be rich in the conditions you are living now. Farming, both arable and husbandry is the only real hope for the continuation of any form of civilisation.

"When I leave here, I hope that Shirley and Emma will be proficient at hunting. Also, when I meet other people and I am sure that they intend to live a life of co-operation, then I will try to arrange that you and they can get together to swap skills and anything else to the mutual benefit of all."

Believer then busied himself with making a further supply of air gun pellets until Eileen and Tammy told them that all that the meal was ready. The food was eaten amid a lively discussion over the future of the group. Believer, on this occasion, was content to listen for the most part.

He felt that if the community was to survive, then they should discuss their own ideas. Besides, by listening he could learn himself. He thought that he had provided a trigger for a much-improved lifestyle and that when he left, their future would be as stable as possible.

Before he arrived, the group had been literally living from hand to mouth with no hope for the future. There had even been some animosity amongst the women, but now, they all seemed to be inspired with a new sense of harmony which could only be an improvement.

During the course of the meal, Believer asked Jimmy what sort of dog he had chased away. Jimmy said that he thought it was a Jack Russell. Believer said th was the sort of dog that would benefit the group most as it was small enough not to need a great deal of food, but also a very noisy breed with a bark loud enough to rouse the group should the need arise.

Day Fifty-Two

At first light, Believer went out with a short piece of rope and a little of the rabbit meat from the previous night's meal. He made a slip noose in the rope and headed in the general direction from which Jimmy had returned the previous day. He had caught sight of the dog about a mile outside the village, so he sat down on an old wall with the rabbit meat in front of him.

The dog had followed the scent of the sheep but was still hungry, so as it smelled the meat, it came closer. Believer could see that it was very thin and emaciated, but still eager for food. It was very nervous and spent a long time coming nearer. Believer had tied the meat to a piece of thin cord and gradually pulled it nearer to him as the dog approached.

The animal stopped every few yards, but finally, hunger overtook it and it made a grab for the meat. Believer slipped the noose over its head while it was eating, but the dog tried to escape as soon as it had grabbed the meat. Believer held the noose and talked calmly to the dog, and eventually, it quietened down until Believer was able to pick it up without fear of being bitten.

"Here's your guard dog," Believer told them when he returned. "He has collar and a name tag. His name is Patch."

The two youngest immediately took charge of it and said that as they were on watch most of the time, it was their job to look after it and train it. Believer agreed with this and told them that they must arrange with Eileen and Tamm for a ration of food for the new member of the community.

Believer then collected his little band of hunter/gatherers and left the village dividing them into pairs as he had before. The only difference was that this tir he took Emma with him and left Shirley with Jimmy. "Did you manage to anything yesterday?" he asked her.

She replied, "Yes, I did my share. I said a little prayer just like you told and I remembered what you said about shooting. It worked. I didn't think would, but it did. You must be right about God helping."

"Do you really think that God helped you? Because, if you do, it means that He has reached you. He has made you aware of Him and one day you will wonder how you ever managed without His help. When you get to that stage, you will be a true believer like me.

"You will be as amazed at the things you can do as I am. When I think back, I know how often I have been helped in the past. The difference is that I didn't know it at the time. Now, when I speak, I know that God tells me what words to use.

"I could not have spoken to you all the way I did in the old days. Now, people listen when I speak. God gives me the confidence to lend authority to my words, but the authority is really God's, not mine. I would just be a mumbling fool without Him.

"Even now, I am being helped. I was a happily married man, but the only woman I was confident with was my wife. I could never converse with a younger woman without feeling embarrassed, couldn't speak without feeling that I would say something that would cause someone like you to dislike me. Now, here am I, alone with a young woman and talking with complete confidence and I know that you will listen.

"I already know that you don't dislike me. You gave me quite a surprise, the other day. I was flattered and pleased, but I think you will agree that circumstances are not right for me to form any attachment.

"When I leave here, Jimmy will come with me, if he wants to, as a companion and pupil. Later, he will go out on his own to spread God's word and try to restore belief and confidence in God. When that day comes, there will be two or more of us travelling around.

"I do hope, though, that there will be people in each community I visit who will keep up the tradition of prayer that I shall try to start. In your little group, Eileen seems to be the most likely to succeed me when I have gone. She will need all the help she can get then.

"When we get back, why don't you have a little talk with her? It will give her great confidence to know that she will have someone to back her up."

The pair continued on their way and were lucky enough to catch a goose which was big enough to feed them all for one meal. Believer decided that they should return and they started back, only stopping to collect some vegetables from the garden of a ruined village. They harvested mostly potatoes and root crops before they had enough for everyone.

"Why are we going back so soon?" Emma asked.

"It's still summertime, even though the weather isn't good. It's difficult to keep food for a long time so we don't want to get too much in one day. Eileen and Tammy will need a long time to cook this bird, and besides, the other pair are likely to bring something back.

"God provides for our needs each day. With prayer, He will look after us, but we mustn't be greedy.

"Greed was the root cause of the problems we have today. Greed for food, money, land or power, mostly power to force a way of life on people against their will. I don't know the real reason for the terrible war we have barely survived, but I should imagine that it was due to greed for power. 'You do what I say or I'll hit you with a big stick' situation.

"I don't even know who sent us the bombs. I don't recall any particular reference or warning. The general public wouldn't have been told anyway. I would bet that those politicians who knew anything were hiding in underground bunkers when it happened. Also, that the first preference for the bunkers would be the politicians and council employees who knew where the secret bunkers were."

"Do you mean that there were a lot of secret shelters for this sort of thing?"

"Of course, there were. I am sure that all major cities had them. Politicians are all the kind of people to look after Number One and never mind the rest of us. You can be very sure that some of them received warnings but did not, or ever intend to give any notice to the general public.

"Just think of the panic it would cause. My only hope is that those people don't surface and try to meddle in our lives again. There is no room for them in this situation where there are only a few of us left.

"Only small groups can hope to survive initially. Your group is about at its maximum level for continued existence. Another reason why I shouldn't stay too long. Two or three hunters can only provide enough food for your daily survival and really only just enough for the 11 of you.

"Jimmy and I will put too much strain on your resources and a small group doesn't need politicians to tell them what to do. Everybody must contribute to the good of you all."

Emma thought about the things that Believer had said. "I've just realised what you've been saying. When you and Jimmy leave, there will be just the two of us to do all the hunting. That will mean that we will be out longer each day, and the days will get shorter as well."

"It's not necessarily true that only you two will be going out. Don't forget that there is a little dog who will warn of any strangers, so Jason and Young Emma will be free to help you and learn from you. Also, I am sure that the men will come out with you from time to time when they are less busy.

"I will mention this to Nick, perhaps, if he feels that is necessary, he can make up some sort of rota. The more people who know how to hunt, the better. When the winter has set in, there will be less for them to do and you might be able to send out two parties. Also, there will be less problems about preserving food so you might be able to stay at home some days."

Emma and Believer had reached the village by this time and immediately gave the goose to Eileen, who started preparing it assisted by Tammy and Emma. The meal looked as if it might turn into a festive occasion.

Pete and Tony were working hard building a fence for the sheep. Paula was helping them as her medical skills were not needed at the moment. Believer went to her and asked her what medicines she had.

She said, "I have some but they are really sparse. I could do with a lot more. As many as you can get for me."

"Come out with us tomorrow and we will see what we can find. It will be an experience for you and you can tell me what sort of things to bring back."

Believer then went to find Nick and found him busy with the building project, helped by Christine. They were working hard and were surprised that Believer was back so soon. Believer said that he and Emma had been lucky and had shot a goose big enough for them all and that the group should not be greedy and take more than they could use.

He had come back early and would be glad to help if there was anything he could do. Nick was glad of the offer and gave Believer a job sawing pieces of second-hand timber from which he had removed the nails. He told Believer that Pete and Tony had taken the task of building the fence as a major priority so that they could let the captive ewe off its tether.

Nick had decided to work on the building as it was a long-term job. Christine was helping him, but as he had to teach her everything about the use of tools, progress was slow. Believer was handy with tools and Nick was glad of his able assistance.

While they were working, Believer raised the point that Emma had made about the girls being happier if they had a man with them when they were hunting. He mentioned the fact that Young Emma and Jason might be able to take their turn, and learn the skills that Shirley and Emma were now acquiring. Nick agreed that he would look at the possibility of sparing one of the men whenever it was possible.

"When do you expect to leave?" Nick asked Believer. "We will all miss you when you've gone."

"A few days yet. When I leave, I will look for a community who might have a small bitch which you may be able to mate with Patch. Dogs only live about 14 years and there is no knowing how old Patch is, so it would be advisable to try and get a replacement as soon as possible. The same thing applies to the sheep you have.

"You must find a ram for her so that you can start your own flock. Perhaps there is a group somewhere who has a ram. If so, you could share the offspring.

"Tomorrow, I am going to take Paula with me so that we can search for medical supplies. She is going to need as much as she can get hold of. I shall hunt at the same time. That way, we shall kill two birds with one stone. Besides, I want to have a good talk with her.

"Nick, you have another big problem that perhaps you have not thought of. You have seven women here and only four males. Eileen is 62 and probably won't be bothered about a mate. Christine is settled with you.

"That leaves five females who have reached or will reach puberty in the near future to three males. I have included Jason and Young Emma in the figures as they are big enough. If the older girls get the mating urge, you must be prepared to let them go elsewhere, otherwise jealousy might creep in. This could be embarrassing for Pete and Tony.

"Jason is a little young just now and there is no guarantee that he will settle with Young Emma even if he seems to be taken with her now. I am not sure, but from what I have seen so far, there might be a general shortage of men. This is mainly because most of the men would have been working in the cities which have all gone. So far, including myself and Jimmy, the ratio is fairly even.

"The last group I was with consisted of four females. I did meet one other young man and sent him to join the others so that makes four to one there. Here it is seven to four. Really, the general population seems to be very sparse.

suppose that I have travelled some 40 or 50 miles and have only seen 17 people. I think that there are probably only thousands left instead of millions."

"There are some others. We were raided once, but we beat the attackers off. I think that we wounded some. I have a feeling that some of them were women, but it was difficult to tell as they were all wrapped up against the weather. When they left, they went towards the North.

"They were after food and I told them we didn't have any spare. There were only about five of them and that was ten days ago. The first thing we knew was that someone shot at Jason as he was running for help. As you know, we keep our guns handy but hoped that we wouldn't have to use them.

"True, we did shoot at young Jimmy, but only to scare him off. Since you came, we think a little differently and we won't try to kill anyone. We still have to defend ourselves, though."

"I regret that you will find that necessary from time to time. I am afraid that human nature, being what it is, provides us with a desperate need to survive at the cost of others. We also tend to be greedy and try to keep what we have. It is very difficult I know, but it is preferable to talk first. Who knows?

"If you meet anyone else, you may be able to help each other. You say that you thought that you wounded some of your unwelcome visitors. If you did, and the wounds were serious, they are probably dead by now. Particularly if they received no medical attention.

"Paula could have provided that if they had stayed. At least better attention than most could provide.

"I know that at the time, you were concerned with defence, but how much better if you could have discussed your mutual problems and perhaps tended the wounded after your encounter."

At this time, the dog started barking and the members of the group who were visible to Believer took cover. He could see that Pete, Tony and Paula had thrown themselves flat on the ground. Eileen and Tammy disappeared out of sight and only Jason was still visible as he was on watch.

He was looking carefully over a wall with his back to Believer. It was he who shouted that it was only Jimmy and Shirley returning after their hunt. They had only managed to get three small birds between them. A crow and two pigeons and were rather disappointed.

Believer told them not to worry as he had brought back enough for all on this day. The hunters cleaned themselves up after the hunt and changed into dry clothes because the day had been wet again. Everybody who had been outside was in the same state so the drying off process applied to Pete, Tony and Paula as well.

It was well into the evening when they all went into the old barn which served as a communal meeting place, church and dining room. It was the only place large enough and with sufficient roof to accommodate all the group. It was the one place where the group could discuss their daily activities and plans for survival.

Pete and Tony told how the fencing was progressing and likewise, Nick described the building work he and Christine were doing. He said that the work was going well but there was still a great deal to be done. Believer broke in with a warning that since they were all using second-hand timber, they should be extremely careful to guard against diseases like tetanus.

Believer then raised the problem of the hunting situation and pointed out that the burden had fallen onto two girls who had no training or experience in the outdoor life. These two would be required to go out unprotected after Believer and Jimmy left in a few days' time. He said that in pre-historic times, it was normally the man's task to do the hunting.

In the present circumstances, all the men were needed desperately for necessary work within the village. This was true, particularly at the present time certainly no one man could take on the job of accompanying the girls on a regular basis. A rota system seemed to be most appropriate. The men should take turn and leave careful instructions as to how their particular task was to be carried out while they were away.

As to the watch keeping, the burden of that had already been eased by the arrival of the small dog. It was now only necessary for one of the youngsters to remain on watch. The dog had already proved his worth twice by barking, first when Believer had returned and then with the arrival of Jimmy and Shirley.

Believer had noted the efficiency of the group when danger threatened. They had all taken appropriate action and were ready to go into defensive position immediately. In particular, Pete and Tony had their guns with them and had been ready within seconds to back up Nick and Christine.

These were the four who had first accosted Believer on his arrival. This meant that Believer had no worries about the defences other than that he deployed the use of violence, which he himself refused to use. So far, he had not needed proper firearm, although he had twice been threatened by them.

The discussion carried on until it was nearly dark, with most of the community contributing something. Even Jason and Young Emma had their say about the watch keeping duties they performed so well. They volunteered to take on the task of keeping and training Patch, and they said that, since they were looking after one animal, they might as well take on the sheep as well. Believer was very pleased at the general attitude of the group and felt that physically, there was not much else he could do.

The spiritual welfare of his new found friends was another matter. He was aware that two or three of them were on the brink of accepting what he said to them. Particularly, Eileen and the older Emma. Nick too, had shown signs that he was being affected by the aura of faith that Believer carried with him wherever he went.

The ex-lorry driver hadn't really thought much of the effect he was having on the people he met. In fact. he thoroughly believed himself that he was helped by God, every step of the way and if asked, always said that nothing he had achieved in recent times had been carried out on his own initiative.

However, helped or not, contact with him left a profound feeling of wonder and confidence. Those he had met so far felt that they had to comply with his requests and that his logic and leadership required instant obedience. Even Nick who had, at first, been very wary on their first meeting and resented his arrival, now thought that if Believer wanted to stay, he would gladly relinquish his leadership.

Nick, therefore, was beginning to understand what drove Believer on. He realised that Believer had a strong compulsion to help everyone he met.

The group's strange visitor had achieved everything he had set out to since he had arrived. He had given the group confidence to look to their own survival and the future which had looked so bleak only three days before.

The amount that had been achieved in three days scarcely seemed possible and all the group, without exception were affected to a greater or lesser extent. Those with whom Believer had spent most time were elated with their own self confidence. Perhaps, the ones who had most fears for the future were Paula and Eileen.

Tammy was a different type of person altogether. She always seemed to be quietly confident and went about her self-imposed tasks cheerfully, but then she was that type of person anyway. She was always helpful and went around offering assistance wherever it was needed. Really, she was unobtrusive, but everyone knew she was there when she was needed and all appreciated her willing presence.

At the various meetings, she did not say very much, but what she did contribute made a great deal of sense. Since she mainly concerned herself with supplies and laundry, she had done her best with one of the major problems. She was a member of a group consisting mainly of women in the age group when child bearing was normally possible.

Even Young Emma came into this category. Tammy had spent some time collecting all the sanitary towels and disposable nappies she could find, and had supplies for some considerable time.

She had also made herself responsible for storing food, clothing and other necessary items. All the things which Tammy did were noted with gratitude by the rest of the community, but when Believer spoke to her, she said that she didn't do much at all.

She was surprised when Believer told her that big Emma and Shirley had felt ashamed by Tammy's activities. She hadn't given any attention about what people thought about her, she just got on with the job in hand. If she felt that it was necessary, she just did it.

She had not noticed that Tony always sat near her or that he often looked in her direction during the busy days which had followed Believer's arrival. Everyone else, including the visitor were aware that Tony was increasingly attracted to this quiet but most useful member of the society.

Believer said nothing to the girl about this. It was not his business to play cupid during his short visit, but he knew that sometime in the future, Tony would make a bid for the girl's affection. Believer thought that they would make a very good match as their dispositions were similar.

Tony was very busy at this time and had many projects on which he was working or considering for the future. He simply had no time to consider any romantic thoughts seriously, so he contented himself with admiring her from afar and to wait till things settle down. He was also wary of being rejected and so far had not acted on his growing attraction for another quietly busy person.

Eileen, when she was not busy cooking or preparing food spent a long time in thought and prayer. Believer noticed that she seemed troubled at times. He sensed that she was worried about the prospects Believer had laid before her.

She was doubting her abilities to take over the spiritual guidance of the community and after the meal was finished, Believer went to her and spent some time discussing the future with her.

"You must put your trust entirely in God," Believer said to her. "Once you do that, you will have all the help you need. You will be told what to say when the occasion demands. Perhaps you should start by initiating a regular Sunday service.

"Try working out the form this will take. Once the first one has been carried out, you will find that things will be easier. If you start a routine, you will have all the help you need from God and also some from the rest of the group.

"I know exactly what you are going through. I felt the same way at first and had to go through the same soul searching when I had to deal with exactly the same emotions.

"The doubts that trouble you are not entirely your own. If you believe in God, it stands to reason that you also believe in the Devil. He will try to undo all the good that God does. As soon as God's influence begins to be felt then the Devil steps in and does his best to stop any progress, which will detract from his own schemes of power.

"That is what is happening to you. It happened to me, so I know what your problem is. Now that you know that, ask for God's help. He will give it gladly. When you take your first service, give a sermon. God will give you the right words to use.

"You may also get help from some surprising quarters, for instance, you may find that Tammy will be one of the most responsive people in the group. She seems to lead a Christian life without realising it. She is just an entirely good person.

"Big Emma and Shirley told me that they felt ashamed that Tammy had made herself so useful while they could only be bitchy to Christine. They both know now that Christine did not deserve their enmity. She was just as unhappy as everyone else and teamed up with Nick for mutual solace."

Eileen said, "I am not narrow minded and feel that people should have what happiness they can get. How do you equate the teachings of your church and mine about their living together? We were both told that this was a sin."

"Did you ever see the film 'The Blue Lagoon'? In that film, two children were cast away on a small island and grew up together. In one version of the film, the couple had a child. What was the reaction of the Churches in cases like that?

"Were the two people sinful? They couldn't get married first, could they? No, as I told Nick and Chris, There is no active church or priest within miles. Surely, the church should regard them as being already married in the eyes of God. The only stipulation is that they should get married as soon as possible. This surely applies to Nick and Chris.

"It may also apply soon with Tony and Tammy. They look very likely to get together if Tony's behaviour is anything to go by. You must have noticed, everyone else except Tammy herself has done. What are you going to do then? I shall probably be gone. I have already told Nick that I shall leave in a few days.

"If you are going to look after the spiritual needs of the people here, then you will have to perform whatever services they need as I must wherever I go."

"But women can't perform marriage services. It would be wrong."

"We have already discussed this. In the Anglican Church, women priests were ordained in 1994 to marry people and many of the Non conformists had women priests. If it is necessary, then do it. God won't forbid it.

"Another matter, education. I am thinking of Young Emma and Jason. Do you realise that they probably don't know simple maths. So far, they have only used computers and calculators.

"Now they will have to work things out by hand and there are not many left who know how to. Tony probably does, but he may be rusty. Teaching must carry on or mankind will stagnate. Have a word with Tony and see what the pair of you can come up with.

"If everyone concerns themselves with just survival, there will be no advancement. The young must be taught and those who have knowledge must pass it on. The hope then is that those who are taught will develop enquiring minds and so learn more than their teachers."

By this time, late in the evening, darkness was nearly complete and most of the community had retired for the night. Believer apologised to Jason and Young Emma for keeping them awake. He had disturbed them while he was talking to Eileen. He then retired to his own shelter in the house that Nick and Christine occupied.

Day Fifty-Three

The following morning, Believer aroused Paula, Jimmy and the two girls, Emma and Shirley. This time, he suggested that Jimmy and the two girls went in one direction whilst he and Paula took another. He had previously unloaded his rucksack and his intent that day was to find as many medical supplies as he could. He intended to hunt at the same time. He knew, therefore that the day would be long.

On the way, he asked Paula how the little group had come together.

Paula said, "I was off duty that day and had been visiting my folks in the village. My mum sent me out to the shop where Tammy worked when the village was destroyed first by fire and then by a violent wind. My parent's house was completely destroyed, but I was sheltered by a large building from the heat flash and the blast.

"I was blown about and had some bruises. Most of Tammy's shop and the house where she lived with her mother were gone but some of the actual shop was left. I could hear someone crying. I went to the ruin and found young Emma with some burns and bruises.

"Jason was further into the shop, unconscious. Tammy was lying behind the counter suffering from shock. She had actually been reaching down for something for Jason when the shop came down about her ears.

"I managed to pull the three of them out from the rubble and did what I could for them, then we went to the old barn which was mostly still standing. I looked around for anyone else and found Nick by the ruins of his house.

"He was holding his wife who was badly burnt. She had been in the garden collecting clothes from the line and caught the heat flash. I told Nick to take her the barn which wasn't far away and he joined the other three there.

"I helped him to carry her and went out again to see if there was anyone else. took a bucket to the stream to get some water and tipped it over Mary. The ter was warm when I got it out. I hoped that it might help her but she was very d.

213

"I couldn't do much really so I went out again, with Tammy, this time. She was still shaking with the shock but she wanted to help. This is typical of her as you know. We found Eileen crawling along what was left of the road.

"She was completely dazed but managed to pull herself out from her cottage which was demolished like so many other buildings. She hadn't got the will to try to stand up, so we helped her back to the barn to join the others. Nick's wife, Mary, was barely alive by this time but I couldn't do anything.

"Tammy and I went out again and spent the rest of the daylight, such as it was, looking around for anyone else. We had nearly given up searching when we saw a car upside down with the driver struggling to get out. That was Pete, he couldn't move because his weight was on the seat belt.

"We couldn't move him because he is a big bloke. I had to cut through the belt with a piece of broken glass. We got him out and went back to spend the night with the others.

"Pete didn't know what had happened, he thought he had been caught in a gas explosion. He couldn't see anything when he came to because his vision was restricted. It was only when we got him out and he saw the damage did he realise the extent of the catastrophe. He was horrified when he found out and grateful to us for getting him out.

"We must have been a pretty sight by then. We were both dirty and our clothes were torn. There were tear stains down our faces and we were still sobbing most of the time. When we got back to the barn, Nick's wife had died.

"We left the barn and huddled together in a cellar to console ourselves. Nick wanted to stay with his wife, but I advised against it because of radiation. Tammy went back to her little shop and managed to find some tins of food and drink to get us through the night, and we settled down to wait for help to come. None did.

"When morning came, Nick realised that help wasn't going to come soon and that something had to be done to organise us all. Up to that time, Tammy and I had done most of the work and we were still exhausted. Though he was distressed over the death of Mary, he took over and started to organise food and shelter for us all. It was soon obvious to us all that Nick was a natural leader and things improved a bit when he took charge.

"We were all worried about radiation and food. I told Nick that any water we drank must be boiled first. Anyway, we all went out and searched for all the food we could find and then we settled in the remains of the village pub.

"There was even some food in there and we were able to raid the freezer for a couple of days. Of course, there was wine and beer to drink. So we didn't have to worry too much about boiling the water.

"Late in the morning, we heard a shout and thought that rescue had come. We were disappointed to see four people coming into the village, they were as dirty as we were and it was obvious that rather than help us, they needed our help more.

"These four were Tony, Christine, Shirley and big Emma. They were the only survivors of a nearby factory. Chris was the receptionist there and the other two girls worked in the offices. Tony, as an engineer was visiting on business there. He was in the reception area when the world was turned upside down.

"Tony had pulled Shirley and Emma from the adjacent office and he and Chris searched the rest of the building for survivors with no avail. All of the factory staff had left for the weekend and only the office staff were left. No one else was found alive. Tony and the three women spent the night in the remains of the factory and when help didn't come, set out to find someone.

"They were distressed to find the damage was so widespread and asked if they could stay here with the rest of us and try to work out some policy for survival. We all thought that perhaps the military would come but we struggled on. We had to go out to find food several times and we found the guns in a ruined house which was owned by a member of a gun club. That is how we armed ourselves.

"We had to move from the pub when the rains came and we split up into our various groups then. We still hoped for organised rescue but it didn't come. You came instead, just when we were getting really desperate. We raided the village where you found Jimmy, and he followed us back and tried to steal some of the food.

"Nick scared him off and he went away. We only found out, when you came here that Jimmy was only trying to get food which we had taken from his village. Poor little mite, if only we had known that he was alone.

"A few days before you walked into our lives, we were raided by a small party of people, both men and women. They didn't know we were armed and they fired on us. They were very surprised when we fired back and left, probably because we were too strong for them. We thought that we wounded some of them."

Believer said to Paula, "You certainly had a harrowing time, much worse than I had. It was worse for you because you knew most of the people you had seen dead, your own family included. This applies to all of the survivors who came from the village, Nick, Eileen, Tammy and the two young ones.

"Just five out of a whole village and none of you related. Tell me, what do you think about the use of guns? What about people who try to take what they want by force?"

"I don't agree with it at all. I want to help people. That's why I became a nurse. I am frightened about the thought of people going about with guns, raiding and shooting at any one they come across just for their own survival.

"We few that are left here have proved that we can work together. True, Nick is prepared to defend our village and it does seem that he has to, but he didn't fire at you, for which I am glad.

"By the way, what did you do during that service? I felt so strange. I imagined that I was setting out on a journey, but didn't know where to. I'm not particularly religious and couldn't understand why so many people in hospital asked for a chaplain.

"That day, something happened to me and now I do think that there is some divine presence. I felt it then but can't really explain it. You know, don't you? You said at the beginning that I was going to have to attend to medical matters.

"I was frightened about that and am still very apprehensive. I patched up the cuts and grazes of all the people as well as I could. I did the same for the sheep Most of the injuries were only minor and would have healed up anyway.

"I wish I could have done something for Mary, but that would have needed greater skills than mine. Still, it hurts me that I couldn't help her at all."

"I don't suppose that a good doctor could have done much better under the circumstances. I'm sure that you helped in many ways, if only by your presence You are a very brave girl. I take my hat off to you. You see, you have already started on your journey.

"You will have to attend to anyone who is sick or injured and you won't be able to help yourself. You will learn from everyone you treat far quicker than you would have done in the hospital because you will not have a doctor to refer to.

"You said that you were not religious, but you were aware that something happened to you the other day. That was the Holy Spirit giving you a little push

I knew He was present. I always do. All I did was to ask Him to make you all aware of Him. Eileen and Jimmy experienced something.

"Nick doesn't know yet, but the Spirit touched him as well and is working on him as He does with all of us. You watch Nick and you will see him wrestling with his emotions often in the near future. I think that will apply to all the others, as in everyone there is a battle between good and evil.

"Evil can only be conquered with God's help and He is always ready to give it. So before you have to make an important medical decision, just ask God. If you have time, pray hard. If the situation is desperate, say, 'Please help me, God.'

"Remember, also that God gives, but the Devil takes. God's help is there for the asking. The Devil will only help to further his own evil purpose. That is why many people are bothered and depressed when they suddenly realise God's presence.

"The depression come when the Devil tries to stop them from turning to God. He knows that those who turn to God completely are lost to him for ever. I know that you will experience this, so put your trust in God."

"You're right. I already have. I felt really frightened about having to do all the medical work and I am still very worried about it. I know I need help but don't know how to get it. Can you tell me what to do?"

Believer stopped walking, looked at her and said, "The Spirit is here now. I felt Him while I was talking and you have asked me for help. I can't help on my own but I can ask God for His assistance now. Kneel down and pray for help now.

"Pray quietly in your mind for a moment and I will add a prayer for you. While you are making your silent prayer, I shall be praying for help for me. When you are ready, look up."

Paula knelt on the wet ground and made her silent prayer. When she looked up, Believer laid his hands on her head and said, "Lord God our Father in Heaven. Your Spirit is here with us now. Permit Him to enter this woman and give her courage to carry out the tasks she will come across from time to time. She has some medical knowledge. Make her also a spiritual healer.

"Give her the power to ease the suffering of the sick and injured in mind or body. Give her also the confidence that comes with the knowledge of your love. I ask this in the name of Jesus, your son who died for us on Calvary."

Believer then lifted the girl to her feet and stood looking at her, saying nothing. Paula was silent for a good half minute, then she said, "Did you say that you felt a tingling sensation in your scalp whenever the Spirit was present? I felt it when you put your hands on my head, very strongly, less now, but it's still there.

"Now I know what you mean and I will pray often in future. I understand about the help you said I would get. I was sceptical, but no longer."

Believer lifted his head and said, "Thank you, Lord." Then to Paula. "Happier now? Shall we carry on? We have a lot of ground to cover and we will have to search every building which is still partially standing to see what we can find in the way of medicines. I asked God to aid us in our search before we left, and now it is up to us."

In the first small village they came to, their attention was attracted by a swarm of flies around a partially damaged hut. On entering, they found the body of a woman who had not been dead very long. Paula found a bullet wound in the woman's leg which had turned septic.

It was obvious that the woman had been unable to walk any further and had been left there to die. There was no trace of any empty food container or any water.

"Paula," Believer said. "Do you think that you could have done anything for her if she had been brought to you?"

"Perhaps, I think she is one of those who attacked our village. I thought that some had been wounded. What sort of people could leave anyone to die like this? Alone with no food. They must have a poor regard for human life.

"I wish they had left her with us. At least, Mary didn't die alone, like this. This is terrible."

"Agreed," Believer said. "That is why I must speak to people like this. Why I can't stay here with you very long. I must find her companions and try to change their outlook. Now I know roughly which direction they have gone, that gives me a heading.

"We must pray for this poor woman and try to bury her. Lord, accept the soul of this poor woman who passed away alone and without friends. Hear us as we remember those who have died in the faith of Christ and also those who did not know you. According to your promises, grant us, with them a share in your eternal kingdom."

The small outbuilding in which they had found the dead woman had been used to store garden tools and Believer was lucky enough to find a spade. He used the to dig a shallow grave, and he and Paula lowered the body into it using an o blanket to cover her. Then Believer said the words of the funeral service which he took from The Alternative Service book. This book was the only thing besides his Bible that he had left in his rucksack at the start of this day's expedition.

When the service was completed, Believer looked round and found an almost complete slate from one of the roofs. He scratched deeply on the slate the words. 'Here lies the body of an unknown woman who was left to die by her companions in misfortune. God has taken her and she is no longer alone.'

Then he pushed the slate into the soft soil of the newly dug grave and the pair continued their search for the medical supplies which they had set out to find.

Paula said, "Why did you bury her when there are so many others left around? Why did you leave that epitaph? The words made me cry."

"I know they did. The intention is to make those who left her think a little about what they have done. You must realise that I cannot bury every dead body that I come across. That young lady has died since the holocaust which caused so many other deaths.

"In the circumstances, which could have been avoided, no one did anything for her. We, who came along not long afterwards could at least do something any Christian should do if it is humanly possible. I wonder how long she lay there alone. She has only been dead about two days and if she was at your village, she may well have been here a week or more.

"Whether her companions stayed here for a while, we have no means of knowing. I felt that we must do something. The important thing is the Christian burial, not so much the actual interment. We have asked for God's protection for her soul because there was no one else."

Paula replied, "We did what we could for the dead we found in the village. We put them all in the cellar of an old house that was totally destroyed, then we filled it in with rubble. Some were completely incinerated, but we buried all we could find, Nick's wife and Tammy's mother among them.

"Those were the ones we could move from buildings that were not completely destroyed. Why were the bombs so powerful? Also, why did so many die instantly?"

"I don't know all the answers to that one. We have been misled by politicians for years because they were too scared to tell us just how powerful the weapons were. The two that were dropped on Hiroshima and Nagasaki were only one kiloton strength.

"I remember people talking about one thousand Kiloton bombs and obviously they would cause so much more destruction, which has been proven.

"The shock wave would have killed a great many that the heat flash missed. The lack of oxygen after the fires would have accounted for many more. A lot of deaths resulted from the collapse of buildings as you have seen. Most of the survivors were in stout older buildings made of stone, not brick.

"Although, I was outside at the time, I was extremely lucky, if you can call it that. I was sheltered behind a large vehicle and in a dip where the flash mostly passed over me. Obviously, God wanted me alive so that I could do what I am doing now, helping other survivors wherever I can.

"These are not happy times and we all have our own griefs to bear. I try to bring hope where and when I can."

"I think you are wonderful. You never seem to stop helping and we were all getting desperate before you came. We had no hope for any future and had given up hope of an organised rescue. Now we can see a chance and we have all worked together much better.

"We are actually doing something for the future instead of waiting for someone to come and relieve us. Our rescue was not the military we hoped for it was a man and a boy with no food to give us. Nothing but a message. What message that was, you told us that God is our solution and it seems that you are right. Where are the armed forces? What happened to them?"

Believer said, "The military bases were all prime targets. In any case, who would give them orders. All the big cities have gone. We have a situation where there have been massive explosions all around us.

"All the country areas have been surrounded by fire storms and the like. What do you think that Salisbury plain is like? I doubt if there are any survivors there at all.

"All the military bases would have been blasted out. Places like Catterick and Portsmouth. All the air fields have gone. Poor old England never stood a chance. I imagine that the destruction is pretty worldwide with possibly some parts of Africa, South America and Asia the safest places.

"We are here and we must make the best of things. This time, we must make it work. There are too few of us left to survive another major war. This is the last ever chance for mankind. If we don't obey God's laws, then there is nothing to live for.

"We have had so many chances in history and we have thrown them all away. We can't do it again. Either we live in harmony with co-operation or we are extinct.

"That is God's task for me. There must be others as I can't do everything. I hope to leave at least one person to carry on with what I have done in each community I visit. In your group, that is Eileen for as long as she is able.

"Allyson was the person in the last group. I believe I have mentioned that she has a spinning wheel. You should bear that in mind if you ever manage to get a flock going and I shall make sure that you know where to find her when I leave."

During this discussion, the pair had moved near to the centre of the village. They came to the ruins of a small general store. This was an old building as was common in the villages. It had generally survived the blast but had been ransacked for food and many other useful items, probably by the group that had left the young woman to die.

There were, however, a quantity of medicines and other sanitary items, and Believer loaded his rucksack with all that they could find. They then carried on searching all of the buildings it was possible to enter, finding quantities of aspirin and paracetamol.

Also, some prescribed medicines like anti-biotics. Some items of food were found in the houses. These were mostly things like rice and other dry goods that were kept in containers. Flour, salt and dried fruit.

Believer and Paula took as many as they could carry. All the canned goods had been removed before they had arrived but the dry goods were a find not to be missed since they would provide some variation of their frugal diet.

Before they left the village, Believer insisted that they put some of the dry goods that they could not carry in the shop in a prominent position. He said that as God had provided this food, they should try to help others and supplies such as these might save a valuable life. Still, he reasoned that any finder should not benefit without knowing that they were being helped by God.

He scribbled a note which he left with the food. The note read:

'This food has been left here in the name of God in order that it might be used by someone in desperate need. If your need is not desperate, please leave it for those less fortunate than yourselves. God loves us all and will provide for all our needs. Trust in Him. Signed: Believer.'

221

Paula said, "Do you really think that anyone will take notice of that?"

Believer's reply was, "Perhaps, maybe not immediately, but I hope that they will read it. If they do, it will be in their minds and one day, they may remember what the message says. They might even tell someone else. Somewhere, somebody might take note of its content.

"When that happens, the Spirit will be active and just maybe, that person will listen to the call. I have to hope that this will be so or I am a hypocrite.

"If by leaving some food for someone, I have made them think of God, I will have done all that 1 can do without personal contact."

"What a marvellous philosophy," Paula said. "I wish I could be like that."

"You are, you know. Why did you join the nursing service? Take the young woman we buried today. Assuming that she was one of the people who attacked your village, what if she had been left with you? Wouldn't you, as a nurse, tried to remove the bullet?

"Might not that have prevented a needless death? If you would not have tried, you are not the person I think you are. I know that you would have done everything you could have done. I do not have your medical skills, I have to do things differently.

"I am no better than you and please don't ever forget that. I try to do God's work in any way that I can. You will do it so much better than me if you can save lives. Do what you do in the name of God and you will find that, really, you are no different from me.

"We just have a different role to perform. Come on, Doctor Paula, we must start back or the rest will all eat without us. We've not finished yet, we have a little hunting to do on the way back."

The pair retraced their steps and Believer managed to shoot a couple of rabbits on the way. Paula carried the rabbits as Believer was now carrying the heavy rucksack. She was silent most of the way back. She was thinking deeply about what had happened during the day.

She, like everyone else who met him, found herself greatly influenced by her companion. She had the feeling that the journey she had thought herself beginning, during the service Believer had held, was now firmly on its way, with the first steps well and truly taken.

Believer had called her Doctor Paula from the first meeting. Now, after the prayer Believer had said for her during their outward trip, she felt that she could begin to face the responsibilities thrust upon her. So far, she had on administered first aid to a few minor injuries and apart from Nick's wife, had not encountered any serious illness or injury she would be required to deal with.

She knew in her heart that she had been unable to do anything for Mary or that it was unlikely that the woman could have been saved even with more skilled attention.

As to the woman she and Believer had buried. The wound she had seen did not seem to have been fatal in itself. Death had been due to aggravation and infection brought about by her attempting to walk with the bullet still embedded.

She realised that if she had been given the opportunity, she would have made an attempt to remove the bullet and, perhaps the woman may have recovered.

By the time the pair had returned to the village, the other party had preceded them. They reported having seen another sheep roaming wild, but on this occasion, had been unable to catch it. Jimmy and his two girl companions had been primarily concerned with obtaining enough food for the day, so they would not undertake an extended chase for the sheep and neither did they get close enough to determine its sex.

Since it had horns, there was a strong possibility that it was a ram. Believer said that he hoped so.

He suggested that Jason should go out with Jimmy and one of the girls to try to capture it. They should make this the prime reason for their next day's excursion, only bothering to hunt when they had succeeded in their purpose.

He, Believer, would take care of the hunting which should not be too difficult as Jimmy and the two girls had brought back sufficient for the day. Believer's two rabbits were surplus to today's requirements.

Eileen and Tawny were delighted that Believer had brought back the dry foods. They found that the commodities like rice and spaghetti were most useful. The meal they all shared that evening was quite enhanced. Believer and Paula had, in addition to the full rucksack, filled their pockets and so had been able to bring back quite a quantity.

During the meal, Paula told the rest of the group about the events of the day and how Believer had buried the woman they had found. When Eileen heard about this, she asked whether he would be prepared to hold a service over the cellar where the group had buried the village dead. Believer said that he would do that willingly. The best time, he said would be before the group's evening meal, providing that both hunting parties had returned.

After the meal and general discussion, which was now accepted as normal practice, the group split up to go to their separate shelters. Believer and Jimmy went off with Nick and Christine as usual.

Nick said to Believer, "Chris and I have had a lot of conversations while we have been working on the building. We have made a decision about our future together. We have suffered like everyone else and I have only recently buried my wife.

"Perhaps, it is too soon but we think that we would like to get married if it is at all possible. We have both experienced mutual attraction and we want to share all our troubles, whatever life throws at us."

Believer thought for a minute. "If that is your decision, then I am happy for you. I am an Anglican by religion, but I don't believe in divorce. I believe in the part of the service which says, 'Those whom God have joined, let no man put asunder.'

"I hold the view that divorce is not a solution to problems in marriage. Marriage is a partnership which requires three things, love, trust and commitment. In the first place, you must love each other. Then you must trust each other.

"You must have commitment from both sides and willingness to discuss any problems between you. You should both share the effort to live together in harmony.

"Are you both sure that this is what you want to do for the rest of your lives? Things are alright between you now, but are you both prepared to share your companionship in old age when one or the other of you might be feeble? Are you also prepared to nurse the other if either is sick?

"Because, in my book, that is what marriage is about. Sex is secondary to that, although it plays a large part. Suppose, for instance that one or the other does not feel like sex for a while. What would your reactions be?

"There should be no forcing or bullying if this should happen. No splitting up just because sex has lost its appeal. I am only interested in helping you if you are both prepared for the other and more important aspects of marriage. Loving companionship and support when things go wrong."

Nick replied, "These are some of the things we have talked about, not the sexual aspects, but how we feel about each other. How we like to just be together as much as possible. We have shared our grief together and literally cried on each other's shoulders.

"We have already decided that sex is not the most important thing in our lives. We have, of course, consoled ourselves with sex, but only when we have both felt like it."

"Good, that is what I wanted to hear. What about you, Christine? Do you feel the same way about Nick? He has done all the talking so far. Are you in complete agreement?"

Chris said, "Yes, I was really hysterical when I came into the village. I thought at first, that it was just the factory, but when I saw all those wrecked vehicles and the burnt countryside and then the village, I wanted to run away. Nick came out from where he had been sheltering with the others and quietened me down.

"I don't know how he could do that. I found out later that his wife had died in his arms the day before. Actually, he told me to shut up or I would set off all the others again.

"He had already spent the night with a lot of people who were in tears and didn't want to go through the day like it. I hated him for that, but Paula told me about Nick's wife and I realised that we were all in the same boat.

"My regard for Nick grew as I watched him looking after everyone else and when we split up into smaller groups, I moved in with him. I took a lot of stick from Shirley and Emma, but only until you came and they are so different now. Anyway, will you give us your blessing, at least."

"What do you really want?"

"A marriage," said Nick. "Or something like it."

"I will carry out a wedding service and sign some sort of certificate in the presence of God and all the people. I will do this if you want it, but you both must realise that an ordained priest might not recognise the marriage. If one should come along, you should discuss the matter with him.

"Some will say that I am some sort of charlatan, but I am only doing this because I believe that God expects it of me or the situation would not arise. On the practical side, it won't be a fantastic wedding with cakes and a reception or even a lovely bridal dress. Just a service carried out in the name of Jesus to join you two together as you have asked.

"All here will be present, I hope, but as I expect to leave here soon, when do you suggest that I do it? Perhaps, just before I go, then I will be remembered with happy memory.

"My last parting was a sad one for everyone involved. I had to leave four people I had come to love and I can tell you, that was one of the most difficult decisions of my life, but it was not really my decision. Others needed me and still do.

"Your group were amongst that category. You needed me for a while, but now you should be able to manage. As I told you, my name is now Believer and that is how l shall sign the certificate. Are you in agreement with this? I can't do any better."

Nick and Christine looked at each other in the failing light, then Nick said, "If you will do what we have asked, we will consider ourselves married in every respect. You will have done us a great honour and favour in addition to all the other things you have done for us."

"I haven't done anything really, have I? You have done it, not me, I have only made a few suggestions."

"Yes, but without you, we would now be completely out of food. There wasn't much left. Most of it burnt up or went bad before we could eat it. You showed us how we could survive and we have succeeded so far. We even have an emergency supply.

"You've given us hope more than anything and now, most of us believe in God to some extent. That is more than before you came and probably before th bombs fell for some of us. We have all seen God working through you. Thos you have spoken to particularly have felt inspired.

"I speak for me and I know Chris feels the same. Emma and Shirley are muc nicer and Paula seems much more confident now. Mind you, she was pretty goo the first day. She worked so hard and I know she was crying all the time."

"You know what was wrong with the two girls, don't you? Because of the work and training, they felt that they had nothing to offer. They felt pret useless. Now, they are contributing to the welfare of you all. They had time feel jealous and resentful. Not now though, because they have a worthwh task."

By this time, it was almost completely dark and Jimmy had already gone sleep. Believer joined him in the room they shared and lay down. He didn't sle very much at first. He was mulling over the implication of his conversations w Nick and Christine and with Eileen.

He spent time in private prayer followed by serious consideration of the fo of service to use for the memorial service Eileen had asked for. The propo wedding posed few problems as this was laid out in The Alternative Service Book and The Book of Common Prayer, both of which he had a copy.

Day Fifty-Four

As usual, the hunting parties set off split into two groups. Jimmy and Emma took Jason with them on this occasion as their primary mission was to try to capture the second sheep that Jimmy and Emma had seen the day before.

Believer and Shirley went off to hunt, but as Believer had brought back two extra rabbits the day before, the urgency was not so great and the hunting did not take as long as usual. The pair were able to return sooner and were able to go in search of the other three to give them any assistance that was needed.

The animal had been cropping newly grown grass in a field which still was almost surrounded by the remains of a dry-stone wall. It was avoiding capture by the simple means of moving away from Jimmy and his two companions whenever they came near it. Believer suggested that they all worked together and spent some time blocking up all the entrances of the field except one.

They achieved this by using any pieces of debris they could find. The last entrance they only partially blocked and Believer hid behind the wall armed with a rope with a slip noose.

Jimmy, Jason and Emma, now assisted by Shirley, spread out in the field beyond the sheep and moved towards it. This made the animal uneasy and it moved slowly towards Believer at the restricted gate. Finally, there was nowhere else for it to go except through the gate and Believer was able to slip the rope around its neck.

The beast put up a terrific battle before the others could come to Believer's assistance and fought all the way back to the village. In consequence they returned amongst a great deal of hilarity.

When they had all returned and secured the animal, they cleaned themselves up and Believer gathered all the group together near the spot where the casualties of the village had been buried. He carried out a moving memorial service and finished the event with the hymn 'Abide With Me'. He was thanked by the group as a whole. Most of the women shed tears during the service, but they were all grateful that it had been done.

Eileen and Tammy started preparing a communal meal and Believer spent some time talking to them while they were working. He said to Eileen, "You could have carried out that service, you know. I only said a few prayers. I didn't do anything special."

Later, when the meal was over, Believer addressed the whole group, "Today, at your request, I carried out a service of memorial to those who passed away in this village. Tomorrow, there will be a happier event. Nick and Christine have decided that they would like to be married. After all, they are almost married anyway.

"They have asked me to conduct the service, which I shall be most pleased to do. I hope that you will all attend and wish them a long, happy and comforting life together. I don't know whether there will be any children, that is in God's hands. I don't even know if that is what they want, but their union is primarily for love and mutual comfort.

"They and you have worked very hard to keep yourselves together as a community and I know that Nick and Chris will continue in their good work. They will need all the support that you can give them. They have decided on a religious ceremony and in the absence of any ordained priest, I will conduct the service. I hope that everybody will be present and witness the union.

"I would like to say that I hope that there will be another union in the village. Thanks to the efforts of Jimmy, Jason and big Emma with some small assistance from Shirley and myself, we now have a ram and a ewe. This is the basis of a flock.

"I think we should all pray now that both will be fertile and lambs will be born to them. I am sure that God would not have allowed us to find them if He did not intend us to benefit, but I think that you will need more ewes in the future.

"You should think about the possibility of meeting another group who have managed to get hold of other animals, and inter breed yours with theirs and share the offspring or arrange some system of barter so that both groups benefit. Allyson, who I was with before, has a spinning wheel and she will be able to help you process the fleeces when you manage to shear them. I suspect that Eileen and Allyson can knit, perhaps some of you other ladies are handy that way. If so, you might well get some new clothes for the future."

"We've already started," Eileen said. 'We have saved all the rabbit skins and we will try to process them for winter clothing. The feathers we get will make good insulation for bed clothes and lining for clothes as well."

"Good for you. Everything you can use like that may save a life. Don't waste anything. Even the smallest things may be of use. Things like rabbit bones can be used for needles if you can't find enough steel ones. It wouldn't be a bad idea to make some anyway while you still have steel ones to make the eyes.

"As for thread, any old clothes made with manmade fibres will provide that. They can be pulled apart. It is nice to see you coming up with ideas of your own. They are all valuable. If any of you get an idea, talk it over with the rest of the group and you can decide on the best way to implement it."

At the end of the evening, Believer spoke with Nick and Christine about the forthcoming ceremony and during the course of the conversation, he warned them and Jimmy that he would depart after the service.

"Jimmy, do you still want to come with me?" he asked. "You realise that nothing will be easy and there will be some danger. If you feel that you want to stay here, I'm sure that Nick won't shoot at you anymore, but if he is willing, I won't force you to come with me.

"Here you will have reasonable comfort, with me you will have to sleep in all sorts of places, and will never know from one day to the next where you will be."

Nick spoke up and added, "You will be welcome. You and Believer have done so much for us and I'm sorry that I shot at you before. I suppose that I was only thinking of myself and this community then and didn't know what sort of a contribution you could make. We will find a place for you if you wish to stay.

"I am only sorry that Believer has to go as well. I know that he said that you both wouldn't stay here long, but we will all miss him. Believer, you are sure you don't want to stay? There will always be a place for you and we won't forget what you've done here."

Jimmy said, "Thank you, Nick, but I think I will go with Believer. I can see what he wants to do and I want to be part of it. Besides, he has a lot to teach me and I want to be like him when I'm older. Excuse me, please, I must go and pack my things."

"He's a brave lad, that one, even if he is small for his age. He will do you proud. Look after him well, won't you and if either of you come this way again will you please drop in and see us."

They said good night and Believer went to the room he shared with Jimmy to pray and prepare himself for the wedding he was to perform the next day.

Day Fifty-Five

Believer awoke at first light as usual. He went to Nick and roused him. "Today is your big day. As I said last night, I am going to perform a marriage ceremony between you and Chris if you still want it. You realise that it will only be a basic ceremony, no lavish reception afterwards.

"There is another matter which you should be the first to know. Jimmy and I will leave immediately after the service. As you will be starting your honeymoon, such as it is, and we are sharing your shelter now, it seems right that we leave then."

Nick replied, "I could see this coming. I thought that you would do that. We shall miss you very much, and Jimmy too. You brought us from feeling very sorry for ourselves to a new hope. We were hoping that we should be rescued, perhaps by the military.

"Now we've seen that the only rescue we can expect is by our own actions. We have to look after ourselves because there is no one to do it for us. Above all, you have shown us how to survive and given us a belief that someone is looking after us. How soon will you want to leave?"

"As soon as the service is finished. I will go and ask Tony if he would like to give the bride away. He brought her here so perhaps he should do the honours. Will you ask Pete to be Best Man? There doesn't seem to be any choice.

"I think that we should try to be as traditional as possible. The only major thing that can't be done is to call the Banns, but everyone here knows your situation and I doubt whether there is anyone who could raise any objection anyway."

Believer and Nick went to arouse the rest of the community and they assembled by ones and twos in the old barn. Tony had agreed to give the bride away and Pete was glad to be chosen as Best Man.

Believer looked around and noted that Shirley and Emma were missing as well as Christine and Tony. He was a little worried about this because he had thought that the two younger girls had made their peace with Christine. Since they had decided to keep to tradition as much as possible, the bride had arranged to arrive later than the rest.

She was to be escorted by Tony, but when they arrived, Believer was pleasantly surprised to see that Christine had asked Shirley and Emma to serve as Bridesmaids. The girls had spent a little time collecting what flowers they could find quickly and had presented Christine with a bouquet of sorts.

Believer followed the service as printed in The Alternative Service Book he had brought with him and the group sang appropriate hymns as well as they could. Then he arranged for a certificate to be made out on a piece of paper that Tammy produced. Everyone signed the certificate because they had all witnessed that ceremony, they all wanted to be part of it, and Believer said it was a good idea.

The service had been the first task of the day, and for the wedding breakfast, Eileen and Tammy produced a meal from what supplies they had. Tony, Pete and Nick made suitable speeches as far as possible and afterwards, Believer stood up and said, "Today has been a happy occasion for us all. I would like you to continue in whatever celebration you can manage. However, there is one sad note.

"As you all know, I promised that I would carry out this wedding for Nick and Chris before I left. This I have done and Jimmy and I have to go on to new challenges. I want to thank you all for the welcome you gave me when I arrived but now, I feel that you can cope without me.

"If I stay, it will mean another mouth to feed so now I will say my goodbye. Jimmy has elected to come with me and I hope that you will remember us with friendship. Remember also that you have a friend who can do far more for you than I ever could.

"Before I go there is one thing I would like you to do. That is to promise greet all whom you meet with a message of peace and give them friendship unless they show animosity towards you."

The community were silent for a few moments, then Nick stood up, "Friends I knew before you that Believer planned to leave. I wish that there was something we could give him. He arrived here with next to nothing and will leave with just what he brought with him. What has he given us?

"You all know exactly what his arrival has meant to us. Life. Without influence, we should be without food by now. He showed us the way to l without the fear of starvation we had before.

"He has given us hope and love and changed our personalities. The proof of that is shown by Emma and Shirley agreeing to be Chris's Bridesmaids. Can you imagine them doing that before?

"He proved that we can live and carry out our own survival, which we have started. I think the biggest gift to him would be for us to carry on with the actions he made us start. We should make the promise he asked of us now and pray that we are strong enough to keep it. Believer, I make a promise in front of all the witnesses here that I shall do my best to live in peace from now on."

Tony stood up, "I would like to add my promise to Nick's, but I think that we all ought to make it together. All agreed?"

"We promise," the rest of the group said in unison.

Believer and Jimmy left to complete their packing. When they came out of the building where they had been staying, they were surprised to find the whole community waiting outside. He called Nick to him and gave him detailed instructions on how to find Allyson, then he said to the group, "May the Lord keep you in peace and love and may His blessing be with you now and for evermore."

He and Jimmy shook hands with them all in turn, picked up their rucksacks and turned to face their next challenge. They looked back to wave just as they went out of sight. Nick and his group settled down to carry on with their lives. Nick and his new bride went to carry on with the building task they had set themselves.

A rather odd way to spend a honeymoon. Emma and Shirley started out on their hunting trip and the rest were left to go about their self-elected tasks feeling a sense of great loss intermixed with a new hope.

Believer and Jimmy headed in the direction Believer had taken with Paula and passed the grave of the young woman Believer had buried. They spent the rest of the day travelling, stopping only to hunt and cook food. They found a sheltered spot to pitch their tent and settled down to sleep just as the light was fading.

Day Fifty-Six

Believer and Jimmy had spent a fitful night after taking leave of Nick's group. Their rest was disturbed in the small hours of the morning by the sound of distant gunfire. They listened for a while, then on Believer's insistence, they packed up their belongings as quickly as possible.

The two travellers started to walk in the direction of the shooting. Believer's intention was to try to stop any conflict he found, and as usual, he had prayed for guidance before deciding on the action he felt he had to take.

The firing had been fierce when they had first heard it. As they walked towards the noise, it gradually diminished until there was only an occasional shot.

Believer said to Jimmy, "It sounds as if there has been an attack which has been repulsed. There is only the odd shot now. This suggests to me that once the attack proved unsuccessful it degenerated into a holding action. We must stop i altogether if we can, but it will be dangerous as both sides are likely to turn or us.

"When we find out what is happening, I want you to stay in the backgroun with our kit. If anything happens to me, I want you to go back to Nick and giv him the news. I need to know that you will do this as I will have enough to do o my own account, and I don't want to worry about you. Promise me that you wi do as I say."

Jimmy looked worried but he agreed and they approached until they coul see a few people in sheltered positions armed with rifles. They were firir occasionally towards a large ruined building from which fire was returne whenever one of the attackers showed themselves to the opposition.

Between the attacking force and the building there was a small stream wi fairly high bank and a Ha-Ha wall on one side, and Believer told Jimmy that intended to use the cover the stream provided so that he could place hims between the antagonists. He impressed on Jimmy that the boy was to ke himself out of sight. He told Jimmy to watch what happened and if Believer was killed or injured, Jimmy was to leave only when he considered himself to be safe.

Believer then took a roundabout route and dropped into the shallow stream some distance away from the scene of the fighting. He worked his way through the water to a point immediately between the two groups. He paused to collect his thoughts and to pray that he be given the courage and strength to carry out the task he had set himself.

When he was ready, he shouted in the loudest voice he could the words. "In the name of God, haven't you done enough killing. Stop your shooting now.' He paused again and then climbed up onto the bank.

"Who are you, old man?" one of the attacking party shouted. "Why don't you go away before you get shot."

"I have come to bring peace and to show you how you can live with each other."

"We don't need your sort here. We take what we want and we shoot anyone who gets in our way."

"Then I suspect that you will shoot me in the end any way. In that event, perhaps you will first hear what I have to say. As you see, I am unarmed. I have no need for arms to protect me. I have God's protection. It will only be by His will that I will be killed. In that case, I will have served His purpose."

"What a load of old rubbish. God is dead, if he ever existed at all. I think I will shoot you now."

"Go ahead, pull that trigger if you dare. I told you that I am under God's protection. If it is His will that I live, then you will be unsuccessful. I do not know the consequences to you if I am right. I am not afraid of the outcome.

"I know that I will be welcomed by Him if I die. Will you? God sent me here to intercede. It is only by His will that I am here at all. I could so easily have died with all the rest, but He kept me alive. For what?

"If you kill me now, it will be a waste of all His efforts so far. No, I don't think you will shoot. You people in the house! Can you see and hear me?"

The answer came, "Yes, we can."

"Good, because what I say applies to both groups. The problem is that it is very hard to shout all the time. I want to talk to both the leaders, but obviously, neither of you trusts the other so I shall have to meet each in turn.

"I ask that you trust me. If you wish, I will remain in full view of you both while I am talking, but I can't communicate property at this distance. I am now going to move towards the people outside."

Believer walked slowly towards the leader of the attacking group and stopped just in front of him so that he could still be seen from the house. He said quietly, "I'm still here and you haven't shot me yet. Are you still determined to get rid of me? I am not quite so easy to dispose of, am I?

"My name is Believer because that is what I am. God has kept me alive so far and He has made me believe in Him as never before. I know that He is there, just as I know that He won't let you harm me unless it is His will."

"Alright, you're here. Now tell me what you want."

"It's not what I want, it's what God wants and to some extent, what you want as well."

"What do you mean by that? what I want."

"Well, you can't tell me that this life you are leading is what you want to do long term. You said that you took what you want. Where does that get you? I presume that you think that the people in the house have something you want. They have. The means of your future survival. In the same way, you have the means of their future. Shooting them is only a short-term measure. What was it that you were trying to get from them? Food? Shelter? They probably haven't got much of either. Then what do you do, go and kill someone else?

"Let me ask you a question. How many people have you lost so far? People who get shot at tend to shoot back and I suspect that that has already happened.'

"We've lost three. The last one was Sue, about ten days ago. She was shot in the leg and couldn't walk any further. We had to leave her."

"A red headed girl about 25 with blue jeans and a red anorak?"

"That's her. Is she alright?"

"I found her two days ago and buried her where you left her. I buried her with as much Christian dignity as I could. She died alone in fear and unnecessarily.

"She could have been saved if you had left her where she was shot. You see I know the people you attacked. All they wanted was to be rescued but you had a different idea, didn't you?"

"Thank you for doing what you could for her, but what do you mean, about her being saved?"

"If you hadn't brought her away, she would have had some sort of skilled medical attention and probably would not have had the infection which killed her. Is that the way you want to end up? I doubt it, but that is the way you will go if you keep up the life you have now.

"At the moment, you are attacking some people in the house there. They have guns, as you do. If you carry on the way you are going, you, all of you, will die in some lonely spot. Perhaps the death will be quick.

"Not like Sue's, slow, lonely and afraid. More than likely, you will die slowly of injury, disease or starvation. You will go one by one until you are all dead.

"There is another way. Whatever your attitude towards other people, you could help the human race to survive. You could provide a useful contribution to all of the remnants of mankind, although, I doubt whether the people in the house will want to trust you. You could help each other instead of killing and taking. What have they got that you want anyway?"

"Food, mostly, we are getting desperate. We have been fighting for food, taking what we've won and then going to find someone else and robbing them."

Believer shook his head. "I can't understand what you hoped to achieve. Don't you realise that there will come a time when no one has anything left. What do you propose to do then?

"The last group I was with had a similar idea, but they didn't go round robbing others, they were trying to live by scavenging and they came up with the same problem.

"Before that, I met someone who just waited to be rescued. Neither plan had any hope of success. There is only one way to ultimate survival. That way involves everyone who is left.

"We must all work together and find ways of producing food. Each group should try to provide for their own food but co-operate with others for assistance when it is needed. There will be no rescue from any official source and there is no future in robbery either.

"I don't know how many there are in your group, but all of you can do something to provide for yourselves. The same applies to the crowd in the house. Perhaps you can work together.

"I have visited two groups of people who were self-sufficient when I left. I want to say the same about you and the others up there when the time comes for me to go to someone else."

"There's four of us left and one of them is injured, he was shot yesterday. That's why we've got to sort out that lot in the house. They can't go around hurting my mates like that and get away with it."

"You aren't much of a one for listening, are you? You seem to think that it's natural to go round shooting at people. Idiots like you caused this mess in the first place. It's because politicians stopped talking and decided to use the big stick that millions of people have died.

"You want to keep up the killing when you should be trying to find a way of permanent survival. You are too cowardly to try any other way. It's only because you think you can beat the people up there that you would dare to try.

"It was a different story when you got Sue killed, wasn't it? The people you met were too strong for you, otherwise you wouldn't have left. Don't let poor Sue's death be in vain. Stop the killing now."

"I suppose you have a point, but it's not fair to blame me for all of this. I didn't drop the bombs, did I?"

"Only because you didn't have the opportunity. Your present actions show that you want to take anything you want by force. How does that make you any different to those who sent us the bombs?

"Whoever they are, they didn't get their way so they went to war instead. Isn't that just what you are doing now, but on a smaller scale. Yes, I do blame you and others like you. You are just continuing the war and helping those who dropped the bombs.

"They wanted to destroy our society and you are just completing what they started. Help defeat the warmongers and stop killing. There is no future in anyway."

"Alright, I'll give it a try. One thing bothers me though, a while ago, you dared me to pull the trigger. You seemed to say that something terrible would happen to me if I did. What would have happened? You implied that I would struck by lightning or something. You said that God was protecting you."

"He is, isn't he? You didn't fire because He made you listen. If God wants me to do his work. He is not going to let me get killed unless my death would serve His purpose.

"That being the case, if He wants me to live and you had pulled that trigger something would have happened to protect me. You would have missed or the rifle would have misfired, anything, I don't know what.

"If I had been meant to die, so what. I would go to join all my loved ones, but you would have been affected by my death somehow, and God's will would be done in any case."

"What do we do now? I'll agree to stop the attack on the house for now. You had better tell me how we can go on from here."

"First, I would like to know who you are. I am Believer. You have someone injured, how bad?"

"Steve is the one who got shot. They got him in the shoulder. Kim is the girl over there, I'm Brian and the other one is Mark. You know who we are now. What are you going to do about it?"

"Talking to you is only half the problem. I would like to try and help Steve, but I don't think it prudent to go out of sight of the people in the house. They have probably been watching me all the time, but they can't see you. If I go out of sight, I might get shot or at least, hostilities will start again.

"In that case, I would have wasted all my time talking. What I suggest is that you make your mate as comfortable as possible and let me go and try to talk to the people in the house. I have to persuade them that you won't shoot anymore, and then perhaps, I can bring you together. Only then can we talk about surviving."

Brian agreed and Believer told him that he would go and talk to the group in the house. He said that he would remain in sight as he had when he had been talking to Brian. Then he turned and walked towards the house.

He crossed the stream by a small bridge near where he had first made himself seen. He took great care to keep himself in sight of the occupants of the house and when he came within speaking distance, he stopped and introduced himself. He asked the defenders if they were prepared to talk to him and received an affirmative answer.

"My name is Believer. I have a task imposed upon me to do my best to prevent any further bloodshed wherever I happen to be. As you will have seen, I am unarmed and I intend to remain in sight of the others out there. This is to gain their trust. I hope I can gain yours.

"It is obvious to me that you have been attacked by them and I understand that you will have a great deal of resentment towards them. They have agreed to hold their fire until I have spoken to you. Now I have to ask you to do something which I know you will find very difficult. I ask you now to regard this as a new period of your life.

"If you want to survive, you all, both parties, have to try to live with some form of co-operation. Somehow you will have to learn to trust each other. I would imagine at this time that you think this is the last thing you could do. They have shown themselves to be some kind of bandit.

"I don't know your circumstances, but as long as you try to defend your lifestyle with guns, then people like that will keep coming. What I realised some time ago is that there is no hope without peace between the remnants of our civilisation. There will be no rescue after this time from anyone in authority. There is no authority left but your own.

"You have been attacked because the folk out there think you have some food that they feel they need. I say to you that unless you work together, both of your groups will disappear one by one. I told this to the others and I believe that they saw my point of view.

"They agreed with me that that is not what they want, and I suspect, neither do you. What I ask of you is to try to put aside any feelings of revenge and animosity.

"Your first thoughts about my proposition will be that you can't forgive or forget what has happened. You probably feel that they are scum who should be eliminated. I would probably feel the same, were I in your shoes. There is help that you can call on if you will listen to me, but you must make the first step yourselves.

"You have to agree to meet before anything can be resolved. If you are prepared to take this first step, I will go back and bring their leader to you. When I return with him, I shall expect one of you to join us outside in full view of both parties. Now, have you anything to say?"

A voice from inside the ruined house said, 'We have heard what you have to say. We have watched you from the moment you first appeared. If you had not shouted from the stream first, you would have been shot. We thought that you were one of them.

"We were amazed when you stood up. First that you would dare to show yourself and then you actually invited them to shoot. How could you do that. know you said something about God.

"We are surprised that you are still here. That took some courage. You are a brave man arid we will agree to talk if you can get the others to comply with your conditions. If you can bring their boss back here unarmed then we'll talk

"Can I have your assurance that you won't shoot. If I have that, I will try.'

"We won't shoot unless they do, go ahead."

Believer turned again and headed back to the attacking group. He arrived at the point where he had spoken and called to Brian, "They have agreed to meet you. Trust has to start somewhere. Are you prepared to come with me, unarmed, just you, Brian, and face that walk up to the house. If you show them trust, they won't shoot."

"How do you know they won't. It would be so easy for them."

"We shall have to reduce the risk then, won't we. Anyway, your risk won't be any more than the risk I took to talk to you in the first place. When I appeared, I could have been shot by either side. I'm still here and you can walk close behind me. If there is any shooting, I will get it first. You must persuade your people not to fire and you should be safe. Are you game?"

"OK, let's get started."

Brian stepped out but was careful to keep Believer between himself and the house, and the pair of them walked slowly back towards the house. Believer said as they walked, "How do you feel, scared? Probably the same as I felt when I first made myself known. I was shaking in my shoes, but it was something I had to try. For your information, I am still nervous and I have been praying all the time."

"You don't show it, you seem full of confidence. I must admit, I am really scared, how do you manage?"

"I told you I pray. I said at the first that I am a believer and if I am that, then I have to trust in God. He has protected me so far and will no doubt carry on doing so."

By this time, they had arrived at the house and were met by a large black man in his forties who stepped out also unarmed.

Believer said, "Hello, this is Brian. Who are you?"

"Barry," was the reply. "Do you think this will work?"

"It must," said Believer. "You are the people who can do it. I can't. You must settle your differences now and start again. Today is the first day of the rest of our lives, so don't waste it, Barry. How many are there in the house?"

"Five, including me."

"Right then, that makes nine of you. You will both find this difficult, but you must pool your resources and work out what each of you can contribute. You will have to hunt for animals and birds to eat and you will have to dig for any vegetables. Forget about radiation.

"God will take care of that. Look! This world has just undergone the most terrible war. You are the few that have been left. I suggest that you think about why you have been chosen. Because chosen you are. With all the many deaths, why are you the ones to be left? God has a purpose for you as He has for me."

Barry said, "What are you, that you feel you have to step in and try to stop the fighting?"

"Me? I suppose that you could call me some form of missionary. I see my task as a mediator between people I meet and between those folk and God. It is my task to replace the clergy who have died. I have to try to bring faith back into a ravished world.

"This is a difficult task as you can imagine. Many people, like Brian here, are not sure that God ever existed at all.

"Everybody who is left has suffered enormous losses and grief. That includes me. I am no different. Like you, my family has all gone. You may think of me as some sort of religious crank. So be it, but besides trying to spread religion, I try to offer practical help.

"Barry, do you have any injured in the house? Brian has one wounded. The first thing we must do together is to try and get some medical attention."

"Yes, two, one is a ten-year-old girl who hurt her leg when she tried to run away. The other, Paul, was shot in the hand."

"In that case, we must send for help as soon as possible. I know where you can get it, but it will take best part of a day unless there is such a thing as a bike around, preferably one for someone about five foot tall. That will save time Brian, what you must do now is to go back to your people.

"Get them to come out and lay their weapons down so that Barry and his friends can see. Then they must all come up here. When they are here, your group, Barry must come out, also unarmed. Then something can be done."

Believer then gave a pre-arranged signal to Jimmy who made himself seen for the first time. "That is Jimmy. He is travelling with me and learning about God at the same time."

Jimmy walked towards the two groups as Brian made his way back to his position. Brian had some difficulty in persuading his group to leave the weapons behind and it was only after a heated argument that they concurred. They made their way back to the house, joined by Jimmy on the way. Steve was in a great deal of pain and was supported by Mark.

Barry waited until he saw that Brian's party had laid down their arms, then he complied with the other part of Believer's instructions. Finally, all the people where gathered together. Sally, the injured child, had been carried out and laid down on the drive.

When both parties were assembled and introductions were made. Barry said that a bicycle was available and Believer thanked him.

"We have a problem. Jimmy and I haven't eaten today and so far, we have nothing. Jimmy has a long ride in front of him which he can't do without eating. I don't like to ask but can either of you provide him with enough for his journey. I will provide for the rest of us."

Barry said, "I have a little to spare, how long will it take him to get back with help?"

"It took us all day yesterday, just to get here, but he will be faster on the bike and I think that Paula will be able to get hold of a bike as well, so he should be back tonight."

Jean, the woman in Barry's party, went back into the house and produced a small tin of luncheon meat and some baked beans which she gave to Jimmy. The boy took it and mounted the bike that Barry had provided for him.

"You know what you have to do, don't you, Jimmy? Go and fetch Doctor Paula and get back here as soon as possible, I saw the odd bike at Nick's place so you should get back by nightfall. Off you go and may God go with you."

Jimmy started his long ride back and Believer turned back to the now extended group. "First, would one of you give me a hand with mine and Jimmy's kit. We left it where Jimmy was hiding."

Mark offered after some discussion and he and Believer walked off, leaving the others talking to each other in an uneasy truce. Believer spoke to Mark about the life they bad been leading and ascertained that this was the band that Eric had fallen foul of much earlier. It turned out that they had another leader at that time.

Eric had disagreed about their methods and an argument ensued. The result was that Eric had fired his gun, more or less in self-defence and had killed the then leader. He had run off and the group had been unable to find him.

Believer said, "I know Eric, I met him and sent him as protector to a woman and three girls. I don't know whether he arrived there, but God told me that he was needed and I believe my prayers have been answered. You see, Mark, everything I do is governed by prayer and I know that this takes some believing.

"Actually, I spend a good deal of my time praying, although it may not be obvious. I am still here and I have faced a few dangers before I got here."

By this time both men had returned carrying the two rucksacks and Believer's air rifle. Mark had queried this when he saw it and was surprised to find that this was the only weapon that Believer and Jimmy possessed apart from cooking utensils.

Believer said, "Steve, would you go and sit with Paul and Sally. There is a task that I must perform before anything else."

He joined the three injured people and examined their injuries. It appeared that Sally had a green stick fracture, and although her leg had been crudely bandaged, no splint had been applied. Believer rectified this defect and turned to the others.

Steve's wound had received no attention at all and Believer asked the two women if they could help and attend to both Steve and Paul. The latter had lost two fingers, but his hand had been bandaged and the blood had stopped flowing.

Having done all that was practical, Believer said, "Lord God, these three persons have received injuries. Please send your healing Spirit to help them. Help them to banish any thoughts of revenge and give your protection to Jimmy and to Paula that they may return here quickly to help you in your healing. I ask this in the name of Jesus Christ, your Son. Amen."

After his prayer, he turned to Barry. "How many habitable rooms do you have in the house. I think that we should all move in. The injured need shelter whichever side they were on. This is the remains of a house big enough to shelter us all and we have to start here with co-operation.

"As to the weapons, do you think you can trust each other not to shoot. suggest the guns should all be unloaded and that one member of each party check those of the opposite group. If you both agree, you will have made a start and will remove some of the tension and the immediate temptation to shoot."

Brian and Barry consulted with their respective followers and an agreement was reached. The two leaders accepted the role of inspecting the weapons and the act was carried out. When this was done to the satisfaction of all, both groups moved into the big house and chose rooms for themselves.

Believer then addressed the problem of food. He asked Mark and Phil accompany him since he felt that by taking one from each side, he could further reduce the tension. By taking both of the fit members and leaving both leaders in charge of the two women and one injured man each, he had left as stable a situation as he could.

The hunting expedition lasted until well into the afternoon and by the time the meal was prepared a degree of harmony existed. Believer insisted that some of the food be kept back as Jimmy and Paula were expected. They actually arrived just when the meal was finished, but Paula, after greeting Believer enthusiastically, insisted on dealing with the injured before she would accept any food. She was very hungry when she finished, and ate the meal that had been saved for her with relish.

When she had eaten, Paula said to the whole group, "You are all very lucky to have met Believer. I know from my own personal experience just what he can do for you if you listen to him. Our group was in despair until he walked down the middle of the road leading to our village.

"We were almost out of food and pretty desperate. Since that day, we have a new outlook on life. Despite being threatened with guns, he just took everything so calmly and started talking.

"He'll talk the hind leg off a donkey, but you had better listen to him. He will surprise you every day, and each day he was with us, he made someone take a new look at themselves.

"I was with him one day, collecting medical supplies when we come across someone who had died from a gunshot wound and infection. He buried her with a Christian ceremony. When I asked why he buried her in particular, he said she had died alone and he hoped that by giving her a proper burial, she would have God's company if nobody else.

Brian said, "That was Sue. I confess that it was your group who shot her, but then we did attack you, and we can't blame you for shooting back, can we? You're right though, he can talk. I have never seen anyone do anything braver than when he stopped us fighting.

"He even made us listen to him. Since then, he has arranged for you to come and help us and he has provided us all with a meal. Thank you, Believer"

Paula did most of the talking that evening. She told the new group how Believer had started helping Nick's party from the moment he had first appeared. She described how the attitudes of some had changed and the whole party listened with awe.

Days Fifty-Seven to Fifty-Nine

When the party awoke the next day, Paula came to Believer and said, "Please can you say a special prayer for me today?"

"Why?"

"Steve is in a bad way. He still has the bullet lodged in his shoulder. I will have to take it out. Also, there is a strong possibility that some clothing has entered the wound.

"If I don't do anything, he will die like Sue, the woman we buried. I didn't want to try last night since it was getting late when I got here. I need a good strong light to see what I am doing. I can't do any operation without some help and I don't know where to get it other than from you."

"God will give you strength, but you will have to have practical help as well. We had better find out who will be able to stand the sight of blood."

Believer questioned the members of the group and the two women agreed to try to help Paula. Believer told everybody what was to happen and asked them all to bear with him and to join him in prayers for Paula and Steve. When the prayers had been said, Steve was lifted onto a table and the women washed themselves thoroughly. Paula had no anaesthetic and had warned Steve that while she had to remove the bullet to save his life, she couldn't help the pain that Steve would suffer.

Believer positioned himself at Steve's head and laid his hands on his temple. Then he said, "Lord God, have mercy on this young man and spare him pain while Paula tries to undo the harm that has been done him. Send down your healing spirit to ease his mind during the difficult time ahead of him. We ask that in the name of Jesus Christ our Lord, Amen."

Paula started working and Steve groaned loudly and then fainted from the effects of the pain. Believer said to Paula, "He's passed out, can you work quickly as you can do with safety."

Paula nodded and worked with an efficiency that surprised her. The delicate task took her the best part of an hour, during which time Steve was unconscious.

When Paula was satisfied that the wound was clean and bleeding freely, she stitched the opening and dressed it. Steve recovered some time later, and although he was weak, was surprised to find that the operation was over.

Paula sat in a corner and was shaking and sobbing with the reaction. The poor girl had just done something she would never had dared to do in her former life. She had spent the previous hour under constant strain, knowing all the time that Steve's life was in danger.

She was well aware that one slip on her part could cause the death of her patient and was now suffering from nervous reaction. Believer went to her and comforted her as best as he could. At the same time, he said a prayer of thanks that Paula had managed to remove the bullet so skilfully.

Believer laid his hands on her head and said to her, "The peace of the Lord be on you." The girl started to calm down after this, but it was a long time before she could speak with her normal cheerfulness.

Believer gathered the rest of the group together and said to them, "I know that some of you may still be sceptical about the power of The Lord. Whether you realise it or not, you have seen evidence of His works, both today and yesterday. Today, our Doctor Paula has carried out the most difficult task of her life. You may have noticed how she was affected.

"She wants all the help and comfort you can give her. Steve was in great pain and I prayed to God to take away the pain of the operation. You all know that Steve fainted and that while he was unconscious, Paula was able to carry on with her work.

"It was only after she finished that she broke down. God's hand was on her too. He helped and guided her actions.

"Paula is no different to the rest of us, but I would have you know that after the bombs fell, Paula did more than anyone to save the people in her village. It was Paula who dragged people from damaged buildings and got them all together. It was Paula who rescued a very big man from an overturned van, and it was Paula who patched up the burns and minor injuries of all the people she rescued.

"Now she has travelled some distance to attend folk she has no reason to love. Steve was a member of a group that attacked her village with the unfortunate result that a woman died. Brian, you understand now what I meant when I said that Sue need not have died. If you had left her, Paula would have tended her wound as she has done for Steve here.

247

"If you ask Paula, when she feels better, she will tell you that she wants no thanks for what she has done today. She will consider that it was her duty. You have a duty to her and to God to try to live in peace with each other. See that you fulfil it.

"Now, our immediate problem is to find food for today. Of the nine of you, you have three who are injured and can't contribute too much to the well-being of the group. In addition, there are three extra people to provide for. This means that I shall have to take Mark and Phil out with me again.

"I suggest that those of you who are fit do what you can to make this place habitable. Barry, Brian, can one of you make some sort of crutches for Sally to use. Paula says that she has a broken leg and she will have to keep the splints on for about six weeks.

"Can you also try and sort out some padding for the splints so that she is as comfortable as possible. Paula will advise you when she can talk to you, but she should rest a while now."

Believer left with Mark and Phil and as he had the day before, he did his best to impress on them the principles of hunting and gathering food. He told them that the use of normal guns was not advisable as the use of these weapons was likely to scare game away. He told them that they should start now to cultivate vegetables. He had already found some growing in the gardens of the big house, and insisted that these be carefully nurtured to provide for the future.

"How do you think Barry and Brian are going to get on with each other? For that matter, how do you two see your future? I would like to know."

Phil spoke up, "I think Barry and Brian will be very wary. As you know already, they have no reason for friendship. You managed to defuse the tension I don't know how you did that.

"You showed us that we needn't shoot at each other, but as to being friends I think that will take a bit of doing. Mark and I? We're together now and he doesn't seem such a bad bloke to work with."

Mark said, "Thanks. I don't know about being friends as Phil here says, but I do understand that we should work together. Brian used to be a bit racist, it will be more difficult for him to relate to Barry."

"He must, if you are to get anywhere. What about leadership? Which one of those two do you think will accept the other? If neither will give way, you will have to have a different system altogether.

"I would suggest that you all have a talk about things very soon and work out how you are going to make decisions. I think the two groups should join together, but I know that it will be difficult. You are basically enemies and it will take a long time before you can trust each other. I realised that and that is why I had you all unload your guns.

"There is another problem. Paula will not want to stay too long. I suspect that she will want to go back as soon as she knows that Steve, Paul and Sally are fit enough to be left. I can't stay too long either.

"Someone will have to escort her, if not for necessity, then at least for common courtesy. It has taken a lot for her to come here and she has suffered a great deal of stress to provide her medical skills for people she has never met."

The trio continued their journey and were lucky enough to catch a goose for the evening meal. They returned and the two women plucked and cooked it ready for the meal. Believer spoke to Paula to find out how her patients were progressing and found that Paul was able to stand and walk about.

Obviously, Paula had been unable to do much more than dress his damaged hand, but the wound was progressing normally. Steve was still very weak and Sally was confined to bed for a while.

While the bird was cooking, Believer called all the adults together around Steve's bed. "What are you all going to do when I leave here?" he asked. "As I have already told you, I move from place to place to try to do two things. One is to bring survivors together. The other is to try to help people make a fresh start and to become self-sufficient.

"You folk here are the nucleus of a viable community. Paula is already a member of another group, but nine is a good size for a start. It is imperative that you all learn to live together. You have only had two days, so far, and it is obvious to me that you are wary of each other. You must resolve your differences now."

Barry said, "I don't trust Brian and I doubt that he trusts me. How do you think we can get over that? I can't see any easy solution, can you?"

Brian added, "I agree with Barry. While you are here, both of us are willing listen to and do what you say. Do you have to go and how soon will that be anyway?"

"Yes, I have to go, but not before you have resolved matters between you and I can see that you aren't at each other's throats. I think the first thing you

249

should do is to find out what your skills are, all of you. Barry, you first, what did you do?"

"I was a plumber. Paul was gamekeeper for this estate and Phil was a rep."

Jean said, "I was just a housewife. We were all living separate lives except for Barry and I and survived somehow. We came together gradually and decided to join up. Sally was with me before we met the others.

"Since then, we struggled for existence, but we found this house and there was quite a lot of food here. We even found some guns so we were pretty set well set up. Then Brian and his gang came along.

Brian said his piece, "I was a stockman in a big store, Kim worked in another one. We both got out when the buildings collapsed. Mark and Steve worked on a building site nearby and Sue lived in a house alongside the site.

"We joined up with a man called Frank who said we should go and find guns and ammunition so that we could take what we needed. Eric joined us as well but he said it wasn't right to go round killing people. Frank said that if Eric didn't agree, then he shouldn't be around to eat food that the rest of us needed.

"He went to shoot Eric, but Eric was quicker and shot first. Frank died, Eric ran away and I took over the job of trying to keep the rest of us alive."

"Well, you have all seen the consequences of trying to live by violence. You have seen also, that it is possible to live without shooting each other. Which do you think is best? You are a mixed group of people with different skills.

"Now you must put them all together. Even Sally can contribute when she better. The trouble is that, through your own actions, you have reduced the efficiency of the whole group. You have three who can't produce their full potential.

"The consequence is that the rest of you will have to work harder compensate for a while. Help each other and start now.

"There is another thing which I am bound to call to your attention. That your spiritual welfare. If you read the Bible, you will find several references the fact that you have to trust God and ask Him for help when you need it. I know He has helped me. You have seen some of the results of my trust.

"Firstly, I am still here against all the odds. Secondly, you saw how Paul was able to operate on Steve. I prayed that he would be relieved of pain when Paula worked. Actually, he fainted and didn't feel anything after the first touch.

"You see that God helped him. If He helped then, how much more will do if you all ask. Strangely enough, the Eric you were talking about is the answer to another one of my prayers. The day I met him, I was able to send him to the assistance of the group I had just left.

"I have been troubled by premonitions from time to time and I had one that day that Eric's presence was needed. Then I met him and told him where to go. I have had no further warning of danger for the family since."

Paula suddenly gave a gasp. "I've just remembered," she said. "Believer said before he left us that I would be needed very soon. He said that I would need to travel to help someone. I forgot what he had said and didn't think about it anymore, not even when Jimmy came back for me. You knew, didn't you, Believer?"

"Yes, I knew, but not how soon or what you would have to do. One of the reasons that I left when I did, was that I knew that I would have to send for you. I had to leave to find out why. Fortunately, and thanks to God, I came here and managed to persuade the people here that it doesn't make sense to kill each other.

"What I don't know is how long this uneasy truce will last. I say to all of you that, no matter how difficult it seems, you have got to find a way to live together. You must forget all feelings of revenge or resentment from this moment.

"You must think before you act. Think that for each one of you who is injured, the others will have to work harder for you all to survive. One pair of hands lost may mean another's death."

Barry said, "What you said makes a lot of sense. I can see that we are the only ones who can make it work. But how? I'm very grateful to you and Paula for what you have already done. Before you appeared out of that ditch, I thought there was no hope for us.

"I thought that either my friends or Brian's would be eliminated. When you showed yourself, I nearly shot you myself because I thought that you were another of Brian's gang. I realise now that Brian must have been thinking on similar lines.

"How did you have the nerve to do what you did? No, don't answer that one, you have already told us the answer. You believe in God and by later events, it seems that you are justified.

"You've helped us when, by all the rules of common sense, you should have walked away. You have made two groups who were fighting each other stop ing and meet. You have linked us with another community through Paula and her you have shown that different groups can help each other.

"Now we know that if we need medical help, we can call on Paula. You said that someone else you met has gone to help the first family you came across. That group is developing an old market garden for the future. If you have done all you say, it seems that you are fulfilling the task you have set yourself, and I wish you all the good fortune you can get when you have to leave here.

"You have a gigantic task ahead of you and I hope you can do it. That doesn't solve our problems now. Please help us to forget our differences."

Brian spoke up, "That goes for me as well. Barry was right when he said that you were nearly shot when you appeared. I think it was the surprise of seeing you that saved you. Like Barry, I can see that we have a chance now. Please help us all."

"You know by now how I think and react. You know that I will say that God will give you all the help you need. You only have to ask him sincerely and you will get some sort of answer.

"This may not be what you expect but if you act on it then you will get the help you all need. As for me, I can't help you personally. Your survival is in your own hands, all of you. First of all, you must want to solve your problems and you must be willing to work together.

"Once that has been established, you must develop some system of communication that works between you. I can't do this. If you insist on fighting each other there is nothing I can do. I have already put my life at risk to bring you together. What more do you expect me to do?

"I can only make suggestions. What I suggest now is that you all have a talk between yourselves without me, Jimmy or Paula being present. We three are outsiders and can't help you since we won't be here when you have to make your lives together."

Believer called to Jimmy and Paula and the three of them went for a walk thus leaving the others discussing their differences without any external influence. They had a reasonable time before they need return since the bird the hunters had brought back took some time to cook. They had gone some distance when Believer stopped and said to his companions.

"What do you think we should do now whilst the others are trying to sort themselves out? I think they need help and that we should ask for God assistance for them."

Paula and Jimmy both nodded and Believer began to pray. "Dear Father heaven. You have brought us all to this place to continue with your purpos

Please grant that Barry and Brian may reach an amicable solution to their problems. Amen."

Paula said, "I expected that you would do something like this. It's typical of you to think of others first. I don't know how you do it. Please tell me how you arrived. I gather from the conversations I have heard that you did something pretty heroic to stop them fighting. Nick and the others will want to know about it when I get back."

"I don't like to talk about heroics or any achievements I might have carried out. You know that I will say that I had God's help. With such help how can I be considered brave? All that I will say about it is that God guided me and through Him I seem to have achieved something worthwhile.

"Jimmy here can give you the details. I am not qualified to make any other comment than the ones I have given you so far."

Jimmy started telling the story as he had seen it from his hideout before Believer called him to meet the people. Believer walked away a little as he was embarrassed by Jimmy's description of his actions. Jimmy spoke to Paula as if he regarded Believer as a hero.

To Jimmy. Believer was just that and was the first man ever to show kindness to the lad who had been so mistreated in his past. It was no wonder, therefore, that the boy idolised his benefactor and his enthusiastic description of events caused Believer some discomfort.

After Paula had heard the story, she said to Believer, "I don't know how you can have done that when you were in so much danger. I couldn't have done anything like it, I would be too scared."

Believer looked at her. "Paula, you surprise me. I know what you did when the bombs destroyed your village. Haven't you today done one of the bravest things I have ever seen. I watched you take a bullet out of a wound when you had no reason to love the person you helped.

"You were willing to come here to help when I sent Jimmy for you. I know that you did this without any thought about your own feelings. I also watched you suffer from the reaction afterwards. Please don't tell me how brave I am when you have done the equivalent or better than I did.

"What you have done is magnificent and there is no way that I could emulate. Don't put yourself down. You are a very important person in the life of those you have come in contact with. Possibly the most important person around."

Paula replied, "I don't know what to say after that. I had never regarded myself as brave before. I suppose that you feel the same way. You and I, we just do the things we have to do and can't think of ourselves before we start. I respected you before and still do.

"I never thought that I would be similarly motivated. I understand now that you have brought it to my attention. Funny, now I think about it. Nick must be similar, and Tammy too. Shirley and Emma have taken to their hunting and are contributing and doing their bit. They must be scared before they start out every day, yet they do it because they must."

"Exactly. We do it because we must. When we see the necessity, we can't think of the implication of our actions, we just have to get on with the task in hand."

The trio were interrupted by a shout from the damaged house telling them that the meal was ready, and they returned to carry on with the conversation about the future of the combined and now larger group.

Barry and Brian said that they had agreed to conduct their affairs with a committee which consisted of all the members. That decision meant that the prospects of disagreement about the choice of leadership were much lower. Believer congratulated them on the good sense they had shown and then asked what they had decided about any commitment to God.

There was a marked silence at this question. The implications had not been discussed. It turned out that no member of the group was prepared to take responsibility for their spiritual welfare. Believer was now faced with a problem he had not foreseen.

He turned to Paula. "You have come here to help these people without any thought about your own safety. You have lent your medical skills but it seem that they are in need of further help. Do you think that Eileen would be able to come and give a service now and then? Do you think she would be up to the journey?"

Paula said, "I don't think that is a very good idea, really. You know how old she is, it would be better if the people here should go there if they wanted, but it's half a day's journey even by bike, and there are three here who can't ride.'

Mark interrupted, saying, "Paula will have to be escorted back, I have suggestion, suppose I go back with her when she is ready. I could take one of the ladies with me and we could have a talk with the people at Paula's place and perhaps we could sort something out."

"Good thinking," Believer said. "That should start off a new relationship between your two communities. You could see how they have started to sort out their own problems and you could also get some good ideas for yourselves. I'm sure that will be for the good of everyone, but you will have to be careful that you don't cause any apprehension or fear.

"Any visits should be made without any enmity. When you can do that, you will find that both groups will benefit."

The day ended with the whole group discussing their future course of action. Believer was pleased to see that everyone contributed, even Sally who was keen to know what part she would be able to play when she had recovered from her broken leg.

The next three days were spent in the group consolidating their relationships and the future pattern of their lives together. Believer spent the time giving advice and helping the hunters to make suitable weapons. He taught them as many hunting skills as he could.

Paula fussed over her three patients and made sure that they were as comfortable as possible. During this time, she frequently checked dressings and the progress of the wounds that Steve and Paul had suffered. There was little she could do for Sally, since once set, her broken leg would take its own time to mend.

The time came for the groups to part company and on the morning of the fourth day, Believer and Jimmy started off in one direction while Paula started back to her home in Nick's village. She was accompanied by Mark and Jean as escorts, while Phil and Kim undertook the hunting for that day.

Believer's time there had been well spent and he had achieved several of his objectives. The most gratifying of these was that through his intervention, Barry and Brian had come to amicable terms and contact had been encouraged between them and Nick's group through the visit of Paula.

Believer and Jimmy walked along searching for signs of more survivors and towards the end of the day began to see signs of recent work in the fields. A few miles further on, they saw some people from a distance. There were about four could see, clearing a field, with two others standing guard. He and Jimmy watched from a distance and out of sight from the folk they could see.

While they watched, one of the workers fell down and Believer was horrified to see that one of the guards appeared to threaten the fallen person until he or she, Believer could not tell which from the distance, arose and started working again.

He turned to Jimmy. "Do you realise what you are seeing here? Slavery. It seems that the men with guns are forcing the others to work. I wonder how the food they have is being distributed. I bet it is two for the guards and one for the workers."

"How will you stop them. What I've seen so far means that you'll try."

"I don't know yet, but you know that I must. We must both pray now that God will help. We will do what we did before. I will try to do something and you should watch from a distance. For the moment, we'll both watch and see where they go at the end of the day. Even slaves have to sleep at times."

The two travellers watched until the light began to fade. They saw that the workers were herded along by the guards to a compound with some relatively undamaged buildings. They were locked in one of them and the guards went off joking amongst themselves.

Believer divested himself of his pack and told Jimmy to wait for one day and then to retrace his steps unless Believer called him. Jimmy was quite capable of catching some food for himself by this time and Believer had few worries about his capabilities.

The older man moved cautiously towards the compound and carefully reconnoitred the area. He could see where the work people had been imprisoned and he crept towards the locked door. When he was close enough, he could see that it was secured by a padlock.

His next action was to hunt around until he could find something he could use to prise the lock and hasp away. He was lucky enough to find an old window latch and he returned and carefully worked on the fitment. He had to work slow because of the noise the screws made when they were forced from the door frame.

The hasp finally gave and Believer eased open the door just sufficient to edge inside. The darkness was almost total and he could see nothing at first. When vision returned slightly, he could see four figures at the rear of the building. They seemed to be cowering in a corner. He whispered. "Peace be with you," and moved towards the group.

He heard a man's voice say, "Who are you?"

"I am Believer. I have come to show you a new life, but you must all leave here now and quietly. Go and hide for at least the rest of the night, but you get as far away from here as possible. I have a friend who will help you hide.

"Go up the ridge in front of the compound and travel for about 300 yards. Then say, "Believer sent us." A boy will make himself known to you and will guide you to a hiding place. Trust him. He has a great deal of experience in hiding. "He has a little food, and he will tell you what to do next. You must be very quiet. Before you go, tell me how many guards there are."

"Three, plus Simon Appleton. He says that he is in charge and he is a nasty piece of slime. He expects us to work and says that he will shoot anyone who doesn't. There is one woman with them."

"You will have to work wherever you go, but in the places I have been to, people work for themselves and not under any duress other than what is needed to survive. I have to try to stop this Simon Appleton and make him change his ways."

"How will you do that?" The voice said. "Are you armed? You would need a pretty strong force to beat him and his men."

"I will have some very able help. Don't you worry about me. Now you should leave. Go quietly and keep in the shadows as much as possible. Crawl if you have to but you must go now."

The small group which consisted of three women and one man moved to the door which Believer opened just enough for them to crawl through. On Believer's instructions, they all went through the narrow gap and lay down beside the wall until they had checked that the way was clear and then left one at a time in the direction Believer had told them.

When the four people had left, Believer closed the door and took up a position inside the building opposite the door. Then he settled down to wait.

Day Sixty

Morning came and Believer could now examine the interior of the hut in which the people had been kept. There were no beds or mattresses and it was obvious that they had been required to sleep on the floor. Sanitation was an evil smelling bucket and the conditions in which the four people had lived was abysmal.

After a while, Believer heard the sounds of movement in the form of footsteps and conversation. He heard the footsteps approach in a normal fashion and then suddenly quicken as the men saw that the lock had been forced. There was some agitated shouting and the door was flung open.

"Good morning," Believer said. "Peace be with you. I'm afraid your guests have left. I should think that they are far away by now, but if not, you had better be very careful when you are out."

"Who the hell are you?" One of the men asked. He was about six foot tall and armed with a rifle which he pointed towards Believer. The other man slightly shorter, about 20, was also armed but said nothing. He stood, like his companion and threatened Believer with his gun.

"My name is Believer. I am here to do God's work in this godless place. Slavery, which you have been perpetuating here, is one of the worst abominations known to man. You have survived so far through the hard work of others less able to look after themselves.

"In future, the hard work will come from you or else you will die. Further, I doubt whether the people who were here when I arrived will be well disposed towards you. They will probably be looking for revenge.

"That is why I warned you to be careful when you go out. Just suppose, for a minute that they manage to get hold of weapons like yours. I would imagine that they will lie in ambush and wait until you aren't looking. When that happens bang! Then you are dead.

"There is another factor. You know nothing about me. you don't know, for instance whether I am alone or if I am not, just how many companions I have

You must consider that my companions are waiting for me to re-appear and that if I don't come out, any other person to do so will be shot."

The big man said, "I don't believe a word of what you say. You are just one middle aged man and you haven't even got a gun yourself. I am going to take you to the boss, then your life won't be worth living."

Believer said, "You must be very brave or else very foolish. I suspect the latter, since you think that guns are the answer to everything. Do you seriously imagine that anyone would put themselves in this situation without adequate protection? I have all the protection I need.

"Certainly, I will go to see your boss. I need to talk to him, but I won't go under the threat of those guns. As I said, if I don't come out of my own free will, who knows what will happen? Look out of the door carefully and see if you can see anyone."

The smaller man peered out of the door and looked around carefully. "I can't see anyone," he said.

His companion snorted. "I thought so, there's no one out there."

"How can you be sure? It would only need one man with a rifle who is a good shot and death for you would come out of nowhere. Here is something else for you to think about. Like you, I have suffered a great deal and lost all the people I have loved.

"What do you suppose my life is like now. It is a life of sorrow with few prospects of improvement. You can be very sure that I will be avenged if anything should happen, but if you shoot me, I will only re-join my loved ones. What will be your future?

"You will be hunted down and exterminated like mad dogs that have become a menace. I promise you that will happen because, besides whatever you may think, this building is being watched."

Now Believer raised his voice slightly in a tone of command when previously he had been speaking calmly. "Put your guns down now or you will not survive."

The two men looked very surprised and fear started to show on their faces. They laid their weapons on the floor. Believer motioned them to move away from the door saying, "Remember that I have to go out of that door first."

He picked up the two rifles and unloaded one. The other he pointed towards the two men and backed out of the door. He motioned to the two men who followed him nervously. Once outside, he told the two men to lead the way to their boss.

Jimmy had been watching from his hiding place and breathed a sigh of relief. He said to the man with him, "He's done it again. That's the third time I've seen him get out of trouble like that and I think he did it once before I met him."

The man said, "Just who is he? How can he do things like that. I couldn't see much of him last night, but he looks just ordinary to me."

"He would say that be is just a man like any other, but he has God on his side. That's what he believes anyway. He believes he can do anything if he prays first and believe me, he prayed very hard before he went down to let you out. The thing is that he talks and makes you think that he can do everything he says."

Jimmy had spoken with the four people Believer had released, and between them, they had decided that two of the women should start immediately and go to Brian and Barry to fetch assistance. He gave them detailed instructions and they had left after a short rest. The man, who was in his sixties, had remained behind because the women had been younger and more able to stand the long walk back.

The man, Fred, he said was his name, had been the person Believer and Jimmy had seen fall. The woman who remained was named Jenny.

"What we've just seen is amazing. He told us that he had all the protection he needed and it seems that he was right. I would have liked to have been a fly on the wall when those two creeps went in and found Believer instead of us. I wonder what he said. You did say his name was Believer, didn't you?"

Jimmy said, "That's his name, but I think he would have told the truth. The last time I watched him, he stood between two lots of people shooting at each other and they stopped when he started talking. I believe what he says and if you don't mind, I will say some prayers for him. He prayed for you, and for me earlier so that is something we can do for him."

Jimmy said the prayers and Fred and Jenny joined him, although Fred was little taken aback by the boy's attitude. He said, "How old are you, lad? You seem to be very grown up and sure of yourself."

"I'm 14. I suppose I do seem capable, but when you've been with Believer for a while, you get to grow up pretty quick. He treated me like a grown up and I've seen him do things you wouldn't understand. He believes in God and now know him, so do I.

"He says he is a missionary and has a task to do that God has set him. When I'm old enough, I want to be like him. He's the kindest man I have ever known and he wouldn't hurt anyone."

"How does he cope when he comes across men like those. They've beaten me and the women, even raped two of them. They are just evil and yet he has just disarmed them and he is taking them to the boss who is even worse. We ought to help but I don't see how."

Jimmy said, "Believer has left one of the guns outside the hut, I think he left the magazine there as well. He knows that we're watching, and perhaps, he means us to go and get it. Look, there's a ditch near the hut, where does it run to?"

"It goes from a hundred yards in front of us, but it's not very big, too small for me. how does that help us?"

"I'm not very big. I'll go. Can you cover me with Believer's air rifle. It won't do a lot of damage, Believer says, but it might put them off a bit."

Jimmy took the air rifle out of its case and loaded it before handing it to Fred. He gave the man some extra pellets and crawled towards the ditch.

He flopped into the two inches of dirty water it contained and crawled along to retrieve the gun.

While this conversation was taking place. Believer was walking behind the two men towards a second building some distance away where another two men and a woman had appeared.

One man shouted when they were near enough. "Tim, Alan, what have you come back for? Why haven't those lazy sods gone out to work? I've told you, if you can't do the job, you'll join 'em."

Believer then made himself visible from behind the two men. He told them to carry on walking and shifted the aim of the captured gun to the man who had spoken. "Mister Appleton, I take it. I thought it wouldn't be too long before someone like you crawled from beneath the rubble."

"Do you know who you are talking to? I am the duly elected councillor for this district. I'll have you shot for this."

Believer looked at him and said with all the contempt he could muster. "A politician, I might have known. I suppose that you had access to a fallout shelter and surfaced only when you thought you were safe. Tell me, where are the people who elected you into power?

"Where is the government and legislation? I know your sort. You think only yourself and not of others. I saw the conditions the others were kept in and have sinned against God and the remains of humanity. May the Lord have mercy on your soul."

261

"You won't get away with this, you know. You have only to turn your back and we'll have you."

"Tell him why you gave up your guns, one of you."

"He says that there are people with guns out there and that if we didn't put our guns down, we wouldn't survive. We believed him because he wouldn't have come without protection."

"You heard, now it's time for you three to put your guns down."

'Why should we? I don't believe you. you are just one man.

Believer said, "You can't know that, can you. Besides, what does it matter to you? You are the man who is going to die first whatever you do to me. I can assure you that you will be the first to go.

"Are you prepared to risk that? I doubt it. You are a number one man and you will fight to the last of your friends. You are not a leader. You are a pusher. As long as you have the advantage, you will stand behind anyone else and keep out of the firing line yourself.

"You are a despicable little man despite your size. Now throw your weapon down before you get into trouble."

Simon looked about him, but could see no one else. He said, "I don't believe you. I think you are on your own. Since you have turned my workers loose, you will have to do their work for them. I suggest that you put that gun down and then you can start work."

Believer sighed and sat down on the floor, still keeping the gun pointed towards Simon. "It seems we have a stalemate here. You are still in great danger of being shot and so am I, but at least, I'm comfortable and you people are going to stand there until you give in.

"Don't forget that whatever happens to me, there is no way any of you will survive. You will be hunted down by my friends and disposed of one by one, not by my friends, then by the people I released. The way you treated them, expect them to come back for you.

"At the very least, they will return the treatment you gave them. The situation is that you will have to look over your shoulders whenever you go out just case my friends or your guests are around. You will never feel safe again and can prevent that."

Jimmy, meanwhile had returned with the rifle Believer had left together with its magazine. He banded this to Fred immediately, exchanging it for the air rifle. Fred loaded the weapon and took guard.

Believer carried on with his persuasive arguments. "You must be complete idiots, all of you, if you think you can control people with guns. What will happen, for instance, when you have run out of ammunition. You won't be able to get any more.

"At that time, the tables will be turned. Then all the hatred you have generated will return to you. You will then have a very bloody end as those who you have dominated won't be too fussy how they finish things. I can imagine what will happen and I don't think I would like to watch."

"Why don't you shut your mouth? You can't do anything against the three of us. One of us will get you."

"No doubt, but you will still be the first to go and the others will be targets for my friends who you can't see. You are not the type to take the risk. You would rather your friend there or the lady did that."

Believer noticed that the woman's expression had changed. "The lady here has just realised the implications of what I have said. While you were in charge and calling the shots, she was in no danger. Now, she knows that if you were in danger, you would make sure that you stood behind her. Lady, if I were you, I would put your gun down as Simon won't protect you if he is in danger."

The woman started to put her gun down and Simon moved his gun to cover her. The movement was seen by Fred and thought to be a threat against Believer. He pulled the trigger and the bullet slammed into the wall behind Simon who then raised one hand and lowered his gun slowly to the floor. The other two raised their hands and Believer relaxed slightly.

"Now, I want you five to move away from the guns and sit down. Remember that my friends are still watching."

Simon and the two others who had been armed moved away, and Tim and Alan joined them. Believer laid his weapon down but close at hand.

"Now, perhaps, we can talk sensibly. I, for one, don't like using guns to prove point. I came down here in the first place without one and I don't like threats. What I am going to say is that there are too few people left in this world.

"We can't have a society where some do all the work for other people. We have all got to chip in. The trouble is that you have created a situation that caused certain amount of enmity. What are you going to do about it?

"For that matter, what are the people you forced to work going to do? I don't know where they have gone, but I doubt whether they feel well disposed to you."

Simon said, "What are you going to do with us now?"

"I don't know. Whatever happens now is largely up to you and the people you had under your control. Firstly, you must understand that everyone has to work if we are ever going to get any sort of civilisation going again. It must be seen that everyone is contributing to the general welfare.

"From what I've seen here, it seems that you expected the others to work for you while you waved guns about. That is hardly a fair distribution of labour, is it?"

"Do you think that we will have any civilisation again?"

"Yes, I do. I have to believe that or I couldn't go on doing what I am trying to do. My name is Believer because I believe that mankind has one last chance to redeem itself. We can't do that with guns. You can hardly say that what you were doing was civilised.

"Look, there are several groups of people I have been in contact with who are trying to rebuild their lives without the threat of guns. Some of them are armed, but only for defence. In one case, I intervened between two groups who were trying to kill each other and they have come to an amicable decision to try to work together. Your case is more difficult."

"How do you mean?" The woman spoke to Believer for the first time.

'Well, there are five of you who seemed to set yourselves above the others. I saw that you appeared to be forcing the others to work for you. There are four of them. I don't know whether they have forgiving natures.

"I have a suspicion that I will have difficulty in persuading them not to take their revenge on you. They will always be suspicious and I couldn't blame them.

"You bloody fool, Simon," the woman said. "You thought everything would be fine, didn't you? You thought that you could take charge and that you would get to run the whole country. I don't know why I believed you. It took a stranger to make me see just what sort of man you are.

"I should have realised it when you built that shelter and put the guns in Everything went fine until last night. Then you lost all your workers and now we are all under threat for our lives. I wish I hadn't gone along with you now can see how wrong it was."

"Alright, you don't have to rub it in. I tried and lost. I'm in more danger than you because it was my idea. You can stop moaning about it. You were just willing at first. The rest of you aren't any better.

"You all backed me up when you had the guns. You aren't any different, Believer or whatever you call yourself. You came here with all your friends up on the ridge there. What does that make you?"

"If you really knew me, you would know just how difficult it was for me to pick up that gun. There is only one of my friends up there, a boy of 14. It was your own fear that made you give in to me.

"I never said at any time that I actually had any friends. I left it to your imagination. I said that there might be. About the threat of revenge, that is probably true since not all of my friends think as I do, and they would know what happened.

"Some of them would have come looking for you, of that I'm sure. I don't know who fired the shot, but the intervention came at just the right time. Whoever it is they are still there and obviously are on my side."

"But you said that you wouldn't have come here without adequate protection. You mean all your talk was false."

"Not all. I did have protection. That is the most difficult thing for you to believe. You see. I put my faith in God and He looks after me. The point is proven, I think. God puts words in my mouth and makes you listen. With help like that, you didn't stand a chance, did you?"

"God is dead, if he ever existed."

"I will have to say that you are wrong there. You see, I am the still living proof. You could have shot me at any time and I would have had no defence because I don't believe in guns. I doubt whether I could have pulled the trigger, but the one on the ridge will."

Simon said, "What happens now?"

Believer was silent for a while before he replied, "I don't know the answer to that. For the moment we are all going to sit here and consider our futures. Whatever happens will depend entirely on whether I will be able to persuade the people you made slaves of not to take any undue revenge.

"I suspect that will be as difficult as persuading you to give up your aspirations of power. Regrettably, we will have to stay here out in the open because I can't trust you and it is obvious that I haven't the physical strength to fight you off in any hand-to-hand conflict.

"I have to rely on our friend up on the ridge to keep me safe. God has placed him there for that purpose and we have to remain in sight of him. You will be no more uncomfortable than me and we shall have to stay here until help comes.

Jimmy will have told your guests where to go for that and I expect it will come before we starve."

"Can't we go into the house. We will be more comfortable and you still have that gun."

"You're not one for listening, are you. We can't go into the house because there might be more weapons in there, besides, one of you might try to overpower me. No. we have to remain here in view of the one on the ridge. He or she is my security. Perhaps, you have some suggestions which might help."

No one spoke for a while, then Believer broke the silence by shouting. "Jimmy, can you hear me?"

Jimmy answered and Believer shouted again. "Come down here, on your own."

Jimmy started down but Believer kept his eyes on his captives the whole time. When the lad arrived, Believer asked him quietly how many were with him. Then he told him to gather up all the discarded weapons and take them back to the ridge.

"When you get there, you had better try to find some food, enough for us all. You will have to go on your own. Feed the others first and then come down here with the rest. It will be hard for you, but you must try. A goose will be best, but if not a couple of ducks will have to do."

Believer turned to the others. "As you see, I spoke the truth about my companion being a 14-year-old boy. I know who has joined him, and they have no cause to love any of you. I think that they will shoot to kill next time, so please don't do anything to provoke them.

"Jimmy will find food for us all and there are others coming. Please be patient until they come. I'm afraid that we will still have to stay here, at least until about mid-day."

"What about toilet needs?" The woman said. "We won't be able to last that long."

"I'm afraid that you have all sacrificed your privacy for a while. I wish that the situation was different, but it is partly of your making. You must understand that I can't do anything else. I've already explained that I can't let you go into the house, otherwise all I have done so far is for nothing.

"I'm sorry, but you will have to put up with some inconvenience until the Anyway, your recent guests had no privacy, so you will be no worse off than them, will you?"

The party settled down to wait. The hours seemed to pass slowly. Believer allowed them to move away a little to relieve themselves, but only one at a time.

Jimmy had been lucky and found a goose which he cooked on a spit over an open fire. Jenny had helped him with the preparation. The three of them ate their share and Jimmy carried the remainder down to Believer. The meal was shared out so that they all felt satisfied.

They settled down to wait again and the day was well advanced when they were joined by Brian, Phil and Kim together with Fred and the three women Believer had released the night before.

The now reinforced party approached Believer with some caution. Fred was quite calm, but one of the women who had come back with Brian was very angry and said that Simon and his cronies should be shot. She was particularly upset that Simon's three male lackeys were still alive.

It turned out that she, Angela, and Louise, the other girl who had gone for help had been taken out one night by Tim, Alan and Charley and had been raped by them in turn. She felt that the men should be punished. Louise just cried but said nothing.

Jenny agreed with her friend to some extent but she had seen the drama unfold as she watched from the safety of the ridge. She had great respect for the way in which Believer had handled the situation, but had been annoyed that Fred hadn't inflicted any injury on Simon. Actually, Fred had missed when he fired the shot.

Believer asked Brian to go into the building and search for other weapons and ammunition. He came out with two more hand guns and another rifle. Believer said to Simon, "You see now that I was justified in not allowing you to the house. I am sorry again for the discomfort you have suffered, but I was left with no choice. I have no doubt that you would have used them if you had got hold of them."

Angela said, "You worry about their comfort? After the way they treated us! Locked up in that filthy hut night after night, having to share the bucket with Fred here. We had no comfort or privacy then. Why should we consider their comfort at all? You must understand how I feel about them."

"Angela, think hard about what you are saying. You have said some pretty bad things about Simon and his friends. With good reason. You revile them and I can understand your motives. What you feel about them now is hatred and revenge.

"You have yourself to answer to later. If you take revenge, that will make you no better than they are. It would give you satisfaction for the moment, but what about the future? Suppose that you shoot them now?

"You are armed and they aren't. You would be shooting them in cold blood and believe me, you will be affected by the action. Revenge will make you hard and bitter and you will end up the same as them. Is that what you want?"

Angela burst into tears. "No, I don't want that. All I wanted was to live as well as I could without interference, but Simon bloody Appleton changed all that. After what his mates did, with his approval and hers, I feel degraded. Louise feels the same, I know. But I don't want to be tarred with their brush."

Believer said then, 'Well now, we have a big problem. You three young ladies and Fred. You have been subjected to cruelty beyond belief. You have the guns now and you feel like taking your revenge.

"You are better people than that and you will make your lives somewhere. I can't expect you to stay here with Simon. You will never trust them. I suggest that you go back with Brian and learn how to live in this new world of ours."

"What about us?" Sarah, Simon's companion, asked.

"I don't know. I shall have to have a talk with God and see what comes up. What you all should realise is that your lives have just been saved. If Angela had given into her first impulses, you would all be dead now. How Fred restrained himself when he was up on that ridge I don't know."

"I missed, that was all," Fred butted in.

"There you are. God helped you then, Simon. Fred has just said that he missed. If he had taken time, you would have been injured at the very least. The problem is that if we leave you all together, you might try again.

"I think it would be better for the world if you were split up. How could we do that. Brian's community will be temporarily swollen by Fred and the girls. The other two groups I've met are only just viable at the moment. The worry is that a group that gets too big will have difficulty in surviving."

Sarah said, "You have told us that your name is Believer. Why? That is a strange thing to call yourself. Just what sort of man are you? You came here virtually unarmed and talked us into giving up our weapons. I don't understand how you could.

"You wouldn't have succeeded if Fred hadn't fired that shot. I might not have survived either because Simon turned his gun on me. One of us would have taken you in the end. Why did you do it?"

"You have asked two questions which I must try to answer. Firstly, you asked why I called myself Believer. I should have thought that was obvious by now. I believe in God and Jesus. I know that He is protecting me as long as I try to do His work. Releasing Fred was God's work. So, I had help."

"Help in what way?"

"God gave me time to talk. He made you listen. I was able to play on your own fears and uncertainty. God made you believe that your lives were in danger if you didn't do as I said. God made Simon threaten you and caused Fred to shoot.

"You all believed me then and I'm still here despite the odds. God also made it possible for Brian to get here and help. On your side, God made Fred miss and Angela to listen to me. Thanks to God's help, you are still alive.

"As to why I did it, I have no choice in the matter, If I see something that needs to be done, I have to try. I can't help myself. God tells me where to go and helps me deal with the situations as I find them."

"Aren't you scared?"

"Believe it, I'm scared, but then I think if God wants me to do this, then he will help, so I'm still around."

Brian spoke then. He had been listening intently. "Believe this man, he works miracles. When he talks, you have to listen. He is so persuasive. He is just incredible. He doesn't seem to consider any danger to himself.

"I know he has done this sort of thing before. He did it to me. He came to us while we were in the middle of a battle and stopped it just by talking. Then he arranged for help for the injured of both sides. He sent for a nurse who we had attacked before and she dug a bullet out of my mate. He proved that we must help each other. Please listen to him."

"Thank you, Brian. Yes, you have got to work together or die. It's no good making other people do all the work, there aren't enough of us. This applies to all. Simon, you have got to forget all dreams of power. You will have to get your hands dirty like everyone else."

Believer realised that the night was drawing in so he arranged for Simon's group to be confined in one room with a shift system of guards. The only exception to this was Sarah who said that she didn't want to spend the night with Simon again. She and the other women shared another room albeit a little reluctantly.

The rest spread themselves into other habitable rooms. Believer walked outside and prayed for a solution for his problems before he retired himself.

Days Sixty-One and Sixty-Two

The greatly enlarged group now consisted of 14 people who all spent the night in a mixture of sleep and uneasy wakefulness. When morning came, they all awoke in fits and starts. The four members of Simon's party had been kept under guard. Sarah with the four women and Tim, Alan and Charley looked after by the men in a separate room.

Brian brought the news to Believer that Simon was missing. A careful search was instigated, but no trace of the man could be found. Believer said that, perhaps, this was a solution of a large problem. He considered that, of all the people there, Simon was most unlikely to accept a life where he would be required to work as hard as anyone else. He would find it difficult to adapt to a life without support and had no weapons.

"There is one thing we must do. That is to warn everybody we can contact to be careful if they should come across him. No one must allow him to get hold of guns if it can be avoided. He will try to take charge again.

"As we've seen here, he isn't too particular about causing suffering. That doesn't necessarily mean that he should be hunted or shot, but people should be warned about his character.

"You and others, Tim, Alan, Charley and Sarah. What do you think about your future? Are you prepared to work for yourselves because really you have no choice? I don't suppose that Fred and the ladies would want you to stay with them, particularly after what happened to Angela and Louise. They will have too many bad memories."

Sarah said, "I, for one, am sorry for what happened, but Simon was so plausible and I think that we all thought he was right at the time. I was his secretary, and a little more, I must say. I was staying at his house when he had a telephone call.

"We went down into the shelter he had built under ground. He had equipped with guns and plenty of tinned food and we've been living on that ever since.

"When we dared to come out, we came across Tim and Charley who were trying to live by scavenging what food they could find. Simon persuaded them to join him and we picked up Alan later. I would venture to say that we were all taken in by Simon's persuasiveness.

"Simon was in charge and he made it very clear that he wouldn't accept any arguments. It was so easy to go along with him and then we came across Fred and the other three. Simon said that we should put them to work for the future in exchange for some food. So we did. We went round collecting all the food we could find and it is stored here."

"Yes, I've seen it. There's quite a lot, we can all eat well today, but it's no answer for the future. Clearing the ground and planting is necessary, but it should be a job that is shared by you all. Look at it this way.

"You had four people doing all the work, while you stood by with guns. How much better if there are eight of you? You will get the job done much sooner.

"There is something else. Jimmy shot a goose yesterday and some of us ate well as a result. We even had some left for the others when they arrived. Most of the people I've met so far are now living by hunting and gathering. That will be the norm for a while. They are all looking to the future and planting for next year."

Believer looked around the area while a meal was being prepared out of Simon's hoard of food. He could see that a small group of people could live quite comfortably. The problem was, which members of the group would agree to live together.

He thought about the characters of all the folk present and he noticed Brian and his companions. Brian had settled on an uneasy peace with Barry. Believer recalled that Brian had been the leader of a group that had attacked Barry. Both leaders were naturally wary of each other and neither could entirely trust the other.

Since Believer's intervention, both parties had worked together for necessity but Believer now looked at them with a new light. There were four people here who would find great difficulty in accepting a life shared with their former tormentors. Better if they could move away entirely, but that would leave a group too small to be viable, and if they simply joined up with Barry and Brian, the group would be too large.

"Brian," Believer said. "I have a proposition to put to you. This concerns all of you here and those where Brian has come from. Phil, perhaps you will be able to give me an idea what Barry, Paul, Jean and Sally will think.

"It must be obvious to you all that Fred and the ladies who were with him can't stay here with Tim, Alan and Charley. It would be too much to ask of them. I think they should go and stay with Barry. That would make one very large community and one too small.

"I think it might be a good idea if you, Brian, moved here with your party in exchange for Fred and the girls. That would remove some of the tension here and at Barry's. Brian can help and guide the people here, and Barry can do the same for Fred."

Brian said, "Can I have some time to think about it before I decide?'

"Of course, all of you should think hard about it. I think that there might be some tension here, but I doubt whether it will be worse than what you have with Barry. What it will mean is that you and Barry can part amicably and then you can work together from a distance.

"What about you four who were with Simon? What's your opinion? You are temporarily under guard. You will have to earn trust from this point on. Will you be able to do that? Otherwise, you may have to leave here without any weapons and definitely no food.

"There is some food here but whoever stays will have to work to survive. If you stay, you will have to work with Brian and learn from him. That is, if Brian wants to uproot himself again."

Sarah spoke up, "I'd like to give it a try. I thought Simon had all the answers, but he has proved to be everything you said about him. He has sneaked off to look after his own skin and I hope he fails. What about you, Tim? Will you give it a try?

"If you and the others agree, we might just make it. We would have to do what Brian says for a while, but that would be no different to obeying Simon, probably easier because Brian doesn't seem so vicious. Shall we give it a whirl? We have everything to gain and nothing to lose now. I don't think we can survive out there without guns."

"You might be right," Tim said. "As of now, it seems to me that we are living borrowed time. If Angela had her way, we should be dead. I can't blame her feeling like that. I would shoot if I had been in her place. I agree with Believer. It would be better if we were separated."

"Count me in," said Alan.

Charley concurred as well.

Believer turned to Phil. "You know Barry a lot better than I do. How do you think he will react when he sees the possibility of changing three men and a woman for the exact opposite? Fred is no young man either, although he seems quite capable."

"I don't know, but it does seem to be a reasonable course of action. I take it that you intend that both groups keep in contact so that we can help each other. There is also Paula and her community. They seem to be doing alright and we can call on them for help as well.

"I think it will work and I'll tell Barry that you recommend it. I know he'll listen to you. As soon as he heard that you might be in trouble, he sent us off to help. He couldn't send any more because Mark, Jean and Paul hadn't got back by the time we left."

"Thank you for coming. As I said, Fred has got his head screwed on and he looked after me for a while. What about you girls? Do you think a move to Barry's place will help?"

Angela had elected herself a spokeswoman. "Yes, it will do. I quite like Barry. We arrived in the early hours and he made us welcome even though he was shorthanded at the time. Louise and I didn't meet the others, I gather that they were taking this Paula back.

"Who is she? She seemed to do a good job on the ones who were hurt. How did that happen?"

Brian answered her. "That was mostly my fault. I decided to take some food from them by force. This bloke, Believer, came and stood in the way. I think we stopped shooting only to shut him up. He made us see reason."

"Paula is a third-year nurse who is the nearest thing to a doctor within a reasonable distance. Believer had met her before so he sent for her to come and help us. Believer seems to know what is going to happen.

"He told Paula before he left her that she would be needed and that she would have to make a journey. That was why he came to us in the first place. He said that he knew someone needed help. If he can do that, he is a man to be reckoned with.

"His actions here have proved that. I still can't believe what I saw when I arrived here. The amount of weapons that Simon and his gang had and they were disarmed by one unarmed man."

"Two," said Believer. "Don't forget Fred. He helped from the ridge and fired a shot just when he was needed."

"That may be, but you still did it. I know you will say that you had God's help. I don't think I could have even thought about it. I think I would have run away," Brian answered.

The conversation moved back and forth for a while and finally Believer's suggestion was accepted subject to Barry's agreement. Phil started back with Fred and the three girls while Brian started to settle in at his new home. There were certain possessions that he and Kim required, but he said that he would attend to that later. Both parties who were to live together sat down to discuss how they would arrange the new period of their lives.

Believer and Jimmy had moved away from the rest of the group because, as Believer said, the sooner the group started to work together, the better for them. As was Believer's practice, he didn't want to influence the relationships, he only intended to advise where necessary.

After a while, Kim noticed that Believer and Jimmy were missing and she made it her purpose to look for them. When her search was successful, she found the pair deep in prayer, so she waited until they were finished before she spoke.

"Believer, what are your plans? You've come here and sorted out another big problem. No one here seems to have given a thought to you. I have, though. I thought a lot about you after you left us and didn't expect to hear from you again.

"When I heard that you might be in trouble, I made sure I came to help. I suppose you will go off again. Don't you and Jimmy get lonely?"

"We don't seem to have much time for loneliness. As soon as we meet one group, there are things to do. We do what we can and move on. As to being lonely, God is always with us so that isn't such a problem.

"This will be the shortest time we have stayed anywhere so far. Our work is done here. Brian and you will tell the others how to make a living. I hope you will find a way to think about God sometimes, but as for us, we have to move on.

"To tell the truth, we are both very tired at the moment. Meeting people under the circumstances we seem to find is very tiring, and I think we will go somewhere quiet and have a long rest and think. Somewhere where we won't have to sort out other people's problems. We'll stop here for the night and be gone in the morning."

"Don't you want to settle down? Do you have to keep moving on? It must be very hard for you to keep saying goodbye."

"That's true, it is, which is one reason for not staying too long. Look at it this way. If I stop, there won't be a day when you or others don't ask me for advice. That won't help you in the long run. You really have to make your own decisions."

"I suppose so, but it does seem hard on you and you drag Jimmy around with you, and he's only young. What about him? Doesn't he want to settle down?"

Jimmy spoke up, "I want to go with Believer. Before I met him, I was hiding from anyone who came near me. With him I'm not afraid anymore. I want him to teach me about life and God and later to follow in his footsteps.

"If I stay, I won't be able to do that. I'll go with him and hope to grow up like him. I think I'm helping and he makes me feel needed."

Kim said, "Point taken, but it still seems a difficult life."

Believer carried on talking. "It is, but it's what God wants of me. The longest place I stayed with people was with a mother and three girls who were starving when I first saw them. I fell in love with that lady and I want to go back to her. That is not to be.

"Later events have shown me what God wants of me and I can't go back Leaving her was the most difficult thing I have ever done. God will tell me when to stop and I think that I will be re-united with her then.

"For the moment, I am very tired but I must go, otherwise I will end up being your leader. That is the last thing I want. I have enough responsibilities already My job is to make people accept each other.

"You can't imagine how hard that is sometimes. Neither do you know the anguish I go through every time I come across people in opposition to each other That is the hardest of all to bear."

Kim answered, "I hear what you are saying and I think I understand. I know you are leaving and half of me wants you to stay. The other half wants to go with you. Is there anything I can do to help?"

"Tell me. What do you believe?"

"I'm not sure. I wasn't very religious before. In fact, I didn't give religion much thought at all. I was christened as a baby, but when I grew up, I thought that people like you who really believe were some kind of crank.

"Now, after seeing what you can do, I'm not so sure. Twice, in the short time I've known you, you have averted a dangerous situation. You say that you a helped by God, and logic tells me that if you can do all that, unarmed, then you must be right and God exists. I want to do more but don't know how."

Believer was silent for a full minute. Really, he was praying for guidance. After a while he said, "Praise the Lord. I know now what God wants of you. Do you remember from the Bible stories what Jesus said to Peter when he first met him. He said, 'Follow me.'

"That is what I will tell you to do. I don't mean to literally follow me. But you can be a missionary like me. God wants you to look after his little flock here and at Barry's place. Can you do it?"

"I'll try, but how can I do it when I don't know what to say or how I can learn about it?"

"I will set you a task. You remember Paula. She believes, but she has a different role in life. As soon as you are settled here, take one of the men and go to her. It's a long way but when you get there, tell Nick, he is the leader there, that I sent you to learn from Eileen.

"She is the lady whom I left there to do what you must do here. She will teach you the basics and then you can come back and start here. Stay one week and listen hard. Don't forget to pray and you'll be surprised what you can do. Perhaps, Steve may be the best choice. He can travel slowly and Paula can have a look at his shoulder."

"How can I learn enough in a week?"

"You can't. Listen to me. I was just a lorry driver. For the first three weeks, I was alone and very frightened. In that time, God spoke to me and I set out on a mission. I don't know enough myself, but God gives me lessons every day.

"All you have to do is to listen to Him and trust Him. But first, you must believe and the best way to do that is to spend some time with another believer. Eileen is the nearest, so go to her for a while. Do it as soon as you can."

"I'll go as soon as Steve gets here. No, I'll go back to Barry's now and go from there. There will be less distance to travel and if I go now, I can catch Phil up on the way.

"I expect that I can move faster than Fred. Then Steve and I can come back here when we leave this Eileen. I'll just go and tell the others about it first."

"Wait a minute. There is something I must do for you. Come here and kneel down."

Kim obeyed and Believer laid his hands on her head. "Lord God. This woman has accepted you without question. Keep her safe and guide her in the task You have set for her. Help her and give her wisdom that she may do Your work with confidence.

"Let Your Spirit inspire her and let her come to know You better. For the sake of Jesus Christ, Your Son. Amen."

Kim stood up. She was surprised at the speed of the events of the past few minutes. "Is that what happens in a conversion?"

"Not a conversion, more a fulfilment. Learn well. The time will come when all you learn will be needed. You have received a call now and you have listened. You will receive another call at some time and all you have learnt by then will be put to the test."

Kim said, "I remember Paula said that you had told her that she would be needed. Are you doing something similar to me? Because that's what it sounds like."

"Yes. I suppose I am. Although I don't know what for. I just felt that I should say it to you but I can't explain these odd premonitions. They frighten me, to be honest. Because they have happened before, I have to believe them.

"All I can say is be ready and prepare as best you can. I don't know when it will take place either, so I'm afraid you will just have to wait and remember what I said. Then, answer the call when it comes."

Kim looked a little worried but turned to go anyway. Believer said as she left. "God keep you and guide you and may his peace be always with you."

Kim made her goodbyes with the rest of the group who all looked puzzled at the strange turn of events. Earlier that morning, Kim had agreed to settle down with them, and now she was leaving very suddenly.

Believer went back to talk to them. "You all know that I am a believer because that is what I call myself. Kim has just discovered that she believes as well. She has been called like I was and she will be away for a week or so.

"When she comes back, she will be filled with God's spirit. Really, she is now, but doesn't know how to accept God's word. That is why she has gone now. She will look after the spiritual needs of you people and Barry's group. hope you will heed her when she returns."

Sarah spoke up, "Why will she have to do that, won't you be here? We will listen to you because we've all seen what you can do. We don't know what Kim can do."

Believer answered, "Neither does Kim at the moment. She has gone to find out. As for me, I am leaving in the morning with Jimmy. My work here is done

God has helped me to stop an injustice and no doubt he will guide me somewhere else.

"Kim will take my place as your spiritual leader. That doesn't mean that she will take over the running of the community, but she will be your mentor and intercessor with God. She will lead you in prayer and I hope you will join her. You have all seen the power of prayer.

"Kim doesn't know it yet, but she will be able to wield the same power. Fifteen minutes ago, she had no idea what her future might be. Now she is a different person and has a purpose to fulfil."

Kim's sudden change and subsequent actions caused quite a stir among the group and was much discussed throughout the rest of the day. This was spent by those who were staying in sorting out the living quarters they allotted themselves. Believer and Jimmy helped where they could, and at the end of the day the building was made as comfortable as possible.

The night was spent in a similar way to the previous one, but there was a more relaxed attitude all round. Since Sarah, Tim, Alan and Charley had agreed to try and live in peace and co-operation, there was less need to impose restrictions on their movements.

In the morning, Believer and Jimmy gathered the people together for a final prayer and chat, during which he said the Blessing. He said as he left, "The peace of the Lord be always upon you." Then he and Jimmy left to pursue their destinies.

A new civilisation and understanding has been kindled.

Statement

There are several references in this story to lay persons taking the role of ordained priests. Also, we have a case where a nurse takes the place of a doctor. I wish it to be known that it is not my intent to usurp the authority of any regular ordained priest. Nor do I wish to suggest that medical practice be carried out by insufficiently trained personnel.

The story is about events which I pray most urgently will never take place. In the circumstances of the story, whereby there are very few survivors, it is obvious that people will take on very different roles to those pertaining in the current situation.

If mankind cannot mend its ways, this might happen.

This story and the views expressed in it are not to be taken as a blueprint for any religious movement. We have adequate numbers of religious sects at the present time.

The peace of Christ be with you always.